IMPURE BLOOD

Also by Peter Morfoot and Available from Titan Books

Babazouk Blues (April 2017)
Box of Bones (April 2018)

PETER MORFOOT

A CAPTAIN DARAC MYSTERY

IMPURE BLOOD

TITAN BOOKS

Impure Blood
Print edition ISBN: 9781783296644
E-book edition ISBN: 9781783296651

Published by Titan Books
A division of Titan Publishing Group Ltd
144 Southwark Street, London SE1 0UP

First edition: April 2016
10 9 8 7 6 5 4 3 2 1

A CIP catalogue record for this title is available from the British Library.

Printed in the USA.

For Rob and Katey

To arms, citizens!
Form your battalions!
March, march!
Let impure blood
Water our furrows!

From the French national anthem,
'La Marseillaise'

PROLOGUE

The boy swung the scythe in a low, slow arc. As precise as a pendulum, it was a movement beautiful in its economy; the blade levelling the crop and gathering it in one fell swoop. With each pass, he edged further into the waist-high wheat, using the old Roman road that ran alongside the field as a guide. Turning at the end of the first swathe, the cut crop lay in an arrow-straight row in front of him.

Hand-scything a one-hectare field gave the reaper plenty of time to think. Or to dream. The boy was imagining himself a warrior facing impossible odds; a lone swordsman pitted against the endless ranks of a vast army. A sudden scuttling in the undergrowth reminded him of the true enemy. Why, he wondered, did a rat disturbed at a field margin almost always head back into the uncut crop? His father had told him that rats were clever, resourceful creatures. But if they were, why didn't they break cover while the going was good instead of retreating into an ever-shrinking island of safety? The last part of the field to be cut, the boy knew, would be alive with the devils. And then, as if in agreement, they would all rush out at once. That's when the fun would really begin. He felt the weight of the shotgun against his back as he worked on.

The main line to Paris flanked the far boundary of the farm. The groan and squeal of a train pulling away made the boy glance up. It was as well he did. Something was moving in the field ahead; something feral among the waving wheat. He couldn't see the creature directly but the parting and closing of the canopy above it pinpointed its position. Whatever it was, it was bigger than a rat. As if attracted to the *shoop shoop* of his slashing blade, it seemed to be heading straight for him. He stopped swinging the scythe. Still the thing advanced. And then he heard it, a whimpering cry among the dry scratch of the stalks. An injured animal was dangerous. A half-dead boar could still kill, he'd heard. His eyes fixed directly ahead, the boy moved back and slowly set down the scythe. With a shrugging motion, he unhitched the shotgun and took aim. The creature didn't appear. Perhaps it had changed course at the last moment. He scanned the whole front rank of the crop. There? No. Just a shadow. There? His trigger finger twitched. The stalks finally parted. The boy stared for a long moment. And then he lowered the gun.

FRIDAY 3 JULY

1.06 PM

A tram materialised out of the heat haze and floated towards the stop at Jean Médecin. On the platform, wilting clumps of passengers picked up their bags and shuffled forward. From a balcony in the adjoining Rue Verbier, Marie Lacroix watched the tram whine to a halt and open its doors. She ran an eye over the new arrivals. None was wheeling a case. Marie glanced at her watch and sighed – the family taking the apartment was now thirty minutes late. Reasoning that if she stopped looking out for them, they might arrive sooner, she decided to check out what else was happening. It should certainly prove more entertaining; her balcony overlooked one of the most cosmopolitan streets in Nice.

Opposite the apartment, a living statue was setting up her pitch under the palm-buttressed north wall of the Basilique Saint Eustache. Made up as a white marble Medusa complete with snake headdress, the girl looked startling. Yet the size of the crowd she was attracting surprised Marie. Maybe they knew something she didn't. Staring blindly ahead, the girl mounted a low plinth, exhaled deeply and froze into a classical pose. Marie looked on for some moments. And? Giving a shrug, she returned her attention to the avenue.

A bald man kneeling at the far kerb seemed far more interesting. In the glare of the midday sun, he wore neither hat nor shades. A bottle of Evian sticking out of the hip pocket of his white linen suit seemed to be his only concession to the heat. But it was the shoelace-tying movement he was making with his hands that really captured Marie's imagination – the man appeared to be wearing slip-on loafers. Rising tentatively, he fingered the screw-top of the Evian bottle as he stared along the pavement towards the tram stop. Then looking all around him, his gaze seemed to settle on the circular billboard, the Colonne Morris, standing on the Rue Verbier side of the avenue. As if compelled to check it out, he hurried across the street towards it.

Surely, Marie thought, *the man must have seen this material before; it's plastered all over the city*. Had been for weeks. The posters were shouting up just one thing: the Tour de France. Two hundred thousand people were expected to attend the opening stage, a time trial around Monaco. But for the Niçois, the real excitement began on day two.

Cresting the ridge of the high Corniche, the 180-strong peloton would fly down the coast road into the old port, file around the foot of the Château Park, and then power out of the city along its palm-fringed hem, the Boulevard des Anglais. A map illustrated the whole stage. There was just one day to go before the Tour began. Two before it rolled into Nice.

Slipping behind the Colonne, the man in the white suit leaned around its circular bulk and peered back across the avenue. Who was he watching so covertly? Marie looked in the general direction of his gaze. There were any number of candidates. None seemed noteworthy.

A shriek rent the air to her right. Marie shot a glance towards the Basilique but before she could make out what was happening, laughter rang out, allaying her concern. Now she understood why Medusa was a hit. While the girl herself remained utterly deadpan, the nest of vipers in her hair had turned into a living, writhing, tongue-darting nightmare. It was so horribly convincing, Marie could hardly bear to look. It was some moments before the snakes froze, prompting sighs of relief tempered with disappointment. The vile creatures would strut their stuff again, wouldn't they? Medusa let the tension build. Just when it seemed there would be no reprise, they squirmed into life once more. A wave of delighted revulsion broke around the audience. There was nothing so entertaining as fear and suspense, Marie reflected, reacting with everyone else.

It was during the next lull in the action that White Suit came jogging into the street. Marie half-expected to see someone chasing him but there was no one. Running in this heat? In playing hide and seek, perhaps the guy had made himself late for a train – Nice's main station, Gare Thiers, was just a couple of streets away. As he jogged past the steps that led to the west door of the Basilique, a bell began to toll and some members of Medusa's audience took their leave. One of them, a bearded young man carrying a rucksack over one shoulder, stepped blindly into White Suit's path. The collision almost knocked the pair of them off their feet. White Suit issued a breathless apology and hurried off, a move that earned a hideous writhe from Medusa's snakes. It drew a big laugh.

As the bell continued to toll, Marie followed White Suit's progress for a moment and then looked past him to the far end of the street. There, a congregation of a different order had already been called to prayer. She'd witnessed the scene before.

The venerable and the vulnerable were always the first to take up places in the prayer room itself. On Fridays, the room filled up quickly and for the rest, there was no alternative but to form ranks on the street outside. Most laid down mats or towels. Others made use of flattened packing materials donated by local shops and cafés. Marie felt a certain sympathy for them. Catholics praying in the vaulted sanctity of the Basilique were often disturbed by sightseers. But Muslims praying in the hustle and bustle of the street had far more to contend with: stray footballs; delivery vans; rubberneckers; abuse hurlers. The solemn choreography of the prayer ritual seemed rather beautiful to her.

Marie's eyebrows rose. Cardboard box in hand, White Suit was one of those joining the outdoor congregation. He hadn't been in danger of missing a train, after all. He'd been in danger of missing midday prayers.

Her mobile rang. In passable French, her client

apologised for his late arrival. He anticipated being with her in forty-five minutes. An hour at most. Marie sighed, thanked him for the update and settled down to watch the service once more. Everything seemed to go smoothly until the final cycle of prayers. At first, she didn't notice the old woman who wheeled her shopping trolley up to the rear of the congregation.

'Look at this!' the woman shouted, fanning herself furiously. 'And taking up the whole street!'

Her observations grew more aggressive as she jolted the trolley off the kerb and set off around the obstruction. Midday prayers being silent, her words carried starkly across the rows of prostrated backs. That they appeared to have no effect seemed to irritate her still further. As she rounded the rearmost rank of worshippers, she turned in sharply, catching White Suit's elbow as she ran a wheel over his makeshift mat. Even if he had wanted to, he couldn't have washed off the smudge at that moment – he'd already used his bottle of Evian to wash his feet. Making a clicking sound with her tongue, Marie shook her head. The old woman tottered off towards the Basilique and another potential hold-up. Marie looked expectantly across but there would be no clash of the soul sisters. Medusa had struck camp, the crowd had dispersed.

Outside the prayer room, a hundred backs were still bent in prostration to the east. Then, as a tram rolled past the end of Rue Verbier, the congregation rose.

All, that is, except one.

2.18 PM

Captain Paul Darac had to queue at Fantin but the wait was worth it. Warm pâtisserie in waxed cardboard; the smell was making his mouth water as he threaded his way between the trinket sellers in Place Garibaldi and headed home. It was going to be a late breakfast; he hadn't got in from The Blue Devil jazz club until 4 am.

It had been some gig, though. Avoiding the runs and chord progressions he'd played a thousand times before had led Darac into some strange territory during a couple of solos. But those moments of being almost lost, of needing inspiration to find a way back to the band, was one of the things he loved about playing jazz. Each return from the unknown had been rewarded with whoops of appreciation from the audience and, a rarer accolade, spontaneous yells of 'yeah!' from veteran club owner, Ridge Clay.

Sightseers were already out taking photos in the Place. Padding like a sleepwalker behind outstretched hands, a prodigiously paunched man in his sixties almost collided with Darac as he crossed in front of the Garibaldi statue.

'Well what do you know?' the man called out in English, finally lowering his camera. 'Garibaldi the Italian patriot, right? It says on the plinth he was born right here in Nice.'

A full ten metres to the man's left was a little nugget of a woman wearing white pedal pushers and a sun visor. Hands on hips, she was surveying the scene with the air of the commander of an invading army.

'Make sure you get the arcades. They're elegant. And check out these apartment houses. *So* Côte d'Azur.'

'Yes they are.'

'But see the balconies?' A charm bracelet jangled as she waved at one of the frontages. 'All that stone decoration? That's Baroque. Like Rome.'

'Rome is right!'

Darac gave a little snort. Those balustrades and pediments were not stonework but brushwork – a painted *trompe l'oeil*. But visitors could be forgiven for being fooled. Many things about the Côte d'Azur were not as they seemed.

As a tram snaked behind him into Boulevard Jean Jaurès, Darac left the Place and disappeared into the whorl of narrow streets and alleyways that made up the old town, a quarter known as the Babazouk. Exuding coffee, fish, flowers and drains, the Babazouk had the feel of the Moorish souk its name suggested – a shaded warren frequented by fast locals and slow tourists. For all its teeming life, the Babazouk was a secretive place. Behind façades washed in tones of cayenne, cumin and turmeric, anything from ratty flats to filigreed palaces could be found. And at every window, swing-wing shutters acted as a sort of niqab against prying eyes.

Street signs in the Babazouk were written in two languages – French and the local Nissart. Embedded in the quarter's northern rim, Place or Plassa Saint-Sépulcre was a grand title for what was no more than a large, cobblestoned courtyard lined by ancient apartment houses on three sides, the rear wall of the eponymous church on the fourth. Darac had acquired his roof-terrace apartment in the Plassa five years ago. It had proved a good move. The pan-tiled canopy of the Babazouk was an atmospheric habitat and it suited him to live suspended between the tangle of the old town and the Nice of the boulevards.

Following the series of doglegged *ruelles* that led off Rue Neuve, he entered the Plassa by a locked iron gate. He hadn't taken more than a few strides before his neighbour Suzanne came hurrying towards him. His strong, broad-boned face broke into a smile as he turned back and unlocked the gate. Adopting a doorman's pose, he held it open for her.

'Late?'

'Sister Lasorgue will murder me. You working today?'

'Certainly am.'

'Then you'll know who to arrest. *Vivà!*'

'*Vivà*, Suzanne,' he called as she disappeared into the *ruelle*.

'Kiss Angeline for me!'

'Sure.'

He could try, anyway. The smell of the cooling pâtisserie fading in his nostrils, Darac re-locked the gate and walked through blue shadows into the Plassa. The sun was blowtorch hot. *It's going to be busy today*, he thought. *An overheated city always brings out the craziness in people*.

And then his mobile rang.

2.33 PM

Downing a triple espresso, Darac swung his unmarked Peugeot into Rue Verbier and hit the brakes. He'd expected one, perhaps two, POLICE INCIDENT – NO ENTRY signs to have been set down across the entrance. Instead, he had to negotiate a slalom course of staggered pairs. After the final gate, cones funnelled him towards a trio of shirt-sleeved officers standing in a shady spot on the kerb. One of them stepped forward and held up her hand. Slowing to a stop, Darac eased the volume on his CD player and lowered his window.

The officer leaned in.

'Quite a production number.'

'Hi, Captain,' she said, smiling as they shook hands. 'They've got the riot squad standing by as well.'

'Wonderful.' Crushing the espresso cup, he tossed it into the empty Fantin box sitting next to him. Crash barriers; riot squad – it all added up to one thing: Public Prosecutor Frènes, the Palais de Justice official who had green-lighted the investigation, wanted the world to see he was committing every resource to what was a 'sensitive' situation. Darac indicated a group of spectators corralled on the opposite pavement. 'It's certainly brought out the fans.'

'Don't know what they expect to see from back here.' She cast a glance towards the far end of the street. 'And we've told them the forensic guys will have their tent set up in a minute.'

Darac followed her gaze. Outside the prayer room, white-clad figures hovered like partially materialised ghosts over the shimmering tarmac. At their blurred feet, a vague white shape lay motionless.

'Meanwhile, they might get heatstroke.' Straightening, she waved him through. 'With any luck.'

Smiling, Darac restored John Coltrane's 'Naima' to its rightful volume and headed for the action.

Nearing the inner ring of cordon tape, he ran an eye over the sheet-draped corpse and the pathology team waiting to examine it. Leading it was a woman with a fine-boned face and the round-eyed alert expression of a small bird. 'Well, well,' Darac said aloud. Professor Deanna Bianchi attending the scene? They *really* meant business. Trailing Coltrane's mournful horn through the on-off crackle of police radios, he slowed to park.

'*Ciao, bella,*' he called to her through his opened window. Her forehead creased as she gave him the merest nod in acknowledgement. Deanna subdued? Unusual.

The ache in the tune demanding a respectful fade, Darac slowly turned down the volume, then pulled on his police armband and got out of the car.

Among the airless, grimy streets clustered around Nice's main railway station, the leafy Rue Verbier formed a welcome oasis. Orientated east-west, the street's northern side was lined mainly by apartment houses, some with ground floors converted into shops and cafés. Its southern flank was taken up entirely by the Basilique Saint Eustache and the car park laid out in its voluptuous shadow.

Occupying the premises of a former bistro, the prayer room was tucked away at the end of the street furthest from the Basilique, just before it opened out into a small marketplace. Here too, Crowd Control seemed to be doing a good job of keeping spectators back.

A little further along stood the phone booth from which the emergency call had been made. 'I'm ringing from the box on Rue Verbier,' the anonymous female caller had said. 'The one outside the pharmacy. A Muslim has just been killed. On the street. During a prayer service.' No further details had been given and Darac still knew nothing about how the man in question had died. Ideally, he would have liked to talk to the caller but unless someone identified her or she came forward, it wouldn't be possible to trace her: the emergency 17 number she'd dialled was a free, cardless call.

As Darac scanned the streetscape, he realised he might not need her. Apart from all those going about their business at ground level, at least fifty apartment balconies and ten times as many windows overlooked the scene. A couple of CCTV cameras set up in the car park might also have a story to tell — perhaps of a shot being fired from one of those windows. A sniper could easily have picked off a stationary target from such a vantage point. And from a silenced rifle, the report would have sounded no louder than a cough.

But it wasn't all good news. A crime scene without witnesses was one sort of problem; a scene with too many could prove a logistical nightmare. Triage was the key and Darac's best man for it, his second-in-command, Lieutenant Roland Granot, had booked the day as leave.

As the forensic examination tent finally went up, most of those looking on from above strolled back inside their apartments. Curtain down for the moment. Perhaps they should have stuck around. In the marketplace, an entertaining shouting match was starting up. Crowd Control and TV news crews often clashed. Recognising the reporter at the centre of it, Darac gave a little smile as he headed off to the inner cordon. He hadn't gone more than a few steps before she caught sight of him.

'Darac! We're in Siberia over here. Do something about it, will you?'

He kept moving.

'You're better off where you are.'

'Better? Hey – this wouldn't happen anywhere else in Europe! Even fucking England!'

'Well this is fucking France.'

The pathology lab technician, Patricia Lebrun, was waiting to sign him into the red zone. On seeing him, she turned to a box containing crime-scene overalls and decided to start counting them. If Darac hadn't known better, he would have sworn she was trying to avoid him.

'Chief? Hold it!'

The voice was as rich as cream-smothered *clafoutis*. And it was one Darac wasn't expecting to hear. He turned.

The moustachioed figure bustling towards him was Granot, alright. At fifty-one, the man was twenty years older than his boss. He was also thirty kilos heavier. On what was the hottest day of the summer so far, sweat stains the size of dinner plates had turned his short-sleeved shirt into a peek-a-boo disaster area.

'Take it easy.'

The big man was breathing too hard to reply.

'And what are you doing here, anyway? You're supposed to be on a day off.'

'Might disappear... later. We'll see... how it goes. Uh... listen...'

'I'll talk – you get your breath back.' Darac turned to the street scene. 'Talk about a cast of thousands... So what have you got? Those worshipping outside at the time of the death; those worshipping inside the prayer room itself; people who may have seen something from shops, apartments and the like, and finally, passers-by?'

Granot wiped a ham of a hand across his forehead.

'Yes, more or less.'

'Top work.'

'No point in separating them individually... They had more than enough time... to get their stories straight... before we got here.'

'What are people saying about how the man died?'

In the background, a young officer questioning passers-by jetted Darac a quick glance.

'No one knows anything.'

'Bang goes my sniper theory.'

Granot seemed in no mood for gags.

'Listen, chief, I've got to tell you something. You're… off the case.'

'Yeah, yeah. Let's go.'

Granot threw out a restraining arm.

'Seriously. You're off the case. Or that's how it's looking.'

The humour that habitually played around Darac's eyes and mouth disappeared.

'How can I be off the case? I haven't got started on it yet.'

Granot gave a sideways nod.

'That's how.'

Outside the prayer room, the squat, grey-suited figure of the public prosecutor, Jules Frènes, was jabbering into his mobile as he paced back and forth. Every few steps, a stubby index finger stabbed the air – a small man laying down the law.

'What's the little arsehole up to?'

'Telling Agnès he wants her to lead the investigation, I should think. He's already told the examining magistrate that's what he wants.'

'The boss lead the case?' Darac's expression regained its characteristic lift. 'What's the problem? Let's get on with it.'

'Uh… it's not just a question of you not leading. Frènes doesn't want you anywhere near…'

Granot was talking to fresh air. Darac was already striding away.

'Don't hit the bastard!'

Outside the prayer room, Frènes was still declaiming

as he spotted Darac. He hurriedly ended the call and stood his ground. It didn't last.

'Not here, Captain – my car.'

'Monsieur Frènes…'

'My car.'

A couple of uniforms smiled as Darac, a light heavyweight, pursued his welterweight quarry to a shiny new Mercedes. He joined Frènes on the back seat.

'Why, monsieur?'

Frènes knew a thing or two about confrontation. He stared straight ahead.

'Are you a good Catholic, Captain?'

Obtuse yet seemingly direct, it was a typical opening from the public prosecutor.

'There's no such thing as a good Catholic, I'm told. I ask you again. Why?'

'No matter. Thanks to the separation of church and state in our system, citizens are not required to observe, believe, or even show respect for the Catholic faith. First and foremost, we are Frenchmen, are we not? Frenchmen first and last.'

Darac ran a hand through his black, wavy hair.

'*Why*, monsieur?'

Frènes continued to address his monologue to the stalls.

'But while showing respect for the faith may not be a requirement, showing tolerance toward it most certainly *is*. You, Captain, have never shown any such tolerance. Indeed, you show no tolerance toward any faith or creed, do you?'

'You really are the king of cant, Frènes. Why…'

Trying not to lose it, Darac took a deep breath and began again. 'Why do you want me off the case?'

Beads of sweat began to dribble through Frènes's sleek, swept-back hairline. As if staunching a haemorrhage, he took a silk handkerchief from the breast pocket of his jacket and pressed it to his forehead.

'Why? Because we are faced with a very delicate situation here. Whatever we may think of our Muslim friends worshipping on the street – practically within sniffing distance of the Basilique's censer, indeed – our investigation must not only be seen to be a thorough one, it must be conducted tactfully, sensitively, diplomatically. Any other approach and *our* streets may descend into chaos. *Our* streets may become littered with burning cars as happened in Paris four years ago.'

As he listened, Darac saw the lean, red-headed figure of his other trusted lieutenant, Alejo 'Bonbon' Busquet, step out of the prayer room and exchange a few words with a uniform. It was difficult to tell what was on Bonbon's mind; his foxy face was invariably creased into a grin. The uniform pointed at the Mercedes.

'*Our* streets.' Darac nodded. 'Uh-huh.'

'Our streets, yes!'

'Okay – first, monsieur, I have no real idea of what's happened here, and as Professor Bianchi is only just beginning her preliminary exam, I suspect neither do you. Second, should the dead man prove to have been murdered during ritual prayers by one of us "real, pure-blooded" Frenchmen, I fully realise I will need to tread carefully.'

As if throwing down the gauntlet, Frènes whipped the silk handkerchief from his forehead and finally turned to face him.

'Tread carefully? If there are toes to be trodden on, Captain, you tread on them. If there are feathers to be ruffled, you ruffle them. You delight in so doing.'

'Bullshit.'

Frènes raised his hands palms upwards.

'There we have it.'

'Bravo. It's still bullshit.'

'I'm sure that your musician friends, and yes, even some misguided individuals in the service, find your irreverent approach amusing, Captain. I do not. We cannot tolerate it on this of all occasions. Understood?'

'"We", Monsieur Frènes? Let me ask you something. How did your superior, the examining magistrate, react to your recommendation I be excluded?'

'As you well know, Examining Magistrate Reboux is not my superior. Our roles run parallel…'

The vein in his temple throbbing with his growing exasperation, Darac got in close.

'Listen, I don't care if you and Reboux run parallel, opposite, upside down or up each other's arses. How did he react to your suggestion?'

A moth flying too close to the flame, Frènes fluttered back into his own space.

'Naturally, he agreed with me.'

'Alright, he agreed with you. I'll bet *my* superior didn't…'

Frènes's eyes were as black and expressionless as buttons. But they slid tellingly downwards.

'...And without Agnès's agreement, you'd have to apply for a formal suspension to sideline me. A suspension on suspicion I *might* step over the line? It's possible you'd pull it off, but it would be a long shot. Am I wrong?'

Before Frènes could reply, there was a rap on Darac's window. He turned. The burning bush had appeared. A sign from above! Either that, or it was the sun catching Bonbon's shock of red hair.

'Am I wrong, monsieur?' Frènes made no reply. 'Thought so.' Darac opened the door. 'How's it going, mate?'

'Not so bad, chief. Yourself?'

Frènes had already heard enough – and not only because he sometimes struggled to understand the syncopated rhythms and altered vowel sounds of Bonbon's Perpignan accent.

'What do you want, Busquet?'

'Oh yes, monsieur.' For the nth time that morning, Bonbon dragged his police armband back up his beanpole of an arm. 'I thought you ought to know something about the dead man before you make a complete... Before you get any further.'

'Well – what about him?'

'What about him?' Drawing out the moment tried Frènes's patience all the more. 'Oh, just that he wasn't a Muslim.'

'But... he was bowing down to the east and all that nons— He was praying.'

'I've just questioned the young guy who was worshipping next to him.' Bonbon's armband was already making the journey south. 'His mind on higher things, he didn't realise anything was amiss straight away. Eventually, though, he became aware that the man on his right didn't know the score. He was just copying everyone else. And that was also the conclusion of a couple of onlookers. They'd spotted it from the start. The guy had no idea what to do, they say. He was faking it.'

'Oh, thank God.' Exhaling deeply, Frènes gave his forehead a prolonged dab. 'But why would anyone do that?'

Darac got out of the car and leaned in.

'That's the first thing I aim to find out, monsieur. I take it you have no objection if I get on with things?'

'Uh... under the circumstances, I suppose you may as well continue. As soon as you know the dead man's religious status for certain, let me know, Captain. Understood? In the meantime, I shall issue a statement to the media about this discovery.'

'That should pour water on any burning rags.'

'Exactly.' Frènes nodded, missing the gibe.

'And you can stand the bully boys down now, monsieur. We won't be needing them.'

'If by "bully boys", Captain, you mean the CRS...'

'Don't look so offended. You'll be saving money.'

'Yes. Well...'

Darac turned to take his leave but Frènes had one further point.

'Bear this in mind, Captain: if it transpires that the dead

man indeed wasn't a Muslim, you will *still* need to tread carefully.' Frènes folded the handkerchief back into his breast pocket almost reverently; silk dampened in the line of duty. 'Should one of them prove guilty of murder, ensure that you do everything – and I mean everything – by the book. If you don't, I shall apply for that suspension anyway.'

There was no need to ask Frènes who he meant by 'them'.

'I'll keep you informed, monsieur.'

As they strode away, Darac gave Bonbon a pat on the shoulder.

'Timely rescue, man – thanks.'

'No problem.'

'Two minutes in Frènes's company and I feel as if I can't breathe.'

Bonbon hoisted his armband up the pole once more.

'Agnès came through for you as well, I imagine.'

'As always.'

'Gangway!'

A black van brushed Darac's elbow as it crept past, heading for the tent.

'God, we're going to miss that woman.'

Bonbon took a packet of wrapped sweets from his pocket.

'Only like we'd miss our right arms. Mint pillow?'

'No Kola Kubes today?'

'The stall in Cours Saleya was out of them.'

'Pass.'

Ahead, a couple of cheerful types hopped out of the van. As one opened the rear doors, the other slid a wheeled stretcher out on to the pavement and locked its legs with a practised flick of the wrists.

'I hate to share even a thought with Frènes...' Darac paused as the morgue boys crossed in front of them with the trolley. '...but why *was* a non-Muslim diving in amongst their prayers?'

Bonbon allowed the softening sweet to roll around his tongue.

'A bet? Or just to see what it was like? Maybe an actor researching a part?'

'What – and someone took offence and killed him?'

'The only person who seems to have taken offence at anything was a passer-by. An old woman.'

'A non-Muslim?'

'As Vichy, by the sound of her. The imam was pretty forgiving about it, I must say.'

Over Bonbon's shoulder, Darac spotted a smiling, dignified-looking figure appear in the doorway to the prayer room.

'That's him, isn't it?' he said, pulling at the hem of his polo shirt to lap a little air around his torso. 'I recognise him from *Nice-Matin*.'

Bonbon turned.

'Monsieur Abdel Asiz, yes. Nice man, warm, urbane – not what you might imagine an imam to be like. And co-operative. He asked all the congregation to stay behind to talk to us, for instance.'

'And did they?'

'As far as we know.'

'He was inside the prayer room throughout the service?'

'Yes, another man, one Hamid Toulé, was leading the outdoor congregation – and by leading I mean literally standing in front of them – but he didn't see anything, either. It's not surprising. They don't look around like people do in church. Even when they're not prostrating themselves.'

Outside the prayer room, a uniform approached Imam Asiz and suggested he go back inside. Pointing at his watch, he exchanged a few remarks before complying.

'He's concerned we might still all be here when the next prayer service is due to start. *Asr*, it's called.' Bonbon spelled it. 'Short and sweet. The word – not the service.'

'When is it?'

Bonbon's elastic band of a mouth stretched into a wider grin.

'All of three hours away.'

Darac let out an involuntary laugh.

'Tell him we should've finished in the prayer room itself by then but the outdoor area will be cordoned off for a lot longer than three hours.' Making a shade of his hand, Darac scanned the area. 'We'll have to find somewhere else for them.'

'That might not go down too well with the local traders. Christ!' Bonbon screwed up his face, suddenly – a meandering trickle of sweat had found its way into his eye. There was nothing for it. Reaching into his back pocket, he unfolded his police-issue cap and corkscrewed it on. Filaments of red frizzy hair escaped its elasticated rim; he looked as if he was wearing a head wreath made of copper wire.

Still scanning the area, Darac pointed to a spot between the apse end of the Basilique and the car park.

'Maybe we could put the worshippers there for the time being. That shouldn't irritate the non-Muslim locals. And if it does, that's just too bad.'

'I'll tell the imam it's sorted.'

'So none of the Muslims saw anything. What about those CCTV cameras?'

'They don't cover the area directly outside the prayer room so there'll be no shots of the incident itself. But we should get the comings and goings either side.'

'Such as that old lady you'd started to tell me about?' Darac's gaze fell on the two lowest-ranked members of his team. Questioning witnesses on the far pavement, the youngsters seemed to be making heavy weather of it. 'What do we know about her?'

'Ah, yes – the old lady. She's out shopping, comes on the congregation, and having to make a detour around them, passes the time by giving them a real tongue-lashing.'

'It happens.'

'I know it happens but this time, there's a twist. As she turns at the end of the back row, she stabs our fake Muslim in the arm. Not that she realised he was a fake, presumably.'

Darac turned back to Bonbon.

'Stabbed? Well then…'

'Don't get excited. She… did it with her shopping trolley.'

'A Ben Hur-style drive-by?' Darac nodded, scarcely able to keep back the laugh. 'So we get a make on a shopping trolley and we nail a killer? Sweet.'

'Absolutely. *But* when the prayer meeting came to an end seconds later, the man *was* dead. And so far, everyone swears nobody else touched him – not the young man praying next to him, nor the one in front, nor any of the other passers-by, or any of the spectators. She was the only one.'

'Someone must have touched him eventually. Or how did they realise he was a goner?'

'No. No one did. He was so still and unresponsive, it was obvious, they say. Like a freeze frame in a movie.'

'Uh-huh.' Darac put his hands on his hips and stared at the floor. 'Just to get this straight, Bonbon... The dead man was the last to join the congregation and he occupied the back right-hand corner position?'

'Yeah – making it easier for him to slip in unnoticed.'

'Anyone see him before the service began?'

'No one in the congregation.' Already uncomfortable in his cap, Bonbon took it off. 'A couple of the onlookers did and there could be others.'

'How did he seem to them? Solemn, neutral, agitated?'

'Nervous, one of them thought.'

'Uh-huh.' Darac pursed his lips as he stared away for a moment. 'This old woman. Do we know who she is?'

'Not as yet. Sounds quite a character. Someone will know her.'

'The one who was praying next to the dead man – he's waiting in the prayer room along with the imam and the other Muslims you kept back for further questioning?'

'Under the watchful eyes and ears of Seve Sevran, yes.'

'Seve? Perfect choice. Have you needed his translation skills?'

'Not so far – I've understood everyone perfectly. And before you ask, they've got my accent down, as well.'

'They can follow that ping-pong Perpignan you call French?'

'Every syllable. And it's not ping-pong. It's table tennis.'

'*Table tennis* Perpignan? Doesn't really cut it.' Once again, Darac lapped a little air around his torso. 'Got a list of names?'

Bonbon took out his notebook and started riffling through pages.

'Seve's wife's in hospital again, you know… It's here somewhere.'

'I heard. Doing a lot better, though, Granot tells me.'

'Can't be easy though, can it? For either of them. Here we go.' He handed it over. Under 'Imam Abdel Asiz' were two lists of names. One was headed 'Praying Close to the Dead Man' and was accompanied by a diagram; the other was 'Seen Dead Man Previously'. There were twelve names and addresses altogether. 'As I said, no one saw anything earlier, but when they looked at the body afterwards, you'll notice five of them remember seeing the man before.'

Darac took out his own notebook and jotted down the names.

'When and where did they see him?'

'Here on Rue Verbier. Just passing by. They couldn't be specific about the times.'

'Okay. The dead man's next-mat neighbour...' Darac checked the notes. 'Young Monsieur... Slimane Bahtoum. He hadn't seen the dead man before, I notice.'

'No.'

Feeling the sun burning through the frizz to his scalp, Bonbon brought out the cap once more. Abandoning the head-wreath look, he opted simply to rest it on his head.

'So what did you make of this Slimane Bahtoum? Despite the fact that no one saw him do anything, he's in Position A, isn't he?'

'He's twenty – a young twenty at that. *Very* nervous.'

'As he would be if he'd...?'

'No, no,' Bonbon shook his head, dislodging the cap. He bent to pick it up. 'If he turns out to be the killer, I'll eat this bloody hat.' He stuffed it back into his pocket. 'I think he's upset because the guy died right next to him. It could throw anyone.'

'Well, we'll see.'

'That's about it for the moment.'

'Thanks, man.' Darac slid his notebook into his back trouser pocket. 'So – body time. Then I'll go over to the prayer room.'

The light in Bonbon's twinkling brown eyes softened for a moment.

'Prayer room... I still think of it as Bistro Carlat. Used to go there a lot when I first moved here. Beautiful etched-glass mirrors – all original.' He scrunched his freckled brow. 'What do you make of it, chief? Muslims praying en masse out on the street and all that?'

'I know diversity isn't the French way but *you* don't have a problem with it, do you?'

'How could I? Don't tell Sarko but I feel Catalan first, French second, myself.'

'Well, then?'

'It must be a question of degree, I suppose. Preferring *suquet de peix* to *bouillabaisse* seems a hell of a long way from prayer mats made out of pizza boxes. It all just seems... a bit weird.'

'It's religions, mate. They're all weird. And if the city had granted Asiz the mosque his congregation seems to need, they wouldn't have to come out here like this.'

'True enough.'

They felt a displacement of air. Granot was bearing down on them, fanning himself with a Tour-heavy edition of *Nice-Matin*.

'Still here, chief? How did you swing that?'

'Mainly through the dead man not being a Muslim.'

'Well, well.' Granot gave the shaggy thicket that was his moustache a contemplative tug. 'What the hell was he doing?'

'Here.' Bonbon reached into his pocket. 'Rest those luscious lips on a mint pillow and it might come to you.'

Producing the sweet packet induced a folded slip of paper to fly out in its slipstream. Deftly catching it with his other hand, Bonbon brandished it as if he'd retrieved a winning Lotto ticket.

Granot eyed it suspiciously

'That from the office sweepstakes?'

'Oh, yes indeed.'

'So who'd you draw?'

Bonbon nonchalantly unfolded the slip of paper. Numbered 22, it bore the name of one Lance Armstrong.

No character actor could portray jowly disgruntlement better than Granot.

'Armstrong?'

'This will be his year again.' Bonbon gave a super confident nod. 'You watch.'

'I don't think he'll win. But he's bound to wind up on the podium. You lucky bastard.'

'It's about time. I've never drawn anybody worth having in the Tour before. Who'd you get?'

'Uh, guys? I know I was late getting here but now we're all…'

Granot had more important things to discuss.

'Some *domestique* from Liquigas I've never heard of. And you get Armstrong – Jesus. Who'd you pull out of the hat, chief?'

The thing was just going to have to run its course.

'Uh… it was a Spaniard… Matador? No… Fundador? Yes, Fundador, I think.'

'Not Alberto *Conta*dor?'

'Contador! That's it.'

More pain for Granot.

'I don't believe it. A hundred and eighty riders in the race and you get El Pistolero? You who know nothing!'

'You've only drawn the red-hot favourite.' Bonbon was still smiling. But his eyebrows were crowding his hairline. 'It's 500 euros for you if he wins.'

'Which he probably will.' Granot made a guttural sound in his throat. 'And failing that, there's 250, and 150, for second and third.'

'Life's just not fair.'

'Fairer for some than others.' A voice calling out, Bonbon glanced back at the prayer room. 'Be there in a second!' The uniform standing guard nodded. 'I'll leave you two to it.'

'See you later, Bonbon. Right, Granot – sign-in and suit-up time.'

'Overalls in this heat? Ai, ai, ai.'

Patricia Lebrun was waiting for them at the red zone.

'So you've got time for me now?' Darac gave her a grin. 'And after all we've been to each other.'

'Sorry, Captain. Just didn't know what to say earlier. I'm glad you're on the case.'

Granot leaned in to her.

'He got Contador in the sweep.'

'I take it all back.'

Darac ducked easily under the cordon tape and held it up for Granot.

'Let's do some work.'

Granot's voice compressed into a hoarse whisper as with all the grace of a beached walrus, he shifted his bulk under the tape.

'This had better be worth it.'

It was a crime scene unlike any either of them had seen before. On the ground, mats and other floor coverings lay butted together in strict alignment to the east. Members of the forensic team were crouched over some of them. Supplication of a different kind.

'It looks like a Bedouin encampment, doesn't it?' Granot said.

'Except some of the mats are cardboard.'

A flash gun went off away to their right.

'Thank you. That's all the shots we need for the moment.'

Darac and Granot shared a look. The cigarette rasp of Professor Deanna Bianchi's voice was a reassuring sound to hear at a crime scene.

The photographer withdrew, leaving her filling in a form over the corpse of a man dressed in a white suit. Darac and Granot slotted in next to her like late-arriving mourners at a graveside. Except for bare feet, the body appeared fully clothed and had been left in the attitude of death: eyes wide open, forehead down on an opened-out, unused pizza box. A further box was opened out under his knees. Darac made a mental note to check their provenance.

Glancing up at the visitors, Deanna performed a double take.

'It was a misunderstanding,' Darac said.

'That's a relief. To us all.' A wry smile gave way to an exaggerated expression of concern. 'Have you ever considered attending anger management classes, Captain?'

Darac indicated the corpse at his feet.

'Listen – bring our dear public prosecutor in here and even *this* guy might lose it.'

Deanna pushed her wire-framed glasses back up her little ski jump of a nose.

'That would be quite some trick.'

Granot took out his notebook.

'Does the gentleman have a name, Professor?'

'Emil Florian. A teacher at the Lycée Mossette in Riquier.' She glanced over her shoulder. 'The deceased's effects please, someone?'

Darac peered more intently at the corpse.

'So what have we got?'

'What we've got is a Caucasian man in his late fifties; lean and fit with no outward signs of ill health – except that his heart isn't beating. Stopped just over forty minutes ago according to a string of witnesses and I would say that was about right.'

Granot noted down the time of death, adding an 'E' for estimate.

'If it weren't for his staring eyes, he'd look as if he'd just fallen asleep.'

'Indeed.'

They were joined by a pleasant-faced young black man carrying a metal evidence case.

'Set it down there, Lami,' Deanna said, completing her form. 'Do you two know our new assistant, by the way?'

Darac gave him a smile.

'We're old friends. Since yesterday.'

Granot's pen was hovering.

'Have you had a chance to check the next of kin?'

'Yes I have, Lieutenant. No wife or children. Both

parents deceased. There's an older brother Jean but the address we have is in Paris. Someone phoned but the number was down or dead. We'll contact the local station and ask someone to call by.'

'In that case, I'll approach the lycée principal to ID the body.' Granot brightened suddenly. 'I'll accompany him, I think. In this heat, I can't think of anywhere I'd rather be than the morgue.'

Lami fished a clear poly bag out of the case.

'Here's Monsieur Florian's *carte d'identité*, et cetera.' He handed over the bag. 'The contents of the wallet are listed separately.'

'Mobile?' asked Granot.

'Already gone to the lab.'

'Thank you. I'll check it now and write you out a receipt.'

'We haven't confirmed it yet, Deanna,' Darac said. 'But it seems Monsieur Florian was not a convert to Islam.'

She pulled down the corners of her small, chevron-shaped mouth.

'So why was he pretending to be?'

'Dunno. Hiding from someone, maybe? Someone he believed wouldn't think of looking for him in such a group?'

Granot ticked off an item on his inventory and looked up.

'He's wearing a white suit, chief. It's a bit of an attention grabber for someone trying to blend in with the crowd.'

'Depends on the crowd. And a crowd that has its head down for long periods isn't a bad spot to hide, is it? But let's say you're right about the suit. All it means is he wasn't anticipating trouble when he left home, no? But he appeared agitated when he tacked on to the end of the group, remember.'

Granot's face creased in doubt.

'So your idea is Florian is walking along Rue Verbier when out of the blue, he recognises – let's just call him an enemy – coming towards him and wonders how best to hide. Seeing a Muslim prayer meeting is about to start, he grabs a mat like some of the others are using, takes his shoes off and dives in among them?'

'It's one explanation.'

'But the enemy spotted him anyway and killed him unseen in front of countless people?'

'Let's go no further than "killed" for the moment. That was the word the anonymous caller used – not just "died". Any thoughts as to the cause, Deanna?'

'Some – but until we get Monsieur Florian back to the lab, I can't offer anything concrete.'

'But say I held a gun to your head or… made you listen to the quintet, or something. What would be your informed guess?'

The new boy looked on, uncomprehending. Deanna seemed amused at the prospect of enlightening him.

'The Captain here plays guitar in a jazz group in his spare time.'

'Oh, I see.'

'Or is it the other way around, Darac? Perhaps playing detective is your hobby.'

'The jury's out.'

Granot finally handed Lami a receipt for Florian's effects.

'There you go, son. A chit for a chit of a boy.'

Unsure of how he was supposed to respond, Lami smiled, picked up the evidence case and took his leave.

Darac gave Deanna a knowing look.

'Alright, you can't be certain. But what do you *think* happened to Florian?'

She drew her latex-gloved index fingers to a point under her nose.

'Alright... consider the following. Under normal muscular control, the man knelt and then prostrated himself with everyone else. But when they eventually rose, he didn't. He was dead. There was no thrashing about, no vomiting, no bleeding. In fact, he seemed so peaceful, it looked as if he'd nodded off in that position, as has been said.'

'If there was ever a "but" coming...'

'Quite. He actually died in screaming agony. But it was screaming no one could hear.'

'Then why the apparent serenity?'

'Massive paralysis. Have you noticed his eyes?'

Granot was the first to answer, his lobster-pink cheeks flushing red as he bent.

'They're bloodshot.'

'Not just bloodshot. When do you often see red splotching like that?'

'In cases of strangling or suffocation,' Darac said, straightening. 'But how could that have happened? Be easier to get away with a strangling in the middle of Place Masséna on a Saturday afternoon.'

'Indeed. I looked for pressure marks, blocked airways and so on, just in case. None. So what might that leave us with?'

Putting his hands on his hips, Darac stared at the floor. 'Poison?'

'Exactly. A form that causes death not by cardiac arrest and so on but by asphyxiation. That's what I'm leaning towards, at least.'

'If it was, how was it administered, Professor?' Granot asked.

'Ingesting or inhaling lethal doses of poisons generally causes vomiting of stomach contents or blood – sometimes both – and that didn't happen. Injection was the most likely method. In terms of the substance itself, the degree of paralysis suggests it was a powerful muscle relaxant – a drug like vecuronium or pancuronium, perhaps. But here's a warning – if it was, it's probably undetectable already. Our best hope is this.' She held up a vial containing a minute sample of a straw-coloured liquid. 'It came from those.' She indicated a poly bag in one of the evidence cases. In it was a piece of cut-up cloth. 'His underpants. He must have peed himself.' Deanna mimed cutting them off the body and wringing them out. 'I may just have got lucky.'

Granot gave Deanna a look.

'So to speak,' she added, pleasantly.

'At least you pulled his trousers back up.' Granot shook his head. 'Poor bastard.'

'If the sample is usable, I'll have a result in twenty-four hours. No sooner, so don't badger me about it, Darac.'

'I'll try not to. Once injected, how long would such a drug take to act?'

'You have always to consider the health of the victim, of course. But just in terms of the injectant itself, onset would depend on exactly what it was, what strength was used, whether it was used in combination with another drug, whether it was injected IM or IV…'

Her sing-song tone indicated Deanna could have gone on listing factors for some time.

'Bearing all that in mind, what's the probability that onset was quick?'

'High. There are more quick-acting variants than slow.'

'And how quick can quick be?'

'Rocuronium injected straight into a vein would take effect in no more than a second.'

'A second?' Darac went to run a hand through his hair before he remembered he was wearing a hood. 'Has anyone told you about the old woman and her murder chariot?'

'Yes, they have. It does sound preposterous, you're right.'

'And yet…' There was a slight tear on the right sleeve of the dead man's jacket, Darac noticed. 'There isn't a wound under there, I suppose?'

'There's an abrasion.'

'Sufficient to conceal a puncture mark?'

'Perhaps. If you would let me get back to the lab, I'll find out for you.'

Darac needed just one more guideline.

'So it's more likely that once injected, the drug would take effect quickly. But go to the low probability end of the scale. What sort of time gap is possible with the slow-acting types?'

'That's much more difficult to say.'

'Seconds? Minutes?'

Deanna shrugged.

'Seconds. Minutes. Hours. Come on, Darac – give me a break.'

'If we have to,' he smiled.

'Oh, there's one thing I haven't mentioned. His feet.'

Granot and Darac studied them for a moment. And then shook their heads.

'There are signs of a residue between the toes. It's faint but see there?'

Now that it had been pointed out, Darac could see it clearly.

'Talcum? Soap?'

'I don't know. I'll let you know what I find. So – okay to move the body?'

'Sure.'

'Boys?'

The men from the morgue unclipped the stretcher from the trolley and began picking their way towards her.

'And where's the photographer got to?'

'Here, Professor.'

'The cardboard mats are almost ready for their close-ups.'

Granot pulled Darac aside.

'This thing is intriguing, alright, but it doesn't look like we're dealing with World War Three here, does it?'

'No, no.'

'Okay, so after the lycée principal has formally identified our friend over at the morgue, I might take the rest of the day off, after all. Alright with you?'

'Sure.'

They watched as the stretcher boys trod their way carefully around the body.

'So, the Shopping Trolley Killer.' Granot tugged at his moustache. 'You're not seriously giving credence to the idea, are you, chief? For one thing, where would an old woman get hold of a potentially lethal muscle relaxant?'

'If she did do it, she's not just any old woman, is she? And the drug got into the dead man somehow – assuming Deanna's right about it, and I'll bet she is.'

'One, two… lift!'

The move was carried out with a precision that belied the morgue boys' brawn. Nevertheless, freeing the body moved both bits of cardboard a fraction. Sticking out from under one of them was the point of something shiny.

The flashgun fired.

'What is that?' Granot screwed up his eyes. 'A needle?'

Deanna's ears pricked up.

'Print kit back here, please! Uncover it, will you, Granot?'

He did so. The shiny point wasn't a needle. It was the tip of a key.

2.55 PM

At first, he hadn't understood why the climate control unit featured two display screens. But then someone explained it to him. The first screen showed the temperature the room should be; the second, its actual temperature. He looked at them. Both read 21.2 degrees. Twenty-one point two, he noted. They go in for precision here. Reassuring.

He drifted off to sleep. He drifted into wakefulness.

Once his slow-mo eyes had finally racked into focus, he noticed that aspiration and performance were still locked at 21.2 degrees. He felt reassured all over again. But then, out of nowhere, a subversive thought hit him. Why should he believe what the displays said? How did he know those figures were accurate? Perhaps the numbers were just stuck at 21.2. Perhaps the thing wasn't working at all. Perhaps it was all a trick. A trick to gull the naive.

No, no — everything was alright. He remembered that a minute ago, or ten minutes ago, or ten days ago, the second display had briefly read 21.1. Yes, that's right, there had been a cold snap. It had been freezing. He'd forgotten that for a moment. He looked at the second screen once more. It was 21.2. Good.

Numbers. Numbers everywhere. Red, most of them. Red numbers and graph traces. The machine next to him looked like a jetliner's control panel. Someone had explained to him what it all meant but he couldn't grasp it at the time. Too soon after the op. Numbers would cease to matter soon, anyway.

A blur of green. A rustle of cloth.

'Hello, darling. How are you today?'

It was the blond girl. All beams and bellows. He blinked once.

'That's great! Soon have you up and running about, won't we? Won't we?'

He blinked once.

'That's the way.'

The fat one was with her. She smiled at him. A gentle hand on his forehead. And then on his endotracheal tube. The smell of soap under his nose.

'The flange is making his mouth sore, look. Couldn't we loosen it a little?'

'Needs to be secure. Besides...' The blond one dropped her voice. '...I don't think he'll feel it.'

She was right. He wouldn't.

'I'll just swab on a little barrier cream, then. And put some gauze under it. Just where it's rubbing.'

Bless you. Bless you for wanting to do something just in case it helps.

The blond one shrugged.

'Alright, then.'

'Won't be a sec.'

For the moment, the only sounds in the room were electro-mechanical: the peculiar hollow thuck *of the ventilator; the beeping of the heart monitor. Then the blond one unsheathed a chart from its scabbard at the foot of the bed. Glances jetted at the equipment. Pen strokes on the page. Brisk. Efficient.*

'Now we've got something for you,' she said, ramping up the volume as she put away the chart. 'You know what the Tour is, don't you? The Tour de France? Cycling?' She mimed riding a bike.

He blinked once.

'Starts tomorrow, doesn't it? Did you know that? Well, it does. And you, young man, are going to be able to watch it. That's right! You're going to have your own TV in here. And it's going to be set up at just the right angle to make it easy for you. You won't miss a moment. Now you'd like that, wouldn't you?'

At last, the blond one had said what he wanted to hear. At last, there would be something absorbing to focus on. Something full of movement and colour. Something he loved. Something, indeed, he was depending upon. Using all the strength he could muster, he blinked repeatedly.

'You don't want it? Oh well, never mind. It will be more peaceful in here without it, won't it?'

No, no, no…

The fat one returned. He smelled her fingers under his nose as she eased the pressure on the holder plate. It gave him a chance to correct his mistake. He tried to move his lips but there was no movement in them. With the tube pushing between his vocal chords well down into his trachea, it would have been impossible to speak anyway.

The smell of salve. A smile from the fat one.

'He didn't even want the TV,' the blond one said to her. 'After all that rigmarole.'

2.58 PM

Darac was already stripping off his overalls as he emerged from the crime-scene tent. Pulling at the hem of his polo shirt, he fanned a little air around his torso as he rang his home station, the Caserne Auvare.

'Agnès – good, I caught you.'

'How's the riot?'

Darac gave her an account of the story so far.

'And thanks for your help with Frènes earlier. How the hell am I going to cope after you've gone?'

'Providing you become a completely different person, you'll have nothing to worry about.'

Darac laughed but he knew she had a point.

'We're all still hoping you'll change your mind and stay on, you know.'

'All?'

Darac glanced into the prayer room's white-painted vestibule. At the far end, a door opened.

'*All*. Better go, boss, Bonbon's here.'

He ended the call as Bonbon joined him on the pavement.

'Learn anything?'

'Nothing further, chief.'

Darac heard a message ping into his inbox.

'Except one thing.' Bonbon dragged his armband back over his wiry bicep. 'They're all dying to meet you.'

'I'll bet. Have you seen Granot?'

'Yes – he filled me in on the unfortunate Monsieur Emil Florian. The old woman still wearing her chief suspect's hat?'

'In the absence of anyone else.'

'We'll do better.' Shielding his eyes, Bonbon glanced across the street. The young officers Yvonne Flaco and Max Perand were still struggling to get through their quota of interviews. 'I was going to do the apartment houses next but…' He gave Darac a look. 'What do you think?'

'I'd give the guys a look first. Or we could be here all day.'

'See you later.'

Darac's text was from his girlfriend, Angeline. There had been a change of plan, it seemed. No jazz club for her tonight. Some of her fellow academics had decided to go out for a drink after the final session of the conference they were attending. Probably turn into dinner. Best make his own plans. She signed off simply: *A*.

Darac stared into space for a moment before replying: *Enjoy it, chérie – Paul.*

Frènes's instruction to tread carefully came back to him as he took off his shoes in the vestibule. Featuring cartoon-like musical notes fighting to free themselves from a page of sheet music, his socks would probably be considered bad form. But he stepped into the prayer room itself doubting anyone would notice them.

A single fan circulating in the middle of the ceiling was doing a good job of stirring up the warm air. The uniform on watch, Jacques 'Seve' Sevran, was a short, chunkily built individual. Raising eyebrows as rounded as Norman arches, he acknowledged his superior's arrival with a wry, conspiratorial smile rather than a salute. He was safe: everyone knew Darac's couldn't-care-less attitude to hierarchies cut both ways.

'How's it going, Seve?'

'Not so bad.' His eyes slid down to Darac's socks. 'Tasteful. No wonder they wanted to kick you off this thing.'

'Frènes hasn't seen these. I'll give you ten euros to leave them out of your report.'

Seve's smile didn't match the strained look in his eyes.

'Listen, we're all sorry about Hélène. But she's doing better, I hear.'

'Practically got a season ticket for that hospital. But yes, she's responding well this time, thanks.'

'That's good.' He waited a respectful couple of beats before casting a glance over his shoulder. 'So you've been in here from the start?'

'More or less.'

'And you haven't had to interpret at any point?'

Seve shook his head.

'So the people in here haven't twigged you can understand what they're saying?'

'No. And why should they? I'm white, low-ranking, middle-aged – just a glorified guard dog, really, aren't I?'

Pursing his lips, Darac nodded ambivalently.

'I suppose they could see it that way. Have they been speaking to each other in French?'

'Not all the time, no.'

'Pick up anything?'

'I'm only really fluent in Arabic, remember. I'm pretty sketchy on most of the West African languages. They've been talking about what happened, naturally. But they seem as bemused by it as everyone else. The fellow who led the outdoor congregation – Toulé? He gives me the creeps, though.'

'Which one is he?'

'Over in the corner, the two talking together? He's the one in the white agbada.'

Darac turned. Toulé was a tall, wisp-bearded man wearing a full-length caftan-like garment. A joyless smile featured a row of long, protruding teeth.

'What's your problem with him?'

'He reminds me of a character in *I Walked with a Zombie*. The zombie, to be exact. And how about those teeth? He could chew a corn cob through a Venetian blind, this guy.'

'Seve, you are a wicked man.' Darac took Bonbon's notes out of his back pocket and consulted the congregation diagram. 'So which one's… Slimane Bahtoum?'

'The kid who was praying next to the victim?'

'Yeah.'

'Over there in the corner. He's the nervous-looking one in the T-shirt.'

'Okay, I've got him. And the guy who was praying next to *him*... Anthar Ibdouz?'

Sevran indicated a fleshy, middle-aged man sitting contemplatively in the opposite corner.

'There – the one squatting with his backside between his out-turned ankles. Ever tried that? Kills your knees.'

'Okay, I'm going to talk to them. But first – a spot of general PR.'

'You?' Sevran grinned. 'PR?'

'I know. But you've got to play with who you've got.'

'I'll be listening. And thanks again, my friend. I'll tell Hélène you were asking after her.'

There were a dozen or so men waiting to be re-interviewed; some talking quietly, others sitting contemplatively on the carpeted floor. The room, a small clean-lined space decorated in creams and sky blues, felt light and calm, an atmosphere very different from the guilty shadows and images of torture and death Darac associated with Catholic churches.

Yet there was little room for error here. A series of wall-mounted clocks specified to the minute the times of the day's prayers, and parallel lines woven into the carpet pointed towards a niche in the room's eastern wall, presumably denoting the direction of the Muslim's holy city of Mecca.

'Gentlemen. I am Captain Paul Darac of the Brigade Criminelle and I have been charged with leading the investigation into the death of the man who temporarily joined your congregation earlier.'

All eyes were on him. In them, he read a range of expressions: acquiescence, wariness, irritation – what he would have expected from any group detained for further questioning.

'I know you have all been questioned separately already and so I would like first to thank you for your patience and co-operation on what I know has been a very trying and difficult day for you. I am well aware of the approach of…' What had Bonbon called the next prayer service? '…*Asr*, but I am confident that if the level of co-operation you have all demonstrated so far is maintained, we should have no problems meeting that deadline. As we speak, a separate area is being cordoned off outside so that the…' For a moment, Darac couldn't think of an alternative to 'overspill'. '…the others can be accommodated there.'

In the corner of the room, Seve Sevran gave him a discreet, reinforcing nod.

Darac picked out the dapper, clean-shaven man wearing a grey collarless jacket and black cotton trousers.

'Alright, I would like to begin with you if I may, Monsieur Asiz?'

'Certainly.'

'Let's get out of the way over there.'

Out of the way and out of earshot of the others.

The imam complied as if delighted at the prospect. It was an impressive attitude, Darac thought. Doubly impressive when he remembered the protracted struggle Asiz had had with Nice's civic authorities to set up the prayer room. He was a cleric with a mission, clearly. But as he turned, Darac looked into his eyes and in them saw humour as well as the determination and intelligence for which he was known.

'Just when I thought the situation incapable of generating any further melodrama.'

Darac was at a loss for a moment. But then Asiz directed his gaze at Darac's socks.

'Ah yes. If you would prefer, I could take them off.'

'No, no, no.'

'Thank you.'

'In turn, Captain, I should like to thank you for your attention to our special needs here. Needs, I feel obliged to point out, that would not exist were the Mairie to agree to our mosque proposal.'

'There is progress on that issue though, I understand.'

The imam smiled.

'It is true that with each month that passes, antipathy to the concept at council level appears to diminish. Whether it is because they have grown tired of us cluttering up a street in the centre of the city or they have become more enlightened, I cannot say. Whichever it is, the Mairie is closer than ever before to "when" rather than "if" on the mosque question.'

'That would be quite a coup for you, personally.'

'The outdoor congregation is our front line, Captain. They are the ones who bear the brunt of abuse on a daily basis. When we achieve our goal, the part they have played will not be forgotten.'

'There's obviously a need so I wish you good luck with it.'

'Thank you. We have indeed been fortunate in your appointment to this case, Captain.'

Bridges built, it was down to business. Darac fixed him with a look.

'I hope you will continue to feel that you have been fortunate if it transpires that one of your congregation is guilty of murder.' He deliberately didn't name Emil Florian: the press and TV might be talking to Asiz later.

As if marking the change in temperature of the interview, Monsieur Asiz's eyebrows rose, slightly. His smile, though, did not fade.

'That proposition is destined to remain untested. Although it would make no epistemological sense to state that one of the congregation could not have killed the man, I am nevertheless certain that none of them actually did.'

'As a cleric, it is perhaps natural that you would put faith before reason, monsieur.'

Asiz reacted with a sort of amused relish.

'I am impressed at the precision with which you express your assumptions. But you will see at least some reason in the timing, surely? We are hardly likely to jeopardise our improved standing at the Mairie by murdering a visitor, albeit an uninvited one.'

'Unplanned murders occur, Monsieur Asiz. All the time. As to timing, what's to say there isn't a renegade in your ranks?' Darac's gaze fell on the leader of the outdoor congregation, Hamid Toulé. Sitting away from the others, the man's eyes were closed, his lips moving silently. 'That's possible, isn't it?'

'In practice, it is quite *im*possible, Captain.'

'I understand that after you learned of the death, you asked everyone to stay behind to talk to us.'

'I did.'

'Was everyone able to comply with your request?'

'They were.'

Darac nodded, pursing his lips.

'According to the statement you made to Lieutenant Busquet, you were in this room at the time of the incident?'

'I was.'

'So you neither saw what happened outside nor even knew who was there.'

Asiz registered the hit with a raised eyebrow.

'It is true that I can't strictly vouch for those who were worshipping outside – you will have to see Monsieur Toulé about that. But for those who were in here, yes, everyone remained.'

The interview lasted for another five minutes. At the end of it, Darac had learned nothing further. But he had come to one tentative conclusion – he'd decided that the imam's genial demeanour was genuine enough. But he felt he couldn't entirely trust him, nevertheless.

Darac turned to Emil Florian's next-mat neighbour, Slimane Bahtoum. Wearing cargo trousers and a plain white T-shirt, the young man was sweating profusely as Darac took him to one side.

'Over here, please.'

Raising eyebrows that ran in an unbroken line, the boy seemed anxious to talk.

'I didn't touch the man on my right – the man who died – at any point, Monsieur,' he said, as if countering an accusation to the contrary. 'I will take a lie detector test, have my fingerprints taken, give a DNA sample – anything.'

In the background, Darac saw Imam Asiz watching them as he maintained what must have been a somewhat absent-minded conversation with another member of the congregation.

'Thank you for volunteering for all those tests, Monsieur Bahtoum.'

'Anything to help. And I'm "Slim" to my friends.'

'However, polygraph tests are inadmissible in law; clean fingerprints tend not to register on cloth materials such as the dead man was wearing; and there are any number of reasons why your DNA may not have found its way on to his person.'

'But I swear, I didn't… do anything.'

Darac was put in minde of a line in Shakespeare. The one about somebody protesting their innocence too much. The boy was hiding something, he felt sure.

'Relax, no one is accusing you of anything.'

'No. Sure. Sorry.'

'I know you've already shown it but I'd like to see your ID card, please.'

'Sure.' Squeezing his hand into the thigh pocket of his cargo trousers, he extricated his wallet, took out the card and handed it to Darac. An apple for the teacher.

Slimane's photo matched the face, and the address

agreed with the one he'd given to Bonbon – the boy lived in an apartment block no more than a ten-minute tram ride away.

'A lot of pockets you've got there.' Darac handed back the card. 'A lot of pockets and most of them crammed with stuff.'

The boy's large brown eyes narrowed warily.

'Yes, I know I put too much in them.'

'It's tempting with cargos – I do the same.'

Slimane managed a smile as he squeezed his wallet back into the pocket. 'My mother is always telling me off for it. "You're not a donkey," she says.'

'But if I knew beforehand that I was going to be kneeling and prostrating myself repeatedly, I would make sure I wore something looser.' Darac looked into the boy's increasingly anxious eyes. 'Like almost everyone else here.'

'It is our duty as Muslims to pray five times a day...' The voice was East African-accented and it faded in from stage left. '...Our personal comfort while doing so is not what is important. I am Hamid Toulé. I was leading the outdoor congregation at the time of the tragedy.'

'You have exceptionally sharp ears, monsieur.' Darac couldn't disguise his irritation that at least part of his exchange with Slimane had been overheard. 'I'll come to you later.' He indicated with a shepherding arm that he required Toulé to step away. 'Please.'

'It's just that Slimane here has been very traumatised by what happened and I didn't...'

'Later.'

Seve Sevran slid in between them.

'Just step over there, please, monsieur. I know you've had to wait for some time already but the Captain will get to you soon.'

Toulé exchanged a reinforcing look with the boy and then withdrew. After a few paces, Darac called Sevran back.

'I'll get to him shortly,' he said, under his breath. 'But first I'm going to take Slimane outside. Watch how they react in here, alright?'

'Watching is what I do.'

'Pay particular attention to the imam, and Messieurs Toulé and the man who was next to Slimane – Ibdouz. Obviously, if any of them try to make a mobile call, prevent them.'

'Anything else? I am on my own in here.'

'This from the man who served in Djibouti, Chad – all over Africa?'

'And a lot of good that did me.'

'I could get someone else in here but I'd rather have you. Alright?'

Sevran still looked unhappy but he shrugged assent.

'Okay, that's all,' Darac said, loud enough for everyone to hear. He turned to Slimane Bahtoum. 'Let's go outside for a moment.'

'Why?'

'It's a bit stuffy in here, don't you think?'

'Not really.'

'After you.'

'Uh… okay.'

As they put on their shoes in the vestibule, Darac could already hear representations being made to Sevran. 'Where are they going?' 'What is he doing with him?' 'The boy hasn't done anything wrong.' Following Slimane on to the pavement, Darac scanned the street for the TV news crew. Luckily they had gone.

Without warning, he clamped a hand around Slimane's forearm from behind. Shocked, the boy didn't try to turn or free himself. Darac dropped his voice.

'Okay, Slim, your minders can't prompt you out here. You're on your own.'

As Darac squeezed a little, droplets of sweat from the boy's arm melted into one and began seeping between his fingers.

'Listen, Captain, I haven't—'

'No, you listen. And listen carefully. It wasn't you, was it? It wasn't you who was praying next to the dead man in your too-tight cargos.'

Feeling energy moving through the boy's body, Darac grabbed his other arm.

'Yes, it was me, captain.' The voice came out in a tremulous whimper. Whatever Slimane Bahtoum was, it was obvious he was unused to skirmishes with the law. 'Who else would it be?'

'That's why you were so eager to be tested to prove you hadn't touched the murdered man. Of course you hadn't. Because you were not here at the time, were you?'

'I was. Ask anyone. Let me go.'

Across the street, one or two of the detained onlookers had started to pay attention to them.

'Ask anyone? Alright – see those people gathered together on the opposite side of the street? The ones talking to the officers? They're doing that because they saw the whole thing. Shall we go over there and see if any of them recognises you?'

He felt the boy's body flex as he gave him a slight push.

'Ask anyone in the congregation, I meant. The man praying on my other side – Anthar Abdouz. Ibdouz, I mean! Anthar Ibdouz. Ask him.'

'You don't want to meet the people opposite because you know none of them saw you earlier.'

'No!'

Behind the onlookers, the two CCTV cameras stood as blind sentinels over the scene. They gave Darac an idea.

'Alright, forget the crowd. We have better witnesses. See those CCTV cameras?'

He let Slimane think about it for a moment.

'We've reviewed the tapes and they prove conclusively that it was someone else praying next to the dead man.'

Spotting that Officer Yvonne Flaco had finally finished questioning the onlookers, Darac gave her a beckoning nod.

'Look, I'll make it easy for you. You're sitting at home or you're out with your girlfriend or whatever when you get a call on your mobile – a mobile I'm going to have examined in a minute, by the way...'

'Examine it! There's nothing there!'

'Deleting entries on a phone's call history doesn't really delete them, Slim. And we have other ways of finding out who called you. Whoever it was – maybe it was your brother or just someone who looks like you – had a favour to ask. A big one. Because *he* was the one praying next to the man who was killed.'

'No. And it was that old woman! She did it.'

'Describe her.'

'Old. Short. Ugly.'

'You were waiting for that one, weren't you?'

'No. I saw her do it.'

'But I think you people have been watching too many James Bond movies. A Rosa Klebb type with a dagger wedged in her trolley? No, no. It was your associate who murdered the man.'

Darac didn't believe it, necessarily. But putting the frighteners on the kid was a good place to start.

'It wasn't!'

Flaco joined them, unclipping her cuffs as her eyes met Darac's. He shook his head.

'That makes you an accessory to murder. Twelve years in prison at least.'

'It was the… woman.'

'Alright, let's say your associate is innocent. Why the call to you? Because he knows he's the more likely suspect. Maybe he's got a police record and we know you haven't. Yet. "The police won't care. They'll fit me up for the murder," he says.'

'No, it didn't happen. I was here all the time. Next to the dead man.'

The boy's head dropped. He started to weep.

'Look, I admire your loyalty…'

From out of left field, a shape streaked across the pavement towards them. Shouts. A swell of noise from the crowd. Warnings. The shape didn't stop. Flaco drew her automatic and with two hands, pointed it at the target. More warnings. The shape was a young man, older than Slimane but resembling him. He called out something in Arabic.

'Hold your fire!' Darac released his hold on the young man. As officers swarmed all around them, the pair embraced. Darac couldn't understand the words that percolated through Slimane's tears but their meaning seemed clear.

There was an onrush of sound behind him. Pursued by Jacques Sevran, Hamid Toulé and several others had come running out of the prayer room. The spectacle stopped them as if they'd hit an invisible wall. In their wake came Imam Asiz. He seemed mystified at what had happened. Darac made an instant decision.

'Okay, everyone – listen. Slimane here and his… brother…?'

'Cousin,' the older boy said, his voice heavy with defiance.

'Cousin. That means you share some DNA, by the way. Name?'

No response.

Darac's expression hardened.

'Name?'

'Narooq. Mansoor Narooq.'

'Thank you. So Slimane and Mansoor have just earned a trip to the Caserne Auvare where they will face charges.'

Darac nodded to a couple of burly uniforms. As they cuffed the boys and led them away, he gave Seve Sevran a questioning look. The man shook his head – no one in the prayer room had made or taken a call. That was one plus, at least.

His expression lacking any trace of its customary humour, Darac turned to the congregation.

'Alright, an exchange has taken place here. For reasons yet to be determined, one cousin swapped places with the other. It's difficult to believe that none of you was aware of the subterfuge.' He pulled Anthar Ibdouz out of the sea of faces. 'You, monsieur?'

'I never paid any attention to who was next to me.' He absently scratched his damp cleavage. 'I am sorry. And until this moment, it never occurred to me that such an exchange *could* have happened. Besides, I've only seen the boy, or boys, on a few occasions and never together until this moment. Even standing there, it's difficult to tell them apart.'

If Ibdouz wasn't telling the truth, he was a skilled liar. Further questioning was necessary but for the moment, Darac was inclined to believe him.

'This is quite, quite wrong, Captain.' Hamid Toulé raised an admonishing finger as he stepped forward. 'Such accusations are completely without foundation…'

For a second time, Darac wondered whether it was Toulé, and not the imam, who was the true leader of the congregation. He knew something about the switch, Darac felt certain.

'They smack of a repressive—'

'You, Monsieur, will also go to the Caserne. To answer questions in a more formal setting.'

'That is impossible. It will soon be time for our next—'

'You can pray in the cells. Flaco – take him. No cuffs.'

'Yes, Captain.'

All eyes were on the young black woman as she stepped forward. Short but powerfully built, Flaco didn't need her *don't even think of messing with me* face to convince Toulé that if he didn't move under his own steam, she would do it for him. She gave him the look anyway.

'But it is twenty-seven times more effective to pray in congregation,' Toulé protested as he walked away. 'Twenty-seven times!'

Darac had to fight a strong impulse to say that he didn't care if it was two hundred and seventy times more effective. He was investigating a murder. And he wasn't being told the whole truth.

'Alright,' he said, looking into the eyes of Imam Asiz. 'Let's start again, shall we?'

3.03 PM

Another sheaf of reports completed, Commissaire Agnès Dantier tossed her reading glasses on to her desk and said a silent alleluia. After six straight hours, she was tired, she was hungry and worst of all, her back felt like a broken deckchair.

Closing her eyes, she interlocked her fingers palms-outwards and slowly extended her arms out in front of her. Then, maintaining the hold, she raised them, and tentatively at first, began reaching up to the ceiling. Five minutes spent on this now, she told herself, would pay dividends later.

Short and slight with wide-set hazel eyes, prominent cheek bones and a small, pointed chin, Agnès had a distinctly feline look. On a good day, she could have passed for a decade younger than her fifty-three years. And if she had wanted to, she could have continued working until she reached sixty. But it wasn't just on days like this that she felt ready to retire. She'd cleared enough paperwork to last two lifetimes.

A ringing desk phone brought a premature end to the stretch routine.

'Yes, Candice.'

'Commissaire, I have Squadron Chief Barbusse of the Gendarmerie for you.'

'Oh… Better put him on.' A click signalled the connection. 'Chief Barbusse.' Agnès was already stifling a yawn. 'What can I do for you?'

'Joel, please. I was just looking down the list of those accepting invitations to the Tour de France security briefing in Monaco shortly and I notice there's no tick against the name of one Commissaire Dantier.'

'Probably because I decided not to attend.'

'Why?'

'The Tour needs the local Gendarmerie to be represented, obviously. It needs the CRS. It needs the Garde Républicaine. It needs the Police Munici—' no holding back the yawn now, '…Municipale. Excuse me. But unless the riders are planning to strangle each other as they pedal along the Boulevard des Anglais or something, it doesn't need a representative of the local Brigade Criminelle, does it?'

'Strictly speaking, no. But wouldn't you *like* to be there? Afterwards, there's a reception. You might meet one of the Greats – Hinault or Eddy Merckx. Or perhaps even Lance Armstrong. He's riding again this year, you know.'

And I might meet one Joel Barbusse, Agnès thought – something she was anxious to avoid since the last occasion. But there was an easy way out.

'Oh… very well. Tick my name.'

'Excellent. Don't forget to ring the Centre de Congrès to confirm. And be quick about it – it starts in just over an hour.'

'Must fly, now. Bye, Barbusse.'

She hung up and blew a kiss at a photo hanging on the wall next to her desk. There would be a Commissaire Dantier attending the briefing but it would not be her; it would be her father, Vincent. Failing eyesight meant he would need a chaperone, but, still active at eighty-eight and a fan of most sports, he would welcome the opportunity. In any case, he would do anything for his Agnès, the cute little tomboy who had eventually followed him into the police. Followed him all the way to the rank of commissaire.

She made three quick calls: the first to her father; the second to his preferred chaperone, Roland Granot; and the third to the Centre de Congrès. Five minutes was all it took to set up the whole thing.

At last, it was time for a break. Her bare feet made little unsticking sounds as she picked them up from the lino-tiled floor and slipped on her slingbacks. Taking a CD from a drawer, she collected her things and went out into the corridor. The jewel case was destined for a clear poly pocket attached to her door. Darac had given her the disc, *Out To Lunch!*, some years ago. At least she'd found some use for it.

The place was quieter than usual; most of her team was still out investigating what Frènes the public prosecutor had earlier referred to as a 'crisis of hideous proportions' brewing downtown. Some crisis. Darac would have rung again if there had been a real problem. Agnès knew there would be many things she would miss about her life in the Brigade Criminelle but having to put up with Frènes would not be one of them.

Charvet, the duty officer, was talking on the phone as she signed out so their usual dialogue – 'off to Bistro Étoile, back in forty-five minutes' – took the form of a mime.

Bzzzzzzzut!

A set of double doors opened and Agnès walked through on to the top landing of an outside staircase. The sun hitting her like a flamethrower, she lowered her shades and descended the single flight into the compound. The steps were bad news for her back but she managed them without the support of the metal handrail. It was a good job too – it would be too hot to touch.

One of several Police Nationale outfits occupying the site, the Brigade Criminelle's Building D stood no more than twenty metres from the main gate. Casually acknowledging the salute of the uniform on guard duty, Agnès walked around the barrier and headed for the street, the Rue de Roquebillière. Before she reached it, a battered Citroën came up alongside her and braked to a sharp stop. At the wheel was a deranged-looking crackhead. His passenger, a hollow-cheeked blonde, looked equally wired. The driver rolled his window. Agnès leaned in.

'Top marks for the get-up, Armani. But do you have to *drive* like a junkie as well?'

Captain Jean-Pierre 'Armani' Tardelli grinned but it quickly faded as he turned his attention back to the street.

'They've strayed a bit off the tourist trail, haven't they?'

A couple of bronzed young backpackers were standing

by the far kerb. Arms pointing in various directions, their faces were hidden behind a folding map.

'It's not your lucky day, guys.' Armani gave Agnès an authoritative nod. 'Users.'

She stared more intently at them.

'What – you can tell that from their knees?'

'Look at the footwear. Sandals *and* socks? They must be on something.'

The map lowered to reveal a pair of shiny, clean-cut faces.

'They look as if they're on vacation from Bible college,' Agnès said. 'But if it makes you feel any happier, I'm going that way so I'll have a word with them.'

Armani turned to his passenger and winked.

'Another bust down the drain.' Before anyone could reply, he floored the pedal and powered away down the Rue de Roquebillière.

Agnès's conviction about the youngsters only deepened as she crossed the street. In an accent she assessed as southern hemisphere English, she heard the boy say:

'The place opposite? It's called the Caserne Auvare. It's a cop shop.'

'If that's a cop shop, imagine what the prisons around here are like.'

'Cop shop' – Agnès loved that. And she could see the shiny ones' point. The Caserne Auvare wasn't exactly the Hotel Negresco. Behind its perimeter wall, thirteen two-storey barrack-like buildings were aligned in strict parallel rows. Four equally severe three-storey structures were laid out across the road.

'If you're lost, I can help,' she said in perfect English.

'Oh, we're not lost, thanks.' The girl was almost off-hand about it. 'Just decided to explore off-piste for a bit.'

'That way, you discover the real city.'

'If reality interests you, you should take a look at the plaque.' Agnès pointed back at the Caserne. 'On the wall outside the… cop shop.'

Unimpressed by Agnès's instant grasp of the idiom, the couple nevertheless followed her pointing finger.

'Next to the entrance on the right, there.'

'Oh yes, got it,' the girl said.

The boy turned to Agnès.

'One slight problem. Not that hot on the old French.'

'No, no, you'll be fine – it's not written in old French.'

The girl gave him a derisory look.

'What my *genius* boyfriend is trying to say is we can't speak French. At all.'

'Oh, I see. Well, what it says is that in August 1942, the Caserne was used to detain Jews rounded up by local police. Over five hundred were eventually deported to a holding camp near Paris. From there, the end of the line was Auschwitz.' Agnès gave them a smile. 'I hope that is real enough for you? Bye.'

'Uh… yes,' the boy said, wrong-footed. 'It is.'

'Absolutely.' The girl nodded. 'Thanks, Madame.'

Agnès had gone only a couple of paces when her mobile rang. It was Granot.

'Boss? I'm over at the morgue with Lycée Principal

André Volpini. He's just formally identified the Rue
Verbier body as that of Emil Florian – a teacher on his
staff, as the man's papers indicated.'

'Good.'

Granot's voice took on a more solemn tone.

'So is it all set for the Monaco briefing?'

'It is and I've wangled you an invitation to the reception
afterwards, as well.'

'Yes!'

Gleeful enthusiasm? Agnès hadn't thought the big
man capable of it. But there was a time and a place.

'I take it you're ringing from the car park, Granot?'

'Not... as such, no.'

'What do the morgue guidelines say? "Respect and
reverence and at all times."'

'But I might meet the Badger.' Granot's words were
carried on a rising tide of excitement. 'Or even the
Cannibal. In the flesh!'

'Cannibals and flesh isn't really helping, Granot.'

'No, I suppose not. But I'll tell you this: if I do get to
meet any of my heroes over in Monaco, I'll show respect
and reverence, then. Big time.'

'I'll take your word for it.'

'Thanks for this, boss.'

'You're welcome. Just don't forget to pick up my
father.'

'Forget? It'll be an honour.'

'Better get to it, there isn't much time.'

'We'll make it.'

It was an upbeat note on which to end the call. But as Agnès crossed the street towards Bistro Étoile, a different feeling came over her. For the third time in as many days, she felt as if someone was watching her. Unwilling to show her hand, she didn't turn around but maintained her stride, glancing in the windows of every parked car and shop window she passed. The reflections proving inconclusive, she was left with little alternative. She took several more easy paces and then spun around, the suddenness of the move paining her back. There was no one. Not a soul. *After thirty-plus years on the force, I've started imagining things*, she thought to herself. *I really* must *let this thing go*.

It didn't occur to her that she should have trusted her first instinct.

3.08 PM

He had lost interest in the temperature now. It wasn't the display's fault. It was that he'd been promised something really interesting to look at, instead. The most interesting and exciting thing in the world, in fact – the Tour de France. The blond one had promised it and then taken it away. Taken it away because he'd been stupid. He should have stuck to just one blink. One blink for yes; two for no. But he'd got overexcited. He'd blinked repeatedly to show just how much he wanted to see it. To see once again something that was part of him. The road winding ever onwards and up. 21.2? Forget it.

It was at the end of his son's previous visit that he'd told him about the TV.

'They don't usually allow it but I twisted their arms. I'll be seeing you, Papa. Or rather, you'll be seeing me.'

Some hopes now.

He could hear voices in the next room. The short one had just come on duty. The short one and his favourite, the fat one. Voices louder. Blurs, smells. They were here. Now was his chance.

The short one's face.

'Hello, my dear. And how are we?'

She had a touch like a forklift truck. His pillows shook as she swung the metal notes case away from the bed end. How are we? How am I supposed to know how you are? Stupid cow. They're nearly all stupid cows. They talk to me as if I'm a child. And they don't really care. That's the thing. Angels? They could be executioners, just as easily. Processing what was in front of them. All except for the fat one.

Here she was.

'Just checking to see if your mouth is any less sore. Is that alright with you?'

He blinked once.

'I'm going to loosen the tube holder plate first.'

Her fingers were under his nose, the plate was loosened. She smiled at him. He tried to speak. But it was impossible to make even a sound. The smell of salve.

Ask me. Ask me if I want the TV again. Ask me if I want it. I'll blink just once.

'Yes, it's doing better. That's good, isn't it?'

He blinked once.

The short one had finished updating his notes. The pillow shook.

Ask me about the TV.

'I'll just tighten it again.'

Ask me.

'Right we're just going to check to see if you have any other sore places,' the short one said. 'Important you don't get bed sores, isn't it? Isn't it?'

He blinked once.

Ask me.

'That's the way.'

For God's sake, ask me.

They took the sheet off him. The short one dropped her voice.

'So he didn't want the TV after all, then? Typical. People get these ideas.'

The fat one looked at him and smiled before the examination began.

When the pair finally left, it was 21.2 degrees in the room. 21.2, yes.

Perhaps it might change later.

4.05 PM

Heading back to the Caserne Auvare from the crime scene, Darac radioed in for a progress summary on Hamid Toulé and the lookalike cousins Slimane Bahtoum and Mansoor Narooq. Each had made a brief initial statement. The feeling was that Toulé knew all about Slimane's post-facto exchange with Mansoor but that it wouldn't be easy to shake his story to the contrary. The cousins themselves maintained that they had consulted no one else before making the switch, nor had they informed anyone subsequently that they had done so. A series of background checks had been started on all three of them.

Once back in Building D, Darac headed straight for the ground-floor office of Jean-Jacques 'Lartou' Lartigue. A strongly built West African with a curiously delicate voice, the scene-of-crime officer had CCTV footage from Rue Verbier cued up and ready to play.

'Okay – what have you got, Lartou?'

Lartigue hit the button.

'As you know, Captain, there's no coverage of the area outside the prayer room itself. This is from the west-facing camera – the one trained on the marketplace. There's nothing of interest until the old woman with the trolley comes into view just… here, look. This is the Before The Incident shot, you might say. Before you ask how I know she's our suspect, I'll show you the After footage from the other camera, shortly.'

She looked exactly as Darac had imagined her: a squat, prune-mouthed pug of a woman wearing a print shift dress.

'How old is she, would you say, Lartou? Seventy?'

'Yes, about that. A little older perhaps.'

She waddled out of shot. The screen went blank.

'I've scoured the frames for anything else of interest – nothing. I'll put in the other disc.'

'So there was no shot of her reaching into the trolley and throwing a spent syringe on to the street, then?'

'One with her full name and address on it? Forensics haven't found one, Captain.'

The disc began to play.

'Disappointing field of view. We're well beyond the Basilique – practically in Jean Médecin.'

'Yes, there's about a hundred-metre gap. Here she comes, look.'

Wild-eyed, mouthing off, gesturing – the woman was still a picture of furious indignation.

'Look at her.' Darac almost laughed. 'Once again, the world has lived down to her expectations, hasn't it? She's the one, alright. Can you get a decent still print of her from one of the earlier frames?'

'Already done.' He handed it over. 'Want me to fly it?'

'Looks pretty good – yes, go for it. Any sign of Florian yet?'

'More than a sign.' He put in a third disc. 'From the camera pointing east again. Watch frame right but don't blink – he's only in shot for a few seconds.'

The man came into view.

'Jogging… not looking around… looks to be running towards something rather than away from it. Play it again.'

Darac watched the sequence five times. Nothing leaped out at him.

'Want a shot of Florian to fly as well?' Lartigue said.

'Please.'

'I'll get on with it.'

'And obviously, it would be useful to know what he was doing before he arrived on Rue Verbier. Do you think you could look at footage from any cameras there may be on Avenue Jean Médecin itself? And you might be able to pick out where the old woman went, also.'

Lartou blew out his baby-plump cheeks.

'That would take a long, long time. *And* the coverage would be far from comprehensive.'

'Well, look – get the thing going and I'll see what I can do resources-wise.'

'Okay.'

Darac gave Lartigue a pat on his bulky shoulder as he rose. 'Now I'm going to have another chat with our friendly neighbourhood Muslims.'

Once in his office, he made straight for the filing cabinets lining the side wall. His beloved Gaggia espresso machine lived on the corner stack. Before the desk sat a man wearing a long white agbada.

'Hope you haven't been waiting long?'

Metal rattled against metal as the man angrily shook an arm. His chaperone needed elsewhere, Monsieur Hamid Toulé had been left handcuffed to Darac's radiator.

'It was either that or the cells. And it's nicer here.' For a couple of beats, the air-con made a sound like lead pellets hitting an oil drum. 'Marginally.' Darac unlocked the filing cabinet and took out a packet of coffee beans. 'And they did leave you one hand free.'

'I was promised water. You people have no undestanding. None!'

'You should have been left some.' Darac turned to see that a cup had been set down next to Toulé's chair. But it was untouched. 'Ah. That's your unclean hand, isn't it? Sorry, Monsieur. That was thoughtless of us.' He went over to him. 'I don't think we need these any more.' A suspicious look was his reward for releasing Toulé's right hand. 'I'll just put them away, and then what would you say to a coffee?'

The man took three sips of water.

'Where is the lawyer?'

On Darac's battle-scarred old desk, a framed photo of Angeline shuddered as he jerked open a drawer. He dropped in the cuffs and rammed it shut.

'Take two,' he said, repositioning the photo. 'Would you like a coffee?'

'No. What I would like is a lawyer.'

'You're being questioned under caution, monsieur – you're not under arrest, as such.'

Darac measured out the beans into the grinder and hit the power button. Toulé waited for it to stop before going on.

'Then arrest me. I want a lawyer. Here. Now.'

Darac couldn't blame Toulé for mistrusting the police. But a lawyer wouldn't help him in the way he probably envisaged. He needed a lesson in French law.

'Let's say I do put you under arrest, monsieur – here's what that would mean.' As Darac began to outline one arcane procedure, he carried on with another – the making of a perfect espresso. 'This case was initiated by a public prosecutor rather than by an examining magistrate. In that circumstance, anyone placed under arrest is entitled to see a lawyer for thirty minutes. The purpose of that meeting is to acquaint detainees with their rights and to outline the legal situation in which they find themselves. The lawyer is entitled neither to read their case dossier nor to be present during questioning, which is conducted anywhere the investigating officer sees fit and without the use of recording devices. Detainees may be held initially without charge for forty-eight hours. This may be extended to ninety-six on the authority of the public prosecutor. Clear, Monsieur Toulé?'

'I am clear that as a system, it is utterly barbaric.'

'It is by no means perfect but let me tell you something about our barbaric system. In certain other countries, guilty parties get away with serious crimes every day precisely because a lawyer is allowed to sit next to them during questioning.'

Toulé seemed unconvinced.

'And think of this – the more money a client has, the smarter the lawyer he can hire. What that means in practice is that if you're rich, you stand a far better chance of cheating justice. You think that's a better system?'

Drawing wisps of beard through his long fingers, Toulé fell into a contemplative silence.

'Neither system is satisfactory,' he said at length.

Darac continued, with the man for another five minutes before he reached the conclusion that there was no compelling reason to hold him.

'Alright, Monsieur Toulé – when is your next prayer service?'

Wearing an expression of deep suspicion, Toulé glanced at his watch. A Rolex, Darac noticed.

'Today, it is five forty-two.'

'I'm going to release you so you can attend it. But I'm going to formally caution you that should you further mislead or obstruct this police investigation, or seek to do so with any inquiry in the future, you will be charged.'

Toulé looked at him as if he was unsure of what was happening.

'You're letting me go?'

'Yes. But I would ask that you remain in the area for the time being and that you make yourself available for further questioning should the need arise. Alright?'

Toulé rose warily, as if fearing a trick.

'I can just… walk out?'

'You will be escorted to the compound where a car

will take you back to Rue Verbier.'

Darac picked up the phone and arranged it, then called the cell block and asked for the youngster Slimane Bahtoum to be sent up. He was saving Mansoor Narooq until last. His story, he suspected, would be key.

4.20 PM

The signature feature of Monaco's Centre de Congrès was its vast glass entrance hall known as La Grande Verrière. To Darac, it had the look of a giant cabochon-cut diamond. No fan of the principality, it was as fitting a symbol for the place as he could conceive.

His second-in-command, Roland Granot, had never been to the Centre before today. As he walked former Commissaire Vincent Dantier towards La Grande Verrière, it looked to him more like a bell jar than a jewel. A bell jar swarming with ants, each wearing an accreditation ID around its neck. A feeling of anticipation rose in his chest. There were giants among those ants.

'Agnès didn't tell me half the world would be at this event.' Vincent may have been pushing ninety but he spoke in a strong, clear voice. 'I thought it was just…' He flinched as a helicopter slid over their heads. 'Good Lord…' He continued in a shout. 'I thought it was just for the likes of us.'

The helicopter set down on the pad a little way to their right. A diverse group of officers disembarked, stooping as they scurried under the *womp-womp* of the rotor blades.

Granot was taken aback by the sight.

'They seem to be on a mission.'

The two men shared a quizzical look and continued on their way.

'You're walking too fast.'

'Sorry, monsieur.'

As they reached La Grande Verrière, the helicopter was airborne once more, a buzzing fly circling the huddled high rises of Monaco. But Granot's eyes were elsewhere.

'Is that…? No.'

Among a sea of faces in the hall, not one proved familiar. But there was time for all that. The reception after the security briefing offered the best chance of rubbing shoulders with his heroes.

'That explains all this hubbub,' Granot said, glancing up at an info screen.

Ploughing his face into furrows, Vincent's mouth gaped open as he tried to squeeze some focus into his eyes.

'Can't see a damn thing at this range. What does it say?'

Granot shook his head, irritated with himself.

'No, of course you can't see it, monsieur. It's saying that the Centre is not only welcoming the likes of us today, it's also home to the entire race organisation. And to the press as well.'

'No wonder, then.'

'Indeed.' Granot scrutinised their tickets. 'Right – where are we headed?'

By the time the pair had got through security, signed in and made their way through the crowds to the conference room – Salle Prince Pierre – Granot realised his hopes for later had been unrealistic. There were just too many people around. Chatting with the likes of Bernard Hinault wasn't going to happen.

After a further check, they were finally admitted to the Salle Prince Pierre; or rather to its lobby, where groups of girls wearing sashes and smiles were handing out meeting agendas. Granot glanced at the five-page document as they joined the slow march into the auditorium itself. He gave a disdainful chortle.

'I'm sure you'll agree with me, monsieur, that individually, each of the forces represented here today knows exactly how to do its job. By the look of it, this meeting is just to make sure that everyone knows where one outfit's role ends and another's begins.'

'I do not agree with you. When disparate police groups have to work together, smooth co-ordination between them *is* a vital consideration. If it's not done well, things might fall apart. And the more there are of these groups, as there are nowadays, the more likely it is to happen.'

'Do I detect, monsieur, that you think there are too many links in the chain of our modern police structure?'

'Perhaps. At one time, you realise, we had just the opposite problem. Everything was monolithic, unwieldy, slow to react. We needed change. But we may have gone too far in the opposite direction. Time will tell.'

Granot glanced at his watch as they entered the auditorium proper. With still just over fifteen minutes to kick-off, there was plenty of time to take in an exhibition of photos lining the rear wall. The shots portrayed celebrated battles from almost a hundred years of the Tour.

'Will you be able to see these alright, Monsieur?'

'I'm not completely blind, Granot.'

After commenting on each contender in turn, they came to a photo depicting perhaps the most celebrated battle in Tour history. Granot gave a long, contented sigh.

'Anquetil versus Poulidor. Puy de Dôme, '64.'

Drawing down the corners of his pinched slit of a mouth, the old man nodded.

'It was good tussle, no question. But there were greater. And greater riders.'

'So who would you regard as the greatest, monsieur?'

'Oh, it must be the Cannibal – Merckx. But my favourite was the Angel of the Mountains. Now who was that?'

Vincent turned, giving Granot a look he felt go right through him. Perhaps a consequence of the old man's impaired vision, the effect was unnerving, nevertheless.

'Charly Gaul,' he said, passing the test somewhat to Dantier's annoyance. 'What a climber. The worse the conditions, the better he climbed.'

'That man was no stranger to suffering. Inspiring – so much so that when he retired, my interest in cycling retired with him to some extent. Although latterly, I did enjoy watching Pantani. Even though he was, shall we say, assisted in his efforts.'

Granot suspected the same could have been said of Charly Gaul but he made nothing of it.

'It was sad, wasn't it – what became of Charly.'

'Losing it upstairs, you mean? Very sad. And then becoming a recluse. Recovering for a time. Losing it again. And all the physical problems. Hospitals. Think – the heart that powered him up all those mountains...' Vincent stared off, shaking his head. 'That heart... failing. Pulmonary embolisms – all manner of complications.' Closing his eyes, he waved a hand in front of his face as if Charly's fate was something he preferred not to confront, or perhaps as an indication to some unseen arbiter that he was not ready to fall into a similar decline himself. 'Let us continue.'

The remaining shots provoked further debate in which Vincent always sought to gain the upper hand, Granot noticed. Competitive to the end. It was a quality he admired.

'Time to take our seats, monsieur.'

Vincent turned and peered into the auditorium. Accessed by three aisles of steps, the stalls tiered steeply down to a stage milling with blurred shapes.

'Which are ours?'

'End of the third row back from the stage. We'll just take this side aisle down and we'll be right there.'

'It's stepped. Bugger.'

'Remarkably, we haven't yet talked about Lance Armstrong. Where would you place him in the overall panoply?'

'Not for the moment. I need to concentrate.'

Cursing under his breath, Vincent held on to the

banister rail and began his descent. As sound in wind and limb as he had been twenty-five years ago, it was only his eyesight that troubled him. His depth perception all but gone, it had turned the everyday activity of negotiating even shallow steps into a nightmare. And the last thing the old man wanted was to take a tumble; especially in front of the Who's Who of law-enforcement officers and Tour officials who would be making up the platform party.

Granot hadn't seen Vincent in some months and watching him feeling his way down the steps gave him pause. Not overly tall, but stocky, he'd been a bull of a man in his prime. A pocket battleship full of energy and ingenuity. By any standards, a great commissaire. And he had been almost as impressive in his retirement. Former senior officers always promised to give their successors help only when asked. Granot couldn't think of another ex-chief who'd stuck to that promise. Even when his own daughter eventually followed him into the commissaire's office, he had never once interfered. And now, as Agnès was herself about to retire, here he was, still turning out when needed.

They had reached the third row.

'We're there, monsieur.'

Granot knew better than to offer an arm as the old man gingerly felt for the tread with his foot. Vincent nodded conspiratorially. He didn't want any of the great and good to be aware of his condition but Granot didn't count. Serving for several years under Agnès, he was family. More or less.

'Now – you want to know where I would place Lance Armstrong?' Vincent finally sat down. 'Well, his record speaks for itself.'

In the adjacent seat was a bronzed individual wearing the uniform of a chef d'escadron of the Gendarmerie Nationale.

'No, no, no.' He flashed Vincent a bullet-proof grin. 'That seat is reserved for Commissaire Dantier.'

'This *is* Commissaire Dantier, monsieur,' Granot said, indicating Vincent's ID.

It took a couple of seconds for the penny to drop. And for the grin to implode.

'Ah. Monsieur, we have never met. Barbusse. Joel Barbusse.'

They shook hands.

'You were expecting my daughter, I imagine?'

'She must have been detained, obviously. Call of duty.'

'No. Just didn't want to come. Wisely, by the look of it.'

As Vincent continued to make Joel Barbusse's disappointment complete, a trio of good-looking, smartly turned-out young officers breezed in and sat in the seats in front of them. Leaning forward, Granot checked the epaulette insignias on their crisp, short-sleeved shirts. He smiled, a feeling of nostalgia drawing over him.

As a young boy, Granot's burning ambition had been to become a top-class footballer. But as he'd grown into his teens, it became clear his ambition was a pipe dream. Chubby, slow and lacking the necessary skills for football, he turned his attentions to rugby but found no greater success. Boxing and then judo were to go the same way.

By fifteen, he realised a change of tack was called for. He needed to aim for a more attainable goal. And then, on Bastille Day 1973, he witnessed a performance by the motorcycle display team of the Paris-based elite corps, the Garde Républicaine. They were fast. They were daring. They were glamorous. He wanted to become one of them even before someone told him that for three weeks every year, an inner corps of forty-five Garde Républicaine officers got to roar around the roads of France helping to police the greatest sporting event in the world.

It made the young Granot drool to think of it. A member of the Garde Républicaine's Tour de France detail got to ride big, fast motorbikes; he got the best seat in the house to watch the race; he got to wear the sharpest police uniform on the planet; and for having all that fun, he got paid into the bargain. And it seemed such an easy assignment. A GR officer at the Tour was basically a glorified traffic cop. His principal role was to alert the race's main bunch of riders – the peloton – to potential hazards on the road ahead. Travelling at high speed in tight proximity to one another, riders in the peloton were in a vulnerable position. Accordingly, GR officers were detailed to take up stations in front of every blind turn, bollard and raised manhole cover on the route. Blowing a whistle while waving a warning flag was all it took. Once the riders had safely passed a hazard, the GR officer in question would remount his bike and buzz past the peloton en route to marking his next assigned position. With the load shared by forty-five guys, what could be easier?

And as if all that wasn't enough to recommend a career in the corps, there was the not inconsiderable promise of sex. Seeing him sitting astride his machine in a pair of the GR's famous knee-length leather riding boots, what girl could have resisted the young Granot?

Chuckling at the recollection, he leaned forward between the seats.

'Still riding BMWs, or have you gone Japanese?'

Heads turned. Gardes Républicaines could be leather-faced, hard-bitten types. These three were a recruiting officer's dream: petrol heads with poster-boy cool. The most senior was a square-jawed man with a cheeky glint in his eye.

'We're still on the Beemers...' He glanced at Granot's ID. '...Lieutenant. Of the Brigade Criminelle de Nice, no less.' He gave a little nod of appreciation. 'Murder, robbery and general mayhem – real policing. Haven't got any vacancies over there, have you?' He reached over the back of his seat to shake hands. 'Senior Officer Yves Dauresse.'

'Roland Granot. Vacancies – what are you talking about? You lot have got the best job in the world.'

'You think the best job in the world would involve waving a flag and blowing a whistle?'

Granot shook his head, disbelieving.

'When I was a kid, I would have given anything to be part of the GR Tour detail.'

'So would I. But I'm not a kid any more. Unlike this one.' Dauresse jabbed the shoulder of the young man to his right, a blond boy with a ready smile. A second handshake introduced Granot to Roger Lascaux. 'Eighteen and never been kissed. According to his mother.'

A cloud seemed to drift into Lascaux's clear blue sky.

'Brigade Criminelle? Not in for any trouble, are we, Lieutenant?'

Granot shook his head.

'No, no. Like you guys, I'm just along...'

'...for the ride,' the trio chorused.

The big man gave an amused harrumph. Of course they'd heard it before.

'Roland Granot,' he said offering his hand to the remaining member of the group.

'David Jarret. Good to meet you.'

In his mid to late twenties, Jarret's features were less chiselled, the eyes more sensitive than the others. But as a student of the checks and balances of human nature, Granot expected his handshake to be the most vice-like of the three. It was.

Over his shoulder, members of the platform party were taking the stage. Jarret turned.

'Here comes the peloton.' Their desks were arranged in a single line across the stage. 'Not a particularly aerodynamic formation.'

Granot ran his eye over them.

'There's certainly enough of our lot up there, although I don't know who half of them are. Don't even recognise some of the insignias.' One face he did recognise was Fréderic Anselme, chief of the Groupes d'Intervention de la Police Nationale, the crack SWAT outfit that maintained a small unit at the Caserne Auvare. Granot gave a disdainful snort. 'Typical that a GIPN man would find his way on to the platform.'

Centre stage was a short, balding man with the deeply lined brow of a professional worrier. Exchanging words with those on either side of him, he seemed to be waiting for a signal to begin.

Back in the stalls, Granot felt a dig in his side. Vincent, finally tired of humiliating Joel Barbusse, was looking for a new game to play.

'Ah yes.' Granot turned to the poster boys. 'Gentlemen of the Garde Républicaine, may I introduce former Commissaire of the Brigade Criminelle de Nice, Monsieur Vincent Dantier.'

As a second round of introductions began, Granot was concerned that David Jarret's steam-hammer grip might pain the old man's arthritic hand. But when it came to it, the young man seemed to realise the possibility and shook it with almost surgical care.

Yves Dauresse gave Vincent the warmest grin as he held on to his hand.

'I've been telling my young colleagues here, Monsieur Le Commissaire, that if we want to see life in France as it really is, we should transfer to the Brigade Criminelle.'

'If you do join the BC, you won't pull half as many women,' the old man said, getting a big laugh.

'Just have to give each one double time,' Lascaux grinned.

The gag provoked comebacks that played under a series of thuds emanating from the stage speakers. The balding man was tapping his microphone.

Dauresse cast a quick look over his shoulder.

'Showtime.' He gave Granot an anticipatory grin. 'Front and centre, boys.'

A hush fell over the hall.

'Suzanne – are you up in the gallery?' the balding man said into his mike. 'Any unauthorised personnel in there with you? No? Okay, good. Jacques? Can we now ensure that our meet-and-greeters are escorted out of the auditorium and the doors locked, please? They are already? Good.'

Wearing the sort of expression TV newsreaders favoured when advising a nation of the death of its president, the bald man took a sip of water and called the meeting to order.

'Thank you. My name is André Soutine and as Security Director of the Tour's Organising Committee, I would like to welcome you all to this briefing.'

'He looks on top form this year,' Granot heard one of the GR boys whisper.

Delivered in a grave monotone, Soutine's introductory remarks followed the familiar pattern of thanks, introductions and announcements and concluded with a short mission statement. Then to business.

'Ladies and gentlemen, I wish first to draw your

attention to item twenty-nine on your agendas.'

Grunts of surprise went up as pages riffled all around the stalls.

'They're starting with Any Other Business?' A side effect of Vincent's incipient deafness was that he spoke much louder than he realised. 'That's a first.'

'The reason for it will become clear, monsieur,' Soutine said, without looking up from his notes. 'I should like to ask Commandant Georges Lanvalle of the DCRI to address the meeting.'

That got everyone's attention. The Direction Centrale du Renseignement Intérieur was the Ministry of the Interior's Intelligence Agency.

A well-coiffed man in his early fifties tapped his mike. 'Is this on? It is? Very well.'

Lanvalle held up a brown envelope and a sheet of A4 paper. On it was arranged text made up of letters cut out of a newspaper. The hall fell completely silent.

'This message was received less than two hours ago. It begins: "To the organising committee of the Tour de France. In two days' time, your riders will pass en masse through Nice. We, the Sons and Daughters of the Just Cause, give due warning that we will reap a bloody harvest in the city unless the following demands are met…'

4.26 PM

Following another tearful performance from young Slimane Bahtoum, Darac sent for Mansoor Narooq. From the moment the young man was led in, the atmosphere in the office changed. Now there was confrontation, defiance, even a sense of threat.

As he sat down, Mansoor's eyes slid immediately to the windows. To assist the air-con they were closed but the latches were simple affairs. Outside, there was only a four-metre drop to the ground and he was a quick, limber young man.

'Forget it.' Darac fixed him with a look. 'They're alarmed.'

In practice, office windows at the Caserne were alarmed only at night.

'And you'd never make it out of the compound anyway.'

Alarms or no alarms, that was almost certainly true.

'And before all that, you'd have to get past me.'

Many had taken on Darac over the years. A few had got the better of him. For a moment, the only sound in the room was the whistle and throb of the air-con.

'I… have no reason to escape.' Mansoor spoke in perfect

French, with a North African accent. 'None whatever.'

'Coffee? I have sugar. And mini bar-style milk.'

'Espresso. No sugar.'

'Sure?'

'Yes, I'm sure.'

Darac tamped sufficient coffee into the holder for two doubles.

'It's a chocolatey little number, this. Guatemalan. Single estate.'

'Chief?'

Officer Max Perand knocked on the open door and loped lazily into the room.

'A note for you.' He handed it over. 'Confirms what you were thinking.' Scratching his armpit, he gave Mansoor a knowing look as Darac read it.

'Thanks. That's all.'

His eye still on the suspect, Perand mouthed 'Busted!' and padded out of the room.

'What did he mean? I've done nothing…'

'You can drop the pretence,' Darac said. 'We know you're staying in this country illegally. As you have tried to do in several others.'

As if a plug had been pulled, all the light and animation went out of the boy's expression. He slumped back, exhaling so deeply, it was as if his life breath was something he felt he no longer needed. Darac drew not one scintilla of satisfaction from the moment. What would it feel like, he wondered, to be shunted around the world, unwanted except in the one place in which you were most vulnerable?

'What's the deportation quota now? Twenty-five thousand a year?' Mansoor's words were heavy with accusation. 'Congratulations, you can subtract one.'

It was a reasonable supposition. But he had chosen the wrong target. Darac hated the whole concept of the quota. Hated it for what it was and for its knowing cynicism. Getting rid of people was so much easier when you reduced them to the status of numbers. And when given numerical targets to hit, law-enforcement officers almost always strove to hit them. It went with the uniform. The plaque on the perimeter wall commemorating the round-up of Jews in 1942 was just one instance of many.

'Listen, I can see how difficult it must be for people in your position. I sympathise.'

'If that is true, then let me go. Give one back from the twenty-five thousand.'

'I can't, quite obviously.'

Mansoor seemed to have another thought. He leaned forward.

'I... could make it worth—'

'Don't offer me a bribe, you idiot!'

The boy slumped back, staring at the floor.

'And I strongly suggest you don't make a similar offer to Immigration when you're handed over. In the meantime, I would ask you to remember that this is still a murder investigation.'

Mansoor sat up suddenly, as if the true precariousness of his situation had only just occurred to him.

'I didn't do it.'

'Let's start with the switch. We know your cousin wasn't praying next to the victim at the time of his death – you were.' Darac knew the answer to his next question but he had to ask it. 'So why did you get Slimane to lie for you?'

'You already know why I asked Slimane to… help.'

On the filing cabinet, the Gaggia began siphoning twin streams of black liquid into a pair of white porcelain cups.

'Still want it black and unsweetened?'

'Milk. And three spoonfuls of sugar. Look, Captain… through nothing but ill fortune, I was present at a man's death and knew I would have to talk to the police about it. I knew that meant my papers would be routinely checked so I rang Slimane and asked him to swap places with me. I didn't think anyone would notice – not even members of the congregation. I'd been to pray there only a couple of times before.'

Darac peeled back the foil from an eyebath-sized carton of UHT milk and squeezed it into one of the coffees. When he turned, Mansoor's eyes were levelled at his.

'Captain, I have never committed a violent act against another human being. Never in my life. And if I had killed that man, do you think I would have put my cousin in the position of chief suspect? Do you think I would have remained in the street and then put myself in your hands the moment you began accusing and manhandling him?'

Darac returned Mansoor's gaze as if the truth of his words could be read in it.

'I've questioned a Monsieur Dhin, the café owner who hands out the pizza boxes some people use as mats. The man in the white suit was very nervous, he said. Kept looking over his shoulder as if he'd seen someone he was afraid of. Was that your impression?'

'I didn't see him beforehand. I was aware that someone had appeared on my right-hand side to pray but I paid no attention to him until later.'

Observing religious practice, Mansoor took three separate sips of his coffee.

'You were aware of the old woman who had to make a detour around the congregation? The one pushing the shopping trolley?'

'Of course. She was shouting.'

Leaning back against the filing cabinet, Darac took a sip of espresso as he studied the young man's face. The last time he'd seen a creature with such sharp-eyed alertness, it was perched on a falconer's glove.

'I have a couple of questions that would never be allowed in court because they call for speculation on your part concerning someone else's intentions. But I'm interested in your answer because even when you're praying, I'd bet you miss very little. Alright?'

Mansoor nodded warily.

'Was it your impression that the old woman ran her trolley into the man in the suit because he just happened to be occupying the most vulnerable position – the corner of the rearmost rank – or was there anything about it that made you believe she had picked him out specifically?'

'I... think it was coincidental.'

'So if he hadn't arrived on the scene, you think the woman would have run the trolley into you, instead?'

'I think so.'

'And if she had, Mansoor, do you think that it would be you lying in the morgue now and not him?'

Mansoor took three more sips of coffee, considering the question. His concentration was broken by a woman's voice from the doorway.

'Captain – a brief word?'

Attaché case in one hand and a couple of loose folders in the other, Agnès Dantier shared a look with Darac and stepped back out of Mansoor's eyeline.

Wearing a resigned expression, the boy proffered his wrist. Darac thought about it as he downed his coffee. Sometimes, trusting a suspect was the way to go.

'I know you'll stay in your seat but I'll be right outside watching you, anyway. Okay?'

'Okay.' His eyes lowered for a moment. 'No, I don't. I don't think it was the old woman who killed the man. She hardly touched him.'

'Thanks.'

He gave the boy's shoulder a pat and stepped out into the corridor.

'Paul – Deanna's office just rang.' Agnès didn't bother lowering her voice – the air-con in Darac's office made an effective sound insulator. 'The first results on Emil Florian are starting to come in. Expect a call from her, shortly.'

'Already? Fantastic.'

'So who've you got in there? The "now you see him, now you don't" Monsieur Mansoor Narooq?'

'The same.'

'And is he the murderer, do you think?'

'I very much doubt it. I think it's just a papers thing. Mansoor's an illegal – cousin Slimane isn't.'

'Hence the switch.'

'Yes. I'm pretty sure Hamid Toulé and some of the others knew about it. But under the circumstances, I don't massively blame them for lying. We've closed ranks around people ourselves, at times.'

Taking a half step, Agnès looked past Darac into the office.

'We have indeed,' she said absently, fixing Mansoor in her feline gaze. The boy's head was bowed, his eyes closed. She moved back. 'He reminds me of someone.'

'Slimane, perhaps? They're practically doubles.'

Pressing her lips together, she gave Darac a chastening look.

'That was idiotic.' Darac gave a little involuntary laugh. 'Sorry.'

Agnès took a second look at the boy, thought about it for a moment, then with a shake of her ash-blond bob, tossed the thought away.

'No, I don't know him. Probably just the type.' She took a deep breath. 'Right. I'm away.'

'Bunking off early? I won't tell that old dragon of a boss, don't worry.'

'Guess where I'm going.'

'To buy your ticket for the quintet's gig on Thursday. We're playing three entire jazz suites.'

'Close. I'm off to the Tour briefing in Monaco, after all.' She raised her eyebrows. 'Summoned officially.'

'So your own little switch routine didn't work either?'

'Sending Papa? Seems not.' She gave a rueful shrug. 'Serves me right, I suppose. See you later.'

He watched her walk away.

'Listen – if you bump into Alberto Whatever-His-Name-Is over there, give him my love. I've got him in the sweep.'

'Forget it. I drew Carlos Sastre. He's getting any love that's going.'

Darac's mobile rang. He kept his eyes trained on Mansoor as he took the call. The boy was still sitting calmly, eyes closed.

'Captain? I've got Professor Bianchi for you. Just hold a second, please.'

'Thanks, Patricia.'

As he waited for Deanna to come on the line, he looked back along the corridor. He couldn't make out what Agnès and the duty officer Alain Charvet were chatting about but whatever it was, it was making them both laugh. An unrepentant sentimentalist, the moment gave Darac pause. The Brigade Criminelle was a disparate bunch of people. That they worked so well together was entirely due to Agnès's stewardship, he believed. Although it sometimes didn't seem like it, he knew this was something of a golden age for the Brigade; one that would surely fade under a standard-issue commissaire.

Following their own submerged logic, his thoughts began to stray to Angeline. How on earth could things...

A rasping voice interrupted his thoughts.

'Darac? Deanna. Sorry for the wait.'

'It's fine. So you've got something on Emil Florian?'

'Couple of things. First: I found that the abrasion on his right arm does conceal a fine needle puncture mark. Tomorrow I'll be able to tell you what the injectant was, possibly.'

'You managed to extract a sufficient urine sample, then?'

'Nobody takes the piss like me, Darac.'

He laughed out loud.

'How long have you been waiting to say that, Deanna?'

'Oh, about twenty years. Anyway – second: remember I found traces of a substance between Florian's toes?'

'Yes?'

'It was sugar.'

'Sugar?'

'Sugar.'

Darac recognised the tone.

'You've got more, haven't you?'

'Indeed I have. A lot more.'

4.55 PM

Commandant Lanvalle gazed into the auditorium over the rims of his half-glasses and took a long draught of water. The man needed it – he'd been speaking for almost fifteen minutes.

Wedged into his seat in the stalls, Roland Granot was tugging angrily at his moustache. So the terrorists were going to 'reap a bloody harvest', were they? On the streets of *his* city. How dare they?

In the seat directly in front of him, Garde Républicaine senior officer Yves Dauresse feinted a punch to Roger Lascaux's jaw and then roughed up his carefully crafted blond hair. *That's good leadership*, Granot reflected. A dose of normality was just what the kid needed.

On the platform, Lanvalle signalled he was ready to continue. The audience hushed.

'Ladies and gentlemen, on the face of it, we can respond to this ultimatum in three ways. We can seek to identify and apprehend the group, the Sons and Daughters of the Just Cause, in time to prevent them carrying out their plan. That would be largely a covert operation, unseen by the general public. However, we have less than forty-eight hours to accomplish the task.'

A voice behind Granot said, 'We'll get the bastards.'

'We'll never get them in time,' said another.

'Alongside that,' Lanvalle continued, 'we can increase surveillance and security on and around the race route itself with the intention of foiling the attempt live, as it were, should the first approach have failed to meet its objective. This would make us a more visible presence, but unless we went completely over the top, the public shouldn't be unduly aware of the situation.' With what looked suspiciously like studied nonchalance, he sat back in his seat. 'And of course, the third response would be to divert the Tour stage away from Nice. Or cancel it altogether.'

Shouts of 'No!' and 'Never!' flew like shrapnel in an explosion of protest. Lanvalle milked the moment with magnificent inscrutability. He waited for the air to clear before going on.

'Bearing in mind, ladies and gentlemen, that the vast majority of you are seasoned law-enforcement professionals, imagine how the public at large might react to such news. The consequences could be devastating and far-reaching.' He let the thought sink grimly in. 'Happily, the solution is a simple one. I want to say this to you unequivocally: the Tour stage through Nice will go ahead as scheduled.'

A relieved buzz; calls of 'Yes!'; isolated pockets of applause – the line was a winner.

The GR trio's reaction was slightly different. Mugging a look of excited anticipation, Dauresse mimed opening an envelope.

'And the winner is… Commandant Georges Lanvalle!' He rolled his eyes. 'What a star.'

Jarret and Lascaux seemed to enjoy the gag. Granot felt too churned up to go with it.

On the platform, Lanvalle took another swig of water.

'These three responses are predicated on a factor we haven't yet touched upon. That factor is the credibility of the ultimatum itself. So should the threat be taken at face value? In a word, we do not believe that it should.'

Another buzz ran around the auditorium. Granot sat forward in his seat, anxious to hear what was coming next. So what that Lanvalle was a pompous windbag? He was The Man.

'I will explain our thinking to you all. The so-called Sons and Daughters of the Just Cause make five demands. Let us consider them.' Lanvalle referred to the sheet of cut-out letters. 'The first is for the immediate severance of diplomatic ties between France and the State of Israel. Second – the immediate imposition of blanket trade sanctions against that same nation. Third – the immediate release from detention in the US Government's Guantanamo Bay Naval Base of one Meier Al Zatdin. Fourth – the immediate establishment of a dedicated mosque in the city of Nice…'

Granot shared a look with Vincent Dantier. The issue couldn't have been more topical.

'…and fifth – immediate relaxation of laws restricting the wearing of hijab dress in any sphere of French society, including schools.'

Lanvalle set the sheet aside and, taking off his glasses, essayed a weak smile.

'Quite a list, isn't it? Let us start with Demand Three. Has anyone here heard of Monsieur Meier Al Zatdin, the detainee at Guantanamo?'

'Have you heard of said monsieur?' Dauresse whispered almost comically to Lascaux. The blond boy shook his head. Dauresse turned to his other colleague, Jarret. 'Have you, David?'

'No.'

Dauresse turned around his seat and raised his eyebrows enquiringly at Granot.

'You, Lieutenant?'

'I have not,' Granot said, keeping his forearms resolutely folded.

'Nor have I.' Dauresse lowered his voice. 'And nor, I think you will find, has Commandant Lanvalle. We've caught this guy's act before.'

'No takers?' Lanvalle asked. 'That is not surprising because to the best of our knowledge – and our knowledge is, frankly, one hundred per cent accurate – there is no such person. Anywhere. We are, of course, continuing to make enquiries.'

Reacting to this latest *coup de théâtre*, Vincent's elbow shot out involuntarily, digging Granot in the gut.

'Now to Demands One and Two. These, by any standards, are unrealistic and unrealisable. On the face of it, Demand Five, the question of the acceptability of Muslim dress, makes more sense. At least it relates to a current issue. As does Demand Four – the question of a first mosque for the city of Nice.'

Vincent leaned into Granot.

'I bet that's what this is really about.'

Once again, Vincent's voice carried on to the stage.

'You are not alone in that view, Monsieur. But let us not jump the gun. Let us look at other factors. No organisation called the Sons and Daughters of the Just Cause is known to exist. No dedicated or affiliated related code name was used.' He held up the sheet of paper. 'And whoever came across a terrorist threat in this form? Letters cut out of a copy of *Nice-Matin*? It looks more like the sort of a ransom note you would find in an episode of *Commissaire Moulin*.'

Tensions starting to ease, a ripple of laughter ran around the auditorium.

'And, consider this, ladies and gentlemen…'

Where security protocols permitted, Lanvalle went on to detail further reasons for discrediting the ultimatum and then called upon the heads of other divisions to give their assessments. One by one, various theories were advanced but none gave credence to the ultimatum as it stood.

Other items discussed summarily, the session ended with the Tour security director, André Soutine, providing a droning summary for anyone who'd been asleep.

Voices rose as informal debates broke out all around the auditorium. Dauresse seemed particularly anxious to get the Brigade Criminelle's take on the letter.

'May I ask what you make of the threat, Messieurs? Do you believe it?'

'It doesn't matter what we believe.' Presenting them with the back of his hand, Granot flicked up a finger. 'The DCRI's Commandant Lanvalle doesn't believe it.' He flicked up a second. 'GIPN's Commissaire Principal Duras doesn't believe it.' A third finger. 'RAID's Brigadier Zacca doesn't…'

'All these initials and acronyms!' Vincent threw up his hands in irritation. 'What's RAID again?'

Lascaux nodded sympathetically.

'Even I get confused, Commissaire…'

Dauresse gave a snort of laughter.

'…RAID stands for Recherche, Assistance, Intervention and Dissuasion. Bunch of nutters, basically.'

Not to be outdone, David Jarret turned to face the old man.

'RAID has perhaps slipped under your radar, Monsieur, because they weren't founded until 19…' He narrowed his eyes, seeking the year. '…1985, I think it was. Which was after you retired, I imagine. It's basically your Police Nationale's counterpart of our Gendarmerie's primary anti-terrorism unit.'

'In other words, it's the PN's equivalent of the GN's GIGN,' Yves Dauresse said, once again playing the comedian. 'So let's all pray UCLAT did their job.'

Vincent's milky eyes seemed to be staring blindly into space.

'Recapping, we have RAID, GIPN, GIGN… and yes, we could argue about the wisdom of splitting up our forces into so many sections. But, and this is the important thing, they are all crack units, aren't they? Highly trained. They hear all and see all, don't they? They know things we don't know. So, providing UCLAT have been doing their job in co-ordinating the activities of the others…'

Impressed, perhaps even surprised, at the old man's perspicacity, Dauresse and Lascaux shared a look.

'…then it seems to me as a former commissaire of the Brigade Criminelle, that we have nothing to worry about.'

'Exactly.' Granot nodded. 'I'll say it again – if the commanders of all these forces are sure the ultimatum isn't genuine, that should be good enough for us.'

Dauresse nodded with exaggerated gravity.

'Rightly so.'

Granot was tiring of Dauresse. A light touch was one thing; not taking matters seriously was another. He felt an urge to straighten the man out.

'And you three? You're the boys on the front line, aren't you? If it turns out the chiefs are wrong and the "bloody harvest" takes the form of say, a bomb going off in the middle of the peloton…'

Dauresse remained utterly deadpan.

'We'd be among the first to know.'

Granot gave him a searching look.

'Well, you hinted you wanted things livening up.'

'I did.' He returned the look with interest. 'Didn't I?'

As staring contests went, it was a non-event. Almost immediately, Dauresse's gaze was drawn to the aisle. Smiling pleasantly, he got smartly to his feet. Granot turned to see what the big attraction was.

'Boss? What are you doing here?'

'Afternoon, gentlemen.'

Vincent stood, aglow with the surprise of it. Stepping aside to allow the old man through, Granot was quick to move back, balking the inevitable advance of Joel Barbusse.

'Gentlemen, this is my daughter, Agnès Dantier, the current commissaire of the Brigade Criminelle de Nice.' They embraced warmly. 'Agnès – these glorified ton-up kids are Garde Républicaine officers.'

Dauresse led the handshakes.

Once again, Granot was able to read the trio's characters in the moment: Dauresse, expansive, playful; Roger Lascaux, all sunny smiles and puppy dog charm; David Jarret, sensitive, a model of correctness.

Meanwhile, Barbusse was trying to shift the bulwark that was Granot.

'Will you please move!'

Granot pretended not to hear.

Vincent turned to his daughter.

'Why *are* you here, darling?'

'I was called in by Georges Lanvalle.' She mimicked him. '"A matter that directly affects your Brigade, madame." Apparently.'

'Directly affects the Brigade?' Vincent gave a derisive grunt. 'Every piece of work a commissaire does directly affects the Brigade.'

'And I told him I still had several hours of it to get through today. It didn't take.'

A uniform appeared. He saluted and asked to check

Agnès's ID. She handed it over.

'As I'm here, Papa, I may as well drop you home afterwards.'

'Are you sure?'

'Of course. It's en route to the Caserne, anyway – more or less.'

Granot seemed as disappointed with the idea as Vincent was pleased.

'I'm more than happy to do it, boss.'

'That's kind but no. And don't make any plans for an early night, Granot. I've called a meeting for 9.30 this evening to discuss all this. Whatever it is.'

The uniform handed back Agnès's ID.

'Thank you, Commissaire. Will you come with me?'

Agnès said her farewells and followed the uniform towards a flight of steps that gave on to the stage.

Getting a filthy look for his pains, Granot finally allowed Barbusse to pass.

'Thank God that's over.' Vincent got to his feet. 'I could do with a drink.'

As the audience filed out along the aisles, most continued to debate the issues raised in the briefing. The exception was the wise-cracking Yves Dauresse. He seemed to be enjoying himself hugely.

4.56 PM

Following Deanna Bianchi's call, Darac detailed a uniform to babysit Mansoor Narooq while he undertook a series of checks. Afterwards, he updated Bonbon on the most significant development in the case so far.

'She got all that from a couple of grains of sugar between Florian's toes?'

'Pretty much, Bonbon.'

'She's hot stuff, our professor. Anyway, this pushes the case further away still from where we began, doesn't it? First we have a provocative anti-Muslim murder on our hands. Then the victim turns out not to be a Muslim. Now thanks to Deanna, it's clear the killing has nothing to do with race or religion at all.'

'Very much looks that way. How far have you got with the Rue Verbier residents?'

'Done about half of them. Flaco and Perand should be back with you soon, by the way.'

Darac took a couple of paces and glanced through the open squad-room door.

'They're just coming in now. I'll update them on Florian and take it from there.'

'Okay. See you later, chief.'

The squad room was the heart of any Brigade Criminelle operation. The Caserne's take on it was an overcrowded, open-plan space furnished with cheap furniture and electrical devices connected by exposed cabling – 'not so much an office, more an officers' mess', as Agnès once remarked.

Darac picked his way over to the youngsters, and resting his elbows on a filing cabinet, wasted little time in getting to the nitty-gritty.

'From a sugar residue Professor Bianchi found between Emil Florian's toes, she was able to isolate a substance that was a form of GHB. Droplets of water in Florian's Evian bottle matched it. He hadn't taken the stuff himself but it was obviously intended for somebody – the sugar added to mask the salty taste.'

'GHB?' Flaco widened her stance as if about to throw a punch. 'The man was a date rapist?'

'Or a supplier to one, perhaps.'

Her heart-shaped face set into a deep scowl.

'So why was he killed?'

'Any thoughts, Perand?'

'Maybe it was a revenge—' He interrupted himself with a yawn. 'Sorry – double shift.' He gave the side of his face, almost black with stubble, a reviving slap. 'Yeah, maybe it was a revenge killing.'

'Not a bad call. Procedures being as they are, rapists often go unpunished – right? So a victim seeking justice might well take the law into their own hands. In this case, causing death by lethal injection, if that's what it turns out to be, has the quality of an execution, don't you think?'

'The old woman with the trolley.' Perand scratched his long chin. 'Maybe she was the mother or grandmother of a victim.'

'I've already got people checking out unsolved rapes, reports of alleged rapes and so on.'

'This old-woman idea, Captain.' Drawing in the corners of her mouth, Flaco shook her tightly corn-rowed head. 'Despite the puncture mark and the timing – she nudges Florian, he dies – it doesn't seem right.'

'I'm inclined to agree. And for what it's worth, so does our Monsieur Mansoor Narooq. But we still need to find her, obviously. Lartou has blown up a still from the CCTV footage of her arriving at the scene. It's not Cartier-Bresson but it's pretty good.'

The youngsters shared a clueless look.

'Seriously?' Darac gave a little shake of the head. 'Google the man. A slog squad will be showing copies of the still all around the area. If they get a hit, be prepared to get back out there to do the interview.'

Perand cast a doleful glance at the stack of papers on his desk.

'Let's look at another question. Florian poured the bottle of water over his feet as if complying with Muslim ablution practices. Now we know about the GHB; there could have been another reason for doing it, couldn't there?'

Flaco nodded.

'To get rid of incriminating evidence.'

'Exactly.'

Perand released a hint of sourness into the air as he raised his arms into a stretch.

'Doesn't that imply that...' Another yawn. '...the people he was hiding from were, well... us?'

'I'm still awaiting replies from further afield but no one from the region had Florian under surveillance. And there's not even a parking violation on his record, remember.' Darac stared off to the side as if his next thought was written on a cue card. 'I'm thinking about the key we unearthed at the scene. It could have just fallen out of his pocket but maybe he was trying to hide it. We have to find out what that key opens. It's for a cylinder lock so it might open an apartment door.'

Perand seemed to think he was on a roll.

'His own apartment, probably.'

'A solitary key? Unlikely. His apartment key was probably on the bunch found in his jacket. I'll get over there shortly and find out.' Darac stared at the floor. 'What was this guy up to? A teacher at Lycée Mossette... A teacher carrying GHB around in the middle of the day... GHB sweetened with sugar...'

'Think it was intended for one of his students, Captain?' Flaco's pencil-thin brows lowered into a particularly severe scowl. 'I used to do all kinds of school activities in vacations.'

Perand shook his head.

'You think he would have trawled his own classes for victims? Sure, he had easier access to them than to kids in general – but it's riskier.'

'Sometimes, risk itself is part of what turns these people on. We'll get a schedule from Principal Volpini – see if anything was planned for today.' Darac went to a related thought. 'What did Florian teach? I didn't pay proper attention to that earlier.'

Perand, who seemed to do a lot of things by halves, gave a sort of half-grin.

'Figure-drawing classes?'

Ignoring him, Flaco picked up her copy of Granot's report.

'It was… literature, Captain.'

'Thanks. What else have you got there?'

'Florian lived alone. He was respected though not universally liked according to Principal Volpini. He himself found him pleasant, quiet and hard-working, though.'

'Granot says the man was in shock earlier. He'll be even more shocked when he hears what one of his trusted members of staff had in his pocket.' Darac shifted his weight back from the filing cabinet and straightened. 'With all this in mind, I gave Frankie a call over in Vice. She's agreed to come in with us on this thing. There's no better officer – full stop. And if it transpires kids are involved, she's particularly brilliant.'

As Darac paused to check his notes, Perand leaned brightly in to Flaco.

'This might be my first child-rape case.'

Flaco gave him a wide-eyed look.

'Hey that's great!' Pseudo-excitement morphed into disgust. 'Pea brain.'

Saving Perand further punishment, the Brigade's IT specialist, Erica Lamarth, pranced into the room at that moment. Tall and slender with a girlish face framed by straight, centre-parted blond hair, Erica was something of a pin-up for the boys at the Caserne. Or most of them. Darac saw her slightly differently: she reminded him of a spectacular Afghan hound an aunt had owned when he was a child. It was a positive association for him but, realising Erica probably wouldn't see it that way, he'd kept it to himself.

'Sorry it's taken me so long to get here.' She set down an evidence bag. 'Tricky computer issue to sort out at Foch.'

'Good to see you,' Darac said, smiling. 'You get all the mobiles?'

'Uh-huh.'

'Before you go on, Emil Florian was carrying a date-rape drug when he was killed. Of course, it may have been something he found and was about to hand over to us. But something tells me not, somehow.'

'So he wasn't just a victim, then. Interesting.' Hooking strands of her blond hair first behind one ear, then the other, she bent to fish the mobiles out of her bag. 'In that case, these may prove even more significant.' She set them down on the filing cabinet. 'Okay, Eenie – Emil Florian's. Meenie – Mansoor Narooq's. Minie – Slimane Bahtoum's. Obviously, I had no pass code for Florian's and the boys were unforthcoming about theirs, but here goes. As I've only had time to have a bit of a play with Florian's, I'll start with his.' She held it up. 'Alright – at 12.10 this lunchtime, Florian made a call. It didn't connect. It was the last call he made and none came in before he died over an hour later. Obviously, we don't know the reason he made that call. It might have been important; it might have been totally insignificant. The intended recipient, though, was not. He or she was designated as speed-dial key one on Florian's phone – so whoever it was, they were obviously close to him. The closest of anyone, presumably.'

'Most likely be his brother Jean,' Perand said. 'Lives in Paris. And his number's disconnected too, we've discovered – hence the call not going through.'

'It's unlikely to be him,' Erica said, re-anchoring her hair. 'Florian called the same number six separate times the day before. All those calls connected.'

Perand shrugged, conceding the point.

'Been any calls from that number in the last couple of hours?' Darac said.

'No.'

'Might be coincidental. Might mean the caller knew Florian was dead. Keep his phone powered up from now on, Erica.'

Wearing an awestruck expression, she pointed at Darac as if he'd come up with the idea of the century.

'*That* is good.'

'Of course you were going to do that.' He smiled. 'Got a name to link with the speed-dial number?'

'Indeed I have. It's listed as "Manou" in the memory. *Man*ou?' she repeated, raising her almost hairless eyebrows.

Darac stiffened.

'Ah.' He had almost made up his mind that the cousins had been innocent bystanders at the death of a man they knew nothing about. But Manou could easily have been a pet name for Mansoor. Or, less likely, for Slimane. 'My friends call me Slim,' he'd said in the prayer room – maybe in an attempt to mislead.

Erica prised open the phones.

'"Ah" indeed. So let's find out if one of these two is Manou.'

Flaco seemed puzzled.

'Erica – why didn't you just run the Manou number past the service provider?'

'Because demos are much more fun.'

Incomprehension turned to surprise on the younger woman's face.

'And they're more foolproof, but I'm just kidding. I did call them initially, but not for the first time, their accounts computer is down.'

It was Perand's turn to look puzzled.

'Uh… how are you going to bypass the pass codes on the phones?'

Erica treated him to the sort of look a benign teacher might reserve for a slow pupil.

'I'm going to read them off the memory chips, sweetie.'

'Yes,' he nodded sagely. 'That'll do it.'

Slimane's mobile was the first to glow into life. Moments later, a customised welcome tone poured a little Afropop into the room.

'Okay, let's call our Manou and see if one of these rings.' Erica picked up Florian's mobile. 'I'm looking forward to this, myself.'

'Hold it a second, Erica.' Darac finally ran his hand out of his hair. 'There's a better way, isn't there?'

'Is there?'

'If Manou turns out to be neither Mansoor nor Slimane…'

'I'll bet you he is.' Perand smiled his lopsided smile. 'Monsieur Manou Narooq to be exact.'

'He may be,' Darac continued. 'But supposing he isn't. The real Manou will think Florian's ringing him, won't he? We could verify the Slimane/Mansoor connection simply by comparing their mobile numbers with the number for Manou on Florian's phone.'

Erica's hair escaped the anchor of her ears as she weighed the point.

'Slightly less showbiz but I agree, it's safer.' She handed over Slimane's phone. 'Here, you take that one, Captain. And you take Mansoor's, Perand. I'll bring up Manou's number.' She began scrolling through Florian's address book, found the number for Manou and left it displayed. 'There you go.'

A moment later, Darac had come up with Slimane's own number. He checked it against the number on Florian's screen. It didn't match.

'Manou isn't Slimane.' With a loose fist, Darac began tapping out a little Latin rhythm on the filing cabinet as they waited for Perand. And waited.

'I can find every shitting number but Narooq's own.'

Erica reprised her teacher's voice.

'From the main menu, find Address Book and then select T for This Mobile.'

'I tell you what's better still.' Perand was tiring of playing the loser. 'Why don't I just ask the guy? He's only sitting ten metres...'

As if in reaction, the sound of Mansoor's voice piped up from Darac's office next door. It was loud and getting louder. Sounds of a scuffle now. Chairs scraping. Shouting. Darac was first out of the door, the others following hard behind.

'What the...?'

They found Mansoor's custodian looking helplessly out of an open window. His gun was still holstered, Darac noticed, pushing him quickly aside. But as he looked down into the compound, the question of whether Mansoor had absconded with a loaded weapon became an academic one, anyway. The boy was lying on his back, his legs twisted under him. There was no blood but he wasn't moving.

'What the hell happened, Dax?'

'I don't know, Captain. He suddenly flipped. Got past me somehow... Opened the window and jumped. Completely out of the blue. I swear, sir.'

'Shit. He's dead,' Perand said, nudging in next to Darac. 'But it's only a few metres down.'

Dax put his hands together as if in prayer.

'I grabbed at his ankle as he jumped and it upended him. He landed... all wrong.'

Looking for any sign of hope, Darac stared hard into the boy's expressionless face.

'Come on!'

Perand stepped back from the window, allowing Flaco in. He turned to Erica.

'Jesus. Frènes nearly had a heart attack when he thought a civilian had killed a Muslim. Now one of us has.'

Figures from all over the compound were advancing towards the body. Darac kept staring, willing the boy to open his eyes. 'Give one back from the twenty-five thousand,' he'd said. Maybe Darac should have tried.

Quite suddenly, Mansoor's face contorted in pain.

'He's alive!' Darac quickly ran an eye over the advancing officers. As far as he could see, none had drawn a weapon. 'And unarmed!' Better safe than sorry.

Mansoor tried to get to his feet as the first officers arrived on the scene. He almost made it but, holding his left shoulder, he slewed and sank back on to his right side. A woman Darac recognised as one of the dispatchers exchanged a few words with the boy and then tentatively tested his limbs for movement.

Flaco looked back into the room over her shoulder.

'He's moving.'

In the doorway, Erica exhaled deeply and uncrossed her fingers.

'But what made him do that?'

Perand turned to her.

'How about hearing his mobile being turned on in the next room? He's our Manou, alright. And he's an all-action guy, you've got to say. Running out of crowds, jumping out of windows...'

The dispatcher looked up at Darac.

'What happened, Captain?'

'It's unclear. What's the damage?'

'Don't think he's broken anything but there is some trauma to the shoulder. And to his right leg. There's soft-tissue damage in a number of places and he's concussed, I think. Apart from that, he looks in reasonable shape.'

'I'm sending someone down. Hang on.' He eyeballed Dax. 'You'll have to pen a detailed account of what just happened. Obviously.'

'Yes, Captain.'

Still standing well back from the window, Erica waved a mobile to catch Darac's eye. Mouthing 'Give me two seconds,' he turned to Flaco.

'In a moment, I want you to get down there and detail a uniform to help you escort Mansoor over to St Roch. Stay with him. Assuming the medicos release him within an hour or two, bring him back here. I'll talk to him later. If they want to keep him in, call Charvet to arrange your relief. Someone must be with Mansoor at all times.'

Realising that with every week that passed, more and more trust was being placed in her, Flaco's full lips betrayed just a hint of a smile.

'Right, Captain.'

'Before you do that, though –' Darac gave Erica a nod '– back to our identity crisis.'

'Hang on a second, Captain.' Perand looked

uncomfortable suddenly. 'The trolley woman – supposing we get a hit from Lartou's photo and Flaco's still over at the hospital. What do I do?'

'Is that a serious question?'

'Well…'

'You'll just have to go and interview the woman without your big sister to look after you, won't you? In the meantime you can catch up with your paperwork.' Eyebrows high in amazement, Darac gave a clearing shake of the head and turned to Erica. 'Finally.'

'Yes – so. This is the Manou number on Florian's phone which we discovered didn't match Slimane's.' Like a conjurer showing an audience a secret card, she let them all see the displayed number. Now she held up the second phone. 'And this is Mansoor's own number.' It didn't match. 'So unless they have other mobiles, which of course they could have, Florian's best friend Manou is neither Slimane nor Mansoor.'

'That is a relief.' For Darac, at least. 'Thanks, Erica. Okay, we'll have a team meeting to discuss progress later on – time TBA. For now, Flaco – off you go.'

'I'll report back, Captain.'

Darac turned to Erica.

'It would still be useful to find Manou. Did the service provider give any idea when their computer will be up and running?'

'They didn't.'

'Okay.' Darac ran a hand through his hair. 'Maybe we'll find out all about him at Florian's apartment.'

'We might be able to take the maybe out of it.' Erica opened a new message on Florian's phone. 'What shall I put – "come to the apartment"?'

'Proactive.' Perand had the look of a punter who knew he'd finally picked a winner. 'I like it.'

'If Manou happens to live in Nantes or Naples or New York, he might find that an odd message to receive.' Darac picked up his desk phone. 'But once I've made a few calls, there is something you can do, Erica. Something far more useful.'

5.10 PM

Still 21.2.

There was a new one on duty. A redhead. Pretty. Scatty. A comedian. Everything was funny to her. Especially herself. 'What am I like?' she kept saying. I could tell you what you are like. You are a moron. At least, I would say it if I could. But I can still communicate. I can blink. Once for yes, twice for no. And I can hear. God, how I can hear. I can hear and understand every puerile utterance you spew into the air. Don't you realise that?

Oh yes, if I stay alive long enough, I will know all about you, won't I? In a few captive minutes, I already know that you don't like fish; that your boyfriend is a plumber; that he's very handy in general and plays football. I know that you fancy William from Télématin *and once dreamed that you shared a hot-air-balloon ride with him over Paris. You were nude. I know your mother had rheumatoid arthritis before a visit to Lourdes completely cured her. And I know that you like your job because it's so meaningful, yet you can still have a great laugh with everybody.*

The moron's face.

'Isn't that right, darling?'

She didn't wait for a response.

'I thought he was getting the TV?' she said to the black one.

'As a matter of fact, he didn't want it.'

No! That is not a matter of fact. It was a mistake.

'Didn't want it?' the red-headed one said, surprised.

Ask me if I'm sure. Please.

Her face.

'I don't blame you, darling. Who wants to watch a lot of stupid cyclists all day?'

I do. I want it more than anything in the world. That's what I'm like.

'Right. He's all done and dusted, bless him.'

Her face.

'See you soon!'

Yes. No doubt you will.

The lovely fat one. She is my only hope.

Wait a minute. Is that 21.3?

No.

21.2.

My mistake.

5.52 PM

Born and bred in nearby Vence and living in Nice itself for the past ten years, Darac was about as local as a local police officer could be. But familiarity hadn't immunised him against the extraordinary beauty of the Côte d'Azur. Nowhere else gave him the same lift. He was driving along the palm-shaded arc of Boulevard des Anglais, a perfect parabola within which the Baie des Anges glittered like shards of silver-flecked sapphire. In his pocket were the keys to Emil Florian's apartment in Magnan. In the passenger seat was Erica Lamarthe. She glanced at her mobile.

'Still nothing from the service provider. You should have let me send that text.'

'We'll get to Manou one way or another, don't worry.'

'It might have done more than just give us an address for him, it might have brought him to Florian's apartment.'

'It might but what if he knows Florian is dead? He hasn't rung his number since, note. Even though Florian tried to call him just before he died.'

'How could Manou know Florian's dead? He couldn't have heard it in the media. A non-Muslim was killed during a prayer service – that's all they said. There was no description – nothing.'

'True, but word can still get around. And what if Manou was there when it happened? What if he was the one who actually killed Florian? All a text message would do is alert him to the fact that we're on to him. Or her.'

Feeling a little too easily outplayed, Erica drew down the corners of her finely lined mouth and shrugged.

'"What if? What if?" Don't you ever tire of asking that?'

'Seeing where "what if" might lead is probably why I enjoy policing. Despite all the crap.'

Boulevard des Anglais' most celebrated landmark, the pink-domed Hotel Negresco, shimmied exotically into view on their right. Turning her back on it, Erica held Darac in an almost accusing look.

'I thought you became a policeman because you have a deep-seated need to right injustices?'

'You're mixing me up with Superman. As unlikely as that seems.'

Erica gave a dry little laugh.

Darac slowed to a halt just beyond the Negresco, waiting for pedestrians to clear a zebra crossing. Bringing up the rear of the group was an unlikely-looking couple: the man was round-shouldered and sported a long grey ponytail, baggy shorts and a Hawaiian shirt. The woman looked to be in her mid-twenties and was wearing her skimpy black bikini with all the panache of an off-duty beachwear model. In the middle of relating something of great importance to her, Ponytail had no intention of hurrying. And neither had Bikini Girl, who seemed riveted by the account and by the elaborate, rhythmical hand mime that accompanied it. As they gained the traffic island in the middle of the road, Darac pulled slowly past them, rolling down his window.

'A broken clock keeps better time than him,' he called to the girl, startling her.

Ponytail appeared in his rear-view mirror, laughing and giving Darac the finger.

'That was Marco. Drummer with the quintet I play in.'

'Ah, yes?'

Erica's tone was bright and approving. His eyes on the road, Darac missed the slightly half-hearted smile that accompanied it.

After a further five minutes of stop-start progress, they finally reached Magnan. Cut in two by the twin conduits of the Nice–Cannes railway line and four lanes of road traffic, it was a mixed, largely residential quarter. There was no 'other side of the tracks' here. It was the degree of proximity to the tracks that mostly delineated the area. Darac had visited Florian's apartment block on a couple of previous occasions. He remembered it as a clean-lined, low-rise building, a short uphill pull from the action.

Erica turned the air-con up a notch as they headed away from the promenade.

'What's his building called?'

'L'Horizon Bleu. Imaginatively.'

'Don't know it. Nice cool underground parking? Say yes.'

'Yes.'

'Thank God.'

'But it's a ground-level lot.'

The lee of a high wall was the shadiest spot he could find.

'Ready?'

'As I'll ever be.'

Thrown in among the laptops and other gear in the boot was a promising-looking box.

'I don't suppose there's anything cool in that, is there? And no gags this time.'

'Of course there is.' He took off the lid. 'Still or sparkling, Mademoiselle?'

'Sparkling.'

'Still?'

'Still.'

They shared the sole remaining bottle, collected their gear and set off at a lazy pace towards the building's canopied entrance.

'This is what it must feel like to be Max Perand.'

'Poor boy.' The thought made Erica chuckle. 'Maybe he'll speed up once he's grown into his strength or something. God, I sound like my mother.'

Darac's mobile rang.

'Chief?'

'Granot – so how's my boy Muntanor looking? Fit and ready to win me five hundred euros?'

'It's Contador, chief. Con-ta-dor. Right?'

'Well how's Contador looking, then?'

'Dunno, haven't seen him. But I tell you who I *have* seen. Half the security chiefs in the country. There's been a terrorist threat issued against the Tour. And Nice is the designated target.'

Darac came to a dead stop.

'What?'

Erica drifted back to his side. Darac put the phone on speaker.

'According to an outfit called the Sons and Daughters of the Just Cause, come Sunday they will – and I'm quoting – "reap a bloody harvest in the city" unless various demands are met.'

'Jesus Christ.'

Erica's hand went to her throat.

'Go on, Granot.'

'But the powers-that-be are absolutely sure it's a hoax.'

Darac let his phone hand fall.

'A hoax.' He gave Erica a look. 'Would you believe it?'

'*Now* he tells us.'

'I know...' He returned the phone to his ear. 'Granot, why the hell didn't you say that to start with?'

'Hey – we had to sweat for what seemed like hours before we got the good word.'

'Well thanks for sharing.' Darac and Erica set off once more. 'Back in the real world, we're just about to search Florian's apartment. You get the updates?'

'Looks like Florian was using the prayer meeting as cover, doesn't it?'

'Looks that way.'

'On the other hand, Florian's pray mate has risked death trying to escape since then.'

'Mansoor's an illegal – that could be reason enough to make a run for it.'

'And what about this GHB thing? I didn't see that coming. Hope it doesn't have anything to do with kids.'

'Did you know Frankie was on board?'

'No. Best news I've had all day.'

'Me too.' Darac glanced at his watch. 'Listen – is Agnès still over with you?'

'Yes – talking with the big brass. There's an aspect of the thing that concerns us, apparently.'

'We're going to be playing Find the Hoaxers, by the sound of it. On top of everything else.'

'No doubt. Anyway, chief – me and Vincent have got canapés and champagne waiting for us. Must fly.'

'Enjoy yourself. Skiving bastard.'

It was banter. Darac believed that if anyone in the unit deserved a break, it was Granot. Despite the ubiquity of screen-based IT, every case the Brigade tackled still generated mountains of paper. Granot, the most indomitable paper mountaineer in the force, had cleared range after range of the stuff over the past few months.

Darac and Erica entered the building.

'I don't expect it but we may yet find the famous Manou waiting for Florian in his apartment.' They stepped into the lift. 'Or perhaps outside it.'

'I'm ready for anything,' Erica said, a nervous catch in her throat.

Darac gave her a smile and hit the button for floor three.

'Anything?'

'Almost anything.'

'It'll be fine.'

The doors opened. They got out. No one was around.

'Almost monastic,' Erica said, as they made their way along the silent, white-painted corridor towards Apartment 38. 'That's appropriate for a rapist.'

Darac reached out and shook her free hand.

'Always glad to meet a fellow cynic.'

'I'm not cynical about everything. I've just got no time for the Church. Or politicians. Or celeb culture. Or corporate America.' She crossed herself extravagantly. 'Except for Apple Mac, of course.'

Until this moment, Darac had had no idea Erica was such a kindred spirit.

'You'll be telling me you love jazz next.'

Erica's one and only visit to a jazz club had proved one of the longest evenings of her life.

'Uh… I wouldn't exactly say "love".'

'Well, you need to hear jazz live.'

'I'm sure that makes all the difference.'

They arrived at number 38. Shepherding her well to one side, Darac rang Florian's doorbell.

'What's our worst-case scenario?' she whispered. 'Manou is Florian's accomplice in the GHB business and he is in there raping some half-unconscious girl?'

'And then he answers the door carrying a syringe full

of pancuronium. That would worsen things a little.'

'Pancuronium?'

'Or perhaps vecuronium, rocuronium. Or one of the other curoniums.'

She looked none the wiser.

'Lethal paralytics. Deanna's pretty sure one was used to kill Florian.'

Erica almost dropped her laptop case. 'I knew I should've stuck to my No House Calls rule.'

'Look, I really don't expect Manou to be in there. And even if he is, he'll probably turn out to be some guy Florian played boules with or something.'

'That doesn't rule out violence.'

No one answered the door.

They let themselves in using Florian's keys and headed straight for his computer.

6.31 PM

It had been a steady 21.2 for some hours now. Since the time of the Romans, possibly. He'd made up his mind. He was ignoring the temperature. He closed his eyes. What was worse, he wondered – being hooked up to a ventilator in an ICU, or pedalling up Mont Ventoux in a headwind? Both made you feel like a living corpse. But it was no contest. The pain of Ventoux was only temporary.

Helplessness. That was the real killer. It felt to him as if there was no difference between having things done for you, and having things done to you. And it was hard to live with the sense that any minute, it may be decided that you have no useful life left. Your ride ended by others.

A swish of linen. A bright face. The red-headed one.

'Letter for you, darling. Shall I read it?'

I don't want you of all people to read it.

But he wondered if he might lose it altogether if he blinked no. He blinked once.

The tearing of the envelope. The rustle of paper. The clearing of the throat.

"'Dear Papa, Well…'"

Her face.

'Have you noticed how often people say "well" as the first word of a letter?'

No, no, no. Just read out the letter. Please.

'Do you know what I mean? Well, here I am; Well, we finally made it...? Oh, what am I like? You don't want to hear that, do you?'

No. I don't. Read or don't read, you stupid, stupid girl. Do not comment. Do not editorialise. And above all, do not interpret what you're reading.

'I'll start again. "Dear Papa, Well..."'

Crash!

The shout came from another room. The red-headed one left immediately, tossing the letter on to his chest like a flower onto a coffin.

6.35 PM

Lycée Principal, André Volpini, was an energetic individual of about fifty, short, and with a head of thinning hair that was too black to be natural. Small, restless eyes shone out of a face so bronzed and glossy, it appeared varnished.

'Captain Lejeune, I... I don't know what to say, as you can see. I cannot imagine that Emil could possibly have been involved in such a sordid – sordid? – *evil* business. It's unthinkable.'

Frankie Lejeune had heard it all before. But she smiled sympathetically.

'You've never entertained any doubts about Monsieur Florian?' Her lullaby-soft voice took the leading edge off the question. 'Not even for a moment?'

Before Volpini could answer, a black cat jumped up on the sofa and decided to make a bed of Frankie's lap.

'Please, shoo Cin Cin away, Captain.' He seemed genuinely irritated on his visitor's behalf but his eyes said he envied the animal. Frankie was a round-figured woman with a head of luxuriant black hair and large, pale-green eyes.

'No, no. I love cats.' As if to prove the assertion, she began tickling its neck. 'You stay, Cin Cin.'

'Then that's... fine. But no, I have had no concerns

about Emil whatever, and I must say, I'm inclined not to believe this. There must be some other explanation.'

'Have parents or any of your students ever come to you or to other members of your staff with questions about Monsieur Florian's behaviour?'

'Certainly not. As I mentioned to your colleague, Lieutenant Granot, Emil wasn't the sort of person everyone liked. He could be difficult. But I always found him amenable, conscientious. In summary, a decent man – yes, decent – and a very good teacher.'

'I see.'

Volpini got to his feet.

'A drink, Captain…?' He smiled expectantly. 'Look, I'm André and I can't keep calling you Captain, can I? A drink…?' He raised his too-black eyebrows.

'No, thank you. We're exploring a number of avenues, of course.'

He sat down.

'Of course.'

'But you do understand that our investigation must include questioning staff at your school, the students, and their families.'

Volpini threw up his hands.

'My staff – well, yes, I see that. But the students and families? No, no. That is unconscionable. In any case, this is vacation time. Many people will be away.'

'The timing is unfortunate. Nevertheless, we must press ahead. Your staff, if available, will be interviewed quite briefly and without fuss. As far as the children and their parents are concerned, a lower-impact strategy will be employed.'

'I don't think so.'

'In the guise of a standard feedback exercise, a questionnaire will be emailed out to each student and family member. Questions will cover a variety of topics relating to what I think your brochure refers to as "the whole school experience".'

Volpini waved the idea away. Frankie continued unabashed.

'Obviously, no reference will be made directly to Monsieur Florian or to this investigation. Nevertheless, those filling in the questionnaire will be given opportunity to air, confidentially of course, any concerns they may have on the theme of sexual harassment, deviant behaviour and so on. Contact details will also be provided for anyone preferring to call, email, or write to us on the issue.'

Volpini was a picture of supercilious amusement.

'Captain – do you realise that clearance from the very highest levels would have to be sought before I could even consider implementing such a scheme?'

'Oh indeed so.' Frankie smiled, as if to mollify him. 'But that's already been taken care of.' She handed Volpini a print-out of an email from the relevant authority. He took it with all the enthusiasm of someone receiving a repossession order. 'And no need to worry about the implementation. We will be doing that. All I need is a copy of the school register.'

'I'm surprised you haven't acquired one already.'

'I tried, naturally. But the relevant office at the

Department of Education was closed and doesn't reopen until Monday. Have you a copy here?'

'No.' In one syllable, Volpini managed to convey that he felt usurped, manipulated and now totally indifferent to his inquisitor's womanly charms. 'I do not.'

'The school is what – a fifteen-minute walk away?'

'You surely don't expect me to go there now?'

Frankie raised her eyebrows pleasantly. Volpini thought about it.

'Well I can't leave at this precise second. I have to wait… until my wife gets back.'

'And when might that be?'

'Soon! Half an hour. An hour at the most.'

Frankie handed him a card bearing her contact details.

'That's very kind, thank you. Use the lower of the two email addresses if you would.'

He grunted.

The meeting was over. At the door, Frankie left Volpini with an even less happy thought.

'In the unlikely event that no progress is made on any fronts of the investigation, we may yet have to talk directly to the children and parents.' A final smile. 'Bye.'

'Goodbye.'

As Volpini went to close the door, Cin Cin's tail gave his leg a disdainful flick as she followed Frankie out into the corridor.

'Get out.' It was a stone aimed at two birds. 'And stay out.'

Shaking his shiny head, Volpini walked purposefully back into the lounge and picked up the phone.

6.52 PM

Darac and Erica left Emil Florian's apartment building and walked wearily through slanting sunlight to the parking area. Neither said much until they had stowed the stuff they'd removed from Florian's apartment.

'Right.' Darac closed the car boot. 'Let's get in and get out of here.'

It would have been cooler to have opened an oven door.

'So glad you parked in the shade.'

Darac set the air-con to maximum and pulled slowly away.

'So what have we learned for certain?' Erica said, fanning herself with one hand, holding her hair away from her neck with the other. 'Florian's gay – that's about it.'

'If he *is* a sex offender, he's not typical. You never find a *small* porn cache, do you? These people collect images like a dead cat collects flies. It's an expression of the scale of their abnormality.'

'Dog.'

'Dog?'

'It's "like a dead *dog* collects flies".'

He looked across at her.

'But I like dogs.'

She gave a little chuckle.

'But now take Florian. Not one pornographic image on the hard drive. Not one shot of him or anyone else abusing a victim. Not one hard copy of anything hideous. Scarcely anything racy, even: photos of a guy who just has to be Manou strutting his stuff in a posing pouch; a book of arty male nudes more or less anybody might own. That's all. It doesn't fit.'

They bisected a Cannes-bound train as it rattled over the viaduct above them.

'And there was no hint of chemicals to make GHB or any other drug. So here's a thought – maybe Florian never hurt anyone. Maybe he did find that bottle of water, after all. Instead of feeling we've wasted our time, we should be rejoicing.'

They turned into Avenue de la Californie and headed for the city.

'I don't think we can break out the champagne quite yet. You're sure no images could have existed on the computer and been deleted?' Darac ran a hand through his hair. It didn't spring back with its usual force. 'Maybe there's a new programme that really does kill stuff on the hard drive.'

'No. None exists. Physical destruction is the only way, believe me.'

'Then there's a second computer. Someone, possibly Manou, may have known Florian was dead, beat us to the apartment and removed it. A laptop probably.'

'No one around saw anything suspicious. And there's no CCTV in the place to help us.'

'It's early days.'

As the air-con began to tame the heat, Darac pulled up in the no-parking zone outside Le Bouton, a takeaway spot known for its *spécialités Niçoises*.

'Leave the engine running. Just starting to cool down.'

'You read my mind. Coffee? Snack? Have to have it on the move, though.'

'Fine with me.' Tilting her head back over the seat rest, Erica let out a long sigh. 'I've got loads to do in the lab.'

'Want to come and see what there is?'

Murmuring settling-down sounds, she closed her eyes. 'You go. I'll stay and guard the car.'

Despite all that was breaking under the surface of his day, Darac couldn't resist a smile.

'So what do you fancy?'

'Uh… a noisette, easy on the froth. And… a slice of *pissaladière*. A large one. And… a tarte aux pommes. And an Orangina. No, water. Sparkling.'

'Anything else for the mademoiselle? *Boeuf en daube*? Nice bottle of Beaujolais?'

Allowing her head to fall to the side, Erica opened her eyes.

'Think they'd have those?'

'I'll see what I can do.'

No sooner had he got out of the car than he was confronted by an arm-waving traffic warden. Following a shouted exchange, Darac had to play his Police Judiciaire ID card to win the debate. Erica lowered her window.

'And don't forget the serviettes!'

Her mobile rang.

'Erica Lamarthe... Oh hello, thanks for calling... Yes, let me have it, please. Just a sec.' Realising her notebook and pen were locked in the boot along with her laptop, she tried the glove compartment. Taking out handfuls of CDs, she found a pen that had rolled to the back. She was just wondering whether to use a jewel case insert to take down the info – a jolly round-faced man named Oscar Peterson looked as if he wouldn't have minded – when she spotted a screwed-up till receipt. That would do. 'Sorry about that. Go ahead.'

In the takeaway, Darac downed a double espresso while he waited for Marcel, the place's veteran owner, to complete his order. Angeline was always telling him he drank too much of the stuff. She favoured green tea. There were several packets in Emil Florian's kitchen, Darac had noticed. The antioxidants hadn't saved him.

Wearing a baggy T-shirt that showed off his stringy, mahogany-brown arms, Marcel grabbed a couple of serviettes from a dispenser.

'So who do you fancy for the Tour, Inspector?'

'It's Captain now – we don't have inspectors any more. The Tour? Uh... Contador. He's the one, I reckon.'

The old man looked incredulous as he handed over Darac's change.

'Good choice. To be honest, I only asked that to get a rise out of you.'

'A string of previous offences doesn't guarantee current guilt, Marcel.' He picked up his stuff. '*Vivà!*'

'*Vivà!*'

Erica welcomed him back to the car with the note.

'It just came in.'

'Manou's details?'

'Swap you for the *pissaladière*.'

Darac read the name out aloud.

'Imanol Esquebel. A Basque, obviously. Apartment 7, La Masarella, L'Ariane.'

'That's in the low rent area, isn't it?'

'It's one of the blocks. The roughest of them, in fact.'

'Bit lower down the social ladder than Florian, then?'

'Practically off it altogether.'

Wolfing down a piece of *socca*, Darac went to the boot and returned with his laptop.

'Let's see who he is. How's the *pissaladière* – good?'

'My own version's better.'

'You don't make a hundred at a time though, do you?'

'In this heat, can you imagine?'

'Here we go – Imanol Esquebel… twenty-six years old… born in Biarritz… string of minor offences… bit of a rough pup by the look of it… no weapons used… bare-knuckle boy… found guilty of aggravated assault three years ago… served four months.'

A photo flashed up. Short but with a weightlifter's tapered torso, Manou's sharp-eyed face smouldered with self-regard. Darac angled the screen for Erica.

'He's the guy in Florian's photos alright.' She dabbed

a rash of crumbs from her mouth. '*Really* street, isn't he? A rent boy?'

'Rent-controlled boy, perhaps – it seems he's been offence-free for the past two years. Judging by the album shots, that's more or less the time he was with Florian.'

'You know, it's in the back of my mind that I've seen him somewhere.' She took a sip of her noisette. 'Maybe it's just the type.'

'That's funny. You're the second person today to say that.'

'Who was the first?'

'Agnès. Of Mansoor Narooq.'

'I only quote from the best.'

Darac shut down the laptop and then, earning a horrified stare from Erica, tossed it on to the back seat.

'It's good for them. Okay, I'm off to L'Ariane. I'll drop you at the Caserne.'

'What – you think La Masarella is no place for a delicate flower like me?'

'Not at all. But you have to be getting back to the lab, don't you?'

'Well, I suppose I do.'

Thank goodness, she thought to herself.

Having dropped off Erica, Darac was on his way out of the Caserne when he ran into Bonbon driving in. They rolled their windows.

'I was going to borrow a local but are you free?'

'Where are you going?'

A car drew up behind Darac.

'L'Ariane. See if I can scare up one Imanol Esquebel.'

'He the Manou of myth and legend?'

'The same. Not a particularly bad boy as far as we know. Twenty-six years old. Born in Biarritz. Street kid. Bit of a hard case. Bodybuilder. Some form but none lately. Florian was sweet on him.'

'Classic bit of rough for the nice teacher?'

'Maybe. Imanol's clean-up act coincides more or less with Manou and Florian being together, interestingly.'

A horn blast from behind. Darac signalled he needed another couple of seconds.

'So the man in the white suit teaches Muscles how to behave; in return, he gets to learn a lot of stuff he never even dreamed of.'

'Could've been that way.'

'Okay, I'm in.'

'Park yours. I'll wait for you by the gate.'

Bonbon's foxy perkiness enabled him to cope with most terrain but his eyes narrowed warily.

'We go in yours?'

'And bring a jacket.'

'You're not planning to put on any...' His face crumpled. '...*jazz*, en route, are you?'

Darac gave a sad little shake of the head. 'Ai, ai, ai...'

'Well, are you?'

'Bonbon, have I ever mentioned Madame Treuil to you?'

'The woman who juggled vegetables?'

'That was Madame Latranne. Madame Treuil was a teacher I had back in Vence. Inspiring, kind – just wonderful. I still see her now from time to time. On the rare occasions I...' He searched for the *mot juste*. '...behaved like a dick, she didn't shout or anything like that, she just looked me calmly in the eye and said: "I'm not angry with you, Paul – I'm just disappointed." Oh boy, did that get to me.' Turning to Bonbon, he rolled out the look. 'Need I say more?'

'I'm chastened.'

'We'll say no more about it.'

'But no jazz, alright? It's a constitutional thing. It turns my stomach.'

Darac threw up a hand.

'Forget it. There's no time for music, anyway. Too much to go over.'

'I'll be ten minutes. Need to grab something from the canteen.'

'And you're worried about your stomach?'

Another horn blast from behind, sustained this time.

'I said, fucking wait! Jesus!'

Darac had Sonny Rollins blasting out when Bonbon reappeared at the passenger door. Like a horse refusing a fence, he came no further.

A deal was a deal.

'Travesty to fade "G-Man" halfway through but we could've been there a while.'

'I'm grateful.'

As they pulled away, Bonbon took a sniff of the canteen's take on a *pan-bagnat*.

'Interesting.' He decided to leave it for the moment. 'So – Emil Florian?'

Darac told him everything he knew.

'Shame there was no corroborating evidence but we'll find something somewhere.' Bonbon took a swig of water. 'And what's the latest on Mansoor Narooq? Flaco call in from the hospital?'

'Yeah, he chipped a bone in his shoulder – that's all, basically.'

'So he's back at the Caserne?'

'Yes. Flaco attempted to question him on a number of issues in the meantime, by the way. He refused to talk to her.'

'Because she's a police officer? Or because she's young, black and female?'

'He answered *my* questions – put it that way.'

Bonbon finally risked a bite of his sandwich.

'Great – it tastes as bad as it smells.'

'Fuel, Bonbon. Just think of it as fuel.'

'Be better off running on empty. So where doesn't young Mansoor want to be sent back to?'

'Didn't specify. Algeria was where he came here from. But I don't think his journey began there.'

'And then it all came to an end on Rue Verbier.'

'Yeah.' It was with some relief that Darac went to a different thought. 'What about you? Anything resembling a lead?'

'A passing resemblance, possibly.'

'The old woman?'

'No – she's proving a bit of a puzzle. Sounded like a real local character, didn't she? Someone everybody knows. "The grumpy old lady with the trolley? Oh, that's Madame Blanche." I kept expecting to hear something like that. But no one I spoke to knows who she is or has even seen her before. Shopkeepers, café owners, the people who live in the apartments – no one.'

'Not local to the quarter, by the sound of it.'

'I'm still a little disquieted. I was hoping to find her so we could discount her from the investigation.'

'Well, we've got Lartou's frame of her from CCTV out there now. Wide coverage. Someone somewhere will come forward.'

Darac turned on to the major route to the north-east, Route de Turin.

'I'm putting this down to the heat earlier, but after she tottered out of Rue Verbier, I pictured her getting into a limo, where divesting herself of her wig, prosthetic make-up and body padding, she turned back into...'

'Johnny Hallyday?'

'I was thinking Juliette Binoche. But you're right. It's ridiculous.'

Bonbon gave up on the *pan-bagnat*. Stuffing its remains into an evidence bag, he dropped it unceremoniously to the floor.

'So what's your possible lead?'

Bonbon flipped open his notebook.

'Number 67 Rue Verbier is an apartment house. Apartment 9 is a holiday place owned by one Marie Lacroix. The young couple who have taken it for the week told me they arrived to find Mademoiselle Lacroix "half-upset, half-angry". At first, they thought it was because they had arrived late for the handover but the actual reason, she told them, was that she'd just seen something happen on the street and it had appalled her.'

Darac gave him a look.

'Go on.'

'However, in the next second, Lacroix had downgraded "appalled" to "discouraged" and quickly changed the subject.'

'Probably worried the couple might look for somewhere else to stay.'

'Perhaps. Anyway, she's going to be interesting to talk to. She's normally home by about 8.30 on a Friday according to the concierge in her building. A Villefranche address...' He glanced at his notes once more. 'Number 1, Quai Mercier – Apartment 6.' Bonbon produced a tattered paper bag from his pocket. 'Aniseed drop?'

'Pass.'

'Wise.'

'I came up with something,' Darac said. I was looking into whether Drugs or Vice had Florian under surveillance, right? It seems neither did but by chance, Armani happened to be in Rue Verbier at about the time Florian arrived there.'

'"About"? Doesn't he know exactly when?'

'He was still off duty at that point.'

'Don't tell me – shopping?'

'For shoes, this time.'

'Well, a drug squad captain can't have enough pairs of handmade loafers, can he?' Bonbon's grin was wider than ever. 'I take it he didn't see Florian.'

'No he didn't. But you know what I'm wondering.'

'If Florian may have seen *him*? And that was why he hid and poured the GHB away there and then.' Bonbon weighed the idea. 'I like it, but isn't there a problem?'

Darac nodded. 'How did Florian know who Armani was? Even somebody who had been busted by him wouldn't recognise him off duty.'

'And Florian's record is whiter than white, anyway. But look – we're only halfway through day one of this case. We'll get there, chief. We always do.'

Darac liked Bonbon's optimism but a high clearance rate didn't guarantee anything. A criminal investigation, like a jazz solo, was a journey into the unknown. Although the analogy had its limitations, one element held true: the more complicated the journey, the easier it was to get lost. And just because you'd made it out and back a thousand times before didn't mean you were going to do so successfully the next time. Therein lay the excitement for him.

Following the course of the Paillon river, Route de Turin described a sweeping right-hand turn as it approached the neighbouring quarters of L'Ariane and La Trinité. Ahead, the three chimneys of the municipal waste incinerator cast long shadows towards the apartment blocks.

'La Trinité,' Darac said. 'A trinity of chimneys.'

'It looks worse than it actually is, I'm told. Which is just as well because it doesn't look pretty.'

'If you offered one of these apartments to Mansoor Narooq, he'd bite your hand off. He'd give anything to be able to breathe that lovely air.'

As they drew up in the lee of La Masarella, Darac broke the news that Granot had landed any Tour fan's dream assignment – a free night out at the pre-race bash.

'I don't want to say Granot always gets the plum jobs…' Bonbon's foxy grin was struggling to cope with the news. '…but he always gets the plum jobs!'

Darac carefully scanned the block's roof as they got out of the car. On a recent visit, a full-sized fridge had smashed into the pavement next to him. Kids being kids.

'Always? Not *always*.'

'Always!'

'He did have to attend the security briefing first. For a while there, he was convinced Nice was going to be turned into a blood bath come Sunday. That can't have been—' Darac's mobile rang. 'It's Perand.' He put the call on speaker.

'Go ahead.'

'Yeah – Lartou's photo of the trolley woman has done the trick. A neighbour recognised her and called in. She's one Corinne Delage, sixty-nine years of age, widow, lives up near the Stade du Ray.'

'Excellent. Delage has no previous, I suppose?'

'Record as long as your arm.'

'Well don't keep it to yourself,' Darac said, sharing an irritated look with Bonbon.

'With one exception, petty thievery and shoplifting seems to be Corinne's thing. That exception is interesting though. In 1998, she killed a neighbour's dog. And she used poison to do it. Warfarin.'

'Administered how?'

'Not by syringe, sadly. She mixed it up in food. She admitted it but claimed she was trying to get rid of rats and Fido got it by mistake. Even though the dose was way in excess of what you would use on vermin, she was believed. She's been a good girl since. Or not caught.'

'Was the neighbour who spotted her in Lartou's photo the same one whose dog was poisoned?'

'No – different. The bereaved dog owner moved away some years ago. The picture I'm getting is that old Corinne isn't a very popular girl. I'm going over to talk to her now. Without my big sister, you'll be glad to know.'

It had been going so well.

'Just do your job properly when you get there.' Darac returned Bonbon's quizzical look. 'Stay in touch.'

Bonbon flicked a film of sweat off his forehead.

'I'm feeling happier about the old woman. But what was that about the sister?'

'Just Perand being Perand.'

Neither of them was relishing the prospect of putting on a jacket. But on the whole, it was a good idea to conceal firearms if you could. They slipped them on and set off for the entrance lobby of the building.

'What's Manou's apartment number, chief?'

'Seven. Ground floor.'

It was Bonbon's turn to scan the roof.

'Come on, kids. Lob another one down. We could do with the ice.'

7.19 PM

It was the short one who eventually plucked the letter off his chest. Paying no attention to meaning, she recited the text in a headlong blurt – a slapdash, thoughtless performance. It suited him perfectly. The girl couldn't have taken in a single word and no one alive was less likely to have read between the lines. But it made his pulse quicken, alright. The heart-rate monitor confirmed it. How he needed that TV!

It was 21.3 degrees now. Hot. Scorching.

Time. Had he been able to see the clock on the rear wall, it would have told him it was gone seven o'clock in the evening. But 7 am or 7 pm – it really made no difference. It hadn't for days. Probably. Tomorrow would be different.

He thought back to his previous experiences of hospital. Life was busy for your average in-patient – an endless sequence of set pieces and ad-hoc events. The first big moment of the day was breakfast. After that, ablutions. Then the first trolley-round of drugs. That safely negotiated, excursions to a clinic or, more exotically, the MRI machine. Followed by the periodicals trolley. And then the drinks trolley. Afterwards, chatting with the fuckwit in the adjacent bed was the form. By lunchtime, you were exhausted. You had to take a nap in the afternoon, partly to get your strength up for the third set piece of the day: dinner. And then, too close for comfort, the fourth: visitors. If you had any. Finally, you might squeeze in a spot of TV before the lights were dimmed for sleep. By God, you needed it.

An ICU was different. A drip-fed patient had no breakfast, lunch or dinner to look forward to. Nor day or night. Everything was homogenous. A prelude to death.

But all that could change. With the TV, it would change. It would give him the Tour. For three whole weeks, his days would have a beginning, a middle and an end. And that would be the least of the excitement. There would be the prologue, the time trials and the road stages. There would be the breakaways, sprints and climbs. He'd be able to watch every moment of the battle for the yellow, green and polka-dot jerseys as they unfolded. Battles that he had a very personal reason for needing to see.

It would be the fat one. She was the only one concerned enough to want to be certain. She had almost asked him about the TV last time, he could tell. Next time, she would say it out loud. Something like: 'You know, the race starts today. Are you sure you don't want that TV?' And he would blink twice to tell her that he definitely wasn't sure. 'So do you want it, then?' He would blink once. Once, not a hundred stupid times. And then they would wheel the TV in and turn it on. A true life-support machine.

Come on, fat one.

Not long to wait…

7.22 PM

'We may as well not have bothered with the jackets, chief. Only a *flic* would be wearing one in this heat.'

At least they had made it into the building without being flattened. The muffled thuds of competing sound systems welcomed them into a shabby, cheerless lobby; cheerless that is, except for the presence of a coffee-skinned woman wearing a vibrant orange bubu and head wrap. Humming sweetly to the child squirming on her outthrust hip, the woman was reading notices attached to a board headed *Your La Masarella*. The child, a girl, appeared much too old to need carrying but as she jerked her head up, Darac noticed the rolling eyes, the tongue exploring the air between her contorted lips. She cried out, suddenly.

'Sshhh… There now.' The woman kissed the child's ear. 'Mama's here.'

'Good evening, madame,' Darac said, giving the mother a warm smile as he and Bonbon went to cross behind her. The woman looked the visitors up and down and returned to the notices.

Passing under a trashed CCTV camera, Darac and Bonbon pushed through a door at the rear of the lobby and entered a corridor of blue-painted brick. American rapper voices came and went as they passed along it towards number 7. The bros were looking to catch up with some skank-ass bitches. They were going to blip them off. Whatever that meant.

It seemed Imanol Esquebel favoured high bpm dance music.

Bonbon gave Darac a look.

'We don't want the full Hollywood, do we?'

'No, no.'

Darac hated guns. And up until a couple of years ago, he'd maintained that you were more likely to be shot, stabbed or have acid thrown in your face if you were brandishing one. That was before he'd stopped a bullet during a routine arrest.

'Just cover me.'

Standing with his back to the wall so he wouldn't be seen from inside the apartment, Bonbon drew his SIG semi-automatic. He kept his eyes trained on Darac as he knocked hard on the door. The music track died in mid-beat. As the seconds passed, no one appeared. Darac knocked again. Finally, the door opened. The smell of Pagan Man-scented sweat hit his nostrils.

He showed his badge.

'Monsieur Imanol Esquebel?'

'Maybe.'

Short, powerfully built and breathing hard, the young man was Manou, alright. A towel around his neck, he was wearing only a pair of Lycra shorts. If he was carrying a weapon, it was difficult to imagine where he might have been concealing it. Darac gave an almost imperceptible shake of the head. Bonbon holstered his gun and stepped away from the wall.

'Sorry to interrupt your exercises, Manou,' Darac said. 'May we come in?'

His black eyes fixed on Darac's, Manou's biceps flexed impressively as he began drawing the towel slowly across his neck. After he had duly conveyed to them that the decision to admit them had been entirely his own, he stepped aside.

'Thank you.' Darac walked past him into a minimally furnished white-walled living space. From the couch to the blond wood dining table, it looked like a cut-price replica of Emil Florian's lounge. A computer sat at a workstation in one corner. It was a year or two older than Florian's – his cast-off, perhaps. Another job for Erica.

Bonbon gestured Manou back into the living room.

'It's alright, I'll close it.'

It was craft disguised as politeness. Leaving a suspect door-side was a non-starter. Manou smirked as he padded back into the room. A dumb trick like that didn't fool him.

'He knows that one, Bonbon.'

'Oh, that's clever, Monsieur Le Flic. Only one problem. I don't know what the fuck you're talking about.'

Manou's accent was almost caricature Basque.

'Listen – you're Biarritz, right? I'm Perpignan. A Basque and a Catalan – we boys from the south-west ought to stick together.'

Manou essayed a look that suggested sticking to

Bonbon was the last thing he fancied.

Darac glanced through an open doorway into the larger of the apartment's two bedrooms. In it stood the multi-gym machine that was the source of all the sweat.

'That's quite some kit.'

'Cut the crap. Why are you here?'

'I believe you know a Monsieur Emil Florian.'

'Emil? So?'

More towelling down. More flexing of the absurdly pumped-up physique. Bonbon sidled off in the direction of the multi-gym.

'Don't go in there.'

'Don't worry. I won't break it.'

'When was the last time you spoke to Monsieur Florian?'

'I dunno. Some weeks ago.' One eye on Bonbon, Manou's surliness was already turning into unease. 'We don't see each other much any more.'

'Have you spoken to him on the phone?'

The sound of clinking weights.

'Don't touch that!'

'Have you spoken to him on the phone, Manou?'

'I could have. Come out of there!'

Bonbon was grinning foxily as he padded out of the room.

'Good job you're on the ground floor, isn't it?' He continued towards the kitchen. 'All that weight.'

'Don't go in there either.' Manou turned to Darac. 'Tell him to come back.'

'Why? You've nothing to hide, have you?'

'No.' He made an effort not to follow Bonbon with his eyes. 'If I'd known you were coming I would've washed up.'

'My partner's an interior-design buff.' Through a chink in the door, Darac could see Bonbon putting on gloves. 'Just wants to see what you've done with the place.'

'Interior design… bullshit. I've heard of *flics* planting evidence.'

'Where did you hear that – in prison? How come you only got four months for aggravated assault, by the way, Manou?'

The man sighed and sat down. As if to ensure he said nothing out of turn, he began chewing the inside of his cheek.

'I've got a whole raft of questions for you but let's go back to the one I just asked you. Have you spoken to Emil Florian on the phone recently? Last night, for instance?'

For a supposedly streetwise operator, Manou was hopelessly transparent. Behind the unimpressed pout, potential responses ricocheted like pinballs. He flipped one.

'No. Should I have?'

'Why not tell the truth? It's easier on the brain.'

Darac had touched a raw nerve.

'What do you think I am?' The words were spat out. 'A fucking idiot?'

Bending slowly forward, Darac got close in to Manou's face.

'You might well be an idiot for all I know. Answer!'

Manou neither flinched nor sought to give himself space.

'You've got a gorgeous mouth.'

Darac straightened, shaking his head.

'When all else fails, fall back on sex. Is that the secret of your success?'

'It hasn't failed. Anyway, there are worse things than falling back on sex. Depending on whose sex you fall back on, of course.' Manou pursed his lips and let his eyes drop to his crotch. 'Twenty centimetres. Send my long-lost pal from the south-west away and I'll let you play with it.'

'Sorry – not gay. Or a homophobe, so there'll be no furious assault to give a lawyer ammo.'

Manou shrugged, the act instantly dropped.

'Look, why are you here? I've got to get ready to go to work.'

'Work? What do you do?'

'That's my business.'

'It's my business also. What do you do?'

'I drive a taxi. If you ask *really* nicely, I'll say "Are you looking at me?" like Bobby De Niro.'

'You just did. Which company do you drive for?'

As if it required thought, he took a moment before answering.

'For... Peerless Taxis.'

'The place down on Rue de Bruges?'

'Yeah, yeah. Now I want you to—' He stopped talking as Bonbon emerged from the kitchen holding a clear plastic canister. In it was some sort of white powder.

'What's this?'

Straightening his arms, Manou clenched his fists tightly.

'What is it?' Bonbon repeated, removing the lid. A circle in red marker ink was daubed on it.

'It's... protein powder.'

Bonbon shook his head.

'It's way too salty for that, my friend.'

'Get dressed,' Darac said. 'We'll carry this on at the Caserne.'

8.57 PM

Agnès was grateful for the handrail — the steps up from the compound seemed steeper than usual. It then took her two attempts to buzz herself in to the building. It was as well the keypad hadn't defeated her a third time. Setting off the alarm was the last thing she needed.

'Béatrice,' she said, resting her elbows on the duty officer's counter. 'Were you to have an espresso sent to my office in fifteen minutes' time, you would make a hot, tired old commissaire very happy.'

'Certainly, madame.'

'Has Captain Darac conducted his progress meeting yet?'

'Yes. The team is questioning the various parties again at the moment.'

'And the meeting call I put out for 9.30 — have Vice and Narcotics managed to get in?'

Béatrice consulted her list.

'Lejeune, Tardelli, Martinet… yes, they're all here.'

'Good.' Agnès picked up her attaché case. It felt heavier than before. First, the steps seemed steeper, now this? And the day wasn't over yet. 'You know what, Béatrice? Make that a double espresso.'

The young woman smiled.

'Of course.'

Like a doctor making rounds, Agnès called in on each of her team in turn. In Bonbon's office, she found Manou Esquebel handcuffed to a vertical pipe. He seemed hardly to register her presence. Free to sit or stand, he was standing, shifting his weight restlessly from one foot to the other. His white T-shirt drenched in sweat, he looked as if his concentration was being stretched beyond its usual limits – a reaction users exhibited. Although there were no drugs offences on Manou's rap sheet, Agnès made a mental note to ask Armani Tardelli about him.

'I tell you, I'm going to kill Emil when I get out of here!'

'Are you?'

'No? Fucking hell…'

'A word, Lieutenant?'

Bonbon joined her in the corridor.

'He thinks Florian is still alive, Bonbon?'

'We're keeping news of his death up our sleeves for the moment.'

'So you obviously don't believe *he* could be responsible?'

'Until we know *exactly* what happened to Florian, and when, we can't rule it out; but we don't believe it, no.'

'Why?'

'Surely the first thing Esquebel would've done if he'd killed Florian, or even if he'd just heard about his death, is to have got rid of the GHB. But he didn't. Our visit came as a complete surprise to him.'

'That's certainly suggestive.'

'And there are other factors.'

'Right. Let's wind him up again and see where he goes.'

Once back in the room, Bonbon showed Manou the key found under Florian's prayer mat.

'So you don't know what this opens. And you can't remember why Florian rang you last night. Maybe you'll remember later. So let's rewind. Again. Your apartment – the one furnished by your boyfriend. Let's talk about the white stuff I found there in the canister...'

Manou let out a groan.

'Our pathology lab will prove it's GHB. You know they will.'

Not until tomorrow, they won't, Agnès thought. The lab stick-dippers would have gone home hours ago.

Manou exhaled deeply and stopped moving. His cuffed hand rattled down the pipe as he sank on to his seat, staring at the floor.

Bonbon's eyes slid expressively to Agnès. It wouldn't be long now. Both remained silent.

'Alright. Alright... it is GHB. Or near enough.'

'We know it is; but that feels better, doesn't it?'

'But I only use it for bodybuilding.'

Bonbon's eyebrows furrowed his freckles.

'Bodybuilding?' He made a derisory sound in his throat. 'What possible use could a date-rape drug have in bodybuilding?'

'You're ignorant, do you know that? Scientists didn't invent GHB to knock people half out and then give them...

uh…' The word search proved futile. '…And then make them forget everything. They invented it for bodybuilders.'

'Really? I don't believe you.'

'No? It releases growth hormone, FYI.'

Bonbon looked down on Manou's one-metre-sixty-seven frame.

'It's doing a hell of a job.'

The cuffs held the boy as he shot to his feet. A rearing cobra might have looked more menacing to Bonbon at that moment. But not by much.

'Fuck you, you ginger fucking wimp. I could take you out with one tap.'

'You probably could. I *am* a wimp. But ginger? Take that back.' Bonbon pointed to the shock of copper wire that was his hair. 'This is auburn. Alright? And tell me this – if you're using the stuff to plump up your bumps, how come *you're* not half-unconscious?'

'It's the dose, you cunt – how much of it you use. Jesus, you're thick.'

Agnès picked up the baton.

'The second thing the lab will prove, Manou, is that your GHB and the stuff Florian carries around in his water bottle are the same. He's no bodybuilder, is he?'

'Think what you like.'

Agnès decided to leave Bonbon to it.

In the squad room, Max Perand and Yvonne Flaco were interrogating Corinne Delage, the Warfarin enthusiast. Sitting unrestrained across a table from the youngsters, the old woman was wearing a look of prim self-righteousness;

something that might have carried more credibility had her rap sheet not been laid out in front of her.

Quite unconsciously, Perand put the question he was posing on hold as Agnès entered. She gave him the nod to continue but now the boss had arrived, Delage had no interest in anyone but her. Her guardian angel had flown in, it seemed; a kindred spirit with the power to straighten everything out.

'Oh, madame – all I did was to run over a bit of muck in the street and these two young... officers are talking about murder.'

'Yeah, well that's not surprising.' Perand gave his stubble a scratch. 'The man died seconds after you left your mark on him.'

Delage cast Agnès a conspiratorial look.

'Honestly – can you believe it?'

'Answer the officer's question.'

Delage's smile faded.

'But...'

Agnès fixed the old woman in her feline gaze.

'Answer the question.'

'Pah!'

Her mouth twisting into a sneer, Delage turned back to Perand.

'No, I'd never seen the man before. And left a mark? That's rubbish. I hardly touched him.'

It was unfortunate but Agnès and the others understood this to be the case.

'Like you hardly touched your neighbour's dog?' Flaco

held up the rap sheet. Delage chose not to look at it. 'You used poison, didn't you?'

'It was an accident. I was after rats and that was proved in court. And listen to me: if this darkie died after he got in the way of my trolley, he must have been dying already.'

Delage sat back as if nothing else needed to be said on the matter.

Flaco shared a look with Perand. She hadn't bought the trolley-killer theory from the outset. Now it seemed the perpetrator hadn't even noticed the colour of Florian's skin.

'Darkie?'

'Yes, *darkie*! Not a black like you but one of…' From sour to saccharin in the blink of an eye, Delage turned once more to Agnès. 'Madame, do I have to explain myself to this—'

'Yes. Yes you do.'

'The dead man was not dark-skinned,' Flaco said. 'He was white.'

Delage's jaw dropped open.

'What?'

Agnès knew the woman to be something of an actress but even so, she judged her reaction genuine. And if so, it was of some significance. If Delage hadn't known anything about Florian beforehand, she could hardly have killed him out of revenge. Other possibilities were up for grabs but Agnès gave them little credence. Yet until Deanna Bianchi came up with an account of exactly how and when Florian was given the drug she suspected killed him, she had no alternative but to continue the questioning of Madame Corinne Delage.

'A piece of advice, madame,' Agnès said. If you further abuse, obstruct or in any way mislead either of my officers, your impressive record of offences is going to bear yet another entry.'

'Yes?' The old woman's mouth twisted defiantly. 'We'll see.'

'Carry on.'

In the next-door office, Darac was interviewing Mansoor Narooq. Leaning inconspicuously against the door frame, Agnès decided to watch and listen for the moment.

'In any pain?' Darac said, placing a cup of water in the young man's right hand. 'If you are, we can postpone this.'

'What difference would that make?' Mansoor took three sips. 'It doesn't hurt unless I move in a certain way.'

Darac's landline rang. An indicator light told him the call was internal.

'Excuse me a second.'

The number was Erica's. Lifting the cord over his photo of Angeline, he went around to the far side of his desk and sat down.

'You still here?'

'Going home now but I've just finished with Manou Esquebel's computer.'

'I wasn't expecting you to look at that tonight.'

'It didn't take long, especially as Manou's password, like Florian's, turned out to be "Manou", would you believe.'

Staring out over the compound, Mansoor gave every

impression he wasn't listening. Darac kept his words neutral anyway.

'I'd wondered if it was a hand-me-down.'

'It was.'

'Anything of interest to us?'

'It was the same as Florian's – clean as a whistle. Not one pornographic file. Hard or soft.'

'Right.'

'But I did discover something unexpected. *I* didn't expect it, anyway. Manou Esquebel can't read. Can barely spell his name.'

'Really?' Darac thought back to his and Bonbon's visit to Manou's apartment. There were some books but that meant little. More indicative, perhaps, were his reactions to digs about his brainpower. 'Are you sure?'

'I found a sound-based Learn to Read programme on the hard drive. Manou's been struggling with it for a couple of years, by the look of it. His answers to some of the questions... Well, I found it sad, somehow. Anyway, no gruesome images – that's the story on page one.'

'Great work – thanks. Now go home. Unless you're coming to the meeting.'

'Not me. I'm half out the door now.'

Darac hung up. Manou illiterate? It must have made driving a taxi interesting.

'Captain?'

'Just be a moment, Mansoor.' Darac got to his feet, conscious that once again, Agnès's arrival appeared to perturb his charge. 'This lady is my boss, by the way. In fact, everyone's boss around here.'

Jetting her the quickest glance, Mansoor nodded and looked away.

In the corridor, Agnès gave Darac a knowing smile.

'On behalf of all women, I thank you.'

'I don't think it will have had much effect.'

'Nor do I.' She glanced at her watch. 'Could you come to my office before the meeting?'

'Sure.'

'Five minutes?'

'Five it is.'

Darac kept his eye on her as she withdrew. She looked drained, he thought. He went back into his office and picked up the phone.

'Seve – you free?'

'For you, Captain, I might be.'

'Come to my office straight away, will you?' Mansoor's eyes slid anxiously in his direction. 'I want you to babysit Mansoor Narooq for a while.'

'The jumper?'

'Yes. You can chat to each other in Arabic.'

Darac found Agnès bent forward in her chair, pulling back the toes of her bare left foot. It looked an uncomfortable position for someone with a back problem.

'Excuse this. *Really* aching feet this evening.'

'So the Tour people have a hoaxer on their hands?'

'Not so much a hoaxer; more a non-credible threatener.'

'Not sure I understand the distinction.' He drew up

a chair and invited her to extend her foot. 'Here – let me. It'll be easier.'

She straightened, wincing slightly.

'I'll explain all at the meeting.'

'Good. Your foot? Left or right – I'm not superstitious.'

Her feet stayed where they were. But she was tempted, Darac could see.

'Paul… Thanks very much but… you know.'

'I know your feet could do with a rub and it's killing you to do it.'

'That's not quite the point.'

'What is, then?'

'Quite apart from the fact that I'm who I am and you're who you are…'

'No doubt about that.'

'—*And*, frankly, I don't think the end of a long July day is really—'

'Don't be silly.' He held out his hands. 'Relax.'

'I think I should probably…'

'Look – as a special treat, I'll let you rub mine as well. How's that?'

She produced her signature laugh, a series of almost silent gasps.

'Oh…' She shook her head, her resistance gone. 'Come on, then.'

Checking her skirt hem wasn't rising too high, she sat back in her chair. Darac took her foot and began working it between his hands with gentle but firm pressure.

'My Aunt Sophie taught me how to do this. Fingers like crowbars. Me, not her. Comes with playing the guitar.'

'Oh my God…' Agnès exhaled deeply. 'Perhaps if you'd done this for Mansoor Narooq, he wouldn't have jumped out of the window.'

Darac laughed but he still felt sheepish about the boy's attempted escape.

'This time, I've put Seve Sevran in with him.'

'Oh, Seve, yes.' Her eyes closed, Agnès's words were already emerging in an adagio monotone. 'How is his wife these days?'

'Up and down. Psychiatric problems are the worst, I think. And it can't be that easy for him, either. Never knowing what he's going to find when he gets home.'

'Indeed… Anyway, before I fall asleep, here's what we're going to do with the Florian people. Mansoor Narooq can spend tonight in the convalescent wing at the Maison d'Arrêt. We'll talk with him here again tomorrow. Ditto Slimane Bahtoum – that alright with you?'

'Absolutely.'

'The odious Madame Delage can go home. We'll resume with her there tomorrow. Our friend Manou Esquebel is bound for the cell block. That boy is as slippery as a sack of eels but he's feeling the pressure.'

'There's more to come from him, alright. It seems he's illiterate, by the way. Erica picked it up, examining his computer.'

'Then he's likely to be particularly resourceful.'

'I hadn't thought of it that way.'

'Anything from Frankie's lycée initiative? I suppose a lot of the staff are away.'

'Actually, most of them aren't and she's managed to speak to quite a few of them already. They seem to break down into three categories: those who, like Principal Volpini, actively liked Florian; those who could take him or leave him; those who didn't seem to care for him at all.'

'I like her online questionnaire idea.'

'Yes and she got it up and running quickly which is important. Once it's known that Florian was murdered, rather than just died – which is obviously what she told the staff she spoke to – anyone who knew or even just suspected the man was a paedophile is hardly likely to come forward. Makes them an instant suspect, doesn't it?'

'Knowledge of his murder might gag someone who hadn't already come forward – true. But it would obviously make no difference to the murderer, and finding that person is our primary goal. Whether they were ultimately doing the world a favour or not.'

Darac smiled. It wasn't the first time Agnès had reminded him not to play God.

'You're right, of course. But a secondary goal has emerged now and in the end, it might prove more important than tracking down the killer of a rapist. If there are individuals out there who have been abused by Florian and or Manou, I want to find them. And I want to ensure that Manou gets no opportunity to carry on the bad work.'

'Absolutely – so long as it remains your secondary focus for the time being.'

'Don't worry.'

With one hand gripping the ball of her foot and the other the heel, he began twisting one against the other.

'Oh yes, yes, yes… Your Angeline is a lucky woman… I don't care what anyone says.'

Agnès needn't have bothered with the decorum-restoring aside. Darac hadn't heard it. He was trying to remember the last time he'd massaged Angeline's feet.

A knock at the door.

'Wait a moment!'

It was too late.

'Here we…' Her eyes averted, the duty officer Béatrice Lacquet advanced into the room as if on rails. 'Your espresso, madame?'

Building K's conference room was the practical choice for the meeting. With desks and stacker chairs formed into a rectangle, the room could seat forty. As Darac took his place, a hand brushed his shoulder from behind.

'One completed questionnaire in already.' Frankie Lejeune's eyebrows rose expressively. 'From a Mademoiselle Adrianna Volpini.'

'Daughter of the principal?'

'The same. Everything's wonderful at the lycée, according to her.'

'It may even be true.'

'It may.' She smiled and headed off to her seat. 'Later.'

A vast and gamey presence materialised on Darac's blind side.

'Plastic chairs?' Once more, it seemed that life had shafted Roland Granot. 'Perfect – if you're built like a pencil.' Hoping for the best, he gingerly lowered his backside at the target.

'Left a bit,' Darac said. 'Bull's-eye. So – some day off for you.'

'Attending meetings isn't really work, is it?'

'Did you see any of your heroes over in Monaco, then?'

'See – yes; meet – no. Glad I went, though.' A cantankerous smile lifted the puckers in Granot's moustachioed chops. 'It would've been better still if someone had given me a nice, relaxing, *intimate* foot massage.'

'Would it?' Darac smiled. 'Uh-huh.'

'Oh, indeed it would.'

'Béatrice?'

'My source shall go unnamed.'

Darac shook his head. What was the Caserne – a police headquarters or a convent school? Five minutes and the story was out. And what was the big deal, anyway?

Unaware of the conversation going on to her right, Agnès pushed off her slingbacks and flexing her still tingling feet, gave Darac's forearm a touch.

'So much better,' she said *sotto voce*. 'Thank you.'

'It was nothing.' Or it would have been if it had gone no further than Béatrice. 'Nothing at all.'

Every seat finally taken, Agnès took one last look at

her notes and, parking her reading glasses in her hair, turned to address the meeting. The room hushed.

'We welcome our colleagues from the Palais de Justice…' She indicated the two soberly suited individuals sitting on her left. '…the examining magistrate Albert Reboux and the public prosecutor Jules Frènes. Welcome, gentlemen. And welcome also to our GIPN chief, Fréderic Anselme.'

Anselme nodded curtly. Reboux and Frènes accepted the greeting with their accustomed hauteur. Frènes appeared slightly irritated at receiving second billing, Darac thought.

'Next, I'm sorry that those of you who were off-duty had to be called in for this—'

'So are we,' Armani Tardelli said, garrulous as usual.

'—but I've been asked to pass on to you the findings of a meeting I attended in Monaco earlier and my arm was twisted so far up my back by Commandant Lanvalle that there was really no alternative.'

Frènes picked up his pen with the relish of a chess player recording a calamitous move by an opponent.

Agnès glanced at his notepad as he wrote.

'I actually said "twisted", not "shoved", monsieur. Could prove important later.'

Frènes made a displacement gesture out of putting down his pen. When he looked up, Darac and his entire team were staring at him. And so was Albert Reboux. Agnès herself seemed unconcerned.

'I'm sure you all know that several hours ago, a supposed jihadist group calling itself the Sons and Daughters of the Just Cause issued an ultimatum to the organisers of the

Tour de France. The group threatened to "reap a bloody harvest" on our streets when the race passes through on Sunday, should certain demands not be met. The various security authorities are as certain as they can be that the ultimatum is not genuine.' She outlined the reasons given at the Monaco briefing. 'However, some believe that it may yet pose a threat to us of a limited sort. Accordingly, just as a precautionary measure – and frankly, I think, to cover their backs should it transpire that they got it wrong – extra resources are being drafted into the area even as we speak. Any questions before we go on? Yes, Frankie.'

'What form do the acronyms from Paris believe this limited threat might take?'

'Amongst those who believe the ultimatum isn't a flat-out hoax, there are two schools of thought. Some – and I have to say I am not one of them – believe it may have been designed as a smokescreen; a means of diverting police resources to the stage route while the perpetrators, who are not terrorists at all but common, everyday criminals, carry out their true plan elsewhere. Others believe the ultimatum has an explicitly political purpose: a local one. Considering the events on Rue Verbier this lunchtime, it's a pretty cogent argument.'

Captain 'Armani' Tardelli adjusted the folded-back cuffs of his crisp white shirt.

'They want to stop me buying shoes?'

Laughs. Even Frènes seemed to find some amusement in the crack.

'No, you're safe,' Agnès said, smiling. 'The issue in

question is a first mosque for Nice. As this is the only realisable demand the group made, I originally thought it represented its sole true objective: the only piece they intended to be left on the board when all the other pieces had been sacrificed. A moment's reflection and then an intelligence report from the DCRI disabused me of the notion.' She turned to Darac. 'Paul has something on this.'

'Yes, I was saying on the way over that the balance of opinion at the Mairie seems to have shifted somewhat. As we know, it used to be tilted heavily in favour of the no-mosque lobby. Now, according to Imam Asiz and his flock – if "flock" is the word – things are more evenly balanced.'

Agnès nodded.

'Probably the most sacred icon of our national life is the Tour de France – agreed? Any group connected with Asiz and company is unlikely to think that threatening to desecrate it would tip the balance finally in their favour.'

Frènes gave Reboux an astonished look.

'What's this? A blanket assessment of an entire community? Tarring all the Muslims in Nice with the same brush? Isn't that the kind of prejudiced thinking you abhor, madame? Just because they worship like automata doesn't mean that they all think and believe the same things. There could be extremists amongst them. Have you ever heard of the phenomenon?'

'I think I may have come across it somewhere,' Agnès said, ridiculing the ridiculous. 'This is where the DCRI intelligence I mentioned comes in.'

When it came to portraying scorn, Frènes was a natural.

'Well? Perhaps you would condescend to share that with us?'

Condescend… Darac's patience with Frènes, already thin, was wearing out fast. But there was little point in expressing it. Agnès had never needed anyone to fight her corner for her.

'Like you, monsieur,' she continued, 'I'm not best placed to answer questions of security. So let's hear from Freddy.'

Darac shared a look with Frankie. They knew Agnès enjoyed using the pet form of Frédéric Anselme's name because it so ill-suited him. A super-fit individual with a shrink-wrapped head, Anselme would lead his SWAT team into the eye of a hurricane and out again if ordered to do so by the Ministry. Darac thought the man was certifiably insane.

'Thank you, Commissaire.' Anselme's voice was an improbably high-pitched affair; an anomaly no one had ever been rash enough to point out to him. 'Shall we just say that the DCRI have mounted a thorough investigation of the local Muslim situation? They found it was clean. As a whistle. Cleaner, in fact.'

'Thank you.' Agnès scanned the room. 'Any further questions at this stage?'

Perand raised a lazy finger.

'Boss – how did the DCRI mount that investigation? Out of interest.'

'I don't know. They wouldn't tell me.'

Frènes made a derisory sound in his throat.

Anselme shook his head emphatically.

'That would be classified information. Even at my level of clearance.'

Anselme's high-pitched piping gave way to Frankie's velvety contralto.

'I have a question, Agnès. If it's generally recognised by those who favour a political interpretation that the threat wasn't made by Muslim activists, then who did make it?'

'They believe it was an anti-Muslim group – either Front National types or just local people worried that theirs might be the neighbourhood earmarked for the mosque. The aim of this, obviously, being to torpedo the Muslims' standing at the Mairie, thereby nixing the project.'

Granot nodded his jowly head.

'This makes the most sense to me. I'd never do anything about it, of course, but if I'm honest, I wouldn't welcome a mosque next door. Some might enjoy hearing the call to prayer five times a day through a tinny tannoy but I'm not one of them.'

The debate found supporters on both sides until Yvonne Flaco brought it back on track.

'How have the DCRI et cetera formally responded to the demands, madame? If they have.'

'As directed.' Slipping on her spectacles, Agnès held up a copy of the evening edition of *Nice-Matin*. 'This is in the personal column. "SAD: we are most seriously considering your requests. Talk to us about it." And then there's a phone number which goes through all manner of electronics to Commandant Lanvalle's people. If the so-called Sons and Daughters are a bunch of half-wits, as many suspect, they may be just dumb enough to ring it.'

'Back on our normal territory, boss,' Bonbon said. 'Why are you disinclined to believe the smokescreen theory?'

'No one in their right mind is going to pull a major job on the day the Tour comes to town, are they? For petty thieves, pickpockets and so on, yes – it could be a field day for them. But we're not talking about that level of activity here. The Tour brings ten times the number of forces into an area than are normally present. By issuing a threat, all the criminals would achieve is to attract more forces still. Highly trained, commando-style forces, at that...'

Freddy Anselme nodded vigorously.

'...Even if the vast majority of them were detailed to line the Tour route – so what? They're still in the area, ready to be deployed.' Drawing her lips together, Agnès shook her ash-blond bob. 'Put it this way – if I were a villain and I wanted to, say, clean out the main branch of Crédit d'Azur, the last thing I would do is issue a terrorist threat.'

Agnès took a long sip of water and then invited the examining magistrate, Albert Reboux, to give his take on things.

The man began in his deep, authoritative tones; a voice made to pass judgement, Darac always thought. He found the content itself invariably less impressive and it came as some relief when after no more than a few moments, his mobile throbbed silently in his pocket. He flipped it discreetly open. The incoming text was from Didier Musso, leader of the quintet in which Darac played guitar.

Where the hell are you? it began – a familiar refrain from his band members and police colleagues alike. Tonight, Darac and Angeline had reserved seats at the Blue Devil – American legend Dinah Graham and her trio were in town. After just one number, Didier was predicting it was going to be one of those special nights. He urged Darac to drop what he was doing and hit the club ASAP. *And what's happened to Angeline?* For some moments, Darac's head was elsewhere. He knew the simple answer: she was out enjoying an impromptu dinner with colleagues. At a deeper level, he had no idea.

It wasn't until Reboux had almost finished speaking that Darac tuned back in to the meeting.

'And so, in relation to the local situation, I agree with your assessment of the smokescreen theory, madame.' Reboux moved his head from side to side suddenly, as if it were weighing too heavily on his neck. 'However, has anyone considered the possibility that the perpetrators' real target may lie further afield? By deploying special forces in the Alpes-Maritimes area, the authorities would obviously be reducing their availability elsewhere. I am unaware of the complements of the various units involved but perhaps our colleagues in Marseilles, Lyon, or even Paris may prove to be the ones in danger of facing a major crime incident with inadequate police resources to back them up.'

Agnès nodded thoughtfully.

'At the earlier meeting, some made that very point. Once again, I have an objection. If I were a criminal seeking to *really* draw forces into our area, I would issue a far more potent threat than the one the "Sons and Daughters" came up with. And I have a further comment. Without wishing to sound too parochial, if the threat did leave another region vulnerable to attack, that's not really our problem, is it?'

'Reading between the lines, Commissaire Dantier, am I right in thinking that you believe the threat to be a hoax, pure and simple?'

Agnès shook her head.

'Not necessarily. I could easily believe that it's the work of disgruntled locals trying to influence the Mairie into cooling on the mosque project. But if it turns out that it's the work of a practical joker, a child, or even what my papa refers to as a "poor unfortunate", I wouldn't be surprised.'

Armani clasped his large hands behind his head.

'A poor unfortunate with a bomb could still blow up the peloton as it pedals by. And several rows of fans to go along with it.'

Untypically, Perand's voice was the loudest in a chorus of disquiet.

'Too right. A bomb's a bomb, for Christ's sake.'

Freddy Anselme dispatched the possibility with a chopping motion of his hand.

'Not going to happen. Firepower. Increased firepower and surveillance. Those are our watchwords. Let them try to detonate a bomb. They'll find out what happens to them.'

'Okay, I think that covers the basics. Just have a few practicalities to go over...' Agnès referred to her notes once more.

'Yes, what does this all mean practically, boss?' Armani said. 'Are we going to be on for the whole weekend? Roaming around looking for action?'

'That's what we do most weekends, isn't it?' his second-in-command, Lieutenant Thierry Martinet, said.

'One way or another.'

Agnès found the relevant note.

'Alright – those normally rostered for the weekend and anyone working on the Florian case will be on. Some officers expecting to be off won't be. Your duty officers will have lists immediately after this meeting. The rest of you will be on standby. No one will be completely off.'

A groan went up. Armani gave Frankie a knowing look.

'Welcome to our world, eh?'

'On that,' Agnès said, 'will you come over to the cell block with us after the meeting? I want you to take a look at a suspect.'

'Sure.'

'And that goes for you too, Frankie, if you would.'

'Certainly.'

'The man in question is one Imanol Esquebel, known as Manou. Name mean anything?'

Neither recognised it.

'But we may have another ID for him,' Frankie said.

Armani pursed his lips.

'Was a blood sample taken?'

'Yes but it won't be analysed until tomorrow. Alright, back to Sunday…'

The meeting rolled on for another five minutes. As it broke up, Frènes made an immediate beeline for Darac. A bad card player with a killer hand might just have looked more pleased with life.

'Do you think he subscribes to *Complete Arsehole Magazine* or does he just buy it at the stand?' Darac said to Granot. 'What can I do for you, Monsieur Frènes?'

'You can tell me how a suspect in your charge came to find himself lying in a twisted heap under your window. Name of Mansoor Narooq. A genuine real-live Muslim.'

'You can tell me how you came to know that.'

'I don't have to tell you anything. Imagine what the press would have made of the incident if they had got hold of it. Imagine what that appalling Annie Provin woman on TV would have said about it on her news programme. Once again, tell me how a—'

Granot had heard enough.

'Narooq was in the care of another officer at the time. Copies of the report are on the way to the Commissaire, to Monsieur Reboux and, finally, to you.'

Frènes's face didn't so much fall as crash.

'How can I put this?' Granot eyeballed him. 'Your intelligence is suspect.'

They left Frènes assessing the degree of the hurt he'd suffered.

'Who do you reckon dropped you in it? To that creep?'

'Someone who wasn't very close to the action. Nor took the trouble to find out what had actually happened.'

'Or someone setting Frènes up for a fall, perhaps?'

'Another hoax caller?' Darac ran a hand through his hair. 'It's an epidemic.' Bonbon came up on his blind side. 'Yes, mate?'

He updated him on Manou's GHB admission.

'Interesting.'

'I got on a bit of a roll so I decided to tell him about Florian's death. He looked straightforwardly stunned. No playacting. Then he cried. Then he laughed when I suggested he might have done it. Then he cried again.'

'So that all adds up to…?'

'I'm ninety-nine per cent certain he didn't know Florian was even dead, let alone murdered him – just like we thought. But we've got him until Sunday evening. Let's see what we get out of him in the meantime.'

'Absolutely.'

Bonbon glanced at his watch.

'It's got a bit late but I'm off to meet Marie Lacroix, the holiday apartment owner from Rue Verbier. You don't need me over in the cells, do you?'

'No, no. That's good – you go and see her.'

'What a carry-on this all is, eh? Terrorists – non-terrorists; threats – non-threats.' Normality returned in the shape of a striped paper tube. 'Lemon honey cup?'

'From Cours Saleya?'

'Of course.'

The pair helped themselves as Armani joined them.

'What's that rubbish you're slobbering over?'

'Have one.'

'And ruin my teeth?'

As they filed out of the room, Armani threw an arm around Darac's shoulder.

'As the man said – I have an offer you can't refuse.'

'If you're fed up with your new shoes already, put them on eBay.'

'Darac, it's nothing to do with my new shoes…' He modelled them. '…which are quite magnificent by the way. No, my offer is this: I will give you fifty euros *right* now in *cash* for your five-euro sweepstake ticket.' He brandished the note. 'What do you say?'

Granot laughed derisively. But he wished he'd thought of the idea himself.

'So you fancy Fun—' Darac hadn't made the mistake in hours. '*Con*tador, do you?'

Cluelessness was one of Armani's least convincing expressions.

'Who? No, no. It's just that you drew ticket twenty-one and that's my lucky number. Fifty for five. How about it?'

Catching Darac's eye, Granot gave a discreet shake of the head.

'No coaching,' Armani said, turning to cut off their sightline. 'The nerve!'

'I tell you what – give me… four hundred and you can have it.'

Armani withdrew his arm.

'Four hundred? First prize is only five! Five hundred after three weeks of anything-can-happen racing.'

'We-ell, it is your lucky number twenty-one.'

'Forget it.'

'Alright. If you're sure…'

'Not even if you throw in a toe suck.'

Darac shook his head.

'I *sucked* her toes now – see what happens? It'll be full-blown sex by tomorrow.'

Armani laughed and threw his arm around Darac's shoulders again. Exchanges with the Italian tended to begin and end physically.

The conversation had moved on by the time Agnès joined them.

'Let's go and see Manou Esquebel.'

They trooped out of the building and took the steps down into the compound. Above them, squadrons of insects were buzzing around the floodlights. It was going to be a humid night.

Armani had a belated thought about the Tour.

'Got a question. What about the riders? Were they told about the threat?'

Granot shook his head.

'They won't know anything. It would only interfere with their performance, wouldn't it? For no good reason.'

A patrol car rolled past them, heading for the street.

'They'll see something's going on though, no? Paris might think the threat's a fake but they still drafted in extra firepower.'

'I don't think the riders will be aware of it,' Agnès said. 'Most of the uniformed units they're bringing in are going to be on standby in the barracks. And armed plain-clothes officers obviously look no different from any other fan.'

Kicking a pebble out of his path, Granot nodded.

'The riders will have their eyes on the road, anyway – not on the fans.'

Darac was entertaining a 'what if?' question from further out in left field.

'You know, this whole thing could be an exercise dreamed up by the Suits, couldn't it? To test force co-ordination in the event of a terrorist crisis or whatever. And we guinea pigs won't find out a thing about it until months later. If we ever do.'

'Interesting idea,' Frankie said. 'You could be on to something there.'

Out on the street, the patrol car blurted a single *whoop* and sped off towards the city.

Agnès watched its flashing light for a moment.

'I must say, similar thoughts have crossed my mind.'

Armani turned to her.

'You really think the threat was penned by some arsehole in Paris?'

'I wouldn't put it past the State to mount such an operation. Would you?'

Darac had a coda.

'Possibly codenamed Operation Peloton or something.'

'Exactly.'

For Granot, conjecture was one thing; idle speculation

another. He brought the thing back into centre field.

'Operation Peloton is what the Garde Républicaine guys are on every day.' There was another pebble on the path in front of him. He tapped it away with his foot. 'Lucky swine.'

'Ah yes.' Granot's pebble had come to rest in front of Armani. He essayed an air shot at it – he was wearing brand-new loafers, after all. 'Those supposedly chic GR boys.'

'No "supposedly" about it. Thanks to the Monaco briefing, I've got friendly with some of them. Pretty cool guys. In the main.'

Darac gave Granot a look.

'*Pretty cool guys*? How old are you? Fifteen?'

The idea seemed to delight the big man.

'Definitely!' He gave it the full phlegm-rattling chortle. 'Where the GR is concerned, that's exactly how old I am. And by the way, Armani? They get to wear the most superb leather riding boots.'

'Calf length?'

'Knee length.'

'See if you can scrounge me a pair, will you?'

They arrived at the cell block.

'Esquebel?' Agnès said to the desk officer.

'Cell… twelve, madame.'

'Go to him on the monitor, will you?'

The officer pressed a button on a control panel, changing the camera shot on his screen.

Darac remembered the cool, menacing Manou who had opened his apartment door earlier.

'Looks as restless as a caged animal, doesn't he?'

Granot gave a snort.

'That's just what he is.'

'Recognise him?'

Armani studied the young man.

'Some physique. No. I don't know him.'

'Frankie?'

'No. Sorry.'

Armani flexed his biceps.

'So let me go have a chat with him.'

Agnès gave him a look.

'What about your cover?'

'Have a uniform tell him a guy from Prisoner Welfare has turned up to see him. Spot check to catch the police arseholes out.'

Agnès gave a nod to the desk officer. The set-up was arranged.

Armani turned to Darac.

'The guy has had his half-hour with a lawyer?'

'They all have.'

Following a further exchange with the desk officer, a guard took Armani off to the cell. The rest of them gathered around the DO's monitor. Despite Armani's convincing performance, the encounter made poor TV and he was back in a couple of minutes.

'He's on something, alright, but it's difficult to say what. There was nothing but the GHB at his place?'

Darac had been waiting for the question.

'A whole sack of stuff went over to the lab.'

Armani grinned at everyone in turn.

'I must be hearing things. There was a drugs cache at the place and you didn't think to call us?'

'We did think of it. But going through it, we didn't find anything suspicious.'

'Oh, *you* didn't find anything suspicious?'

'It was mainly just caffeine tablets and things.'

'Was it? How would you know?'

Agnès sighed in exasperation.

'Boys?'

'And you, of course, might have come up with more, Armani. But whatever the other stuff was, the lab will let us know, anyway.'

Looking only partly placated, Armani gave a shrug.

'The blood result will come first. That will tell us what he's on. But he might wind up telling us himself before then. He might scream at us to get him some.'

Darac winced. Of all the many and various expressions of human frailty, drug addiction touched him particularly. Some of his jazz heroes would have sold their souls for a fix.

Agnès glanced at her watch.

'I think he'll tell us all he knows about Florian well before that point. Anything else strike you about him, Armani?'

'One thing did, yes. I didn't recognise him, as I said. But I'm pretty sure he recognised me. I think he knew I was in Narco the moment I walked in.'

10.38 PM

It was a good thing the Blue Devil jazz club didn't rely on passing trade. Occupying the site of an old print works, there were few outward signs of the joint's existence. By day, a set of garishly graffitied roller shutters hid the place from the street, Avenue des Diables Bleus. By night, there were no neon signs or flashing lights to draw the eye – just a few photos lining a stairway that led down to a pair of scruffy, red-painted doors.

But then you saw it. Captioned *Blown Away by the Brass Section*, the club's signature poster was based on a photo taken at the Blue Devil in 1963. For Darac, no other image better conveyed the atmosphere of a hot live jazz date. He never entered or left the place without reaching up and touching it for luck.

In the lobby, the American club owner, Eldridge Clay, was sitting at the battered card table that served as the Blue Devil's cash desk. Absorbed in the day's *Nice-Matin*, the big man's eyes stayed on the page as Darac's shadow fell over it.

'Garfield.' Ridge's pet name for him emerged in a distracted murmur, the pitch of the voice somewhere down with the double basses. He held out a hand. Darac slapped his palm into it. 'You shoot anybody today?'

'No, but it's still early,' he said, looking down on the man's head, its nap threadbare as old baize. 'Are you door-keeper as well as everything else now?'

'Pascal went out for a second.' Ridge folded the paper and tossed it to one side. 'Miss Dinah Graham.' He nodded reverently. 'You see her in the States ever?'

'Tonight's a first.'

'Then go learn.' He held the look. 'I'll join you in a minute.'

There was a good house in for the veteran singer. Her trio began the intro to Ellington's ballad 'Solitude' as Darac circled round the back of the room and made for the bar. He wondered how many times the band had played the tune. Drums, bass and piano sounded like one instrument – that was how many times.

Dinah stood centre stage, listening with a rapt smile on her lined, heavily made-up face. Squat and square in her gold lamé dress, she looked almost like a parody of what she once was. But then she started to sing.

'In my solitoooooood…'

The voice sounded less smooth than in its silky prime, and after just a few bars it was clear her range had shifted south a little. But the simplicity of her approach to the song's melody and lyrics conveyed its theme of isolation and longing so palpably, it brought Darac out in goosebumps. As the final notes died away, all he could think of was Angeline.

A hand touched Darac's shoulder as the room erupted in applause.

'Hey.'

Darac exchanged greetings kisses with Khara, the club's Senegalese waitress. Without asking for his order, she opened the chiller cabinet behind her.

'How's it going?'

'Fantastic.' She opened a Leffe Tripel and turned to pour it. 'You?'

'Not bad.' He gave a little nod at the stand. 'What do you think?'

'Sublime. Nice lady, too.'

At the mike, Dinah began to introduce the next number.

'Sorry, folks, I can only do this in English. Ridge Clay and I are New Yorkers, right? The Bronx. Anybody ever been there?'

A few voices called out.

'And you made it back. Congratulations.'

Darac shared a smile with Khara as he took his drink.

'Well, he and I first met in 19...' She flicked a finger across her lips, blurring the rest. '...Okay? Now if you'd told me that the man would move to Nice, France, take on a club and run it for twenty-five unbroken years, I would have said you were ca-ray-zee. So come on – put your hands together for Ridge. The guy's a hero.'

There were no dissenters. The Blue Devil was just about the last old-style jazz club left in the South of France. Its longevity was all down to him.

'So this next one's for Ridge.'

As if on cue, the man came into the room as the band

went into 'All The Things You Are'. Darac turned to Khara.

'And a cognac for Ridge on me – his favourite.'

Khara's eyebrows rose.

'It's Mapin XO, you know.'

'Make that his almost favourite. How many of the quintet are in?'

'Two, three…' Khara closed one eye. '…seven… nine with you.'

A collective of local players anything from three to twelve in number, it was their little joke always to refer to themselves as a quintet. Darac spotted the bandleader, Didier Musso, sitting at a table with their alto sax player, Charlie Pachelberg. Opened-out LP sleeves were draped over the two chairs next to them – the club's way of denoting the seats were reserved. For a moment, Darac was back with the pizza boxes on Rue Verbier.

'Put a round together, will you, sweetie? I'll be back in a minute.'

'I'll bring them. The guys are dotted all around the room.'

Darac touched base with Marco the drummer until Ridge's number ended, then picked his way around to Didier's table.

'Finally.' The two of them embraced. 'No Angeline?'

'No Angeline.'

Darac slipped *Our Man in Paris* off his chair and bent to kiss Charlie.

'My God, she's missed something special,' she said,

her Berlin-accented French just about intelligible. 'Such a shame.'

'Yeah.'

On the stand, Dinah began a lengthy introduction to a number designed to showcase her long-time pianist, Wilfred Jones. In time-honoured fashion, she left its title until last.

'So people, close your eyes and drift away to the beautiful… "Blue in Green".'

The announcement itself brought a prolonged ovation. The man began to play, the melody emerging through the fading applause like a butterfly from a chrysalis.

Didier disobeyed Dinah. His eyes were wide open.

'Wilfred Jones… Talk about touch! He's barely breathing on the keys.'

'Wilf's barely breathing, period,' Ridge said, joining them. 'Thanks for the drink, Garfield.'

A few numbers later, the band proved they could still tear a place up as they ripped through 'Squeeze Me' at break-neck speed.

Didier's quiff nodding in time with his clapping hands, he leaned in to Ridge.

'Got a question for you – something only an American club owner would answer.'

'You want to know how much I'm paying these geniuses for the gig. Right?'

'Exactly.'

Ridge took a slow sip of his cognac.

'More than stoop labour; less than a living wage.'

The faintest lines creased Didier's boyish brow.

'They're playing just for expenses?'

It wasn't the first time American artists working the summer festival circuit had done this. A favour to Ridge, a gift for everyone else.

Darac stayed until the final encore. Dinah was alone when she returned to the stand. One hand on the piano, she closed her eyes.

'You... don't know what love is...'

Immediately, Dinah was speaking to each member of the audience as if only the two of them knew what she was feeling. She was certainly speaking to Darac. Three minutes of shared pain later, she brought the number to a close, her voice fading as if she were taking her final breath. Silence. And then the place erupted. The trio waited a good couple of minutes before following her out on the stand. More rapturous applause. And then Ridge joined them, hugging Dinah until the ovation finally subsided. He turned to the audience.

'Now go home,' he said, eliciting laughs. But he had a word for Didier. 'Didi – round up the guys and stick around, will you?'

A perfect evening just got more perfect. It seemed Dinah and the boys were up for an after-hours jam session with the quintet. Only Darac declined the invitation. Nothing lost. He'd played with legends before. There would be another one along sometime.

* * *

Angeline was in bed by the time he arrived home. Unsure of how deeply she was sleeping, he slipped in next to her as gently as he could. But she stirred anyway, her arm brushing across his chest as she turned towards him. She was sound asleep.

Feeling her breath against his cheek, he lay there looking at her in the half-light: the face he knew better than his own; the body whose rises, falls and hollows were hidden under a nightdress.

You don't know what love is... But Darac knew, alright. He had known what it was for the past four years.

11.59 PM

It was almost midnight before Agnès Dantier arrived back in her home patch of Cimiez. Laid out on a saddle of rising ground in the north of the city, it was an elegant quarter; an enclave of shady avenues, stuccoed mansions, bright new apartment blocks and, most impressively of all, classical ruins.

Agnès passed the Roman arènes feeling she was something of a ruin herself, this evening. What a day. She thought back to her encounter with the young Australians she'd met outside the Caserne. Bright, shiny, their lives in front of them. She wondered if they had found the 'real city' they had been searching for. Though somewhat irked by them at the time, she felt a little guilty now at the way she'd directed them to the wall plaque. It had been a brutal way to make a point. Am I turning into a bitch? she wondered. A ruin *and* a bitch – fabulous.

The sky was crystal clear overhead and as she turned at the head of the down ramp into her building's parking garage, she caught a glimpse of Mont Alban away to the east. Rising from its wooded ridge, a telecom mast rigged with red warning lights pierced the night sky like a giant, blood-beaded syringe.

She parked, stretched out her back and set off up the footway that followed the ramp back on to the avenue. It wasn't surprising she was feeling overwrought: predictions of race riots on the streets, of carnage at the Tour. And once more, she had had to defend Darac against the Palais. How many times had she pointed out to them that his clearance rate was the best in the region? She hoped to God he would never falter because he would be gone in a minute. Gone with his integrity still intact, though, no doubt. She loved Darac for his honesty; for his refusal to be anything other than he was. The greatest compliment she could pay him was that of all the officers she had known, he came the closest to measuring up to her father.

And who but Darac would have volunteered to massage the hot, unwashed feet of a exhausted fifty-three-year-old? And then to have done it so carefully and without fuss?

Blinking deeply failed to clear her tired eyes as she gained the top of the ramp. Through the blur, she didn't notice the parked van nor hear the footsteps hurrying behind her.

As the telecom mast came into view once more, a gloved hand clamped over her mouth. It was the last thing Agnès felt before she stepped into a pit of infinite darkness.

SATURDAY 4 JULY

7.46 AM

Every year, 100,000 fans flooded into Monaco to attend the Formula One Grand Prix. Twice that number was expected to show for the opening stage of the Tour de France. Although for many, the race didn't begin in earnest until the 182 kilometre second day, the 15 kilometre individual time trial had an excitement all of its own. Above all, it meant the Tour was under way for another year. Three weeks of drama, fun and probably scandal lay ahead.

The time trial, in which competitors set off singly at timed intervals, ran to a different timetable from a normal stage. The first rider was not due to leave until 2 pm, hours after the field was usually rolling out from the start line all together. But for the Tour detail of the Garde Républicaine motorcycle squadron, the later start made no difference – it was business as usual. By 7.30, all forty-five of them had showered and breakfasted.

Whether they were going to cover 15 kilometres or 215, the day for every GR officer began with a maintenance check of his motorcycle. Although a peloton-less 15 kilometre circular course offered little in the way of a challenge, the mood in the locker room was upbeat, fuelled by a crossfire of banter. More exciting days lay ahead.

'Hey, Cognard – I'll get you a date with my sister if you do a wheelie off the start line.'

'He's already dating your sister, Bertrand.'

'Everybody's dating her.'

'Including Bertrand.'

The gags volleyed back and forth as the men changed into their inspection overalls. For once, the joker in the pack, Yves Dauresse was taking a back seat: he had his phone's radio tuned to the France Info radio station. A piece on the Tour was revealing some interesting stuff.

'Any bombs go off, yet?' David Jarret asked him, peering into a mirror attached to the back of his locker door. *I look a little red-eyed this morning*, he thought.

'They don't reckon any of the French boys are going to do much this year,' Dauresse said, not hearing Jarret. 'Mightn't win a single stage, they're saying.'

'No?' Roger Lascaux ran a comb carefully through his blond hair. 'One of our guys will do something fantastic. You watch.'

France Info going to an ad break, Dauresse pulled out his earphones.

Jarret turned to him.

'Any changes in the orders likely for tomorrow?'

'Why – scheduled in a little action with one of the promo caravan girls?' He smiled, his words punctuated by locker doors closing all around the room.

'Me?' The idea seemed to amuse Jarret. 'No, I was just wondering.'

'Have you seen that redhead on the Fromages de

France float?' Lascaux waved a loose fist. 'Ai, ai, ai.'

Dauresse put his hand on the boy's shoulder.

'Roger, as you've only done one Tour, here's a word of advice. A giant Camembert does not make a good bed partner. Even one with red hair. Go for the Emmental girl instead.' He raised an eyebrow. 'Think about it.'

As the youngster did so, a shampoo bottle came winging out of the showers towards him. He kept his eyes on Dauresse as he threw up a hand, caught the missile and tossed it aside in one seamless action.

'Emmental!' He creased up, finally seeing the gag. 'Holes!'

Dauresse turned to Jarret.

'Brain of a worm; reflexes of a cobra – got to love Lascaux, haven't you?'

'Yes. Tomorrow?'

'No changes scheduled. As yet, anyway.'

'So we've still got the Boulevard des Anglais stations?'

Dauresse nodded his shaved head.

'Unless we get out of sync, that's where we'll be.' He gave Jarret a look. 'It's the destination target par excellence, isn't it? If there *is* anything to the threat, we'll be the ones who get blown up, shot, have fish pinned to our backs or whatever.'

'No one's going to take *me* out.' His comb standing in for his automatic, Lascaux mimed firing off a clip. 'Fucking blow them apart.'

A couple of the boys roughed up his hair in passing.

'Arseholes!'

'Alright.' Dauresse picked up his toolkit. 'Let's go tighten our nuts.'

They made their way out on to the barracks square. Since Lascaux and Jarret had returned from their pre-breakfast jog, the mist veiling the surrounding mountains had lifted, carried out to sea on the back of a steady offshore breeze. Six hundred metres below, the exclusive tenements of Monaco glinted in a tight, teeming mass.

In chatting with Granot at the briefing, the trio had learned that the principality wasn't every local's idea of heaven. For some, it was an ugly growth in the body of an otherwise beautiful landscape. Dauresse had particularly enjoyed hearing Granot's immediate boss's take on the place: 'a modern-day Babazouk for the rich but without the charm'. Yes, Dauresse liked the sound of Granot's Captain Darac. He hoped their paths would cross sometime. The sooner the better.

Lascaux shielded his eyes as he surveyed the scene below. There was no doubt where his sympathies lay.

'They call it filthy money, don't they?' He set down his kit by his bike. 'Doesn't look filthy to me.'

'Can't see the attraction, myself.' Dauresse reinserted one earphone. 'Give me Cannes any day.'

Like an inquisitive puppy, Lascaux's eyes were already elsewhere.

'Funny-looking water tower.' He pointed towards a structure perched on a high escarpment a couple of kilometres away to the west. Dauresse followed his gaze. Hit by the early morning sun, the building appeared to glow as if lit from within. Perhaps it was the distraction of half-listening to his radio but when he spoke, Dauresse sounded like a different person.

'It doesn't hold water. It holds power. The power of the Roman Army. The Trophée des Alpes, it's called – a reconstructed triumphal tower.'

'How do you know that?' Jarret drew his bike back on to its stand. 'You said you'd never been here before.'

All around the square, four-stroke engines began to throb into life.

'How do I know? Because unlike you two morons, I am educated.' Catching something on France Info, Dauresse held up a hand. 'Quiet a second.' He listened, then pulled out his earpiece as if he'd finally caught what he'd been waiting to hear all along. 'Guess how many people are going to be watching us on TV today? Throughout the world.'

Lascaux turned his engine over.

'Listen to that baby purr… The world? I'd say… twenty million.'

'Jarret?'

'Eighty.' He fired up his machine. 'At least.'

Dauresse gave them a level stare, his china-blue eyes wide.

'Try three hundred and seventy million.'

'What?' Lascaux gave his throttle an involuntary tweak, over-revving the engine. 'Thank fuck they're going to be watching the riders and not us.'

Dauresse smiled as he turned over his engine.

'Absolutely.'

8.02 AM

Darac's breakfast pâtisserie smelled less enticing than usual as he left Fantin and set out across Place Garibaldi. There were fewer trinket sellers around this morning, he noticed. A purge, perhaps. No such problems for the pavement artists. If anything, there seemed more of them around than usual.

God, he felt flat.

It was on a very different Saturday morning a couple of years ago that a watercolourist had painted Angeline's portrait. 'You realise you're a dead ringer for Audrey Tautou?' he'd said with only partial justification as he'd begun setting down the basic architecture of her face. Fifteen minutes later, he'd succeeded in producing a stunning likeness – of the actress, not of her. 'What's your name?' he'd asked as he signed the work. 'Audrey Tautou, of course. I thought you recognised me.' Darac gave a little smile at the memory.

As he disappeared into Rue Neuve, he recalled the first time he'd shown Angeline the Babazouk. It was an unusually cold day in January and they were on their second date. A Bordelaise just three months into a lectureship at the university, she'd enthused about the shops and restaurants she'd already visited in the quarter. But it was its ancient apartment houses that really fascinated her. 'I live in one of the oldest,' he'd said. 'Would you like to see it?'

It was as they entered Place St. Sepulchre that Darac had realised just how deeply he was falling for Angeline. She was warm, sexy and fun. Her blade-sharp mind fizzed with ideas and connections and yet she was an attentive listener. Above all, she was open and alive to things in a way he'd never encountered to quite the same degree before.

When the time came, his apartment house did not disappoint her. The lobby was a plain, almost drab affair. But as they emerged into the ornate, groin-vaulted stairway at its rear, the look of joyous surprise on her face was something he felt would always stay with him.

'This is magnificent,' she'd said, continuing to examine the mouldings and rib work as they climbed the stairs.

'Better watch your step.' He took her arm. 'The lady who cleans these steps once left a bar of soap on them.'

He mimed the result. She smiled her dimpled smile.

'I have the top floor.'

'It feels warm on the stairway but there are no radiators.'

'That's our thermosiphon system. Do you know about that?'

'No. But I hope I'm going to.'

'It's all about understanding how hot and cool air currents move. Everything here is designed to aid convection and ventilation. The orientation of the streets, the gratings above the doors, the passageways – even the swing-wing shutters – it's all part of it. The Babazouk is like a giant chimney in a way. It works so well, it's warm in winter and cool in summer – much less variation than the rest of the city.'

'That's really interesting.'

As Darac put the key into his lock, he'd turned to find Angeline smiling at him.

'What?' he smiled back.

'Nothing. I'm just… enjoying myself.'

That was four years ago.

Angeline had showered and dressed in the time it had taken Darac to return with their breakfast. She was waiting for him stretched out on a sun lounger on their roof terrace. A modest twenty-five square metres and with no palm tree or pool, it was hardly a rival for the roof garden at the Negresco. Nevertheless, it was their favourite space in the whole apartment. The way sounds floated up from the streets; the glimpses of Château Park and the Baie des Anges; the unobstructed views of the surrounding mountains – it was perfect. And by a happy accident of orientation and sightlines, not one window overlooked it.

It was already warm enough to sit out nude, though Angeline had donned shorts and a blouse. On the tile-top table they had made themselves, she had set a jug of freshly squeezed orange juice and a cafetière of their favourite Delta Diamante. A wicker basket awaited the pâtisserie. Darac emptied the box into it and sat opposite her. She wasn't looking daggers at him; she wasn't puffing anxiously on a cigarette, rehearsing what to say. And yet, Darac sensed that this might be the morning they would begin the conversation that could have only one outcome.

She bit into a pain au raisin.

'How can a simple pastry taste this good?'

He picked up a croissant.

'They mix amphetamines in the dough, I think.'

'They're probably just fattier, saltier and sweeter than anyone else's.'

'That's probably it.'

His eyes fell on her bare foot. The safe thing was to do nothing, but a sort of emotional vertigo came over him. All at once, he felt compelled to stray near the edge, to flirt with destruction. He closed the fingers of his left hand around her toes and gently began to bend them back.

'It was an interesting meal last night,' she said, withdrawing her foot. 'Despite having a flaming row with a guy from the Sorbonne about—'

'What's happened to us, Angeline?'

Five words were all it took to burn off the veneer of normality under which they had been hiding. Angeline swung her legs off the sun lounger and sat up, her large brown eyes staring through her sunglasses, through the floor, through to the centre of the earth. He leaned forward.

'Let's make love. Now. Out here.'

At length, she turned to him.

'Hitting someone. Playing your guitar. Making love.'

Her words came out evenly, almost gently. 'Those are your three solutions to any emotional crisis. But not everything can be solved that way. It just can't.'

She got to her feet.

'Angeline...'

He watched her walk away.

'I love you,' he called out, a flare fired into the chasm.

Once again, she made what seemed a conscious decision to turn and face him.

'Yes, I know you do.'

She continued into the apartment.

Darac was aware of gravity suddenly, a colossal weight pressing down on him. Hitting someone. Playing the guitar. Making love. No, she was wrong about that, surely. He dealt with crises much more subtly. Didn't he? He looked at his hands. They were balled into fists. Opening them, the remains of the croissant fell like scattered ash on to the table.

8.42 AM

Darac left the apartment and walked through stark sunlight to the Théâtre Esplanade car park. It might have been cold and raining for all he noticed. Turning the Peugeot's ignition fired up the CD player. The opening salvo of Louis Armstrong's 'West End Blues' ripped across his lowered spirits. There was an energising joy in those phrases, a clarion call to life. But even the genius of Armstrong couldn't lift Darac this morning. As the number settled into the reflective mood of its verse, he turned it off.

What had just happened back on the terrace? For the first time, he and Angeline had acknowledged there was a problem. A major one. But mightn't there be a way back? Nothing terminal had been said.

His earlier relationships had ended in no-holds barred, cathartic bust-ups; typical Act Three scenarios that had left both parties feeling at least energised. On a couple of occasions, it had even rekindled things for a while. This morning had been the opposite. No resentment. No smashing of objects. No shouting. Instead, a few short sentences, heavy with sadness and disappointment. He couldn't bear the thought that this could be the end. He loved Angeline. It was as simple as that.

He pulled into the Caserne and showed his ID at the barrier.

The guard on duty gave him a look.

'CD player bust, Captain? I could get you a new one for nothing. More or less.'

'No, it's fine, Berthoud.' The barrier rose. 'Headache, that's all.'

Darac knew that if he let it, the situation with Angeline was going to resonate through his day like a held-down organ note. He made a resolution not to think consciously about it. He had a murder to solve. And, possibly, a series of date rapes.

After three seconds, he was right back there. It was about four months ago that he'd become aware of Angeline's diminishing feelings for him. At first, he wondered if she had found someone else. He was enough of a realist to accept the possibility; enough of a Frenchman to think it inconceivable. The debate hadn't lasted long. He felt with some certainty that Angeline would not have broken their bond of trust. The fault line ran through different terrain.

He parked in the space marked with his name and rank.

Perhaps unusually for a left-leaning intellectual, Angeline had never voiced disapproval of the police *per se*. And she had seen immediately that Darac was a totally different animal from the average career officer. Nevertheless, his role as a detective had worried her from the start.

He got out of the car recalling the innocent way in

which the issue had first surfaced. He and Angeline had just started sleeping together and the morning had begun wonderfully. Darac's pre-breakfast routine never changed: once out of the shower, he picked up an old Hofner f-hole guitar he kept leaning against the living-room wall and played through several choruses of a favourite number. However many times he worked around the changes, he endeavoured never to play the same solo lines twice.

'Why do you always start your day like that?' Angeline had said.

'It's my morning detox.'

On that particular morning, he was wearing only a pair of boxers.

'The guitar leaves marks,' she had said, running a finger around the parallel indentations on his thigh.

'Well, you have to… suffer for your art.'

He'd never known such passionate sex.

Afterwards, she had voiced an observation about Darac no one else had.

'Do you know what I find strange? About you, I mean.'

'Keep it to one thing – I'm sensitive.'

'Seriously – it's that you're both a jazz musician and…'

'A *flic*?'

'…a creature of habit. A love of improvisation and a love of predictable pattern – it seems inconsistent.'

'Maybe one can't exist without the other,' he'd replied, initiating a debate on the nature of contradiction, paradox and meaning. Angeline left the question of how he could be both a musician and a policeman until later. And it was to become the centre of most of their rows over the years.

'Have you ever hit a suspect?'

'Have you ever shouted at a lazy student?'

'Of course but that's not the same thing. Have you ever hit a suspect?'

'I've never hit an innocent one.'

On and on. But their arguments never ended with a sense that their differences were irreconcilable. It sounded like a line from a bad pop song but their love had always been strong enough to see them through.

'Would you rather I gave up the police and became a jazz musician exclusively?' he'd once asked her. 'It would mean a slight cut in salary, of course. Of about ninety-five per cent.'

'The money has nothing to do with it. You could no sooner be just a musician than you could be just a policeman. You're a *poète policier* – that's your truth. That's who you are.'

Poète policier... Darac had first come across the term in the written press. Regarding the phenomenon – with some complacency – as peculiarly French, commentators saw *poètes policiers* as making a unique contribution to the life of the nation. At least in the popular imagination, artists were self-absorbed types who led indulged, ivory -ower existences; in contradistinction, *poètes policiers*, often equally gifted, risked their necks fighting crime for the benefit of all. It was a win-win combination.

In one sense, Darac agreed with Angeline about his

'truth'. Leading a double life was something that held a natural appeal for him. It wasn't, he believed, that he was afraid of commitment; it was just that it seemed more interesting to inhabit two entirely different worlds.

He was less sure of its value to others. Was the condition of being neither one thing nor the other really worthy of celebration? Angeline seemed to have thought it was. Until recently, anyway. For his own part, Darac sometimes wondered if he had put a positive spin on his inclinations. Perhaps living on the cusp was really a form of sitting on the fence. And perhaps the world would have been a better place if he had sought to emulate the genius of Agnès Dantier *or* Sonny Rollins – not both.

A female voice brought him back into the moment. The attitude was pure Cagole.

'Morning. Hot night, no?'

Carrying a sheath of papers, the woman was wearing the uniform of an APJA, an officer's assistant. A smile played around her thin, coral-glossed lips.

'Yes... Adèle. Sorry, I didn't see you there.'

'*Really* hot. Hardly slept a wink. Might need a nice back massage later. So – thong on or off? What do you think? I've brought a towel and—'

'For fuck's sake, has no one got anything better to do around here than...'

Her eyes flared.

'I've got plenty to do, as it happens, Captain.'

She walked away.

Darac's apology got no further than a raised hand and

an open mouth. Abandoning the pose, he walked up the steps of Building D wondering how to play it with Bonbon and the others. Would they realise he wasn't his usual self? They wouldn't be the greatest detectives in the world if they didn't. Should he say something? If so, what? He recalled that Granot had once turned up at the Caserne with two black eyes and a face the colour of a red traffic light. His then wife had hit him with a fire extinguisher and turned it on him. Compared to that, Darac's 'Angeline and I had words this morning. The future's looking uncertain' might seem a little tame.

Lartigue, yesterday's crime-scene co-ordination officer emerged on to the landing above him.

'Thanks for sorting out my backup, chief. It's making life a lot easier.'

'Sorry I could only get you a couple of guys, Lartou.'

'No, no, they're invaluable. I was beginning to see Avenue Jean Médecin from different angles even when I *wasn't* looking at the monitor.'

Darac sympathised. Reviewing CCTV footage for long periods was a lousy job.

'Any further clips of Florian or Delage?'

'None. We've still got several options to look at, though.'

'Let me know if anything comes up.'

As Darac signed in at the duty officer's desk, Bonbon emerged from his office further down the corridor.

'Chief?'

'How did it go with Marie Lacroix?'

'It didn't – got there too late. I'm going over there now.'

The pair met each other halfway.

'Manou Esquebel is waiting for you in your office. He seems calmer this morning, interestingly. More information has come in on him, by the way. Statements from neighbours, I think.'

'I'll look at them in a second. Mansoor Narooq?'

'He's in with Granot. Immigration want to know if they can come for him this afternoon. They obviously wouldn't start the deportation unless we gave the word but I doubt he has anything more to tell us. A guy just in the wrong place at the wrong time, wasn't he?'

'I think so. Slimane Bahtoum?'

'Flaco's putting the frighteners on him but for practice more than anything. He doesn't know anything about the murder, does he? He wasn't even at the scene at the time. Immigration will no doubt want a word with him, though. He knew his cousin was an illegal, after all. And he said nothing.'

'Getting more like Vichy-fucking-France every day, this country. Madame Delage?'

'Perand's gone to see her. Finally had a shave, by the way – Perand, not Delage.'

'Good. That all?'

'Think so. Oh, one thing – Florian's older brother, Jean. Our hard-working colleagues in Paris still haven't been round to his place yet. So although it happened yesterday, he still doesn't know about Emil's death, presumably.'

'Unless he did it.'

Bonbon's elastic grin widened. 'There you go – case solved.'

'Seriously, we do need to be apprised of his movements. In terms of giving him the bad news, I don't think a day's delay will matter much. There wasn't a letter, photo or even a reference to the guy anywhere in Florian's things so they obviously weren't close.' Darac made to move away. 'Boss around?'

'Not in yet.' A knowing look in his eyes, Bonbon stood his ground. 'So how did you leave it?'

'Leave what?'

'The big problem you're having with Angeline.'

Darac ran a hand through his hair.

'That obvious?'

'Not at all. I'm a brilliant detective.' He proffered a pink paper bag. 'Sherbet belly button?'

'Pass.'

'You haven't had a row with her or you'd be stomping around and acting mean. It's more serious than that. On the other hand, it's not completely…'

Darac held up both hands, palms outwards.

'Save it. You're right. I think it'll be okay, though. In the end.'

Bonbon gave an encouraging nod.

'Sure.'

'Yes, I think it'll be okay. Definitely.'

'As you think there's hope – welcome a word of advice?'

Darac gave an unconvinced shrug. 'Sure. Why not?'

'The two of you need to undertake some sort of project. It doesn't matter what it is just so long as it takes time and you do it together. Painting the apartment is a good one.'

'Is this why your place always looks so pristine?'

'No.' The twinkle in Bonbon's tawny eyes glinted a little more sharply. 'The wife's lover is a painter and decorator. Honestly – think about it.'

'See you later, man.'

Darac gave Bonbon's cheek a pat and continued to his office. He found Manou Esquebel in the custody of one of the Caserne's burlier uniforms.

'Morning, Poitrard. He give you any trouble?'

'This little arsehole?' The man snorted disdainfully. 'Am I relieved, Captain?'

'You're relieved.'

Manou extended a leg as Poitrard moved past, tripping him and earning a stiff kick on the shins as a reward. In what seemed a conscious caricature of camp, Manou yelped loudly, and then bent to rub away the pain. When he spoke, his words emerged in a furious bleat.

'That is police brutality. Police brutality!'

Poitrard glowered over him.

'Shut the fuck up or I'll kick your pretty little face in as well.'

'I'll tear your foot off first, you fat cunt.'

'Thanks, officer.' Darac shepherded him away. 'For now.'

'For now? You saw that, Captain. He kicked me. I'm bringing charges.'

Darac decided to take a different tack with him.

'You're an intelligent guy, Manou. So don't play games – alright?'

Caught off-guard, Esquebel seemed to decide that complying might be a good way to go.

A framed photo of Angeline lived on Darac's desk. His eye went to it as he picked up the interview file. He opened a drawer, hesitated a moment and then closed it again. An added distraction or not, the photo could stay where it was.

Telling Manou to remain quiet, Darac settled down to read through the account of his interrogations so far, and the reports from a slog squad detailed to talk to his neighbours. After no more than a couple of minutes, he picked up Angeline's photo and laid it carefully in the drawer.

As he had expected, only a few of the neighbours had given statements. Of those, a few reported seeing Florian at one time or another. One, a Madame Griet, a widow whose ground-floor apartment was on the opposite side of the building to Manou's, had a little more to report. Ad hoc football games took place most weekends at La Masarella, she said. Seeing them as 'breeding grounds for trouble', she felt obliged to keep tabs on them by casting occasional glances from her window. At any one time, as many as thirty players might be involved in games which could go on for hours. Most were teenage kids but 'the one they call Manou', something of a hero to the youngsters for his physique and for his 'madcap stunts', often joined in. Two Saturdays ago, Madame Griet remembered a man she later identified as Florian watching a game from the sidelines. She'd noticed him because he'd seemed a fish out of water. Manou seemed to know him.

The following Saturday, Madame Griet was waiting in for a friend when she spotted Florian hanging around again. It was about 10 am but this time, Manou didn't seem to be playing. She'd remembered Florian particularly because he'd got a plastic bottle stuck in his pocket and had gone comically red in the face trying to extricate it. At that moment, her friend had knocked on Madame Griet's door so she got her things together and left with her to go shopping. No further dramas. End of story.

Closing the folder, Darac tossed it on to the desk and sat back with his hands behind his head. He felt as if he'd come to a fork in the road – the next step would be an important one. He had always been impressed by Agnès's ultra-logical approach to questioning and, on her behalf, advocated that method to the officers he was mentoring. By instinct, though, he was a devotee of the Try Everything You Can Think Of school. And he had a useful edge over Manou if he could think of a way of exploiting it.

'You're feeling better this morning. Not so feverish, not so at the end of your tether.'

'So?'

'We'll find out from the lab later today what you're on. But it might expedite things if you told me now. It can't be anything particularly heavy or you would be suffering.'

Bored by the question, Manou shook his head.

'How many more times? What I'm *on* is GHB, steroids, caffeine tablets and shit. Nothing else.'

Darac was still sitting back in his chair, hands behind his head, relaxed.

'All for bodybuilding?'

'And for energy. I overdo it sometimes. Makes me weird.' The pout disappeared. 'Works, though.' The handcuffs fettering his left wrist rattled up the pipe as he flexed his biceps. It made him look like a performing monkey. 'See?'

'You've already admitted to possessing GHB, which is a controlled substance. You do realise that?'

The monkey slid down his pole.

'I bought some years ago. I don't think it was against the law then.'

'It is now.'

'I know! Jesus. Give me a break.'

Free to move, Darac continued to remain absolutely still; tethered, Manou was all restless movement.

'So the stuff is well past its use by, is it?'

'It dissolves like shit but it still works.' He heard the implication. 'As a growth hormone releaser, I mean. For bodybuilding.'

'There are no drug offences on your rap sheet, are there?'

'Not one.'

'In fact, you've never even been questioned in that connection.'

'Not even when Tard—'

Manou extended his free arm, grabbing at the air as if trying to take the remark back.

'So you know Captain Tardelli. He visited you last night in the guise of a prison liaison officer, didn't he? How do you know what he looked like? How do you know his name?'

The air conditioner marking the moment with a loud, off-beat clatter, Manou's mental pinball table came into action again. Full tilt. But then, quite suddenly, he seemed to abandon the game. If it was a play, it was his most convincing yet.

'Some guy I met had ID photos of the Narc and Cock squads. A full set with names and everything. And a couple of other people who work here. Not you or your little ferrety friend, in case you're wondering. I would've remembered.'

Darac pursed his lips. The story had the ring of truth. But how the hell had anybody gained access to them? Records had never suffered a break-in, as far as he knew. A hacker? Erica had once told him no police file was hack-proof. Another, less technical possibility suggested itself.

'Who was this guy you met?'

'Just some piece of meat off the Ajaccio ferry. One-night stand. I came across the shots when I was going through... when he was asleep. I thought they might come in useful so I took photos of them on my phone.'

'How had he come by them?'

'You think I asked him? It's obvious though, isn't it?'

Manou rubbed his thumb over his fingertips. 'Someone here took a nice backhander, didn't he?'

That was probably true, too. An inquiry would have to be launched. On top of everything else.

'You've heard about Florian, I gather.'

'What about him?'

'That he's dead.'

'Yeah, I heard that. Too bad.'

'And you didn't do it?'

'Pur-lease.'

'Well, we can go into that in just a little more detail later. The photos you mentioned. Did you show them to Florian?'

'I didn't even know Emil then. I met him the month after.'

'But you showed them to him eventually. Why?'

'I don't know. Just a bit of… show and tell, you know. To pass the time.'

'"If you ever see these guys, pour the stuff away quick." That the idea?'

'No.' Manou was outraged. 'No way.'

Things were starting to cohere. As Darac had already begun to suspect, it was Armani Tardelli's appearance on Rue Verbier that had been the catalyst for the prayer-meeting scenario.

'Who do you think killed Emil?'

'Dunno.'

'His older brother, perhaps?'

Manou's eyebrows became part of his hairline.

'He had a brother? First I've heard of it.'

'I repeat. Who do you think killed Emil?'

'I've got no idea. And I tell you something else. I don't care.'

'You don't care?' Darac shook his head. 'I've seen quite a few photos of you two together. You looked close. And unless he got rid of them, there were no photos of anyone else before you.'

'No. I was the first proper lover he'd had.' The miniature muscle man looked horribly coy, suddenly. 'He wasn't the first to think he was straight before he met me.'

'So you turned him on to all sorts of new pleasures?'

'Did I ever. And he was very good to me. Better than anybody else has been.'

'Really? He didn't have you move in with him. And although he put a few sticks of cast-off furniture into your place, it's not the same as setting you up in a nice little love nest, is it?'

'He was a school teacher, not a fucking millionaire. Anyway, I like L'Ariane.'

'You like L'Ariane. And you loved Emil. And now you don't care who killed him.'

Manou shifted uncomfortably, then leaned forward, putting his hands palms together between his knees.

'That was before… That was before.'

Darac was still sitting back almost horizontally in his chair.

'Before what?'

'Before we split. Nothing lasts for ever. It was over. Finito.'

The held-down organ note grew louder.

'Relationships end for a reason. What was it?'

Manou sat back, crossed his arms and began tapping his foot.

'I just... got tired of him.'

Darac had Madame Griet's material to work with. It was time to take it and improvise.

'Because his timid ways were a liability on the street? How did you work it, Manou? You join in with a bunch of kids skateboarding, playing football – whatever. You're an overgrown street kid yourself so you fit right in. You gain their confidence easily...'

This was all too fast for Manou. Shaking his head, he began to squirm.

'...As the game goes on, everybody gets hotter – especially you because you've got your eye on one kid in particular. You wait until he's had enough and decides to go. This is where Florian comes in. You need him to turn up with the GHB water because you don't want to carry the stuff yourself. You're much too smart for that...'

'No. No. It's not true.'

'...There's no sign of the police faces you both know so well, so as you walk off the pitch, you turn to the kid you've picked out and say: "Listen, I know that old guy – we can blag a few euros off him, come on." You and the kid go over to your timid benefactor for a moment...'

'It's a fucking lie. It never happened. Ever!'

'…"Here, gimme some of that water, I'm hot," you say, grabbing it out of his pocket. You pour some over your head. Maybe you feign drinking some. You pass it to the kid…'

Manou got to his feet, the veins in his arms and neck rope-taut.

'No!'

'…The kid drinks. I don't need to tell you what happens next, do I? Did you get to go first or did Florian? Maybe you alternated.'

Just as it seemed Manou might come apart, he found something. Focussing his eyes into the distance, he set his feet shoulder-width apart and began taking even breaths, in through the nose, out through the mouth.

'This is one weight you can't lift. The weight of your own guilt.'

The words should have worked like punches, but rehearsing his pre-lift drill had helped Manou. When he sat down, he seemed a degree or two calmer.

'It's. Not. Fucking. True.'

'I repeat. Who do you think killed Florian? A parent of one of your joint victims? Maybe a brother?'

'I don't know who killed him. All I know is I never did anything.'

'You never did anything…'

'Fuck off! Alright?'

'We've shown a photo of Florian to a lot of people. Our opening question was a very simple one: "Have you ever seen this man?"' Darac sat forward and opened Madame

Griet's file. 'Here's an eyewitness statement by someone who had seen him. Dated and signed. Last Saturday morning at about ten o'clock, this witness saw Florian standing outside La Masarella watching a football game – just as I described earlier.'

Manou began chewing the inside of his mouth.

'This time though, the routine didn't go smoothly. Florian got the bottle of water stuck in his jacket.' Madame Griet could help no further. Darac was on his own. 'But he got it out eventually, didn't he? After it was all over, our witness reports... now what's the exact quote?' Darac consulted the statement, moving his finger over a line. 'Yes, here... "I saw the boy walking across the lobby. He looked sick and drowsy. Too much exertion in the sun, I thought. But now, I realise what had really happened. He'd been drugged." And there's more.' To preserve her anonymity, Darac obscured Madame Griet's name with one hand as he rose and showed the page to Manou. 'You can't dispute it. It's here in black and white – look.'

Manou's eyes slid across the page like bald tyres on ice. After some moments, Darac withdrew it, sat back and fixed him with a hard, level stare.

'You raped that boy together and no doubt you raped others. We'll find them and then you are going down for a long time.'

'I never did it! I told you, I never used GHB for anything but bodybuilding.' His voice took on a more urgent, intense tone. 'Listen – I've been no angel since I was fourteen years old. And I like it that way. But I've never raped anybody. I've never fucked a *kid*. Men are what I go for.' Tears now. 'You've got to believe me.'

'So it was just Emil.'

Ears cocked, Granot appeared in the doorway. Darac beckoned him in. There was a look suspects adopted before confessing: a sort of fear-relieving resignation. Sensing that such a moment was coming, neither of them said a word.

Manou dried his eyes with the heels of his hands.

'Emil…' The word was dredged up as if from a pit of hatred. 'Emil was… mad for young boys. "Cherub meat", he called them. "Moist little morsels." He had seen videos by the score but that wasn't good enough for him. He wanted the real thing. But he was way too scared to do anything about it. Then he read somewhere about GHB. The answer to a prayer, he called it. Especially as he knew I used the stuff.' He looked at Darac with a sort of injured pride. 'He thought I would join in. He was wrong. He thought I would at least give him some of the stuff so he could do it. He was wrong again. So the bastard stole some from me. Mixed my pots up when I wasn't looking. I never gave him any help. Ever, understand? I'm not… an accessory to anything he did. I told him not to do it or we were finished.'

Darac ran a hand through his hair.

'So a whiter than white, straight schoolteacher meets you. Two years later, that same man is drugging boys so he can rape them?'

'Yes! That is exactly it.'

'Did you ever witness him committing rape?'

'No. I told you. I didn't even know he had finally done it until you read out that eyewitness report.'

Granot gave Darac a look. He knew no neighbour had reported anything half so incriminating.

'What did he say had happened that morning, then?'

'Nothing, according to him. Once he'd fucked up the pass, he went back into the city, he said. Lying bastard.'

Darac had little doubt that that was what had happened.

'The *pass*?' he said. 'That sounds pro.'

Manou gave him a look that would have played to the rear stalls at the opera.

'I know words for stuff you wouldn't believe but it doesn't mean I do them.'

Granot caught Darac's eye. He nodded, putting him in.

'Where were you when all this was happening?'

Manou seemed happier with life, suddenly.

'I'm so glad you came in, big boy. I was waiting for *him* to ask me that. I wasn't at the apartments last Saturday morning. Not at the time you said. You can check.'

'We will. Check with whom?'

'I worked from eight to eight in the evening at Peerless.'

'Driving a cab? By no means a perfect alibi.'

'That's where I've got you, again. From eight until two, I was in the squawk box.'

'What's that – some sort of club?'

'Are you listening to me? I was working. The squawk box is what we call the booth at the back of the office. I was taking walk-ins, answering calls, organising the drivers. Six hours straight, I did that.'

Darac picked up the baton.

'Point by point through your questioning, you've denied anything that might incriminate you until we've shown it was pointless to persist. And all through, you have been at pains to dissociate yourself from Florian. You even maintained you hadn't seen him for months at the beginning. Remember?'

'I would still be denying it now if somebody hadn't seen him and the kid last Saturday. What do you expect? I knew you would think we were in it together. And what with him being a teacher and everything, I knew you'd think it was me who'd tried to talk *him* into it. Especially as I had the GHB.'

'We've only got your word for it that you didn't. Florian's dead. You know you can say what you like about him.'

'But I wouldn't do. You'd catch me out. Being such clever boys.'

The air conditioner suddenly made a sound like a labouring helicopter. Darac reached back and slapped it with a practised hand. It whined for a moment, then resumed level flight.

'And so-ooo butch.' Manou was beginning to enjoy himself. 'Yowzer.'

'Records show you took a phone call from Florian last thing on Thursday evening,' Darac continued. 'Recount the conversation.'

'Can I have a coffee? That's not what he said. I just want one.'

'Answer the question.'

Manou sighed extravagantly, a performance that made Granot squirm. Manou the hard man, he could tolerate. Manou the queen, he couldn't. 'I'm not anti-gay,' he'd once said to Darac. 'But camp makes me really grit my teeth.' He was feeling that way now.

'Am I getting under your skin, darling?' Manou was enjoying himself more and more. 'Good, because I dreamt you got under mine last night.' He rolled his tongue around his lips. 'You weren't very caring, you naughty boy.'

Granot's teeth were gritted practically to stumps. But he knew better than to rise to the bait.

'Just answer the question.'

Another deep sigh.

'We-ell… because of the way things were going, I told Emil it was all over between us. He told me not to be so silly. *Him* tell *me* that! He said he wouldn't involve me in any of it so all I had to do was turn a blind eye. I promised I would never shop him but it didn't change anything. It was over. Then he said, no, we were meant for each other and he would buy me a nice present to prove it. I said he could buy all the presents he liked, it wouldn't make a difference. I put the phone down, saying I was never going to speak to him again. And I was as good as my word. If you've got records, you'll know he rang me yesterday about noon – right? I was in at home, working out. When I saw whose number it was, I didn't bother answering.' He smiled triumphantly. 'But you know that already, don't you?'

'We don't know you were at home when you got that call, do we?' Granot said. 'You could have been standing right next to Florian.'

'But I fucking wasn't. Alright?'

'In that Thursday-night call, did Florian mention what plans he had for the day after? What he intended to do?'

'No. I'm getting bored with you, Fattie.' He turned to Darac. 'Where's that coffee? You've got a machine there.'

It was time to put the squeeze on.

'Let's go back to the previous Saturday morning,' Darac said. 'If Florian had succeeded in drugging that boy, where would he have taken him?'

Manou sat upright.

'What's this? You told me he *did* succeed. That eyewitness saw the kid…'

'We don't know all the facts. Maybe the boy did have heat stroke, after all. I repeat the question. Where would he have taken him? Your apartment?'

Pinball.

'Might have.'

'So how was he going to get in? You were out and no key to your place was found on Florian or among his effects.'

'Uh… no, he did have a key then. But… I got it back off him in the week. I didn't want him having it any more. Like I said, it was over between us.'

Darac opened a drawer and took out a small poly bag. Manou peered at it then seemed to freeze in his seat.

'When you were still maintaining you knew nothing

about anything, you said you had no idea about this.' Darac allowed the key to slide out on to his hand. 'It was found under a mat. A mat made out of an opened-out pizza carton. Now tell us more.'

'I can't. It's… just a key.'

Darac looked into Manou's black eyes. They stared back at him with such studied innocence, he was convinced he was lying.

'Florian was trying to hide it from someone. We've already tried it in doors at La Masarella and L'Horizon Bleu…'

'Trying doors? That's a waste of time.' Manou started tapping his knee. 'There must be a million doors in Nice. You can't go round them all, can you?'

'Relax,' Darac said, smiling.

Manou stopped tapping.

'I am relaxed. Get me that coffee now. No. Not coffee. Water.'

Granot gave him a knowing look.

'With or without GHB?'

'Don't get funny with me, you mountain of fucking…'

'Lard?' Granot said, happy to be back on track with Manou.

It was time to increase the pressure by seeming to ease it. With someone as labile as Manou, Darac realised, it might prove particularly effective.

'I'll get you some water.' Darac got to his feet. 'That's if our cleaning lady has remembered to replenish the cup dispenser. Looks as if she has.' He kept his eyes on Manou as he stood at the cooler. 'We don't intend to try *every* door in Nice, obviously.' He pulled a paper cup from the stack. 'But it would be remiss of us to leave out your...' He turned to Granot. 'Some water?'

'No thanks.'

'Sure?'

Tension was starting to knot Manou's back muscles. Like a horse nodding to release its bridle, he raised and lowered his head suddenly.

'Yes, it would be remiss to leave out the workplace... what's it called?'

'Peerless Taxis, you mean, chief?'

Staring straight ahead, Manou took in a long breath through the nose.

Darac shook his head as if Granot's suggestion were ridiculous.

'No, no – not Peerless.' The tension in Manou's shoulders eased slightly. 'Florian's workplace – the school. He did work there for the last eight years, after all.'

'The Lycée Mossette?'

'That's it. Don't you think so, Manou?'

'Well... if you're going to try doors.' He wiped his free hand over his chest. 'That's the one place it might be worth it. Must be plenty of rooms he could have used. Store cupboards and shit.'

'Thank you.' Darac handed him the cup. Compressed by Manou's grabbing hand, water sloshed over the rim. 'That's helpful.'

So helpful, it had decided Darac on his next move.

9.47 AM

'We'll take my car.'

Granot's eyes narrowed.

'No jazz?'

'Philistines – the lot of you.'

They signed out at the duty officer's desk.

'Anything from the boss, yet?'

Alain Charvet, who was manning the desk, shook his greying head.

'I can call her, if you like.'

Darac remembered how tired she had been the previous evening.

'She isn't late for any appointments or anything?'

'No, no. She wouldn't have been in at all today if it weren't for this Tour business.'

'Alright. We'll leave it for a while.'

Bzzzzzzzut!

It was crazily hot on the steps.

'Muscles is spinning quite a story, isn't he?' Screwing up his chops, Granot slipped on the one classy element of his entire summer wardrobe – his Ray-Bans. 'The street scum didn't degrade the culture vulture – it was the other way around! You don't buy that, do you?'

'I don't trust Manou as far as you could throw him. And yet...' Darac left the thought hanging.

'You *do* buy it?'

'No, not necessarily. But he's a strange one, isn't he? Homo-erotic tough one minute; limp-wristed simperer the next – I've never met a gay man quite like him.'

'Let's hope we never meet another.'

Granot had to make an effort to keep up with Darac as they set off across the compound.

'You certainly got lucky with that statement bluff.'

'It did have some basis in fact. And I had a bit of a head start on the part I made up.'

'Don't get you.'

'I didn't just tell him what I wanted him to think was in the statement. I let him read it. Or at least look at it.'

'Still don't get you.'

'He can't read but he didn't know I knew that.'

Granot gave a throaty chortle.

'Well, well... Let's put Manou's possible role in the GHB business on the back burner for a minute. Are you absolutely certain he didn't kill Florian? He has no alibi.'

'Well, we don't know whether he has or hasn't, do we? Not until we know exactly what happened to Florian. And when.'

Granot looked unconvinced.

'Maybe, but Manou told Bonbon he got up at ten, alone, and then stayed alone in the apartment until the pair of you got there. That's *hours* unaccounted for.'

'If I'd killed somebody, I'd have furnished myself with a better alibi than that. Especially if I were a hustler like Manou.'

'Perhaps.' Granot was already sweating profusely. 'Maybe there was no arm he could twist.'

'Manou – are you kidding?'

'You know what I mean. Manou could be your murderer.'

'No, no – I'm with Bonbon on this one. I think he's guilty of something but I very much doubt it's Florian's murder.'

As they reached Darac's Peugeot, he spotted Adèle Rousade, the officer's assistant, coming out of the archives office in Building G. Their eyes met. He gave her a smile. She blanked him.

'What's wrong with her? She was as happy as a lark earlier,' Granot said, pulling the passenger seat back before getting in.

'There's nothing wrong with Adèle.'

'So that just leaves you, then, doesn't it? Don't tell me. I can guess.'

With the Gare Thiers rail station at their backs, they walked down stone steps into the dreary Rue de Bruges. Peerless Taxis was halfway along the street, sandwiched between a sex shop and a kebab place. Only a hundred metres or so from the palm-studded elegance of Rue Verbier, they could have been anywhere in backstreet Europe.

'This hasn't just started,' Granot said, folding his copy of *Nice-Matin*'s *Tout Sur Le Tour* into a fan. 'You and Angeline.'

'It's been going on for a few months now.'

The pavement was slick with stepped-on vegetable matter from a nearby stall. As if signifying a broader need to tread carefully, Granot picked up his feet.

'Relationships. Difficult things. Take a word of advice from someone who knows?'

'Paint the apartment together?'

'Forget her. Let's face it, Angeline has always hated the fact that you're a *flic*.'

'It's more complicated than that.'

'Have you ever complained about what *she* does for a living? Forget her. Someone just as bright and beautiful will come along in time.'

They had arrived at Peerless Taxis. Mercifully.

'Work to do, Granot.'

Darac offered Florian's key to the latched-back front door.

'Another one it doesn't open.'

They walked through streamer curtains into a strip-lit bunker-like space with a door and a customer window set into a cinder-block rear wall. It was not even 10.30 am and there was a pool of fresh vomit in one corner. Above the window was a queuing-system counter surmounted by a soiled polystyrene plaque that read: PEERLESS – WHEN ONLY THE BEST WILL DO. Next to it, a handwritten sign advised: WE NEVER HAVE ANY CASH HERE EVER.

On first impression, the large black woman sitting

behind the squawk-box window was poorly cast. The gravity of her mien reminded Darac of the queen of American gospel music, Mahalia Jackson. Granot leaned into the window.

'Take a ticket.'

'Point one: we're the only people in here and—'

'Take a ticket.'

'Point two: we're from the Police Judiciaire, sweetheart.' Granot showed her his badge. 'Open the door and let us in or I'll give you a different kind of ticket.'

Indicating that each move was an intolerable imposition, the woman removed her headset, rapped down her pen, and dragged back her chair before hauling herself up on to her feet.

'That's the way.'

'Ask her if she knows "Amazing Grace", Granot.'

Exiting stage right, the woman disappeared from the window. In the meantime, Darac tried the key in the door's lock. No go. After a moment, the door jerked open from the inside. They stepped through into a square ,lobby-like space. To their left, a short corridor led back to the squawk box; ahead was a kitchen area and toilet. Staff lockers, eight of them, lined the side wall to their right. They were battered-looking but surprisingly, each seemed to be fitted with a proper cylinder lock.

'Madame,' Darac said as the woman closed the door. 'Which one of these lockers is Imanol Esquebel's?'

She waved a hand in the direction of all of them and retreated back along the corridor.

'Thank you.'

Darac tried the key in the first locker. It didn't fit. Ditto, the second. It was the same for the others.

Granot shook his jowly chops.

'Don't get it. Manou was practically shitting bricks at the thought of us coming here.'

They looked around. There were no other connecting doors in the place and the toilet door had no lock.

The phone rang in the squawk box.

'Peerless.'

As the woman dealt with the call, Darac slipped his mini-tool roll out of his back pocket.

'Shield me.'

The big man backed into the space. A pile of sandbags would not have blocked the woman's view of the lockers any more effectively. Darac picked each lock in turn until he found a locker containing a couple of body-building magazines, a hooded jacket, a toilet roll and a bottle of Pagan Man. Darac grabbed the jacket and quickly went through the pockets. Tissues, condoms, an unpaid bill... Then in an inner coin pocket, he felt a promising shape. He took it out and held on to it while he fished Florian's key out of his own pocket. Laying them side by side on his palm, he turned to Granot.

'They match.'

11.00 AM

A petite brunette wearing a short orange sundress answered the doorbell.

'Mademoiselle Marie Lacroix? Lieutenant Alejo Busquet, Police Judiciaire.' Bonbon showed her his ID. 'At last.'

'Ah yes,' she said, ushering him in. 'I got your message.'

The place was full of light and furnished in pastel colours. A Dufy painting come to life. Something of an antiques buff, Bonbon's eye was drawn to a round, marble-top coffee table standing a little way inside the room. On it was arranged a collection of shells, pebbles and what looked like a small bird's skull.

'This is lovely.' He looked at it more closely. 'Josef Frank?'

'The table?' she said, immediately disarmed. 'I think it's by somebody called Sven Ten. Or that's what an old boyfriend of mine said, anyway.'

'Ah, no. Sven*skt* Tenn.' Bonbon smiled warmly. 'It's the name of the department store Frank made a lot of stuff for. In Stockholm. It's early fifties, this. Be worth quite a lot of money, I should think.'

Marie cast him a quizzical look.

'Are you sure you're from the Police Judiciaire?'

'We're allowed one hobby each.'

'I like the table too much to sell it.' Marie did a pretty good line in smiles, herself. 'Unless I have to at some stage. Drink?'

'Just some water would be fine. Sparkling if you have it.'

'I have. Why not sit out? It's what I was doing.'

Shading his eyes against the light, Bonbon walked out on to a balcony that offered an unobstructed view of one of the Côte d'Azur's most perfect bays, the Rade de Villefranche. Across the water, the humpbacked silhouette of Cap Ferrat looked like a whale breaking the surface.

'Wonderful apartment. Is it yours?'

'I own this one and the one I let to holidaymakers in Rue Verbier. Glass or bottle?'

Bonbon heard the muffled rattle of a fridge door opening.

'Bottle's fine. Yes, it was in talking to your new people that we found out about you.'

She returned with an opened bottle of San Pellegrino.

'Thank you, mademoiselle.'

'Sit, please. And shall I lower the awning? The sun's hot and you're very...'

'Auburn, yes. Where's the...?'

'I'll do it – it's tricky.'

'If you're sure.'

There were two cedar-wood recliners on the balcony. A pair of white-framed sunglasses sat on a half-read *Nice-*

Matin on the seat of one of them. Bonbon chose the other, pulled its back upright and sat down. The handle for the awning was set into a niche in the wall. Accompanied by a series of squeaks and rasps, a vaguely sylvan atmosphere descended as a canopy of two-tone green canvas unfolded overhead. It seemed an inappropriate moment to begin the questioning.

'You know, I think a lot of people in your position would choose to live at the Rue Verbier apartment and rent out this one. Top-floor situation right on the old quayside and with a view to die for, you could charge the earth for it.'

'I did for a... time,' Marie said, the effort she was putting in showing in her voice. 'But I prefer it... this way round. Money's... not everything, is it?'

'As with keeping the Frank table.'

'I suppose so... yes.'

The awning finally lowered, Marie went to sit down. Tossing the paper aside, she put her shades back on and adjusted her seat forward.

'Now, Lieutenant Busquet, wasn't it? How may I help you?'

Bonbon indicated the copy of *Nice-Matin*.

'Pretty vague, isn't it? The report of the death of a non-Muslim at a prayer service. Could you add anything to it?'

'Uh, yes. Sorry I didn't identify myself at the time but I was the one who called you that day.'

11.01 AM

Voices out in the corridor told him the mid-morning shift was coming on. He could hear the short one clearly. He tried to blank her out. She didn't matter. She would never ask him if he'd changed his mind about the TV. Not that she was lazy. On the contrary, she was all action. That was the trouble. She had no time to think of extraneous matters.

He heard another voice, sweeter, lighter. But did it belong to his beloved fat one? It didn't sound quite like her. But they were still outside. It was too early to tell. 21.2 degrees it was. That much was certain.

The bed jolted.

'Good morning!' the short one said, out of his line of vision. 'And how are we today? Let's look, shall we?' Riffling of paper. Pen scratches. In a lower voice she said, 'Heartbeat is faster.'

'Let me look.'

No! It was the horrible blue-eyed one. She hadn't been on duty for ages. The horrible blue-eyed one who hardly ever said a word to him. Where was the fat one? Now there was no chance. The Tour was gone. No Nice stage. No Mont Ventoux. No following Contador, race number 21, all the way to Paris. It was back to watching 21.2 degrees all the way to nothingness.

But perhaps there was still a chance. Maybe the fat one would come on at lunchtime.

The short one's face.

'Feeling alright today?'

He blinked once.

'Good. You're comfortable?'

He blinked once.

'Heart's only marginally faster,' the horrible blue-eyed one said. 'Everything else looks normal.'

The short one's face.

'Have you had a letter from your son today?'

He blinked twice.

'And no one's just re-read yesterday's to you, have they?'

He blinked twice.

Face gone. Dropped voices.

'It's not that, then.'

'It's a response to something.'

Where was his beloved fat one? He knew she would have asked about the TV.

'He's probably excited because you're back,' the short one said to the doorway – the horrible blue-eyed one had already left. 'They all love you.'

The bed jolted as the notes went back into their scabbard.

The short one's face.

'Happy to see Josette again, yes?'

He thought about it. He blinked twice.

'No? Ah – I know, you're missing Hortense. You like her, don't you? The large girl?'

He blinked once.

'Well, she's moved to another department now. So you'll just have to make do with us!'

No, no, no. She was the only one. The only one who cared.

A heavy rolling sound. A large black screen. Flickering. Trains at a station. Flickering. A woman reading the news. Flickering. Actors in costume. Moving images, one after the other.

'I know they don't start riding for hours but what station is the Tour coverage on? Is this it?'

What? It couldn't be.

On the screen, a woman stood holding a mike. A banner saying DÉPART fluttered across the road above her. He could hardly believe it. This was what he'd been hoping for, praying for…

'Oh, I didn't tell you,' the short one said. 'He didn't want the TV after all.'

'No? I've just brought it in here. As if I didn't have enough…'

'Perhaps it could go in the day room?'

'It can't go in there. It's all set up so he can watch it lying here. I'll just put it back.'

A finger jabbed at the case. The screen went blank.

Not just given and then taken away. Put right in front of him and turned on. He wanted to be dead now. It felt as if his whole hellish life had just taken one last lick of flame.

The horrible blue-eyed one's face.

'Are you sure you don't want it, dear?'

Yes I do want it! But just a minute, now. This was important. How should he answer? One blink or two? Would one blink mean 'Yes, I'm sure I don't want it'? Or 'No, I do want it'?

Should he not blink at all, prompting her to reformulate the question? Too risky. She might just lose patience and take the set away. The horrible blue-eyed one was like that. Two. It should be two blinks. If she understands grammar, two blinks would mean he wasn't sure.

He blinked twice. Her face looked as blank as the screen. Come on! Be clever enough to understand what I mean.

'So... you do want it?'

He knew he wasn't, but he felt he was smiling.

He blinked once.

'You do want it after all?'

He blinked once.

'Oh. Okay. That's alright then.'

The horrible blue-eyed one had come through for him. The screen flickered into life once more. And in his head, so had he.

11.02 AM

Darac swivelled up his shades as the Peugeot plunged into the *voie rapide* tunnel.

'I'm worried by the delightful Madame Peerless,' Granot said. 'One word from her and the plan doesn't work.'

'She won't say anything to Manou. She detests him.'

'She detests everybody, by the look of it. She might mention our visit to him just to spite us.'

'I don't think so. Besides, she didn't see us open his locker. All she saw is that we tried a key in it and it didn't work.'

'You've got a point.'

Darac's mobile rang.

'It's Deanna,' he said, glancing at the ID screen. A call from her was always significant. Coming as they emerged into the light at the end of the tunnel made it seem doubly so.

'We're listening, Deanna.'

'I've got the low-down on Florian's COD.'

'Excellent.' Darac put the phone on speaker. 'Go for it.'

'Florian died as a result of an intramuscular injection into his right bicep—'

'The same bicep Madame Delage rammed with the trolley? Tell me it wasn't her.'

'Will you let me continue?'

'Continue.'

'Yes, the same bicep. The injectant was lancuronium mixed with neostigmine. The effect of the latter drug was to substantially delay the onset of the former, a lethal paralytic in the dose administered. Before you ask, I would say the injection was given between twenty to sixty minutes before death occurred. *Fin*.'

'You are quite brilliant, Deanna. I hope you realise that.'

'Save it – I'm busy Thursday nights.'

'I'll get you to one of our gigs yet. The timing seems to rule out our trolley killer doesn't it?'

'Indeed.'

'How do you think the injection was given?'

'The needle used was a very fine one so Florian might not have even felt it.'

Darac was already entertaining theories involving poison-tipped umbrellas and the like. He pitched a few of them to Deanna while Granot rang Perand and told him to abandon his questioning of Madame Delage. Once Darac's call with Deanna had ended, he rang the duty officer, Charvet.

'We've got some significant movement on the Florian case. I think we need a team meeting. Send out a call, will you? Squad room in an hour.'

In the meantime, he had some permissions to obtain from Frènes.

The mood was upbeat as teams connected to the Florian case began to assemble. Only the boss herself wasn't there.

'What's happened to Agnès D.?' Armani said, filing into the room alongside Darac and Frankie Lejeune. 'No, don't tell me. I'll bet she was scared you were going to paw her again.' He turned to Frankie. 'All over her body, he was.'

Grinning, Granot squeezed between them. Flopping down in the seat next to Darac, he began riffling through a stack of papers.

'All over her body?' Frankie turned to Darac. 'What's this?'

'Her feet were aching.' He downed the industrial-sized espresso he'd brought with him and set down the cup. 'Feet.'

Hands on hips, Frankie nodded ambiguously.

'You gave Agnès a foot massage?'

'Exactly! That's all it was.'

'All – uh-huh.' Her large, pale-green eyes hardened slightly. 'I worked with you every single day for nearly three years. You never did that for me.'

Armani raised his hands palms upwards.

'Never did it for me either. And God knows I've asked him enough times.'

'Remember that day up at Saint-Jeannet?' Frankie was getting into her stride now. '"Hell on the rock" they called it afterwards. I would have *killed* for a foot massage at the end of that.'

'Listen, if either of you wants to make an appointment, see my lovely assistant.' Darac indicated Granot, who was taking a crafty sniff of his armpits.

Without looking up, the big man nodded approvingly.

'Roses,' he said.

Frankie shared a grin with Granot as she went to sit down.

Armani turned back to Darac.

'Seriously, where is the boss?'

'Having the morning off, I guess. I'm going to ring her straight after the meeting, though. Give her an update on things.'

Armani draped a crisp, cufflink-sleeved arm around Darac's polo-shirted shoulder.

'Just before we get going – the Tour. I've been thinking about your lucky number twenty-one sweepstake ticket.'

'The one that just happens to correspond to red-hot favourite Alfredo Contador.'

'*Alberto*. That is the one. Seventy-five euros for it. And that's my final offer.'

'Sorry. No can do.'

Laughter over by the window. Passing a mobile backwards and forwards over his coppery head, Bonbon was in demonstration mode with Erica Lamarthe.

'See, my hair is so charged, it affects the signal. Look at the meter.'

'It's a hot spot in the room, you idiot.'

'Oh.' He slipped the phone into his shirt pocket. 'You won't believe this but you're the only one who hasn't fallen for it.'

'I do believe it.'

As Darac called Bonbon over, Armani gave it one last try.

'Be reasonable, okay? Seventy-five is a top offer.'

'It is. But I've already been offered eighty.'

Granot finally found the papers he was looking for.

'*Voilà*,' he said, brandishing them with a flourish.

Armani shot him a filthy look as he went to join his Narco colleagues. He had no doubt Granot was the rival bidder. And the idea hadn't even been his.

Darac took Bonbon to one side.

'Anything useful from Marie Lacroix?'

'Plenty.'

'Good. I'll open on Manou, go to Deanna, and then hand over to you, okay?'

'Fine. Been out to buy paint yet?'

Darac gave a little shake of the head.

'Granot thinks Angeline and I should call it a day.'

Bonbon's eyebrows made a bid for the wire.

'I love Granot like…' He thought about it. '…somebody else's brother. But he is to relationship advice what a sledgehammer is to a nut.'

'Probably so.'

'Decorate the apartment – I'm telling you.'

'Okay but we'll do this first, shall we?'

The buzz in the room subsided as Darac called the meeting to order.

'Okay – there are a number of developments, so let's get on with it. As we know, the Florian investigation has two possibly connected points of focus: one – Emil Florian's murder by person or persons unknown; two – the probability he was involved in drug-assisted rapes. Granot and I visited Manou Esquebel's workplace earlier. There, we found a key identical to the one Florian was trying to jettison at the time of his death – a key Esquebel was most anxious we didn't go looking for.'

'"There's a place for us,"' Armani sang, in a passable Basque accent.

'Exactly. There's an apartment somewhere, isn't there? Or probably just a room that Esquebel shared with Florian for purposes we can guess. This morning, Esquebel told us that it was Florian who was the degenerate rapist and that he, Esquebel, was guilty only by association. He says he tried to persuade Florian not to go ahead with his newfound hobby and ended the relationship when he refused. We need to find the room they shared. When we do, their true activities will be clearer.'

'So what are we going to do, chief – sweat the bastard?' Narco Lieutenant Thierry Martinet had a face like a club hammer and a manner to go with it. 'Esquebel will sing ,given the right persuasion.'

'Or he might not,' Bonbon said.

'We've got a better idea,' said Darac. We're going to release him and let him take us to the place.'

Almost asleep at his desk, young Max Perand finally sat up.

'Follow him? It'll have to be at some distance, won't it?' The smile was more of a sneer. 'One way or another, he knows what most of us look like.'

'I've already approached Cauteret at Foch. He's giving me a good tail guy. But in the event he loses him, or if Manou Esquebel gets on to him, I want a backup. Erica – could you fit a GPS transmitter into Esquebel's mobile?'

'I could, but there's one in it already. There's one in every modern mobile.'

'One that transmits whether the phone is on or not, I mean.'

'Ah.'

As if the relevant calculations were written in the heavens, Erica tilted her gaze upwards.

'Ten euros says she can,' Armani said to the room. There were no bets.

Forehead scrunched, lips pursed, Erica nodded slowly as the solution seemed to come to her. And then she tossed the mask aside.

'Just did that for effect. Of course I can. And hide it so he won't be able to find it.'

Darac smiled for the first time that day. And then he felt guilty, as if escaping his cell of sadness for a moment constituted some sort of betrayal.

'Catch,' he said, shaping to toss her the phone.

'I'd rather not have to repair the thing first.'

Darac handed it to Granot who passed it on.

'We'll probably be releasing Esquebel tomorrow evening, so how long do you think it will take you? I already have the warrant from Frènes, by the way.'

'How long? No interruptions – four hours. Reality – twice as long. I can get straight on it.'

'Excellent. And how precise can you make it?'

'Using EGNOS MTO/2 – it'll be accurate to within about four metres.'

'I don't know what that means but it sounds fantastic.'

Granot gave Erica a look.

'Couldn't fit one into my wife's mobile, could you?'

'Seems only fair, I've fitted one in yours for her.'

Laughter all round. Almost. Darac gave her a look.

'Will you let me know immediately when you've done it?'

'Sure.'

'That's great, Erica, thanks.' Glancing at his notes, he got to his feet. 'So now on to our primary focus – Florian's murder itself.'

Writing the words LANCURONIUM and NEOSTIGMINE on the whiteboard, Darac outlined Deanna's findings.

'She shoots, she scores,' Granot said. 'As always.'

Darac parked his backside on the edge of a desk.

'So, Bonbon – want to come in here?'

'Yes, I've just returned from interviewing the woman who rang in the original tip-off call from Rue Verbier, one Marie Lacroix. From a third-floor balcony opposite the Basilique, she saw Florian join the prayer meeting; she saw the old woman, Delage, hit him with her shopping trolley; she saw him bend forward as if in prayer, and not get up again. But, and this is the important thing now we have a handle on the time frame, she also saw Florian arrive on the street before all this happened. Before Lartou's CCTV footage kicks in, in fact. In retrospect, I think we can piece together what happened. It seems Florian first saw you, Armani, on Jean Médecin. He hid behind a Colonne Morris. Then when you disappeared into a boutique on Rue Verbier, he decided to leg it – especially as there was the cover of a small crowd of people on the pavement between him and you. They'd gathered to watch one of those living-statue street performers.'

'I was only collecting a pair of shoes, so I went into the place and came out again almost immediately. I did notice that crowd on the pavement opposite.'

'And then you walked off in the direction of the prayer room?'

'Yeah.'

'That, I think, is when Florian really panicked. He thought you were following him.'

'Instead, I went into a place to look at some shirts. I didn't see Florian at any point.' Feeling all eyes on him, Armani stiffened. 'Look, I was off duty, right? Get off my back, all of you.'

'No one's on your back, man,' Darac said. 'Go on, Bonbon.'

'So Florian dived for cover in the prayer meeting. He seems to have had only one good idea in all this – he poured away the incriminating GHB water in his bottle in a way that looked natural for a Muslim about to pray. He needn't have bothered, of course. But then he didn't know he had such a short time to live.' Bonbon took a pink-striped bag out of his pocket. 'In light of Deanna's findings, let's go back to the crowd who were watching the mime. Marie reports that Florian was jogging past, when one of them, a young bearded man carrying a rucksack, peeled away. Florian ran straight into him. It was quite an impact. Both of them were almost knocked off their feet.'

Bonbon let the implication take as he unwrapped a sweet.

Darac was listening with his hand to his chin.

'Florian collided with the bearded man, Bonbon? Not the other way around?'

'It takes two to collide though, doesn't it? All you need is timing and a bit of nerve to walk in front of somebody who's running to make it look as if the impact is their fault. Ask Granot – half the defenders in his beloved l'OGC Nice get away with it every match.'

Exhausted patience was one of Granot's signature looks.

'The paranoid ravings of a typical Barcelona fan. But he is right.'

'Okay.' Darac nodded, picturing it. 'She – Marie – saw nothing more conclusive than that?'

'She didn't say so but I didn't press the point. We didn't have Deanna's findings at that stage so I was gearing my questions mainly to what happened at the other end of the street.' Bonbon looked at his watch. 'She may still be at home. What say I ring her?'

'Yeah – do it.'

Bonbon made the call, asking questions à la Agnès in a logically ordered sequence. At the end of it, he had learned nothing conclusive but several points had resonance: Marie agreed that the bearded man could have engineered the collision as Bonbon had outlined; that the impact had been to Florian's right-hand side; and that he had collided with the bearded man's rucksack rather than his shirt-sleeved arm. Further, the rucksack had looked substantial and appeared fully packed. She hadn't seen where the bearded man had gone afterwards.

'Great work, Bonbon,' Darac said, running a hand through his hair. 'Questions? Comments?'

'I have one.' Frankie broke the seal on a bottle of water and took a sip. 'I'm not sure I believe this MO. If I were, for the sake of argument, a vengeful parent, I would seek to flatten Florian under the wheels of my car, bludgeon him to death, stab him with a knife. Perhaps all three. What I wouldn't do is hang around with a rucksack-mounted syringe full of poison on the off chance he passed by me on the street. Passed by at a run, conveniently. It's too outlandish, isn't it?'

As if it were essential to the process, Darac shifted his point of balance as he weighed the idea.

'It is, yes – but there are other outlandish aspects to this thing we know to be true. Take the composition of the drug cocktail used on Florian. I also think his being there wasn't just chance. Florian frequented Rue Verbier – we know that from the statements of the Muslim worshippers, several of whom had often seen him there. They won't be the only ones who knew it was part of his stamping ground. Fair?'

Canting her head to one side, Frankie drew down the corners of her full mouth.

'It's fair, certainly, but… Armani – give us your take on this.'

'Thanks to La Professoressa Bianchi,' he said, transparently seeking to regain lost ground by emphasising his tribal connection to Deanna, 'we've got a meaningful timing for the lethal injection. And I have no problem buying the concealed syringe idea. None at all.'

'By running,' Frankie said, 'Florian made it easier for the bearded man to pull off the collision trick, true? But how did he know Florian was going to do that? He couldn't have anticipated Florian was going to see someone who would spook him. Or perhaps Beard had beaters of his own secreted around the corner, you think?'

Bringing his thumb and fingertips together, Armani shook his hand. 'Frankie – the fact that Florian was running was coincidental. Remember Deanna said that the superfine needle used might create no more than a mildly irritating sensation on the skin? Florian mightn't have noticed he'd been jabbed even if he'd been standing still.'

'Deanna did say that, yes. Still seems a *little* strange.'

'We've had stranger MOs than covert injections.' Armani swapped the shaking hand for the double palms-up. 'Many stranger ones.'

'Well, that is true. Especially by some of you Italians.'

'We're an inventive race. The point is – this bearded man: every effort must be made to find him.'

Darac nodded.

'Yes, I think he may prove to be Florian's killer. A couple of things might help us with this. First: the human statue may have got a good look at him. Second, there could be footage from CCTV cameras in Avenue Jean Médecin. We need to look at any new material and review what has already been reviewed.' He gave Lartou Lartigue a sympathetic look. 'I'll arrange a whole squad of film critics to assist you.'

'Thank you, chief. I'll need them.'

'The stuff you've already looked at, I don't suppose you remember seeing…'

'What – a man with a beard and rucksack when the brief was to find a man in a white suit and an old woman?'

'Forget I asked. As soon as the meeting is over, I'll set that up, okay?' Lartigue gave him the thumbs-up. 'Bonbon – the human statue. Do we know anything about him or her?'

'It's a her. I haven't had time to make any enquiries yet but finding a marble Medusa complete with all-singing, all-dancing snakes shouldn't tax us too much.'

Erica clicked her fingers.

'*That's* where I've seen him. Manou Esquebel, I mean.' She gave Darac a look. 'Do you remember I said he looked familiar?'

'Yes, I do. Go on.'

'Last Saturday afternoon, I took my nephew to the children's carousel in Jardin Albert. On the promenade just opposite, Medusa was… performing, if that's the word, and she'd drawn quite a crowd. Manou was one of them.'

Yvonne Flaco finally felt able to join the debate.

'Was Manou's interest just focused on the act, Erica? Did you see him arrive or leave?'

'I didn't notice – he was just a face in the crowd. Look, I know I'm a techie and not a detective…'

Several voices supported the assertion.

'Guys?' Darac said, raising a hand. 'Go with it, Erica.'

'I was just going to say that the crowd was made up mainly of kids. It seems a bit of an odd coincidence that Manou and Florian were both seen around this Medusa character. Perhaps that's why Florian was heading for Rue Verbier yesterday. Street artists stick to a timetable and he may have known she would have been there at that time and that she acts like a magnet for the sort of … prey he was interested in.'

'Grazers go for the low-hanging fruit, don't they,' Max Perand said, still smiling his lopsided smile. 'The easy pickings.'

Darac had an expert on sex crime to call on.

'Frankie?'

'The easiest pickings of all are to be found in the family home.' She gave Perand a look. 'That's where the vast majority of paedophilic activity takes place.'

The young man stirred in his seat.

'Sorry, but there *are* paedos who abduct kids from playgrounds, et cetera. Aren't there? Or what are we putting a bug in Manou's phone for?'

'They exist — certainly. Florian and Manou may be among them. And they may have latched on to Medusa as someone who attracted kids — a sort of Pied Piper on a plinth.' Expressed in Frankie's talc-soft contralto, the phenomenon sounded even more sinister. 'But let's break it down into age groups. The picture may change but no one in the city or in the wider conurbation has reported that a young child has obviously suffered abuse or gone missing recently. So that leaves us with unaccompanied older kids and teenagers. A big problem there is that teenagers who have been drugged and raped are often too ashamed to tell anyone about it. For a variety of reasons, this holds especially for boys. So even if you know for a fact that someone has been attacked, you often have to gently tease the info out of them. That's why I devised the questionnaire for the Lycée Mossette in the way I did.'

'Anything from that yet, by the way?' Bonbon said.

'Nothing conclusive so far. To get back to the question – there are hundreds of places where kids congregate. Medusa's various crowds would just be one more to add to the list.' She gave Erica the sort of look that had attracted Principal Volpini's cat to her lap. 'The connection you're trying to draw is a little tenuous, I think. And Florian, don't forget, was often seen on Rue Verbier.'

'True, but maybe Medusa having a spot there was the reason for that.'

'But he didn't pause by the crowd even for a moment. He ran straight past.'

'He'd seen Armani just seconds before, though.'

Armani shook his head.

'Sorry, Erica, but I don't see where this is getting us.'

'I was just wondering if Medusa was part of the set-up. Perhaps the three of them were in it together. She, Florian and Manou.'

'If she was,' Darac said, 'she'll have to be a sharp one to conceal it from us when we talk to her. You saw her a week ago today, right?'

'On the promenade opposite Jardin Albert, as I said.'

'When?'

'About one o'clock but she'd been there a while

already, I think.' She looked at her Swatch. 'She might even be there now.'

'We'll get over there in time.' He scanned the room. 'Any questions or comments?'

No one responded.

'Alright, that's it for the time being.'

Papers riffled. Chairs scraped.

'In other news,' Frankie said, getting her things together, 'we saw Freddy Anselme's SWAT team leaving for Monaco a little while ago. Judging by the expression on his face, he thinks World War Three has started.'

Granot sidled up.

'He hasn't had any special orders, has he?'

Armani shook his head.

'No – they're just taking up station in the barracks.' He adjusted his button-down collar. 'Hyped up? I tell you, a cat dashes out in front of their vehicle – two seconds later, there'll be six thousand bullets in it.'

'Here's to our men in uniform,' Darac said, raising his empty espresso cup. 'Okay, my team – who's been neglecting their paperwork as much as I have?'

Flaco raised Perand's hand for him. He couldn't stop her, Darac noticed. And his own efforts to follow suit failed miserably.

'Alright – you're as strong as an ox,' Perand said. 'Happy?'

'Yes.' But Flaco's face had fallen slightly as she returned Darac's look. 'I'm behind as well, Captain.'

'Okay, so you're not free.' His scanning eye fell on Granot

and Bonbon. They shook their heads so synchronously, it looked rehearsed. 'And neither are you two.' Options were running out. He felt a hand brush his shoulder.

'See you later, Frankie.'

After a moment, he picked up his stuff and hastened after her.

'Hold on.'

'Well, I suppose a five-second gap does constitute "later".'

'Got a minute?'

'Certainly.'

'And would you have another one in about half an hour? To come and interview Snake Girl with me?'

She scrunched her forehead.

'I'll need to check in with my guys first. Should be alright though, I think.'

'Call me if you can't,' he said, as they headed out of the door.

As stealthily as a pickpocket, Armani slipped in alongside.

'Ninety. Ninety euros is absolutely my final offer.'

'Seventy-five was absolutely your final offer.' Darac flipped his mobile and keyed in Agnès's mobile number. 'Wasn't it?'

'This is absolutely *final* final.'

Granot took up closer order behind them.

'Don't listen to him, chief.'

'Ninety, Darac.'

'I'll... think about it.'

Armani smiled like a suitor who had just secured a winning advantage over a rival.

'It's not over,' Granot whispered in his ear, 'until the fat lady sings.'

Charvet's voice called down the corridor.

'Captain – a couple of officers from Immigration are over in the cell block. They want to take Mansoor Narooq and to talk to Slimane Bahtoum. Is that alright?'

Mansoor's dig about repatriation quotas played in Darac's head.

'Have they been cleared?'

'Just a second.'

Charvet said a few words into his headset.

'Yes, they have.'

'Alright. Give them the go-ahead.'

Darac was getting no answer from Agnès. He left a message and called her home phone. He left another message.

'Charvet? Has the boss rung in?'

'No.'

For the first time, Darac began to feel uneasy. He thought about giving Vincent Dantier a call. Granot, he knew, had his numbers. The big man was already tackling the lower slopes of the mountain of paper on his desk.

'Got your address book there? I want to give Agnès's father a call.'

Granot handed it over.

'Waste of time. She's turned her mobile off – that's it. We all do it.'

'Let's hope you're right. She hasn't rung in, either.'

'That's unlike her but there could be hundreds of reasons. She's probably at the osteopath. Or the chiropractor.'

He grinned wickedly. 'Or getting a massage from some nice young man.'

As Granot continued with his papers, Darac rang the first of Vincent's numbers.

'I am unable to take your call at the moment. Please…'

He left yet another message and tried his landline. Same result. He stared into space for a moment.

'We may just call in at Avenue Marguerite after the interview with Medusa.'

'We?'

'Frankie and I are doing it.'

'Like old times. But I should forget it if I were you. Agnès isn't home – end of story.'

'Nevertheless.' Several scenarios played in Darac's head. 'Do you remember me telling you about my father's mishap in the shower? It happened… let's see, he was still freelancing, then…' He swatted the question away. 'About ten years ago, it doesn't matter. The point is, he slipped getting in and put his back out. The slightest movement was agony so he just had to lay there waiting for…' He searched for the name. '…well – whichever lady friend he was living with at the time – to come home from work. Nearly an hour went by before she did. Remember me telling you that?'

Granot nodded.

'Ten years ago? Oh yes, we're still talking about it.'

'Things like that happen, is all I'm saying.'

'If the boss is lying on her bathroom floor, you'd better send Frankie in.' A second thought hit Granot. 'No, go in yourself – the laugh *that*'ll give us will run and run.'

12.44 PM

Lunch was an invariably snatched affair for those working a murder case. But at least Darac and Frankie were snatching theirs on the terrace of Café Parfait. Superb *moules farcies* was one draw. Being able to keep Medusa in plain view across Boulevard des Anglais was another.

'I don't know what the effect is like close up but from here it's uncanny.' Frankie extracted a final pesto-infused morsel from its shell. 'How does she make the snakes do that? She doesn't move a muscle.'

Darac set down his fork.

'They're on a timer? Dunno. We'll ask her in a minute. Espresso?'

'Coffee kills. Especially in this heat.' Frankie's smile was a radiant thing. 'You have one, by all means.'

'I'm making it a double for that. Then you'll be sorry. Water?'

'Please.'

He ordered the drinks as a Petit Train Touristique trundled past the terrace. Prompted by the recorded commentary, passengers were moving their heads from side to side like spectators at a tennis match – until they caught sight of Medusa.

'It's game over for the rest.' Darac could see the appeal. 'Maybe they ought to feature *her* in the commentary.'

'Best not arrest the girl, then.'

Making references to the case and banter – on the surface, everything seemed normal. But in the silence that followed, a darker reality floated up from the depths.

'Haven't seen Angeline in a while,' Frankie said, with slightly loaded emphasis. 'Her university teaching going well?'

'Oh, fine.'

'And...' Her pale green eyes locked on his. 'How is she in herself?'

Darac flipped his mobile.

'Just going to try the Dantiers again.'

'Uh-huh.'

Nothing was said while he listened to the familiar recorded messages.

'Still no answer. Yes... Angeline's very well, thanks.'

'I have a shoulder, you know. Two, in fact.'

Darac should have known that Frankie, of all people, would have divined something was amiss. It would be a relief to drop the pretence.

'Offering relationship counselling, now?' Propping himself on an elbow, he lowered his head into his hand. 'It's very sweet but if truth were told, I don't really believe in it.'

'You don't think relationships sometimes need work to succeed?'

Darac fell very still, suddenly.

'It's catching, this statue thing.'

'Seems so.'

'Work to be happy, Frankie? No, I don't believe you can. And Angeline shares that view, I know. We've always been a bit… smug, I suppose, about how right we seemed to be for each other.'

'No relationship can be perfect. As she ought to know better than most.'

'Thanks.'

'I just meant that hers is a very postmodern take on things, isn't it? No place in critical theory for concepts like ideal love.'

'I think most people understand nothing is perfect. And there have always been some quite big differences between Angeline and me. But they've never really got in the way until now.'

'You feel the relationship is failing?'

'I know it is. On her side, anyway. Me – I'm still very much…'

The drinks arrived. As they were set out, Darac picked up the bill and paid it. Nothing else was said until the waiter cleared the plates and left them to it.

'It's come in well under the allowance, look.'

'You were saying.'

Darac exhaled deeply.

'I take it you do believe that people can work to save a relationship?'

'If both parties ultimately want it, I do.'

'But then they wouldn't have found themselves in that position in the first…' Darac slapped the idea away. 'Look

– this is the crux, Frankie. All the contradictions and other little things that Angeline used to find fascinating about me now seem to disappoint her. Added to that, my horizons have come in. I hit people, I make love, I play the guitar – those are the triangulation points I use to navigate through life. Or through life's crises, at least.'

'According to Angeline, that is.'

'Yeah.'

Across the promenade, Medusa's snakes writhed, sending an amused shudder through the crowd.

'At first, I thought she was wrong about that. But maybe she isn't. Maybe my emotional options have been pared down. Maybe it happens to all homicide detectives – a reaction to the chaotic world we spend every working minute in.'

'Adopting simplicity at home as an antidote to all the complexity we face at work? If that's the dynamic, I don't see anything too terribly wrong in it.'

'Adopting simplicity is one thing; behaving simplistically is another. But that's only part of it. Whether my role in the police is at the root of it or not, Angeline has come to the conclusion that I lack qualities she realises she needs in a partner. I can't see a way back.'

Once again, Frankie's eyes seemed to see right into him.

'It's far too early to say that. When did you first notice something was wrong between you?'

'Four months ago. Or so.'

Her eyes didn't leave his.

'Don't give up on it.'

Darac's expression took on a flintier quality. It was a look she knew well.

'I believe people can change, Frankie. I've seen it many times. But it must come from within. Changing just to fit someone else's perspective? No. I'm not doing that. Not even for Angeline. Love me, like me or loathe me – *this*...' He jabbed a thumb against his chest. '...is what I am.'

'Yes – change should come from within but in relationships, you have to make some compromises, don't you? As long as there aren't too many of them and they go both ways, I can't see a problem. Bend a little, Paul.'

'Bend...' The tablecloth claimed his attention once more. 'And at what point does bend become bend over?'

'I'm talking about making compromises, not... shafting yourself.'

Nothing was said for a moment.

'Working at a relationship.' He shook his head. 'I don't know.'

'I do,' she said, almost inaudibly.

Darac gave her a look.

'You and Christophe have never had to work at it, have you? Strongest couple I know.'

Frankie's eyes finally left Darac's, drawn over his shoulder to Jardin Albert. She couldn't see its celebrated carousel – a stand of trees was in the way – but she could hear its calliope piping away as it turned.

'Yes, I suppose there is some strength there. But just over two years ago now, we did have a problem.

Correction, *I* had a problem – Christophe was unaware of it at first. But then he noticed certain changes in me and that's when it became a problem for us both.'

Darac ran a hand through his hair.

'This was going on at the time you were putting in to leave my team?'

'Yes,' she said, as neutrally as she could manage.

'I wish I'd known about it. I wouldn't have kept going on at you to stay with me.'

Frankie turned her gaze on the promenade.

'I... didn't think I could confide in you at the time.'

'Of course you could have. But hey – it all worked out for you, so that's great.'

'Yes indeed.'

After a couple of beats, she smiled and turned back to him.

'The important question now is: where do you both go from here?'

'Where indeed?'

'Has Angeline mentioned the S-word?'

He looked at her, confused.

'Space,' she said. 'Needing it.'

'No, she hasn't but if she does, that's what it will mean – space and time apart. It won't be a cover, an easy way of walking out for good. If she wanted to do that, she'd say so.'

A round of applause drifted across the boulevard. Medusa's show was over. A few people were already stepping forward to have their photo taken with her.

Darac got to his feet.

'Better get over there.'

Frankie gave his hand a squeeze.

'I said it was resolvable and I'm sure it is. But if it doesn't work out that way, you *will* get over it.'

Darac thought he could see tears forming in the corners of her large, expressive eyes.

'I don't know what André sees in you.' He laid his hand on her cheek. 'Now for fuck's sake, let's go and do some police work for a few minutes.'

By the time Darac and Frankie had crossed the boulevard, the photo session beneath the marble-effect paint was over. Medusa was a slender, keen-eyed girl in her early twenties. Wearing an elaborate headdress was clearly a tough call in the heat. As she took it off, her blond razorcut was stiff with sweat. She shook a hand through it, then pulling her face into chimp-like grimaces and grins, stepped off the plinth and went into a series of stretches.

'A statue looks far more weird moving than standing, don't you think?' said Darac.

Frankie didn't reply at first; her eyes were fixed on the headdress.

'Even fake snakes are hideous.' She gave a little shudder. 'Which is why the act works so well, of course.'

'Indeed. We'll let her finish her stretches.'

Keeping her legs straight, the girl extended her arms above her head, clasped her hands together and then slowly lowered her torso until it lay flat as an ironing board against her legs.

Frankie gave a nonchalant shrug.

'I could do that if I wanted to.'

'Really?'

'Of course not. Lovely peplos, though, I must say.'

'If I knew what a peplos was, I might agree with you.'

'That cute little garment she's wearing.'

'So not her cute little bottom, then?'

'No,' Frankie said, with some feeling.

The stretch routine finished, the girl returned to the plinth and lifted off its top. Using this as a tray to support the headdress, she carefully set it down on the pavement.

Darac stepped towards her.

'*Chapeau.*'

The girl reached into the plinth, took out a litre bottle of water and drained about half of it before replying.

'Pity you didn't catch the act itself. Every euro helps.'

'How do you know we didn't catch it?'

'Because I see everything,' the girl said, encouragingly. 'There's not much else to do, you know. When you're just standing around.'

Darac took out his wallet and dropped a five-euro note into her tips bag.

'You didn't see quite everything. We were watching you from across the boulevard.'

'No one's perfect.' She reached into the plinth and took out a pair of rollerblades. 'Even a goddess.'

Frankie indicated the plinth.

'Not so much Medusa as Pandora.'

Once more, the girl shook a hand through her hair.

'You think my skates are evil?'

'Sorry – didn't think it through.' Frankie's self-deprecating smile was a disarming thing. 'I just meant it's not just a plinth, it's a box.'

'Ah.'

'And it's crammed full of stuff.'

'You're right, there.' The girl smiled, incising hairline cracks into her matte-white make-up. 'You notice the weight going uphill – put it that way.'

Darac was dumbfounded.

'You don't mean you skate from gig to gig carrying that thing, surely?'

'See the fluted pilasters on this side? They're actually webbing straps that pull out.'

'The box goes on your back?'

'Like a rucksack.' She reached for a skate. 'Wait one minute and you'll get a live demo.'

'We were hoping for more like ten minutes.'

Medusa stopped lacing up the skate, a wary look opening up a few secondary cracks around her eyes. Since one or two spectators were still hanging around, Darac shielded his ID as he showed it to her.

'And my colleague here is Captain Lejeune.'

'Jesus! A sting operation for five euros?' Her face fractured like a dropped plate. 'Yeah, well you're out of luck, *flic*. I've got a permit to perform and to collect tips here. Fucking hell!'

'Hey, hey, hey – we're not here in connection with your licence or anything.'

'What, then?'

'We've got no problem with you at all. We just want to pick your brains about something.'

Medusa held up a hand.

'Listen – I'm sorry, okay? But we do get that kind of hassle from time to time.' She stood. 'What do you want to know?'

Darac didn't reply for the moment. His eye was taken by a cyclist freewheeling up behind her. Riding a pannier-laden touring bike, the man was in outline a dead ringer for Roland Granot. But blue-and-white-striped pedal pushers were not his old friend's style.

'Uh… We're here because of what happened on Rue Verbier yesterday lunchtime. You were performing outside the Basilique?'

Medusa made a pistol of her hand and shot herself in the temple.

'The man who was killed – of course. Did I see it – is that what you want to know?'

'Uh-huh.'

'It – no; him – yes.'

The groaning whine of brake blocks heralded the arrival of the bike. The rider adjusted his long red pigtails as he dismounted.

'Got a problem, Astrid?'

'No, no. Start getting ready, Alex, I'll only be a minute or two.' She turned back to Darac and Frankie as the man parked his bike. 'Look, I probably should have come forward but…'

'It's alright, Astrid.'

Darac hadn't seen Frankie work in some time. Getting more than just a nostalgic kick out of it, he gave her the nod to continue.

'Astrid *what*, by the way?'

'Pireque.' She spelled the name as she bent forward and began fishing around in the box.

'Just tell us anything you remember about the man in the white suit.'

'Do you mind?' she said, finding her Gitanes. 'Gasping.'

'Go ahead.'

'Well, he ran across my pitch. Right in front of me.'

'Had you ever seen him before?'

'Several times.'

'On Rue Verbier?'

'I've been doing this for three months now. I've seen him most weekends.'

'I'd like to show you a photo.'

As Frankie reached into her bag, Darac glanced across at Astrid's would-be champion. Although he was stamping on a foot pump connected to a lump of flattened grey plastic, Alex the cyclist was as convincing an Obelix the Gaul as could be imagined.

'Just so we're clear, Astrid – is this the man?'

'It's him. How...' She frowned, as if she only half wanted to know the answer. '...did he die?'

'In a way, he died as a living statue. A paralytic drug killed him.'

Looking more than a little unnerved, Astrid took a long drag on her cigarette.

'Everyone's getting in on the act.'

'Apart from yesterday, did he always stand and watch your performance?'

'The first time I saw him, he did. Not since. Unless he watched from behind, of course. But people don't do that.'

'So recently, you've seen him only in passing?' Frankie's honeyed voice made it seem as if they were talking about a mutual friend. 'Was he ever with anyone?'

'Always by himself.'

'Thank you.'

Frankie gave Darac a look. A little eyebrow semaphore between them put him back in.

'Back to yesterday,' he said. 'After you saw the man, what happened then?'

'Well, I had quite a good crowd going. One of them was a guy with a beard. He peeled away eventually and the man in the suit ran straight into him. They nearly went down, the pair of them.'

'Anything stick in your mind about the man with the beard?'

Astrid gave a dry little laugh.

'Oh yes. If somebody watches your act for like, half an hour and then goes without giving you a cent, they stick in your mind, alright.'

'How long do people usually watch for?'

'Five or six minutes. Ten is a long time to watch somebody standing still. Even with the snake shtick.'

Frankie made a mental note to ask her about that later.

'So Beard was there for thirty whole minutes. Was it your

impression that he was waiting for the man in the white suit? Did he keep looking towards the Avenue, for example?'

Astrid took a deep drag on the cigarette.

'He did that, yes. A few times. But I don't know if he was waiting for the man in the suit, particularly. And when he came jogging up, he didn't shout, "Ah, here's Charlie!" or whatever.'

'Were you looking at them at the moment the guy peeled away and they collided?'

'Not the exact moment. This real looker had just arrived and I was giving him my death stare.'

A shadow fell over Darac.

'Come on, guys, you're eating into my time,' Obelix said, stowing his foot pump into one of the many panniers on his bike. Behind him, the flattened lump of plastic had turned into a bulbous lump of plastic. 'My menhir's pumped up. *I'm* pumped up – so will you move, please?'

Darac took out his wallet and handed him a ten-euro note.

'Five minutes?'

Obelix gave an unimpressed shrug but he took the note.

'Just a second. We're from the Police Judiciaire. Do you ever work Rue Verbier?'

'Only Astrid goes that far up Jean Médicin.'

'Is it alright if my colleague shows you a photo just in case?'

Another shrug.

Concerned she might laugh at the surreal nature of the situation, Frankie duly handed Obelix Florian's photo.

'No. Never seen him.'

'Our other friend, Frankie?'

Obelix ran his eye over Manou Esquebel.

'No. But in my act, I never look at the audience, anyway.'

'Pity.' Darac glanced at his watch. 'So five more minutes.'

'Five.' Obelix sloped off. 'And no more.'

'We were talking about the collision, Astrid. I know you didn't see the impact directly but who do you think was responsible for it?'

'Neither of them was looking where they were going. But the man with the beard's back was turned and the other guy was running so you'd blame him, I suppose.'

'Who came off worse – Suit or Beard?'

'Suit. He really yelped – that's what made me swivel my eyes back toward them. Beard was carrying a rucksack and I think it was *that* Suit ran into. There must have been... tent pegs in it or something.'

Darac shared a look with Frankie.

'Then what happened?'

'Suit hurried off down the street towards the market place. The guy with the rucksack walked off in the opposite direction. Towards the Avenue.'

Darac looked into Astrid's eyes.

'Would you recognise him again? The guy with the rucksack?'

'I remember every square millimetre of that cheap bastard's face, believe me.'

'We have a sketch artist at the Caserne Auvare. Think you could—?'

'No need, Captain… Darac, was it? I'm a Fine Arts graduate – I'll draw the guy for you.' Elegantly shaping her white marble hands, she struck a dramatic pose. 'This shit is just temporary.' She took another cheek-hollowing pull on the cigarette. 'I hope.'

'You do look fantastic,' Darac said, sounding lame. 'The drawing – could you come in to the Caserne to do it?'

'Not just at the moment, I can't. But later today – definitely.'

'We'll send a car.'

They took down her contact details.

A little to their left, Obelix was starting to look restless – odd preparation, Darac thought, for someone who was about to stand stock still for minutes on end.

'Finally – have you ever seen this other guy?'

Frankie handed over the photo of Manou. Astrid gave a little snort.

'Torso Boy – sexy but short. Yes, I've seen him. Here. A few times.'

'How many is a few?'

'Four, five maybe. Always pays. Not much, but something.'

Darac was coming to the conclusion that Astrid Pireque was one of the most useful eyewitnesses he'd ever come across.

'Alone?'

'No. That is, he doesn't arrive with anyone. But he's left with someone a couple of times. Different people, I mean.'

There was genuine appreciation in Frankie's smile.

'This is really helpful, Astrid. Did anything strike you about these encounters? Could you describe or perhaps even draw the people he went off with?'

'One was a horse-faced boy of about eighteen or so – I could draw him. The other was a girl about the same age, I suppose, but I didn't get a good look at her. A black girl. Tall. Big shades. Red Crocs.'

'You've got one minute!' Obelix called out, deftly kicking his menhir from one instep to the other.

Darac gave him a wave as he continued.

'A boy *and* a girl left with him? In what manner?'

'Just chatting.'

'Flirting?'

'A little. With the girl. Maybe even with the boy.' She picked up her water bottle. 'Why do you want to know this?'

'There was no reluctance on their part to going with him?'

'No.' She gulped down the rest of her water. 'Didn't look like it.'

Frankie gave her a look.

'Must be murder wearing the headdress in this heat.'

'Tell me about it.'

'Did Torso Boy ever have a bottle of water or anything with him?'

'I didn't see one but he had a bag. Could have been in there. Look, I better stow my stuff and get out of Alex's way.'

'If we have any further questions, may we ask them when you come in to the Caserne later?'

'Sure.' She picked up the headdress and carefully lowered it into the plinth. 'Don't suppose you need a second sketch artist at your place, do you?'

'Not that I know of.'

'Shame.' She began lacing up her rollerblades. 'Anything would be easier than this.'

'Astrid, uh…' Frankie risked peering at the snakes. 'How do you make them move?'

The girl looked astonished.

'Make them? I don't make them – they're real.'

On cue, the snakes writhed. One hand patrolling her skirt hem, the other going to her throat, Frankie emitted a sharp cry and took several backward steps.

'I'm kidding!' As proof, Astrid flicked one of the beasts in the eye. 'But I'm not going to reveal how I do it. You alright?'

Frankie took a deep breath.

'Of course.'

Still grinning, Astrid put her tips bag into the plinth and strapped it onto her back.

'Thank you,' Darac said. 'If everyone were as observant as you, our job would be so much easier.'

'You wait until you see how well I draw. Nice to meet you both.'

The girl took a few swaying strides and began carving her way down the boulevard.

'Quite a sight.' They finally left the pitch to Obelix. 'A classical goddess on blades.'

'And what a witness.'

'Absolutely.'

'Paul – the snakes. She obviously operates them remotely – but how?'

'Did you notice that ring on her left hand? '

'Which one?'

'The ruby. There was a pea-sized bump on the palmside of it. I think I saw her push her thumb against it.'

'A switch for a radio-controlled transmitter? Bluetooth?'

'Maybe. Where's Erica when you need her?'

Frankie gave him a look.

'I was only pretending to be scared, you know.'

Darac's habitual half-smile disappearing, he nodded with obviously faux sincerity.

'I know that.'

'I was!'

Laughter from behind suspended the debate. They turned to find Obelix juggling the menhir in a series of increasingly extravagant passes. And then, with a concluding flourish, he tossed it onto the end of his upturned nose and froze.

'*That's* why he doesn't see the audience,' Frankie said, shaking her head in disbelief. 'Impressive. In its way.'

'Let's just hope he doesn't get a slow puncture.'

Releasing a wave of kohl-black hair over her shoulders, Frankie threw back her head and laughed.

Darac gave her a look. 'Shame to break this up, don't you think?'

'Agnès's apartment?'

'Want to come?'

'Try and stop me.'

1.48 PM

This was the moment he'd been waiting for. God bless the TV!

Everything was in place. The introductions had been made. The interviews given. The experts had pontificated. The promotional circus had paraded along the stage route. From motorised bananas, boats and bottles, the crowds had been pelted with trinkets. Giant hand-shaped gloves appeared to be among the most prized.

Made of soft green foam rubber, spectators loved to wave them at the peloton. It was all part of the fun. The riders saw it differently. If you were pedalling in train at fifty kilometres per hour, a foam finger could rip your arm open like a shard of glass. It was all part of the pain.

But there would be no peloton today. Each rider had his own race to ride. The stage was going to be quite long and hilly for an opening time trial. A fifteen-kilometre knee-breaker up and down, out and back. A testing overture to the symphony that was to come. Tomorrow – that was when the piece would really begin. One hundred and eighty-two kilometres with all the riders going off together.

The first rider was in the start gate. Eyes focussed a few metres beyond the ramp. Long, lung-filling breaths. Thighs flexing to power the bike away. A human spring ready to uncoil.

My son has made all this happen, *he said to himself. My son who bought a TV and had it specially adapted so I could watch it lying flat on my back. After everything I've done to him.*

Five, four, three, two...

Thank you.

1.50 PM

Three separate rings having failed to bring anyone to Agnès's door, Darac slipped a couple of picks out of his tool roll.

'You don't have a key?' Frankie said. 'With all that skin-to-skin contact going on, I would have thought...'

He halted the conclusion with a look. But Frankie had more.

'And if Agnès *is* in and has put the security chain across?'

'I'll just get you to bite through it.'

The door opened cleanly.

'No post on the mat, look.'

Frankie took a tentative step inside.

'Agnès? You home?'

There was no sound from inside the apartment as they walked through a short lobby into the hallway.

'You take the bathroom and the bedrooms.' Darac indicated three closed doors. 'And yes, I know which is which.'

'So do I – it's alright,' Frankie said, tiring of the game.

Darac walked through into the lounge, a large L-shaped space flooded with light.

'The curtains are all open in here,' he called out.

'The bathroom's clear. You know, Agnès is going to go up the wall when she hears about this.'

'I wasn't planning on telling her. There's nothing in the lounge'

Darac craned his neck into the kitchen as he heard Frankie open the first of the bedroom doors.

'Because you've made me paranoid, I'm going to try the closets.'

'Okay. Kitchen looks normal.'

He stepped back into the lounge and walked through it into the dining room. Sitting on a sideboard was a collection of photos, a record of Agnès and Vincent's respective rises through the ranks. One, a twin of a shot in Agnès's office, showed a young Vincent standing in front of his locker at the Caserne, a senior officer presenting him with his certificate of promotion and dress uniform. Thirty-plus years on, a companion shot replicated the moment with Agnès centre stage. But pride of place was given to a shot of the two Dantier commissaires taken together. The look on both their faces was touching; apples of each other's eyes.

Darac heard a sound behind him. He turned. It was Frankie, her olive complexion an ashen mask.

'Her bedroom,' she said, all the silk stripped from her voice.

In the two seconds it took Darac to reach the doorway, a horror show of images flashed across his brain. He'd seen headless bodies, burned bodies, bullet-riddled, stabbed and strangled bodies. But with the exception of his mother, who had died when he was just twelve, Darac had never seen the dead body of anyone he was close to. But there wasn't time to steel himself. He rushed in.

There was no corpse on the bed, on the floor, anywhere. And then he saw it. A sheet of A4 paper was lying on the pillow. After almost fifteen years in the police, Darac's instinct was still to pick it up. He stopped himself in time. The message, formed in cut-out newsprint, read:

Our cries were not heard so neither will hers be heard. You have until 3pm on Sunday. The Sons and daughters of the Just Cause

The crime scene was a hive of activity, and that was the only thing about it that felt normal. In the bedroom, the senior forensic investigator, Raul Ormans peered at the message and shook his large, patrician head.

'I should have stayed on leave.'

Bonbon Busquet's foxy face was all pinch points and pain.

'It's tricky, R.O.?'

'Tricky?' The word emerged with all the subtlety of a sonic boom. 'Unless we get very lucky, this message is not going to tell us anything. Anything of significance, anyway.'

'But you've extracted DNA from stamps stuck to

envelopes... you've lifted clean fingerprints off paper... you've traced rare inks, esoteric newspaper fonts – all kinds of strange things.'

'Strange is easy. It's mundane that's difficult.' He pointed a thick forefinger at the newsprint. 'I'm pretty sure they cut this from *Nice-Matin*, but even if we prove that, what good would it do us? The paper's on every stand in the city. And beyond.' He transferred the page to a bag and sealed it with a conclusive pull on the zip. 'There's no envelope here, ergo no stamp. Further, the glue used to gum down the words, I think, is from a stick you could buy anywhere. So unless the people who did this drooled invisibly on the paper, there'll be no spit to extract DNA from. Prints? I can run more sophisticated tests for them in the lab but I'm not hopeful.'

'The consensus was that these fucking Sons and Daughters were more or less harmless,' Bonbon said. 'Possibly even kids.'

'I don't know anything about this group or even if they really exist...'

A voice rang out in the doorway.

'They're in there, monsieur.'

Jules Frènes, the public prosecutor, bustled into the room. In his all-in-one crime-scene overalls, he looked like a bad-tempered baby.

'Busquet. Ormans. Where's Darac?'

'Down in the parking garage, monsieur.'

Frènes grunted.

'The message?'

Ormans laid it out on the bed. Frènes peered at it, shaking his head.

'A "non-credible" threat – that's what they said it was. They were certain. Certain!' He straightened, wagging an accusing finger at the air around him. 'Commandant Lanvalle will have something to say about this, no doubt. And I will have something to say to him.'

A uniform craned his neck around the doorframe.

'Monsieur Frènes? The examining magistrate, Monsieur Reboux is here.'

'Ah.'

In the reverberant space of the garage, radios were crackling on and off, the synaptic firings of the mind of the investigation. One forensic team had been detailed to comb the area in metre squares while another had carried out a preliminary exam of Agnès's Citroën. A technician reported the findings to Darac as a low loader carried the car away for further tests. Preceded by a couple of official vehicles, the procession had the feel of a funeral cortège.

'There's nothing so far, Captain,' the technician said. 'But Commissaire Dantier could have been abducted anywhere.'

'We had to start somewhere.' Darac's face was tight as a fist. 'Her car was here so it looks as if she got home last night. And the note was on her bed.'

'Right, but it's unlikely she's still on the premises.'

Darac's face tightened still further.

'So you want to overlook that possibility, do you?'

The technician shook his head.

'No sir.'

'Good. Where's the dog handler got to?'

'He'll be here shortly. I have to go, Captain.'

'Get back to me if you learn anything.'

Darac glanced at his watch. It was now almost half an hour since he'd dispatched Granot and a six-strong team to Avenue Celestine, a quiet cul-de-sac on the slopes of Mont Boron. If Vincent Dantier was at home, he still wasn't answering his phone. Nor was he answering his mobile.

Flaco appeared, accompanied by a man whose short, greased-back hair and wide-eyed expressionless face gave him the look of an antique ventriloquist's dummy.

'Captain – this is La Marguerite's security chief, Monsieur Alphonse Potrain.'

'If anything has happened to the lady, Captain, I can assure you it didn't happen because my system or one of my team was—'

'Be quiet and listen.' Darac pointed to Lartigue. 'See that officer? The one drawing a sketch map of the garage?'

Potrain complied immediately as if his will was something out of his personal control.

'This officer…' He indicated Flaco. '…will escort you to him. You will then take him on a tour of your on-site CCTV setup. Immediately afterwards, you will give him unrestricted access to your control room. Understood?'

'How dare you talk to me in that manner?' Potrain's voice was an indignant bleat, his face an unreadable mask.

'I'm going to write to your superior... uh... I mean I'm going to...'

To stay his temper, Darac stood very still.

'Flaco?'

As she led the man away, Darac's mobile rang. His stomach tightened a little.

'Granot? Go ahead.'

'The bastards have got Vincent. Left the same note as yours but for "hers" read "his".'

'Shit.'

'I would've rung a couple of minutes ago but we were buttonholed by a neighbour, an old boy by the name of Eric Taglier. Interesting stuff. It seems he calls on Vincent most Friday evenings. The pair are in the habit of toddling down to the old port, having a couple of slow cognacs and then taking a taxi back. But when Taglier got to the house last night, there was no answer and, this is the interesting part, there was a long-wheelbase Mercedes panel van parked in Vincent's drive. White, unmarked. Taglier could think of no reason why it would be there. Especially as it seemed to be all quiet within and no one answered the door.

It was no more than a crumb of encouragement but Darac eyed it hungrily.

'This could be good, Granot. What time was that? Did he notice?'

'Precisely 8.56. Taglier – may Mary Mother of Jesus keep him – looked at his watch.'

'Fantastic. I don't suppose he also—'

'He didn't take in the registration number. But he said

he would have noticed if it had been a foreign plate, though.'

'Did he notice anything else about the van? Was it new, old, pristine, battered?'

'It was in good condition and no more than a couple of years old, he thought. One detail: the owner's manual was sitting on the passenger seat – as if the driver had had to refer to it.'

'Open or closed?'

'Open, pages down. Like a tent, he said. Obviously, the driver had been consulting it.'

'Suggests the vehicle was new to them. That could help us hugely.'

'Check recent sales, you mean? Not necessarily the case. You might also need the manual the first time you have to replace a light bulb or something. The guy might have owned it for a couple of years.'

'Yes, point taken. Anyone else up there likely to have seen the van? We need to fly as good a description as we can, as soon as possible.'

'Avenue Celestine is a cul-de-sac of just fifteen houses, right? I've split my guys into pairs and they're already talking to anyone who's at home. It won't take them long.'

'Good.' Darac pictured the sparse road layout on the wooded hill that was Mont Boron. 'What's the likely access and egress from Avenue Celestine? For a van, I mean.'

'It had to come off Boulevard Carnot. No one would pay any attention to a white van on a busy road like that but from Carnot to Vincent's place there are only two... no, three possible routes. Quiet residential roads. We need to widen the search on the ground.'

'Agreed, and let's hope someone noted the registration or got a good look at the driver. But we can't rely on that. I hate to say it, but I think we do need to go down the provenance route, even if the van *is* two years old. And we'd better add on another two for safety.'

'Check Mercedes long-wheelbase van sales for four whole years? In just over twenty-four hours?'

'This *is* the age of the phone. But you're right. It's clutching at straws.'

'Straws? It's a hell of a long shot, chief. Dealers, garages, private sales… And then there's the van-hire market.'

'Hire companies tend to plaster ads all over their vans, though.'

'It could have been re-sprayed. We need to include rentals.'

'And we should check out garaging, lock-ups and so on.'

'Ai, ai, ai.'

'We've traced other things with less to go on, you know.'

'It's the deadline that worries me. Just over twenty-four hours? It's nothing.'

'So let's make the most of the time we have. I think we should call just local outlets to begin with. If we don't come up with anything, we'll gradually cast the net wider.' He consulted the duty rosta in his head. 'Flaco's co-ordinated phone searches before. I'll brief her in a minute. She and Perand can head-up the teams.'

'Perand? Are you sure?'

'She'll keep him on track, don't worry. Look, I've got a slog squad going door to door here. I'll update them about the van, circulate the description such as it is and get more people sent over to you. They can doorstep lower down the hill.'

'Fine.'

'Then I'll ring Charvet and ask him to start drafting in people for the phone-athon.'

'I'll get back to you the minute I have anything more.'

Darac sent out Granot's update as an open radio message and then made two calls. As he rang off, the dog handler arrived.

'Did you copy that message, Roulet?'

'I did, Captain. Sounds like a good break with the van. Still want us to go ahead?'

'Absolutely. Have you done the scent control yet?'

'Yes, from a pair of Madame's shoes.'

'Right. As you can see, some of the car boots are open. They belong to the owners we've been able to find. But that leaves quite a few still locked. I can't unlock the electronic ones. Erica Lamarthe *could* do that and she is on her way. But as speed was of the essence I sent for you as well. It's a belt and braces approach, and probably a wild goose chase, especially now we know about the van, but I don't care. Alright?'

'I know how important it is to find the boss, Captain. Just a word of caution. Félix can detect the scent of a live or dead body through the metal of a closed car boot. And he can detect whether there has been a body in such a place or even an object that belongs to the person we're looking for. But he can't if that body or object is or was sealed away in some container. That goes for drugs, explosives – anything.'

Darac ran a hand through his hair.

'So the search can be conclusive but only one way.'

'Exactly. If we find something, we find it. If we don't, you will still have to open the remaining boots.'

'Understood. The boss's own car has just gone to the lab for further tests, by the way.'

'I know it has. It was all I could do to stop Félix from jumping on board.'

'Félix couldn't detect the boss's most recent trail down here, could he?'

'Yes but *we* wouldn't know if it was the most recent or not. She will have walked up and down these footways on to the street and into the building every night and morning for years.'

'I'm not thinking – of course. Okay, go for it. I'll be down here for a little while longer.'

'It should only take a minute or two.'

Darac looked on dry-throated as Roulet let Félix off the leash. He felt an odd kinship with the animal as it began following its nose through a criss-cross of true and false trails.

'I'm back, Captain. Potrain's co-operating fully.'

The words were Flaco's, returned from her escort duty.

'That's good. Now I've got a much bigger job for you. It's going to be arduous and it might give us nothing in the end.'

Flaco's eyes flared. Whatever it was, she was already relishing the challenge.

Darac spent some minutes outlining the phone-trawl plan and how best to manage it.

'It's just the same as you've handled before but on a far greater scale. Alright?'

'Yes, Captain.'

'Clear on everything?'

'I am.'

'So get Perand and decamp to the Caserne. The duty officer is already starting to draft in the help you're going to need. If we find out any more about the van, I'll let you know immediately. One more thing.' He held her with a look. 'I know *you* will be exhaustive and systematic. Make sure Perand keeps to the script as well, yes?'

'I'll make very sure, Captain.'

A uniform arrived as she took her leave. The young man had the apologetic look of someone who knew he was on a fool's errand. Needing time to think, Darac didn't welcome the interruption.

'Sir, the building supervisor is waiting outside and wants to know when the garage will be back to normal. Some of the residents are getting annoyed.'

'Nallet, isn't it?'

'Yes sir.'

'Nallet, tell the building supervisor to go fuck himself

with my compliments. When the cordon tape comes down, he can have his fucking garage, and not before.'

'Yes uh… it's a woman, sir. A Mademoiselle Fort.'

'Well tell her to go fuck *her*self, then.'

The boy saluted and left at the double. Lartigue and Potrain followed him up the ramp, en route to the camera stationed at the entrance.

'A white, long-wheelbase, unmarked Mercedes van, chief?' Lartigue called. 'There are a lot of those around.'

'We only need to find one of them. How are the cameras looking?'

'One more to check at the top here and then I'm going to the control room.'

'Coverage?'

'If all the cameras are working, it should be wall to wall.'

'They are, I keep telling you,' Potrain said. 'Everything here is state of the art.'

'Keep me posted.'

Lartigue gave an affirming wave as Darac's mobile rang.

'Granot?'

'Most of the neighbours were at home last night. It seems just two were out. The family who live in the first are away on holiday; the couple who live in the other are out somewhere. I've left a note asking them to contact us when they return and I'm going to post a guy, I think, just to make sure. So far, including Taglier, only four people noticed the van. They thought it a bit unusual but that's all. No one saw it arrive or leave but putting the accounts together of when they saw it wasn't there, it arrived no earlier than 8.30 – just after Agnès must have dropped Vincent off – and left no later than 9.30.'

'Only a sixty-minute window? That's useful.'

The sound of scuttling paws signalled Félix's return. Darac's pulse speeded up.

'Listen, I'll send that out in a second, Granot. Got to go now.'

'We found nothing,' Roulet said, managing a smile.

Darac exhaled deeply.

'Thank God, eh, Captain?'

Darac unpeeled his gloves and stroked Félix's head as he padded to and fro at his feet.

'What a crying shame this all is,' Roulet said. 'The boss set to retire and everything.'

'Yes.' This wasn't the time. 'Thanks, Roulet.' They shook hands. Darac sent out Granot's update and then repaired to a quiet corner. Energy flowing through him like an electric current, he leaned back against a roof pillar and started to think.

What was really happening here? Motives, targets, timing, a number of questions needed working through. He began by dismissing the idea that the whole thing might be a government exercise. Staging fake kidnappings? Not even the current administration would go that far. But if the kidnappings were real, he was more than ever convinced that the Sons and Daughters of the Just Cause were not. Not as a terrorist group, at least. So where was the truth? Paths led off in all directions but there wasn't time to explore them all. He needed to be decisive. And he was. Only one interpretation made sense to him.

'While Rome burns, you hide? I must say I'd expected—'

It was one sneer too many. And it was the wrong time. Seven years of frustration with Frènes surfacing all at once, Darac grabbed the man's overalls at the collar and shaped to slap his face. A familiar voice cried out.

'Darac – don't!'

It wasn't Erica's words that halted him. It was the horrified look on her face.

Hit someone. Make love. Play the guitar.

Darac pushed Frènes away, sending him into a spluttering spin.

'He chose the wrong moment. I can't be dealing…'

Erica shook her head.

'I don't want to hear it.'

Clutching his forehead, Frènes sank to his knees and vomited. Erica went over to him, laying a hand on his heaving back.

'It's… the heat,' he gasped between spasms. After a further outpouring, he righted himself and wiped his mouth with a handkerchief. Silk soiled in the line of duty. 'Thank you, Mademoiselle. That was kind.' Breathing heavily, his face had the appearance of wet clay. Holding the handkerchief to his mouth, he turned to Darac. 'After this is all over, you will be required to attend a disciplinary hearing. You face suspension and the likelihood…' He paused to catch his breath. 'The likelihood that criminal charges will be brought against you.' At last, it seemed Frènes had a winning hand. And Darac himself had dealt him the cards. He smiled. 'I have a witness.'

'Fine,' Darac said. 'What's done is done. Let's pick it up. Erica, I'm not sure we really need you on this but now just so we cover every angle…' She was still not looking at him. 'Erica?' She turned to him but it was as if there was a shutter in front of her eyes. 'There are about twenty cars in this garage with locked boots. We've had a sniffer dog go over them from the outside but just in case there's anything, can you get into them?'

'We have a warrant?' she said to Frènes.

'Duly issued.'

'Okay.'

She picked up her case and walked briskly towards the first vehicle. Frènes, recovering fast, turned to Darac.

'I came looking for you because I wanted to formulate our response.'

'To?'

'To the DCRI and to the Tour de France authorities, of course. When this threat business was being discussed in Monaco, neither I nor Examining Magistrate Reboux was consulted. We were not even informed about it until it was concluded. Did we object? Yes. Did we complain? No. And now look what's happened.'

Darac recognised the progression. In a few short sentences, Frènes had gone from righteous indignation through pain nobly borne to triumphalism – the turgid trajectory of a stunted spirit.

'Our first priority is to get on with the search, monsieur. And why should we make any response to them, anyway?'

A car alarm sounded a single stentorian note, a full stop to Darac's point. Silencing it, Erica opened and then closed the boot and moved on to the next vehicle.

'Why?' Frènes seemed genuinely astonished. 'Because the terrorist group they so loftily pooh-poohed have struck. And they will strike again. Possibly at the Tour peloton, tomorrow. The race must be stopped, clearly.'

'Think.' Darac looked Frènes hard in the eyes. 'The Sons and Daughters are not a terrorist group. There's no intelligence whatever to support that conclusion.'

Another stentorian full stop.

'Then who do you think has kidnapped Commissaire Dantier?'

'Why would a terrorist organisation threatening the Tour want to kidnap Agnès? She isn't the mayor. Or the Tour chief. Or even the most senior police officer in the city. And think of the timing. Using a cut-out note of all things, the so-called SAD issued the threat on Friday afternoon. In the manner requested, the authorities responded saying they were seriously considering their demands and asked them to get in contact. They failed to do so. Instead, only a matter of hours later, SAD leave notes saying "Our cries have not been heard." For one thing, there had scarcely been time to hear them, had there?'

'Notes? Plural?'

'Yes. Vincent Dantier has also been kidnapped.'

Frènes brightened.

'The current *and* a previous commissaire. That constitutes high profile, surely?'

Darac ran a hand through his hair.

'Their snatching Vincent Dantier as well as Agnès convinces me more than ever the notes are a smokescreen. Not in the way originally envisaged but a smokescreen, nevertheless. Kidnapping the commissaires *is* the crime. The root of it is personal, not political.'

'Personal.' Frènes made an unconvinced sound in his throat. 'Why?'

'The most likely thing is that someone they put away, or perhaps an associate of that person, is exacting revenge by taking *them* away. Nothing else makes sense.'

Another car alarm. Frènes pointed a stubby finger at Darac.

'If what you say is true – that a released convict or a relative is out to settle a score – why have they gone to the trouble of erecting this whole terrorist charade? Why haven't they just abducted the Dantiers and had done with it?'

'To send us off in entirely the wrong direction, thereby wasting precious time.'

Frènes assumed the look of a conjurer pleased with a deft sleight of hand.

'But no one believed the threat from the outset.'

'That's true, and I can't explain why they didn't put forward a more convincing case. Perhaps they're imbeciles. We've both come across our fair share of them over the years.'

Frènes nodded, conceding at least the possibility.

'But I still feel that Lanvalle at the DCRI…'

'Look, you go telling him and the others to call off the race and you will be laughed at and vilified in equal measure. They *know* SAD is not a terrorist group.'

'Concerned for my well-being all of a sudden? I wonder why?'

'My only concern is the search for Agnès.' He hadn't intended the obvious implication. 'And her father. I think we in the Brigade Criminelle are best placed to conduct it. If you make formal advances to the DCRI, they may be obliged to deploy people here, perhaps even take charge of the investigation. That would be intolerable.'

A vein ran like twisted blue string in Frènes's temple. It began to throb visibly.

'Darac the irreverent. Darac the maverick. Darac the friend of the rank and file. You're just as hungry for power as anyone else, aren't you? You don't want the DCRI involved because *you* want to be the man in charge.'

Darac looked Frènes in the eyes.

'They'll laugh at you.'

A stand-off. Frènes's mobile rang, breaking it.

'Commandant Lanvalle?' He turned away from Darac. 'Yes sir, the situation is very difficult. Very difficult indeed.' He listened. 'Theory?' He gave Darac an anxious look. 'Uh…'

'They'll laugh,' he said.

'Uh, we think one possible motive is revenge against the Dantiers.' He listened, brightening by the second. 'Personal. Yes, absolutely. I think we can discount the political argument. Totally.'

Another alarm made a truncated clarion call across the garage. Darac left Frènes to it and walked quickly across to Erica. As he caught up with her, she moved off to the next vehicle.

He indicated the torch-like device she was using.

'Build that yourself?'

'The trick is to point the transmitter beam down through the roof.' The car's locks opened, triggering an alarm. The press of a second button killed it. 'Otherwise several might open at once and there would be a real cacophony down here.'

Darac opened the boot. A holdall containing tennis kit was its only contents.

'Look, upsetting you wasn't on my to-do list today. I'm sure you're upset enough with the kidnapping.'

'It's horrible.'

'But it matters to me that we get on well and so I want to say I'm sorry for what happened just now.'

'It's fine.' Still avoiding eye contact, she moved on to the next vehicle, an Alfa Romeo.

'It clearly isn't. But I hope it will be.' He glanced across at Frènes. The man was finishing his call. 'I need to get out there.'

She pointed the torch once more.

'I've fitted the live GPS into Manou Esquebel's phone, by the way. I'm on with the tracking to map software, now.' The Alfa's locks opened. 'Just needs another hour or two.'

Manou Esquebel. The Florian case now seemed a world away.

'Very well done, Erica. That's quick work.'

'Yes. It is.'

'I'm going to ask Frankie if she'd like to lead the tail group on the ground. Providing it's not all hands on deck with the kidnapping, we'll go for it tomorrow.'

'Alright.'

There was nothing of interest in the Alfa's boot.

Erica finally turned to face Darac. When she spoke, her words had an unfamiliar directness.

'I always thought you were strong *and* sensitive.'

'Erica…'

'You know what? I've heard a couple of women at the Caserne say they're turned on by your hot temper. It suggests exciting possibilities to them. I don't know whether it suggests that or not. But I do know *I* don't like it.'

Darac didn't care a great deal for it himself.

'We've got work to do, Erica. Let's get on with it.'

Another alarm sounded as he walked away. He flipped his mobile.

'Granot? Keep everything going up there but I want you to abandon your post and return to the Caserne.' He outlined his revenge theory. 'I'll join you there later but in the meantime, start pulling up all cases that the boss and Vincent Dantier worked on together. Cases that resulted in long convictions, especially. There's not *that* much of an overlap so it shouldn't take for ever.'

'This feels right, chief. Terrorists? It's nothing to do with that. I can think of…'

Darac continued listening as he hurried towards the cordon tape. Sharing a concerned look with pathology lab technician Patricia Lebrun, he scribbled his signature on her sign-out sheet and ducked into the street.

'Sorry, Granot – what was that?'

'I said, Vincent once killed a guy.'

'Did he?' Darac cast a eye over the small crowd that had started to gather. 'I didn't know that.'

'Name of Maurice… Brosse. Mid 1970s – not long before he retired. And Agnès was definitely on the force then. It was a bank robbery. Vincent saved a teller's life by shooting Brosse but I guess the villain's family might not have seen it that way. Why they're taking revenge now after all these years might be a good question, mind you.'

'Absolutely, but we must follow up anything like that. Commandeer anyone sensible to help you. I'll get there as soon as I can.'

Ending the call, Darac spotted Frankie emerging from La Marguerite's sister building across the street. She had a man on her arm – a halting, elderly figure with a slightly stoned expression. She called Darac over.

'This is Monsieur Georges Dalot. He lives on the fourth floor of this building. His is just about the only apartment that commands a view down the ramp of La Marguerite's parking garage.' She turned to the old man. 'Tell Captain Darac what you told me, Monsieur.'

As if it would give his account greater credibility, Dalot relinquished Frankie's arm.

'Excuse my woozy ways, Captain. It's the tablets. Side

effects are as bad as the condition I take them for, practically.'

This looked as if it was going to take some time. Time Darac didn't have. He gave Frankie a questioning look. She nodded, implying the wait was going to be worth it.

'It's quite alright. Go ahead.'

'A couple of days ago, I was looking out of my window when I saw a fellow park his van at the top of the ramp, there – parked it this side of the barrier. It was a white van. Quite big. I've already told your colleague I couldn't tell the make. Now from any other vantage point, no one would have seen what happened next because the van would have been in the way, but from mine, you could.'

'Excellent.'

Dalot took a moment to mop his forehead.

'Anyway, I thought nothing of it when the driver got a stepladder out of the van and set it up under that closed-circuit camera, there.'

Dalot smiled, indicating a twist was coming.

'Interesting. Go on, monsieur.'

'I assumed he was from some firm. Repair man. Anyway, he goes up the ladder, just seemed to stand there looking out for a second, came down straight away, got in the van and drove off. Now explain that.'

'When was this?'

'Thursday. Be about five past eight in the evening.' Dalot raised a cautionary finger. 'Now I don't live at that window like some nosey old woman. Sorry, my dear…'

Frankie humoured the old man with a smile.

'…But I was going out and as you can see, I'm not

so good on my legs these days so I'd called a taxi. I was looking out for it. That's how I know what the time was.'

'By any chance…'

'Can I describe the driver, Captain? You see, I'm not stupid. Uh… no, I can't. But he was wearing dark-blue overalls. He was young-ish, I suppose, judging by the way he skipped up and down the ladder. Medium height. Medium build. Clean-shaven, I think.'

'Go on, you're doing well.'

'But that's it. I couldn't tell you what colour hair he had or anything.' He wiped his forehead again. 'He was wearing a cap. Blue. Or black, maybe. The peak was down quite low over his eyes.' He leaned forward slightly. 'What's gone on here, anyway? A murder or something?'

'A white man, was it, the driver?'

'Ah, you're not sure yet – I get you.' He straightened. 'The driver? I think he was white. Couldn't say for sure, though. Some of your Beurs are very light-skinned for example, aren't they?'

'Can you remember anything else about him at all?'

'Sorry. In all conscience, I couldn't recognise him in a line-up.'

'Any writing or designs on the overalls? Or on the cap?'

'Not that I could see.'

'Was he wearing gloves?'

'Now that you mention it, he was. I couldn't see them to start with but when he was on top of the ladder, he took them off. Then after a moment or two, he put them on again. Then he went, as I said.'

'What did he do in the gap between taking off his gloves and putting them on again?'

Dalot shook his head a fraction, as if a greater effort might collapse his scrawny neck.

'He had his back to me. I couldn't see.'

'The van, now. Was it your impression that the man in the overalls was used to driving it?'

Dalot was delighted by the question.

'Funny you should ask that. I don't know if he wasn't used to it or not but he did have a problem reversing it out. Stalled it twice.'

'Uh-huh. One final point…'

'I haven't seen either the man or the van since. That what you want to know?'

Darac smiled, extending his hand. Dalot's handshake was surprisingly firm.

'You've been a great help, monsieur.'

'Always glad to help the police.'

'Can you make your own way back to the apartment?'

'Of course I can.' Leaning precariously in to Darac, the old man essayed a wink. His eyelid stuck halfway. 'I'd rather she came with me, though. Like Elizabeth Taylor in her prime, isn't she, eh? A beautiful, proper woman. Not like these stick insects. If you take my meaning.'

'I take it. But I need her to come with me.' He turned to her. 'That's if you're finished in there, Elizabeth?'

'Yes I am, Richard.'

'We may need you again, monsieur.'

'That's alright. The young lady has my details.'

Conveying a sense that it had been the most exciting afternoon he'd experienced in years, the old man turned and tottered back into the building.

'Good find, Frankie.'

They turned and headed back to La Marguerite.

'What did you make of what he saw? The man in the overalls didn't seem to have had sufficient time to disable the CCTV or anything. He didn't even touch it, according to my admirer.'

'The business with the gloves is puzzling as well. But I'm hoping all will be revealed when we look at the footage from the camera. I'm going off to the control room in a minute.'

'Good luck. We never get *quite* what we need from CCTV, do we?'

'There's bound to be a first time. Listen, Frankie – the Manou Esquebel tail operation. Remember that?'

'Just about.'

'Anyway, Erica's on schedule with her...' He searched for the term. '...phone GPS tracking thing...'

'Excellent.'

'So it's set for tomorrow, provisionally. I'd love you to lead it. Will you?'

Darac tended to stare at the floor when he was thinking; Frankie favoured thin air.

'I'd like to – providing I'm not needed on this.'

'We'll have to see how things pan out. But if you could do it, you'd have two Foch guys in cars just to begin the tail.

How many do you think you'd need at the business end?'

'Four more. Four plus Erica.'

'Can you take a couple of your own people off what they're doing?'

'I hope so. But there'll be time to decide that later.'

Darac had another proposal to make. He outlined the brief he'd given Granot.

'Martinet's back at the Caserne,' she said. 'Why not ask him to help?'

'At times, we've all missed things ploughing through lists, haven't we? Martinet misses more than anyone. You wouldn't do that.'

She pressed her lips together, another aid to thought.

'I'm on my way. Keep me posted.'

'And vice versa.'

As Frankie left for the Caserne, Darac noticed the crowd had expanded a little. He turned his back on them as he sent out an updating radio shout, then called over the callow Officer Nallet. The boy's shaved head was beaded with sweat.

'I'd stand under one of the palms if I were you. You'll get sunstroke.'

'I'll be fine, sir, thanks.'

'Okay.' He indicated the crowd. 'It'll probably grow. Keep them back. If they get in the way, disperse them. Can you do that?'

'Yes, I can.'

Darac gave the boy a parting pat.

'By the way, sir,' Nallet called out, 'I did tell

Mademoiselle Fort to go fuck herself. Not in those exact words, though.'

'Good call.'

Potrain's much-vaunted control centre was in the basement of the building: two air-conditioned rooms full of high-tech gear. Darac had to admit the place looked impressive. But looks could be deceiving.

Potrain waved an arm across it.

'It's as I told you, Captain. This is a state-of-the-art surveillance system. Extensive in here.' Another arm wave. 'Discreet out there.'

Darac caught Lartou's eye, a look inviting *his* take on the set-up. He gave it a guarded thumbs-up.

'Okay.' Darac ran a hand through his hair. 'You all heard my account of what Monsieur Dalot witnessed from across the street?'

They had.

'I take it the man in the white panel van isn't part of your maintenance staff, Monsieur Potrain?'

'You take it correctly.'

Lartou was sitting at a multi-screen console next to one of Potrain's employees, a serious-looking individual whose name badge identified him as 'Alain Drut, Senior Security Officer' – the man who had been on duty overnight. Darac turned to him.

'You were on duty last night?'

'Yes, Captain. From 10 pm. I've already made a statement but, in short, I didn't see anything untoward either on foot patrol or on screen.'

'Have you seen any of the footage yet, Lartou?'

'Just about to. When do you think the boss arrived home last night? Every frame is time-tagged so we can be precise about it.'

'Time-tagged accurately?'

'Really!' Potrain's poker face set new standards for the genre. 'Within a tenth of a second accurate enough for you?'

Darac ignored him.

'Béatrice's record shows Agnès signed out at 11.47. Add two minutes for the walk to her car – that means driving straight here, she couldn't have been back before 11.55. To be on the safe side, start running the footage a couple of minutes before.'

'From the camera at the top of the ramp? The one the man in the van looked at?'

'That's the one.'

'What else?' Potrain said. 'Talk about obvious.'

Darac gave him a look.

'We don't need you any further, monsieur.'

Potrain stood his ground for the moment.

Darac eyeballed him.

'But here's one final thing. Don't breathe a word about what's happened here today until the story is released officially. If you do, you will be in serious trouble.'

Potrain walked briskly away but he paused at the door.

'Run the playback at eight-times speed, Drut, or you'll be here all afternoon.'

'Run it at normal speed, Alain,' Lartigue said.

Potrain threw up his hands.

'Six properties, we manage. Six. And we've never had a single…'

Darac fixed him with a look.

'Goodbye.'

'If they sequester any of the discs, make sure you get a receipt, Drut.'

'Yes, monsieur…'

The door closed behind Potrain.

'…Tosser.'

The review finally began. Like a family engrossed in a TV programme, the trio kept their eyes on the screen as they talked.

'Don't envy you working for Potrain.' Lartigue gave a little snort. 'What's wrong with his face? Stroke?'

'Botox. He thinks the injections make him look younger. He looks like a living corpse, if you ask me.'

'At what time did you look around the garage before this?' Darac said. 'On foot, I mean.'

'Eleven-thirty on the dot. And then one-thirty was the next time. Regular as clockwork. I take pride in what I do, Captain. I never bunk off, never sleep, read, watch TV or drink on the job. I want you to know that.'

Darac had never come across a security guard who *did* admit to doing these things. But most of them had, at one time or another.

'And you saw nothing strange? Nothing at all?'

'No. I had a spin round all the parked cars, as well. Sometimes, a resident who knows they're not going to be needing it will lend their barrier key to a friend and they use their space. They're not supposed to do that and we tick them off about it. But not last night – every vehicle in there was the authorised one. I'd swear to it.'

'That's good work. But of course, you can't be everywhere all the time, can you?'

'No. This is what we keep telling them. We need more staff. But what can you do?'

'On your way to and from the garage, you didn't see this white van Monsieur Dalot saw parked in the street?'

'That was the first thing Officer Lartigue asked me when you radioed in. No, I didn't. And I always look up and down. Especially since we've had the kids.'

'Kids?'

Their eyes were still glued on the screen.

'Shining those laser beam things. Into drivers' eyes. Little arseholes. But we haven't seen them for a day or two.'

'Ah.'

They didn't have to wait long for a familiar grey Citroën to appear at the top of the ramp, the barrier closing behind it.

'Here's Madame's car arriving. But of course you know that.' Drut looked overcome suddenly. 'It's destroyed me, this has. Beautiful person. Always had a word. Always…'

'Yes.' Darac nodded. It wasn't the time to give in to his feelings. 'Let's keep watching. Closely.'

Lartigue noted down the time from the monitor as the Citroën descended the ramp and turned at the bottom. Almost immediately, the image blipped and lost focus. When it returned, the picture lacked sharpness.

Lartigue's brow lowered.

'Is that the monitor or the camera?'

Drut squinted at the image through his sleep-deprived eyes.

'Must be the camera. But it doesn't do that normally. The kit here is pretty good, I will say that for them. The van driver must have doctored it.'

After a couple of minutes, the image blipped and returned to its original sharpness. They waited another ten minutes for Agnès to appear on foot. She didn't.

Darac turned to Drut.

'Which camera covers her parking space itself?'

'Camera Two. This is Camera One we're looking at.'

'Go to Two and rewind fifteen minutes.'

Drut did as he was asked. The footage showed the Citroën turn into shot and stop. Darac's heart grew heavy as he watched Agnès get out of the car, quite unaware of what awaited her. She stretched, took a couple of bags from the rear seat and set off along the side wall towards the footway. As she disappeared around the corner, Darac asked for the sequence to be replayed.

'Now Camera One again.'

They watched the whole thing again – from Agnès's arrival in the Citroën to her failure to appear around the corner at the bottom of the footway.

'Note down the exact times of those blips in the image, Lartou. Because it was in that slot that they grabbed her.'

'What?' Drut said. 'But there's nobody there.'

Lartou put a hand to his chin.

'You're thinking the van driver did what, chief – put some sort of jammer on the camera that made it lose five minutes? No, that doesn't work, the time tagging displayed is continuous.' He snapped his fingers. 'A device that made the camera shoot the same five-minute sequence twice? No – same problem.'

Darac sat forward in his chair.

'To defeat the time tag, they needed something really sophisticated or really simple. I think they went for the latter.' He stared at the floor. 'How's this? On Thursday evening, van boy draws up and takes a photograph from the exact point of view of Camera One. That's why he was so quick, why he didn't appear to touch the CCTV camera, and why he took his gloves off and put them back on again in the way he did.'

'Ah yes,' Lartigue nodded. 'You can't operate most modern cameras with gloves on. The buttons are far too fiddly.'

'Right. Then last night, they somehow interposed the photo he took in front of the CCTV camera's lens. That's the blip in the image we're seeing. The autofocus then tried to do its job but the photo must have been a little too close and that's why it isn't properly sharp.' He pointed at the screen. 'Also, the framing is a little different, look. But it worked well enough for their purposes.'

Drut nodded.

'So unseen and unrecorded, he or they apprehend Madame while the camera is broadcasting the image of the photo.'

'And then when they've got her safely in the van, someone removed the photo and off they went.'

'It could have been worked like that, monsieur. Without question.'

'Stop the footage there, would you?' Darac unclipped the radio from his belt. 'Let's take a closer look at the camera itself. I'll call R.O. and Erica.'

'I'll get a stepladder, monsieur. And... I'm sorry I didn't see those blips and things but I was patrolling at the top of the building at that time.'

'Not your fault. Even if you had been sitting here in front of the monitors, it's probable you wouldn't have noticed. No one would.'

'Thank you, Captain.'

Erica and her boss Raul Ormans were already in position by the time they arrived.

'The abduction — it happened just here?' Patricia Lebrun said as Darac signed her sheet.

'Looks that way.'

'I can't get over it. To happen to her of all people.'

'I know, Patricia.'

Armed with a print kit and other tools, the four-square figure of Ormans climbed the stepladder while Darac steadied it.

'What are you seeing, R.O.?'

'Give me a chance... Alright, there are scratches in the metal. Linear. Grooves, really. They're more or less parallel and they appear on the upper... and lower sides of the camera body.' He took out a magnifying glass and torch. 'There's a slight build-up of paint flecks in the grooves at either end.' He looked down at Darac. 'It's clear that something tight-fitting and metal, let's call it a frame, has been pushed on to the camera from the front and then dragged back again to remove it. Fits with your theory. It was a frame for holding the photo, wasn't it?'

'I'm sure it was.'

'Gloves or no gloves, I'm looking for prints,' Ormans said. 'But if there's anything to help us further with this camera, I would be surprised.'

Darac glanced up the ramp towards the street. As he'd feared, the crowd of onlookers had grown exponentially. Young Nallet had at least judged that the time had come to disperse them. But he appeared to be having little success.

'Where's Seve Sevran?' Darac said to Lartigue. 'He'd shift that lot in ten seconds flat. And keep everybody else in order. In four different languages.'

Lartigue looked a little sheepish, suddenly.

'Forgot to mention it with all this. Seems he's been suspended. Came through while you were interviewing the Medusa girl.'

'Seve suspended? Why?'

'With immediate effect. Serious, by the sound of it. I don't know what for though.'

'He's been arrested, not just suspended, I heard,' Patricia Lebrun broke in. 'How his wife will cope with it, I don't know. Poor woman.'

Scowling with exasperation, Darac ran a hand through his hair.

'Well there's no time to get into that now.' He turned to Erica. 'Frankie is up for the Manou tail, by the way. You can fill her in on the technicalities later.'

'I will.' She seemed a little more engaged with him than before. 'Good work on the camera stuff.'

'Thank you.'

Ormans descended the ladder.

'I've got prints here. Probably not the van driver's. I'll run them anyway, of course.'

Darac's mobile vibrated in his pocket. A text. He looked at it.

This is the hardest thing I have ever had to do. I won't be home when you return tonight. In fact, I have decided not to...

That was as far as he got. His hand dropping to his side, he stood like a stunned animal. It was over. Over without discussion. But surely... No, he couldn't allow himself to think about it. There was no time for anything now but action. Agnès's life depended upon it.

Erica's face was a mask of concern. Unconsciously, she put her hand on Darac's forearm.

'What's the matter?'

Ormans looked him in the eye.

'That was a text? Not about Agnès, surely?'

'No. It was nothing to do with the case.' Darac flipped his mobile. 'It's fine. Let's go and check out the footage from the building.'

The held-down organ note in Darac's head grew louder with every step as they hurried back onto the street.

After four years she ends it by text? No. Not good enough. Fuck you, Angeline.

Their radios clicked on.

'Denfert. Third floor completed. Going to the fourth. Over.'

'Uh… Lartou?' Darac's face was hard as a shield.

'Yes, chief?'

'Well done on sorting out the radios for us non-uniforms.' His words emerged as if on autopilot. 'They work much better than mobiles at a crime scene like this.'

'Yes,' Lartigue said, sharing a concerned look with the others. 'And uh… secure too, on our own encoded frequency.'

'Indeed.'

Erica caught Lartigue's eye.

'What's wrong with him?' she mouthed, silently.

They took the shallow steps that led to the building's revolving front door. As it came around, Erica slipped into Darac's quadrant.

'Sorry, Darac, but what's happened? Has someone… died?'

'No. No one is dead. It's okay. Really.'

'If you say so.'

'I do.'

They swept into the lobby. Darac turned as Ormans and Lartigue emerged after them.

'Whoever put that note on Agnès's bed may have got careless. Let's get to it.'

4.05 PM

A team of twenty clerical assistants and other officers were helping Perand and Flaco trace Mercedes van sales and hirings. Between them, they were creating an impressive list.

Perand struck a line through a directory entry and picked up the phone in one continuous action.

'Like working in a call centre, this.'

'Can you think of a better… Oh, good afternoon, this is Officer Yvonne Flaco of the Brigade Criminelle in Nice. We're interested in tracing anyone who has bought…'

Across the other side of the squad room, Frankie and Bonbon were helping Granot trawl through cases in which the Dantiers had played a significant part.

'Here's another candidate.' Frankie added the sheet to her stack. 'Found guilty of two murders. Stabbed his wife and her lover. He got twenty years but died in prison after twelve. That was 1992. Kidney failure and other complications. Maintaining his innocence to the end, he accused Vincent of fitting him up.'

Granot made a grunting noise as he downed his fourth espresso of the afternoon.

'I remember that case. He was guilty, alright. His name was… Albert, no, Alain Monceau.'

Frankie took a long draught of Vittel.

'Alain, yes. His younger brother Cyrille sent Vincent a couple of threatening letters at the time of the death. The old boy was retired then, of course. No note of any further harassment. And no indication that Agnès was ever contacted – although she was in-post both during the case itself and when Monceau died.'

'It's worth a follow-up, certainly.'

Sweet wrappers littered Bonbon's desk like confetti. A couple slid off a file as he brandished it in the air.

'This is interesting. Greuze, Benoit. Huge grudge against Agnès. Said she tricked him into confessing to murder. Released only last June.'

'The Greuze case,' Granot said. 'Another possible, definitely.'

Arriving back from La Marguerite, Darac was taking a call on his mobile as he craned his neck around the squad-room door.

'Better continue on my office landline, will you, Lartou – this thing's about to…'

The mobile's battery died before he could finish the sentence. He stuffed it into his pocket and turned to Granot.

'Any progress?'

'So far, we've got…' He looked down the sheet. '…twenty-four names of people who might or who actually did hold a grudge against the Dantiers. Armani's leading the team talking to the parties concerned. But we need to get out there ourselves, soon – maybe just retain a couple back here to keep the trawl going. If not, we're in danger of creating a backlog that will take too long to clear.'

'Agreed. We'll get on that.' He looked across at Flaco. 'Van sales and hirings?'

'Similar story, Captain. But multiply the number of names by about twenty.'

'You got national coverage sorted?'

'There are uniforms and clericals all over the country approaching the buyers we've come up with. But as we cross one name off the list, another two possibles come in.'

'How many companies, agencies and so on have you still to contact?'

'About… eighty or so. So there's an end to it. And then Perand and I can get out on the street, as well.'

'What about the garaging aspect – lock-ups and so on?'

'We've put together a long list. Uniforms are checking them.'

'Good. I need to go next door but I'll be right back.'

The desk phone was ringing as Darac walked into his office.

'Go ahead, Lartou.'

'I've got another of those blip and refocus sequences, chief. It's from the camera on the boss's corridor on the fifth floor. For less than a minute, it happens.'

'But we looked at footage from that camera.'

'We looked at it for the time around the abduction. This blip happened at 5.46 pm.'

Darac ran a hand into his hair and kept it there.

'Whoever stole in and put the note on her bed did it *before* they took her?'

'Several hours before.'

Darac swivelled in his chair and gazed out of the window. Rows of identical barracks buildings made a useful alternative to the blank canvas of the floor.

'What about footage from cameras on the other floors around that time? Don't they show anything?'

'No. But if you go into the building through the service entrance and take the back stairs up to the fifth floor, you don't encounter any camera until the one that was doctored.'

Darac dragged his hand out of his hair.

'State-of-the-art system…'

'Indeed.'

'You know, in *some* ways, it makes sense to leave the note first – especially if it turns out SAD is just a couple of people. Or even just one. If you kidnap someone in a parking garage, bundling them perhaps noisily into a van, the last thing you would want to do then is enter the building, go up five floors, pull the stunt with the camera, gain access somehow to the apartment, et cetera, et cetera. You'd want to get away from the scene as quickly as possible, wouldn't you?'

'I think you would, yes.'

'But how did they know somebody wouldn't go into her room in the meantime? How did they know someone wouldn't find the note and tip us off? Agnès herself could have found it, conceivably.'

'They must have been au fait with her movements somehow…'

Darac swivelled back to face the room. His jaw dropped when he saw who was standing before him. It didn't make sense.

'We'll… talk later, Lartou. I have to go.'

The visitor was wearing a grey suit and matching tie.

'Hello, Captain. I'd like one of your excellent espressos if there's one going.' Mansoor Narooq slid his hand inside his jacket. 'No milk or sugar. How I managed to stomach it last time, I'm not sure.' He showed an ID, put it back and extended his hand.

Darac ignored it.

'DCRI. Uh-huh.'

'It's quite natural that you feel…'

Darac's chair fell over backwards as he got to his feet.

'Don't tell me what I'm feeling, you fucking bastard! You sat there…' He jabbed a finger towards the radiator. '…watching us struggling to make sense of the case…'

'I work undercover. It's my job.' He smiled as if bewildered by Darac's reaction. 'Calm down.'

'"Congratulations – you can subtract one," you said. Well congratulations, whatever your name is, you can *add* one to all the case teams you've fucked over, you time-wasting bastard…'

Darac's whole body was flexed as he moved around the desk. Everything that was welling up in him was going to release in one huge explosion. There was no way he could stop himself this time.

Shapes banged in through the doorway. Arms enveloped him from behind.

'Chief! Chief! Relax,' Granot shouted. 'He was… just doing his job.'

They struggled into the centre of the room as one heaving entity, for the moment Granot's massive strength subduing Darac's tensile power.

'Help me!' Granot shouted, his face already colouring with the effort. Perand threw his lanky carcass at the scrum but failing to find purchase, slid ineffectually onto his knees. Head down, Bonbon managed to hold on, at least, but immediately disorientated, began to push Darac towards his target, rather than away from it. It was Flaco who made the difference, tackling the heaving pair head-on. Caught in a pincer movement, Darac felt the check, but still he pressed forward, his eyes locked on the man who had misled them and wasted all their time; the man who was looking on now, almost within reach; the man whose cocksure nonchalance could be erased with just one decent dig to the jaw; the man who stood in for everything that was causing Darac pain.

And then quite suddenly, the view of the target was gone. Cut off. Her hands clamping his face, Frankie made him look into her wide, imploring eyes.

'Stop it. Stop it now.'

Darac made one last flexing effort but then, juddering with a different kind of emotion, he subsided completely. A feeling of defeat came over him. Defeat in more than just this battle. Defeat in almost every area that mattered.

'It's fine… It's fine… It's… over.'

Granot's questioning eyes met Frankie's.

'He's alright.'

Chest burning, Granot released his hold and slumped back into a chair by the desk. Darac and Flaco disentangled themselves and stood to regain their breath.

'Your team value you, Captain,' the visitor said. 'I'll note that.'

He turned to the others.

'For those of you who didn't catch it, I am Lieutenant Efe Santoor. Of the DCRI. Paris.'

'And we are investigating the abduction… of Agnès and Vincent Dantier,' Darac said, his voice cutting through a groundswell of resentment. Clenching and releasing his shoulders, he went over to the water cooler. 'Do you people… know anything about that?'

'We know nothing about it. But we agree with your assessment. It's not political. It's criminal.'

'So you can confirm that the… Sons and Daughters of the Just Cause are neither a terrorist organisation… nor a figment of some bureaucrat's twisted mind?'

'Unreservedly. I came in today to let you know that.'

'Good of you.' Darac turned to Flaco. 'Water?' Blowing out her cheeks, she shook her head. Pouring one cup, he gave her a pat on the arm as he carried it back to his desk.

'I can't wait to hear what your story is, Lieutenant Santoor,' Bonbon said. 'But every minute could be crucial, so if you'll excuse us?'

'I understand. You'll all be receiving my report in due course anyway.'

Granot was still in Darac's chair, breathing hard.

'Speaking for... myself... I can't... do anything... for the minute.'

'Alright then.' Santoor glanced around the room. 'Where's your guest chair? I'll give you the bare bones now if you want to hear them.'

Darac handed Granot the cup of water. In lieu of a handshake, he gripped the big man's shoulder.

'You alright, man?'

'Pussy like you?' Granot wiped his forehead with his forearm. 'I could keep that up... all day.'

Santoor had found the chair he'd graced during his pointless earlier interrogation. For old times' sake, he set it down next to the radiator.

'As some of you may have already worked out, one of my principal duties in the DCRI is to investigate – undercover – potentially subversive Muslim cells.'

Bonbon eyeballed him.

'Is this the investigation into the "local Muslim situation" Lanvalle mentioned to Agnès but wouldn't give her any details about?'

'It was part of it, yes. Concerns about Hamid Toulé led me to infiltrate the prayer group. But I had found no evidence to support those concerns at the time of the incident with Monsieur Florian. I can honestly say that the evidence I gave to you all was absolutely as I witnessed it. I did not see Florian beforehand; I did not believe the old woman caused his death; and I had no idea who or what did. Now fact and fiction diverge a little.'

Frankie shook her head.

'I bet they do.'

'My superiors saw Florian's death as an opportunity for me to push things with Toulé. They believed that we might find out more about his potential criminality if we promoted the idea of Mansoor Narooq's own. "I'm illegal – they'll send me back," I told him. Then I came up with the idea of the exchange with Slimane, who really is my cousin, by the way. And of course, although he doesn't know what I do, he does know I work for the government. I put the idea to him and then we approached Toulé.'

'Did anyone else know about it?' Darac said. 'The imam?'

'I think he was aware something wasn't right and I don't think he likes Toulé very much but he knew nothing about it. In terms of encouraging Toulé to open up a whole new side of himself to me, the plan didn't work. In fact, he advised me to face the consequences of questioning and only went along with it because I insisted.' He essayed a look of exaggerated sympathy. 'I do hope the prayer group's mosque will be granted them one of these days, don't you?'

'Yes, yes, yes.' Bonbon was essaying a look of his own – one of sheer incredulity. 'But where are you at, Santoor? When you ran out of the crowd that day and didn't obey calls to stop, Flaco here almost shot you.'

'Nice to see you again, Yvonne.'

Flaco's scowl was of Jesuitical severity.

'Five more steps and I would have pulled the trigger.'

'That's fine – I was going to stop after four had the Captain not intervened.'

Darac exhaled deeply.

'Cut the bravado. Why did you do that?'

'I hadn't expected you to discover the switch with Slimane at all, to be honest, let alone so quickly...'

Spitting out a mouthful of air, Granot shared a comradely look with anyone who would have it. There were plenty of takers.

'I should never have involved Slimane. He let me down. Badly. I could see he was on the verge of blowing my cover in front of everyone.' He fixed Darac with his hawk-like stare. 'Blowing it just to bring an end to the routine questioning you, Captain, were subjecting him to. I couldn't allow that. Apart from anything else, it would have completely compromised any other covert activity we may plan for Toulé and company in the future.'

Risking a stubble fire by giving his chin a scratch, Perand looked animated to a degree no one in the team had ever seen before.

'Two things. Surely, you should have told *us* who you were? Secondly, you nearly killed yourself jumping out of the fucking window. Sir.'

Santoor smiled.

'Beautifully put.' The smile was switched off. 'Naturally, I didn't intend to fall so heavily. But the escape itself was all part of my new brief. Plan A was dead so we'd moved to Plan B.

'How did you receive the order?' Darac said.

'Through my one allowed phone call, of course. You should really start monitoring them, don't you think?'

Darac exhaled deeply.

'Tell us about Plan B.'

'Obvious, isn't it? My arrest presented me with a perfect opportunity to see what you people were up to from the inside. As it were. The DCRI being the DCRI, a false ID trail was laid immediately and I got to it. I'm still working on my report but so far, Commandant Lanvalle has found it most interesting.'

Frankie levelled him with a look Medusa herself might have envied.

'*Chapeau.*'

'Thank you. In short, you've done some things well, others very, very poorly.' He indicated Darac's desk. 'Although I'm glad to see you've already corrected one error, Captain. It's strictly against guidelines to display an image of a loved one where it might be seen by a suspect. An identifiable loved one is a security risk both to the officer concerned and, by extension, to the entire Brigade.'

Darac opened the drawer and tossed the absent photograph on to the desk. In the shot, Angeline was wearing a trilby pulled low over her brow, dark sunglasses and a heavy moustache. It was Darac's favourite photo of her. Despite everything, it would probably remain so.

'Oh, that's funny.' Raising a sardonic eyebrow, Santoor nodded. 'Very knowing of you both.' All at once, his sharp features took on an even keener edge. 'Leaving a suspect unfettered and unsupervised while audibly discussing case developments with a superior officer *and* a senior pathologist – those and other errors won't be so easy to answer for.'

'I've heard enough,' Darac said. 'We've got work to do. Get out.'

'In relation to the Dantier case, you need to hear one more thing. Commandant Lanvalle has instructed me to tell you that should your own resources prove inadequate to the task, you may approach him.' He gave a phone number. 'We have special resources in the DCRI. Resources and powers. Assistance, where possible, will be provided.'

'What sort of assistance?'

'Door-stepping, for instance. I like your term "slog squad", Captain. They could slog even harder if more bodies were thrown into the mix.'

'How many could we have and how soon?'

'The simple things are often the hardest, aren't they? The numbers and timing would have to be determined by committee. And we'd require adequate notice, obviously. And there would have to be—'

'No time for red tape. Can you do anything else?'

'Now it gets easier. We can obtain fast-track warrants, we've got expert hostage negotiators – anything in that line we can do quickly.'

'Thank Lanvalle from us for that – we may need it.'

'So that concludes our business.' Santoor got to his feet and as if bidding the radiator farewell, gave it a pat. 'It's just not the same without the handcuffs. *And* the air-con's behaving itself. Disappointing.' He moved to the door. 'Bye for now.'

'One second, Santoor.' Darac's *what if* mind had come up with another connection. 'Jacques Sevran. AKA Seve.'

Santoor shrugged, uninterested.

'Yes?'

'Beat officer. Hugely experienced. Linguist. Babysat you in this office. The office in which you offered me a bribe...'

The team could see where this was going. A further wave of condemnation broke in Santoor's direction.

'...A bribe *I* refused. Now Seve is under arrest. What do you know about that?'

Santoor thought about it for a second.

'I cannot discuss an ongoing investigation, Captain – you know that. Goodbye. And good luck.'

'You can wait another second.' Fully recovered, Granot got to his feet and walked slowly across to the young man. 'It's a good job for you I weigh 115 kilos and Flaco there is as brave as a lioness or you might not have been able to complete that report of yours for some time.'

Santoor gave Darac an evaluating look.

'I'd have taken my chances.'

'It's not just the job,' Frankie said. 'You really are an arsehole, aren't you?'

Santoor grinned, turned on his heel and was gone.

'Seve, you bloody idiot.' Darac picked up Angeline's photo and, triggering a crossfire of glances between the others, returned it to the drawer. When he looked up, they were all looking neutrally at him. 'But that's for another time. As is so much else – including properly expressing my thanks.' He caught Bonbon's eye. 'Even to you and Perand, you wimps.' As the smiles faded, he glanced at his watch. 'Agnès is out there somewhere. Let's pick the tempo back up.'

4.44 PM

In the haze-veiled hills above Monaco, Yves Dauresse's work was almost over for the day. Pursued by a team car and a posse of camera-wielding outriders, the final competitor out of the start gate was approaching the Garde Républicaine motorcyclist.

Even had Dauresse not been on station, it was doubtful that any of the 180 lone starters would have failed to see the hazard he was there to indicate – a section of kerbed pavement suddenly appearing on the inside of a dropping hairpin bend – but safety first was the brief even when there was no peloton to worry about. His whistle clamped between his lips, he held his yellow warning flag in both hands above his head. Dauresse began to wave it slowly from side to side.

The sound of his pedalling masked by the crowd and by his motorised entourage, the rider flew safely past and began his snaking descent into Monaco. For Dauresse, Stage One was over. Throwing his leg over his BMW, he radioed his status to the team co-ordinator and set off down the mountain. Twelve years he'd been doing this. Twelve long, tiring, uneventful years. This year was going to be the last.

6.03 PM

Nurses had come and gone. Presumably. Come and gone in 37.5 degree heat for all he knew. The Tour had occupied his entire consciousness. And it was just a taste of what was to come.

For the second year in succession, Cancellara had won the time trial. The trunk-thighed Swiss had blasted around the course a whole eighteen seconds faster than Contador. If Cancellara could climb the really big stuff, he mused, he would have no equal as a Tour rider. What a powerhouse he was on the flat. And what a descender. Fearless. No one riding a motorbike could catch him going downhill. A GR man had once tried it. A 1000cc engine under his backside and he got nowhere near.

The short one's voice. Saying something, out of his line of vision.

The bed jolted as the notes went back into their sheath.

'I said, did you enjoy that?'

He blinked once.

'Lovely! And did you see your son?'

He blinked once.

'Did he win?'

Idiot.

He blinked twice.

'No – never mind. You must be very proud of him, though.'

He blinked once.

Especially if what had been planned for tomorrow went as he'd hoped.

6.47 PM

The landing was strung with lines of washing. As a Las Planas-bound tram whirred along the boulevard below, Darac brushed between a pair of beach towels and made for the apartment's front door. Before he could knock, a child of no more than three emerged backwards through it. Giddy with terror and laughter, he shrieked as a shaven-headed man in his mid-thirties appeared suddenly, issuing threats in a pantomime roar. Both were clad in the black knee-length shorts of Nice's football club, OGC Nice, known as Le Gym. The boy shrieked again and turned to run off.

'Sorry, mate – didn't hear you knock. Be with you in a second.'

The bogeyman swept up the boy and carried him upside down back into the apartment. Darac heard a woman's voice from inside.

'How am I supposed to get him ready for bed now?'

'You've never had any problems getting men into bed. Has she, Poupou, eh?'

'You arsehole… Shut the fuck up!'

'I've told you – no swearing in front of the kid! And we've got a visitor.'

A whispered exchange. Darac couldn't make out the

words but they sounded to the point. The man reappeared at the door.

'Sorry about that.' He adjusted the hang of his balls. 'Women, eh?'

Darac showed him his ID.

'Cyrille Monceau?'

The man's face hardened.

'What do you want?'

'I want you to answer some questions.'

Monceau cast an anxious glance back into the apartment. Putting the door on the latch, he stepped outside.

'I haven't stolen so much as a newspaper in years, *flic*. Not since I've been married.'

'I'm not interested in years. I'm interested in the past twenty-four hours. Talk me through them.'

Inside, Poupou was already rebelling at the prospect of bed. He wanted Papa.

'Talk you through them why?'

'Look, I've got no time, no time at all, to mess around. Answer the question or you'll be spending forty-eight hours at the Caserne.'

Monceau cleared his throat and spat. The gobbet landed nearer his own bare foot than Darac's shoe; he just about got away with it.

'Alright – for ten of those hours I was at work at EDF – I'm on the maintenance team at the plant. You can check.'

'Don't worry, I will. What time did you start?'

'Eight. Eight until six this morning.'

'Did you leave the site at any point in between?'

'In my job, you can't just leave the site. I was there all shift. Several people can back that up.'

Assuming this checked out, it meant Monceau could not have taken part in either abduction. But he could still have been behind them.

'What did you do immediately after your shift?'

'Had breakfast in the canteen, then came home to bed. Yvette doesn't work today so she can vouch for that.' He looked at his watch. 'I'm off again in an hour or so.'

Inside, Poupou's tears were turning to temper. Darac pictured Yvette reaching for a bottle of something tranquilising. Perhaps for them both.

'Now we can go back years. To 1992 to be exact. When your brother died in prison, you wrote two letters to the officer responsible for his conviction. You told Commissaire Vincent Dantier to watch his back. Because you were going to kill him.'

Monceau shook his head.

'1992… Jesus. Look – my brother and I were close and he was stitched up by that bastard. Then he didn't get the proper medical treatment in the nick. When he died, I was eighteen. What do you think I'd do? Write to Dantier and say: "Never mind, monsieur, I forgive you."'

'You threatened his life. Twice.'

Monceau's narrow-set eyes widened brightly.

'Has somebody iced him? Best news I've had!'

'Sorry to disappoint you. But threats have been made against Monsieur Dantier and his daughter.'

Yvette appeared with Poupou. Without a word or a

look, she handed the livid little bundle to Monceau and went back into the apartment. He held the child to his chest like a badge of honour.

'Threats – so what?'

'Serious threats.'

'Look, I feel sorry for Dantier's daughter. It's not her fault she's got a bastard for a father.'

Darac called time on the interview five minutes later. He had everything he was going to get from Monceau for the time being. He called Armani as he took the steps down to the lobby.

'Anything yet?'

'I'm bringing in Jacqueline Dutillieux as we speak.'

Darac's grip on the phone intensified.

'Bonbon's find? Go on.'

'I put him on to it. Our Jacqui's got a classic rap sheet for a heavy female user. Theft, deception, prostitution. No hint of violence, mind you, but here's the thing. It's Agnès D. she blames for having her kids taken away from her. She's been out and clean now, more or less, for a year or so but the kids still don't want to know her. So she hates Agnès with a vengeance and I'm quoting.'

A tram accelerated away from the stop as Darac emerged onto the boulevard.

'So that's motive. Means and opportunity have got to involve a guy.'

'The van driver himself, yes. There is a boyfriend but beyond saying she was with him last night and this morning, she refused to give me any more on who, where and why.'

A rollerblader was sitting on one of the platform benches. Eyeing Darac's mobile, he looked interested, suddenly.

'What's your gut feeling?' The boy stood. 'Forget it, kid.'

The kid sat down.

'What was that?'

'Nothing. Go on, Armani.'

'My gut feeling is no. But we'll see. Your guy?'

'I'll check it but he looks to have a solid alibi. As for any other involvement, I don't see it.'

'Right. Where next for you?'

'Saint-Laurent-du-Var. The son of one Maurice Brosse. Keep me posted, Armani.'

Dead end. Brosse was on vacation in Mauritius. Had been for a week. As the hours wore on, lead after lead receded back into the woodwork. By eight o'clock, most of the team were back in the squad room at the Caserne, seeking to tease a second tranche of suspects out of the records. What else could they do?

It was just before nine when Flaco's desk phone rang. Rubbing her eyes, she almost dropped the receiver as she picked up.

'Yes?' As if it had a life of its own, the pen she was holding began to tap, pocking the margin of her pad. 'What a mess.' She stopped immediately.

'What was that, Flak?'

'Nothing. Go ahead.'

'It's Partin, here. I'm with the team up on Mont Boron.

I've just spoken to the Alledargues.' He spelled the name. 'They're a retired couple who live next door to Commissaire Dantier. They were the ones who weren't in when Lieutenant Granot called round earlier. To cut a long story short, Madame Alledargue, the little beauty, spotted that the van we're looking for had a Département 31 registration. 31 is Haute-Garonne, where she's from. That's why it stuck in her mind.'

Flaco punched the air.

'Fantastic, Partin.'

Across the other side of the room, Darac looked up from his case notes.

'There's more, Flak. She's certain "A" was the letter immediately before it. "A for Alledargue" she'd thought at the time. The woman may be egocentric but she's observant.'

Flaco smothered the phone.

'Listen up, everybody.' One or two voices continued. 'Quiet please!' Silence. 'The van has a Département 31 plate. And "A" was the final letter.'

Fist pumps, silently mouthed thank-yous, raps on desks – the news was celebrated all around the room.

'I wish we'd known that before we dug up all this.' Perand waved a hand at the piles of paper crowding the work table in front of them. 'And sent the pavement pounders out.'

As Flaco continued the call, he and the rest of their group began pulling out the A-31 plates from the follow-up stacks.

'Anything else from Madame Alledargue?' Flaco began tapping on her pad in earnest. It had worked last time. 'Or from the husband?'

'Plenty. All of it irrelevant.'

No more tapping.

'So they didn't see the van arrive or leave or see the driver?'

'No.'

'Too much to hope for. But that's great work, Partin,' she said, unconsciously copying Darac's manner.

As the call ended, Perand handed her a greatly reduced stack of follow-ups.

'With all the non-A-31 plates taken out, it leaves just two buyers and one hirer to check out, *chief.*' He smiled his lopsided smile, enjoying the rib. But it disappeared as he took back the top page.

'Jesus Christ!' He showed it to Adèle Rousade. 'Did you pick this one out?'

'Hours ago, darling. It's an A-31, no?'

'That it is.'

Adèle's features fell like a dropped lipstick.

'So what have I done wrong?'

'Not a thing.' Subsiding into his chair, he held out the page to Flaco. 'It's just that if either of us two had got this one, the buyer's name would have jumped straight out. As you say – hours ago.'

At their desks, Darac's team was following the exchange like spectators at a play.

Frankie spoke for them all.

'Don't drag it out, for God's sake. Who bought the damned van?'

Holding up the page for everyone to see, Flaco announced the name. No one quite believed it. But it was there in black and white.

9.34 PM

Rue Vaulesne was one of a network of streets linking Boulevards Cessole and Auguste Raynaud in the north of the city. An essay in vernacular architecture, there were scarcely any two structures in the street that looked as if they belonged together.

Outwardly, the two guys strolling along Rue Vaulesne didn't seem much alike, either. Exuding an attractive mixture of warmth and sensitivity, one was dark, strongly built and moved with a sort of easy confidence. The other, a skinny individual with wiry red hair, had the mischievous alertness of someone who was used to taking his chances. But they had at least one thing in common. They enjoyed a joke. Or that's what it would have looked like to anyone watching.

'I suppose it was too much to hope the van would be parked outside,' Bonbon said.

Darac laughed and gave his mate a punch on the arm.

'Can you see us?' he asked.

Lartou Lartigue's voice buzzed into his earpiece.

'Yes we can, chief. We just rang the landline again — intending to pose as the phone company, this time. Still no answer.'

'Anything else we need to know?'

'Nothing.'

'Everyone in place?'

'Everyone.'

Darac and Bonbon were still shaking their heads and chuckling.

'Let us know immediately if anyone comes back to the house. Otherwise, don't come on again until I get back to you. And no more calls to the landline – we'll know soon enough if anyone's home.'

'Check. Good luck, chief. Out.'

'It's the next one.' Overdressed in the heat, Bonbon paused to mop his brow. 'No lights on.'

'Not necessarily.' Just smiles now – the gag seemed to be wearing off. 'They could be using blackout curtains.'

The target address was a semi-detached, two-storey townhouse rendered, where it was adhering, in stained lavender-washed plaster. On one side, the property abutted the end wall of a dreary three-storey apartment block; on the other, a half-closed wrought-iron gate gave on to a path that led to the rear of the house.

'You go round the back, Bonbon. I'll wait a second, then try the front door.'

'Got your safety off?'

'Oh yes.'

Bonbon opened the gate and, leaving it at the same angle he found it, disappeared down the path. Darac turned to the door. Listening for sounds inside, he stood at a right angle to it and knocked. He heard nothing. No lights came on as far as he could tell. He knocked again. Still no one came to the door. But he heard muffled steps on the pavement behind him. With any luck, it would be just a passer-by. Darac had every confidence in Lartou and the others but earpieces could go down and so could the links to them. Feeling anything but relaxed, Darac essayed a smile and turned. Moving with the exaggerated care of someone walking a tightrope, the interloper proved to be a frail old man carrying a bag of shopping.

'Evening, monsieur,' Darac said.

His eyes fixed determinedly ahead, the old boy said nothing as he shuffled on his way.

A third knock unanswered, Darac went to join Bonbon in the back yard. Bounded at the rear by a flat-roofed outbuilding, it was a scruffy, utilitarian space. Terracotta pots proliferated. Some were planted up, most were stacked against the outbuilding's cinderblock front wall. In the fast-fading light, they looked like clusters of clinging barnacles.

Overhead, a corrugated plastic canopy connected the outbuilding's roof to the rear wall of the house. A shield against prying eyes, perhaps, as much as a shelter. Stumbling over a partly demolished wall, Darac adopted it as a redoubt as he looked around for Bonbon. He couldn't see him.

'Bonbon?' he whispered into his mouthpiece. There was no reply. 'Bonbon?' Still no answer. He was nowhere to be seen. 'Psssttt!'

The outbuilding door opened. A figure slipped

stealthily out into the open; open, that is, to the yard and to anyone looking out of the ground-floor window of the house. The figure looked thicker-set than Bonbon. But it was him, alright – he and Darac were both wearing bullet-proof vests under their shirts. The figure disappeared momentarily and then reappeared at Darac's side.

'You had me worried there for a minute.'

'I was talking into my mouthpiece but it must be down.' Bonbon's expression conveyed none of its usual whimsicality. 'So no signs of life at the front?'

'Armani shuffled past on the pavement. That was it.'

'Doesn't seem to be anyone in at the back. That outhouse concerns me, though. The floor's concrete and there's a small pile of broken bricks in one corner.'

'How small?'

'Too small to conceal anything like a body. But it could cover a Gartreuix-style hatch. It would make too much noise to shift a pile of bricks now, though.'

Shards of ice chilled the sweat running down Darac's back. Bonbon had worked on the case of Jean-Marie Gartreuix, a killer who had concealed the remains of his many victims in an old wine cellar that extended under his garage.

'After we've checked out the house, we'll get right back out here.'

'I know it's… Just a second.' Bonbon took the whisper down a notch. 'Did someone just open that curtain a crack?'

Keeping very still, the pair stared at the ground-floor window of the house.

'That's how it was, I think.' He gave Bonbon a tap on the knee. 'Alright, let's do it. Quiet and careful, now. Or we may as well have sent for Freddy Anselme.'

As far as they could tell, nothing stirred inside the house as they ghosted their way to the back door. It took Darac precisely three seconds to pick the lock. Standing well to the side, he gave the door a gentle push but it opened only as far as a security chain allowed. It took another ten seconds to retrieve the wire lasso from his tool roll, hook it around the track bolt and disengage it. The door swung wide open. For the moment, they remained still.

Poised to fire if necessary, Bonbon slipped quietly inside. The lobby was dark but his eyes were sharp. No one was there. Torch in one hand, automatic in the other, Darac swept quickly past him and through a half-open door into the kitchen. No one there either. And there was no sound from the rest of the house. He gave Bonbon a beckoning nod.

'Bread and bleach,' Darac whispered, sniffing.

'You're supposed to say "clear".' Bonbon's eyes darted between the two doors that gave off the room. 'Santoor might be lurking around here somewhere.'

'If he is, he might just get his head blown off. By mistake.'

The living room was next. No one. Silent. And dark enough for Bonbon finally to switch on his torch. Alternating entry and cover, the pair worked their way through another three rooms until there was just one left – the larger of the two bedrooms. They shared a look and then went in together. Torch beams criss-crossed as they pierced the silent gloom.

'Jesus Christ.'

The two of them almost sank to their knees but they knew the relief they felt was no more than a temporary respite. They still had no idea where Agnès and Vincent were; nor even if they were alive.

Nor had they encountered the owner of the house – Madame Corinne Delage.

Bonbon wasted no time in peeling off his shirt.

'At least we can get out of these vests now.' They headed back down the stairs. 'Before we do anything else, I'm going to shift those bricks. Only take a minute.'

'Take half a minute if we do it together.'

Darac didn't believe in an afterlife from which the dead could somehow communicate with the living. But he knew from experience that places in which a violent death had occurred, or in which a victim's body had been dumped, sometimes retained an atmosphere of pain and hopelessness that could live on for years. Atmospheres, though, made very unreliable witnesses. As he and Bonbon stepped into the outbuilding, he detected nothing whatever out of the ordinary except to wonder what use an old woman like Delage had for a pile of broken bricks.

Resting the torches on a couple of battered old paint tins, they donned exam gloves and set to work, picking at the pile. Reliving earlier memories, Bonbon hesitated as they finally got down to the base layer. He hadn't known any of Gartreuix's victims. Agnès was a different story.

'It's going to be alright, Bonbon.'

'Yeah.'

They shifted the bricks, then swept away the rubble and dust.

'Fucking hell.'

It *was* alright. There was nothing. More relief. More temporary respite.

Darac was already speaking to Lartigue as they walked back through the lobby.

'There's no one here, Lartou. Get that? Not Agnès, Vincent or Corinne Delage, for that matter. So send Roulet and the dog in and get Flaco on to the neighbours. Tell her to begin with the one who identified Delage in your photo.'

'Check.'

'It would make life a lot easier if we could put the lights on in here. The curtains seem pretty thick.'

'Go for it. We're watching.'

Bonbon's torch found the wall switch.

'They're on, Lartou.'

'You can't tell from outside.'

'Good. Keep watching – we'll turn some others on.'

One by one, Darac and Bonbon put on as many lights as they thought useful.

'That's all good, chief.'

'Excellent. Keep Ormans and the others back until I call again, okay?'

'Will do. Out.'

'Let's start in the kitchen.'

The various cupboards and drawers revealed nothing of interest. Then in a pantry, Bonbon found several keys hanging from a row of hooks. One of them caught his eye.

'Sweet Mary... Look at the serration profile.' He handed it over. 'Familiar?'

'Shit... And there's us thinking Delage was only incidentally linked to Florian and therefore Manou.'

'Looks as if she's a keyholder to their secret world.'

'Let's be sure.'

Darac took Florian's key from a pocket and put the two together. 'Yes it...' He looked more closely. 'No, we're wrong. It doesn't match. See?' He indicated the one incongruent jag. 'It should go in there, not out.'

'Yes it should.' Bonbon rubbed his eyes, feeling tired suddenly. 'Jumping to conclusions. Let's calm it down.'

'Especially as there's a hell of a lot to do here and we don't know how long we've got.'

Bonbon put back the key as sounds behind them signalled the dog-handler's arrival. He was dressed casually, as if he were out walking his pet.

'How's it looking on the street, Roulet?'

'No one would know there's a surveillance op going on, chief. If and when Delage or anyone else comes back, they'll walk right up to the house, no problem.'

'Armani or Martinet would grab them first.'

Roulet's receding hairline receded still further.

'They're not out there, are they?'

'Yes they are. Okay – let Félix do his stuff.'

The dog set to work, laying down a soundtrack of

scampering and sniffing under Darac and Bonbon's own searches. As the seconds ticked by, the one thing they had wondered if they would find was conspicuous by its absence.

'Still out shopping at this time of night?'

'Maybe she ditched the trolley.' Bonbon shook his head. 'Pointlessly, if she did. She never denied ramming it into Florian.'

Nothing else leapt out at them in the kitchen. Félix was already exploring the stairs as they moved through into the living room. An impressive flower arrangement caught Darac's eye.

'They look fresh.' He lifted the bouquet carefully out of the vase. 'And so does the water.' He sniffed it. 'Fresh today, I would say. So Delage has been home.' He lowered the arrangement carefully back into the vase. 'Or someone has.'

'Where has the old girl got to?'

Looking for anything at all that might help them, they examined the room in more detail. Modestly furnished, it was clearly an older person's domain. But apart from a few framed photographs and a small collection of ornaments on a sideboard, it wasn't a space in which the past spoke louder than the present. Because of that, Darac decided to look first at what few mementoes there were.

'Do those ornaments tell us anything about her, Bonbon?'

'They're country pieces, interestingly enough. Sentimental value only...' He picked up a plain cylindrical pot. 'This is worth a couple of hundred euros, though. It's a confit jar. Salt glaze, probably early nineteenth century.'

Darac glanced at the object and then turned back to one of the photographs.

'It's the one in this photo.' He held it up. 'Isn't it?'

'It's just like it, certainly.'

'When was it taken – early 1950s?'

In the photo, three adults and a child were sitting around a table in a farmhouse-style kitchen. The adults were a couple in their late forties, large-boned, with kind faces, and a lad in his early twenties who was the spitting image of them. The mother was simply dressed and wore a crucifix. Father and son looked as if they had just come in from working in the fields. The child was aged about eight and she was tucking into a huge plate of something hearty. The confit pot was sitting in the middle of the table.

Bonbon looked more closely at the little girl.

'That's a young Corinne, isn't it? The age is right and although it must be sixty or so years ago, you can see a resemblance.'

'That squashed little face. Like a pug. You're right – I'm sure it's her.' Darac turned the photo frame around. His luck was in – there was a note written on the back: *The whole family. Mama, Papa, Antoine and me. Summer 1949.* Darac shook his head. 'Family fun on the farm? That's not the childhood I'd have pictured for someone as bitter and twisted as Corinne Delage.'

'They look serene there but who knows? They could have been at each other's throats the rest of the time.' Bonbon took a wad of papers from the inside pocket of his jacket. 'Let's see what light Perand's case notes shed.' He straightened the paper. 'Here goes: "Delage née Groismont. Birth re-registered as 10 October 1940, Grandeville, Île-de-France".'

'Grandeville? Never heard of it.'

'It's fifty kilometres south-east of Paris, according to Perand. He continues: "Grandeville sounds the sort of place that if it had a horse…" What?' Bonbon's brow creased in incomprehension. He had a second stab at it. '"Grandeville sounds the sort of place that if it had a horse… it would rise to the status of a one-horse town." He looked at Darac. 'Bloody idiot. He means…'

'It's a small rural community, yes. I'll have a word with him.'

Bonbon went back to the notes.

'"Corinne's parents Jeanne and Albert Groismont were thirty-nine and forty-four at the time of her birth. Tenant farmers. She had an older brother, Antoine…"' Bonbon closed his eyes to aid the calculation. 'Fifteen years older, in fact… "All now dead. Corinne married one Yves Delage 2 June 1970 in Paris. No children. Divorced 1978. Yves Delage died 2001."' He turned the page. 'Her rap sheet we know about… "Lived in Nice since '79. Patchy employment history. Worked mainly as a florist."' As if there were a need to illustrate the point, he indicated the flower arrangement. '"Retired seven years ago through ill health – rheumatoid arthritis."'

'Fifteen years is quite a long gap between siblings with none in between.'

Sitting on the mantelpiece was a shot of Corinne

aged about twenty. Smiling at the photographer, she was behind the wheel of a battered Renault Dauphine. Darac picked it up and checked it for an inscription. *My first car – June '65.*

'She's twenty-four in this shot. About as old as Antoine was in the one of the kitchen.' Darac looked at it once more. 'They don't look a thing alike. In fact, she looks like no one else in the family.'

'Adopted? There's nothing to indicate that.' Bonbon checked through the paperwork. 'No – not a thing. But there is one detail worth noting – the Groismonts' birth certificates are re-registrations. The originals were lost during the war, it seems.'

'The same thing happened to my maternal grandmother's family. *Mairies* lost scores of documents through shelling, bombs, fires, et cetera.' A bureau stood in the corner of the room next to the window. Darac went over to it. 'What's in here might help us.'

'How does Delage connect to the boss, though? That's the pressing question.' As Darac patted ineffectually around, Bonbon pressed a pair of catches hiding under the overhang of the lid. The bureau's writing slope released. 'And Agnès met her, remember – at the Caserne just last night when Flaco and Perand were questioning Delage. According to them, there were no fireworks, no flash of recognition or anything. On either side.'

Félix padded into the room, back from his searches upstairs.

'Yes but that doesn't necessarily mean—'

'Gentlemen?' Roulet wore the expression of a man who knew he had an important message to deliver. 'I'm as certain as I can be that the boss was never here. We had a scent control for her father this time, as well. He was never here either.'

'Thank you.' Darac was already thinking through the implications as he flipped his mobile. 'Lartou? Send the others in now, please.'

Bonbon gave Félix's ears a scrunch as Roulet put him on the lead.

'He's earned one for the road, hasn't he?'

'Always.'

Bonbon tossed up a kola kube. The dog caught and crunched it in one.

'That was really helpful, Roulet.' Darac turned back to the bureau. 'Thanks again.'

'Just before I go.' He brought Félix to heel. 'I know you discounted Delage from the Florian killing but since it turns out she almost certainly provided the vehicle for these kidnappings, are you revising that? The cases must be linked, don't you think? It's too big a coincidence.'

'They're linked at some level, yes. But all we can say for sure is that we need to find the Dantiers as soon as we can. If anything about the Florian case can help us do that, we'll follow it up, believe me.'

'I know you will.' He led Félix away. 'All the very best, gentlemen.'

'And to you.'

The contents of the bureau looked promising.

'Marcel will be here in a second. He can photograph all of this.'

Bonbon took out an embroidered case that was plump with correspondence.

'Difficult to disagree with Roulet, isn't it?' He unfastened its pink ribbon tie and began laying out the pages on a gate-leg table. 'Though it's weird to think Delage could hold the key to this thing.'

'*A* key, perhaps,' Darac said, picking up another useful find – Delage's address book. 'And because of that, I think we ought to release Manou this evening. I was only delaying it until tomorrow because we're concentrating on the abductions. Now we know there's some sort of link, we should do it.'

'So Erica's finished the project, then?'

'She has and all the tails are in place.'

'In that case, let's go for it. I don't suppose any of us was expecting to see our bed tonight, anyway.'

The organ note blared. Bed? What did that mean to Darac now? His mobile rang, halting the slide into mawkishness. If there was any wallowing to be done, it could wait.

'Granot – you au fait with everything?'

'Lartou's just filled me in. Thank God you didn't find…'

'Yes, yes, yes.' He put the phone on speaker. 'What've you got?'

'A couple of things. Giraud, the guy from Croix Noire Autos in Saint-Laurent confirmed no one accompanied

Delage when she bought the van.'

'Didn't he think it odd that a woman of that age was buying such a vehicle?'

'He did but she seemed to know what she was doing. She stalled it several times when she drove the thing away, mind you. But now we come to the interesting part. Have you located her bank statements?'

'Not as yet.'

'First thing you should've looked for. Anyway, I've got copies here. Listen – on January 17th, €9,500 was paid into her savings account. That was the week before she bought the van for that same sum. And there's no corresponding withdrawal from any of her other accounts.'

Darac and Bonbon shared a look.

'So Delage was a front for someone else.'

'For the true purchaser of the van – indeed. The van driver himself, perhaps – the man with a way with CCTV cameras.'

One name was all they needed.

'How was that money paid in, Granot? Say it was by personal cheque and I'll never make you listen to Ornette Coleman again.'

'Bloody hell, I'm tempted to say it was. But it was a cash deposit. She paid it in herself. Mixed denomination notes.'

'Shit.'

In the doorway, the booming voice of Raul Ormans heralded the arrival of his forensics team for the night. Erica and Marcel – the unit's long-serving photographer – made up the trio.

'You had two things to report, Granot?'

'Yes, I've looked through Delage's rap sheet...'

In her light, prancing gait, Erica moved purposely into Darac's eyeline and, pointing at Delage's landline phone, raised her eyebrows enquiringly. Still sensing there was some sort of issue between them, he smiled and nodded.

'I can't see any contact with the boss or with Vincent,' continued Grant, 'Hers is far too petty a record to have interested the Brigade Criminelle.'

'Not the cat poisoning?'

'It was dog poisoning. No – Foch dealt with that. And she got off.'

'What do you think the relationship is between Delage and the true buyer of the van?'

'Hard to say, isn't it? At this stage.'

An unpalatable thought struck Darac. Leaning back in his chair, he ran a hand through his hair.

'Let's hope they're closely related or at worst, friends. If it turns out he was just a guy she met in some bar or whatever, it's going to be a lot harder to crack this thing.'

'In other words, it's better for us if they're in it together – all the way.'

'Absolutely. Keep digging, Granot. Listen, I've decided to have Manou released this evening. Unless events overtake us.'

'Yes – why not? Perand's having a little tête-à-tête with him as we speak, by the way.'

'Drop in on him, will you?' Darac could picture Granot's reaction. 'I want to be sure he's exploring the possible Manou–Florian–Delage link properly.'

'Do I have to do everything around here?'

'Can you think of anyone better?'

'I'll be in touch.'

Flipping the mobile shut, Darac finally ran the hand out of his hair. It seemed to release an idea.

'How's this, Bonbon? Prepare yourself – the reasoning's thin. It could be Delage and the van purchaser *are* close.'

'Go on.'

'The van cost €9,500. She paid in €9,500. Not 9,750, 10,000 or whatever. Where's the margin? If she were doing it as a business proposition, there would be commission of some sort, surely?'

'Maybe he gave her that separately. Up front, possibly.' Bonbon gestured Marcel over to the table. 'Or in kind.'

'Told you it was thin.'

'It may yet be right… Marcel – can you photograph all these letters I've laid out? And there are more in the case.'

'Sure.'

Brandishing a call list, Erica joined Darac at the bureau.

'Already? That was quick.'

'I feel dirty but before we left, I went to your friend Santoor at the DCRI. He had the records ready and waiting.'

'Not just empty promises, then.' He took the printout. 'There's no computer to worry about so that will save time.'

'And she has no mobile either. I just checked the answerphone – nothing. And nothing recoverable on the cassette. But the tap is already on the line.'

At the table, Marcel's flashgun began to fire.

'A tap – just like that?' Darac held the first page so they could both read it. 'Outgoing calls first.'

Erica leaned forward.

'There are no speed-dial numbers on the phone, by the way.'

'Right.'

Nothing seemed significant.

'Let's look at the incoming numbers.'

Again, the cupboard was bare. But finally, by dint of their absence, a couple of things did strike them: Delage hadn't made or taken a call with anyone on the day of Florian's killing, or of the Dantiers' abduction.

'In fact,' Erica said, re-anchoring her hair as she straightened, 'for a woman of her age, Corinne Delage doesn't use the phone much.'

'She never had children so there are no daily or weekly chats to them or to grandchildren. Not many friends either, by the look of it.' Darac folded up the pages and slipped them into his pocket. 'When we get out of here, Erica, I'm going to release Manou. How confident are you your tracking device will work?'

'One hundred per cent.'

He loved her certainty.

'Have you had time to brief Frankie on what she has to do?'

'Absolutely.'

'What does it involve, exactly?'

'Basically, just following a cursor around a map on a laptop screen. There are one or two trickier aspects but she's got them down. If any user issues do arise, I'll be in the car with her, anyway.'

'Depending on how we progress tonight, so might I.'

'I've had a chat with one of the live tails we're using from Foch, by the way – Officer Terrevaste.' She smiled with comedic insincerity. 'He thinks my tracker isn't necessary, won't work and while we all flap around uselessly, it will be him and his mate who save the day.'

'Well you'll show them.' A different thought gate-crashed the party. 'Listen, before that all gets underway, have you got time for something?'

'Depends what it is.'

'Could you cross-check all the Delage numbers you've just given me against the phone records of the other principals? That's Florian, Manou, *and* Agnès and Vincent. You'd be looking for links, obviously. It's not your job, I know.'

'I thought Granot was king of the paper chasers?'

'He is but he's on other stuff. Could you do it?'

'I've got to go back to the Caserne first but yes – no problem.'

'That's great – thank you.' He fished Delage's phone records out of his pocket. 'And I'm going to have her address book photographed in a minute. I'll email it over.'

'Right.'

'So keep me posted, yeah?'

'I will.'

She didn't move.

'That's it,' Darac said lightly.

'Yes, I'm going.' Colour flushing her cheeks, she smiled awkwardly. It seemed there was something she needed to say. But couldn't.

'Just keep me posted, okay?' Darac gave her elbow a squeeze. 'Thanks, Erica.'

'Uh… sure.' She turned to go. 'See you later on, maybe.'

Darac returned to Delage's address book. Leafing quickly through it, he found no entries of obvious interest.

'Marcel – can you photograph this as well, please?'

'Double page per image okay?'

'As long as it's all legible, I don't mind how you lay it out.' Darac tossed it over to him. 'You get anything yet, R.O.?'

Raul Ormans was dusting the telephone for prints.

'Haven't found a match with any of our principals – including Florian and Esquebel. A man has been in this room, though. At least one.' He gave a nod to the sofa, an overstuffed two-seater with wooden inlays on the arms. 'They sat there. Delage sat in the armchair. I've already emailed the prints to Archive. Probably nothing, but you never know.'

'Absolutely.' A nagging question returned. 'Bonbon upstairs?'

'I can't see him down here.'

Darac found him going through a chest in Delage's bedroom. He gave a little snort.

'There's one of these in each of the drawers.' He held up a wave-shaped bar of turquoise-coloured soap. 'Sweet, eh?'

The held-down organ note suddenly became a huge chord in Darac's head. The soap, he knew, was from a boutique savonnerie in Villefranche, a favourite of Angeline's. Darac's antipathy to Corinne Delage grew even stronger. It seemed all wrong that the old crone shared anything with his lover – particularly something as personal as a scent; the smell of their shower, an undernote of sex. And now of memory.

'People do strange things.'

Bonbon nodded.

'Make a good title for my autobiography if I ever write it.' He took a last look around the room. 'That's it for in here. You came looking for me?'

They started back down the stairs.

'Yes. Did Paris ever get back to us on Florian's brother? They must've contacted the man by now.'

Bonbon stiffened.

'No they bloody haven't…'

Darac's mobile rang.

'…Haven't got back to us, I mean.'

'We should follow that up.' He glanced at the caller ID. 'It's the duty office.'

'Béatrice Lacquet, Captain. I have Astrid Pireque here – the street performer you asked to come in and draw the bearded man and a couple of other likenesses? She's done them but says she's remembered something else about the

Rue Verbier incident. May she…'

'Yes, put her on.' Darac smothered the mouthpiece. 'It's Medusa.'

'Captain?'

'Hi, Astrid. Happy with your efforts?'

'Albrecht Dürer couldn't have produced a better likeness.'

'Then we'll use them straight away. You've got something more?'

Bonbon came in close.

'Yes. About the incident on Rue Verbier. I don't know why I didn't remember this earlier but when the bearded guy walked off after the collision with the man in the white suit, a woman hurried after him. To ask him if he was okay, I assumed.'

'Had the woman been watching the act also?'

'No. She had just arrived.'

'Describe her.'

'Didn't see her face. But she was small, old, a bit bandy-legged.'

'Wearing?'

'It was… a green cotton dress. A flower print. Hibiscus, I think it was supposed to be.'

'Delage,' Bonbon whispered.

'What happened next?'

'The bearded guy either didn't hear her or deliberately ignored her. I think it was that, actually. Anyway, he carried on walking. Quite a lot faster.'

'Was she pushing a shopping trolley?'

'No. Should she have been?'

Darac kept his eyes on Bonbon.

'This is very important, Astrid. Did you see the old woman and the man in the white suit together at any point?'

Bonbon nodded, seeing the implication. Astrid's recollection had put Delage right back in the frame for Florian's murder. If Beard could have injected the man on the run, so could she.

'Together in what way, Captain?'

'Within touching distance.'

'No, she came into the picture after he'd run off.'

'You're sure?'

'Absolutely certain.'

'We just need a positive ID on this old woman we're talking about. Would you ask the duty officer to show you a flyer of one Corinne Delage?'

It was done.

'Yes, that's her. Definitely.'

'Thank you, Astrid. Once again, you have pointed us in a very useful direction. And saved us a tremendous amount of time.'

'I should be on commission.'

'Yes, I don't know what form this might take but we owe you.'

'Give me a job, I keep telling you.'

'Make sure they give you a ride home. Thanks again.' He gave Bonbon an encouraged look as he flipped his mobile shut. 'It's coming together.'

'The bearded man and Corinne Delage...' Bonbon's foxy eyes twinkled – there were chickens in the yard ahead. And a nice hole in the fence. 'How's this? Delage was there when Beard injected Florian. Afterwards, she follows the victim, perhaps hoping to be there when he drops dead. Then she sees him join the prayer meeting – joins it in the vulnerable back right-hand corner position. A sitting duck. She goes off, acquires the shopping trolley somewhere and comes back. Good, she thinks, he's still alive. Then she rams him in an attempt to destroy the evidence of the puncture mark on his arm. Or maybe she did it just to add insult to injury. She is the despising type, let's face it.'

'Yes...' Darac was staring at the floor. 'The bearded man didn't want to know her earlier, did he? He hurried away from her, anxious no one saw them together. Why?' He looked up. 'Maybe because of what he was planning to do next – the kidnappings. With Delage's name on the sales receipt for the van, it was essential she remained in the wings. Instead, she put herself centre stage.'

'Where's Delage got to, eh? Twenty minutes with her and we could be halfway to finding Agnès and Vincent.'

'No good plan would include a cannon as loose as Delage, would it? I'm wondering if we'll even find her alive.'

'Be a lot better for us if she isn't dead. And let's hear it for our Astrid, by the way. Talk about the value of eyewitness testimony – the girl even produces likenesses of the suspects.'

'Absolutely.' Darac gave an approving little nod. 'She's got a case, hasn't she? Perhaps we should try and get her on the strength.'

His mobile rang.

'Granot again.'

Darac updated him on the Delage development. Then it was his turn.

'We've just finished questioning Manou. He's never even heard of Corinne Delage, I'm certain of it. Of course, that doesn't imply the reverse – especially as it seems she did have some knowledge of Florian.'

'All we can do with Manou is let him go and see where he takes us.' Darac picked up the photo taken in the farmhouse kitchen. There was young Corinne at the family table, a spoon stuck in her squashed little face. 'But whatever happens, I suspect there are depths to this thing we're only just beginning to plumb.'

For Granot, the 'what next?' question trumped 'what if?' every time.

'So when shall we kick the boy out?'

'I'll get back to you on that in a minute.'

Darac ended the call and made another.

'Frankie? It's go.'

SUNDAY 5 JULY

1.05 AM

By one o'clock in the morning, the Brigade Criminelle had been on duty for seventeen hours. No one had gone home. No one except Manou Esquebel. Everything was in place.

Working out of Commissariat Foch, Alain Terrevaste was a slightly built, slightly balding, slightly bland individual. But not too bland – that might have made him more conspicuous. And remaining as inconspicuous as possible was the stock-in-trade of a tail man. Following subjects on foot was his speciality. As things stood, the brief was a simple wheel job but he was certain his talents as a pavement artist would be called upon before the night was out. He was parked in a side street off Avenue Romaine, a kilometre or so south of Esquebel's apartment.

'What's he doing?' he said into his mobile. 'He should have driven off by now.'

His partner from Foch, Denis Sôtenne, was parked within sight of Manou himself.

'He's had the bonnet up. Now he's on his back underneath the vehicle. Looking for a tracker, obviously. Suspicious bastard. No need to get yourself all dirty – it's in your mobile, you nonce.'

'He's got it with him, then? Pity.'

'Trouser pocket. Front right.'

'As far as I'm concerned, he can find Mademoiselle Lamarthe's little toy.'

'Now don't be like that, TeeVee. She's a sweetie, that Erica. Sweet and slinky. I'd like to track her right into bed.'

Terrevaste sighed heavily.

'Keep what passes for your mind on the job.'

'I *have* got my mind on the job. I'm thinking about our so-called command vehicle. Erica and Frankie Lejeune in harness. Now can you imagine a threesome with those two? The girl and the woman; the skinny-assed blonde and the busty brunette…'

'Sôtenne – do me a favour, will you? Don't talk again until Esquebel moves off.'

'Just winding you up, you miserable sod. Hang on, looks like we're in business. Yes… he's shimmying out from under… he's getting in… and he's driving away…'

Sôtenne allowed Esquebel to get well clear before he pulled away from the kerb.

'He's heading into the city on Boulevard L'Ariane. I'll just wait to see if he takes Turin or Raybaud.'

'Check.'

'It's Raybaud. Okay, mobiles off, let's go public.'

'Let's show them how the professionals do it.'

'Oscar Quintal One – suspect moving south on Avenue Raybaud. Copy everyone? Over.'

Sôtenne's radio message registered simultaneously in three other vehicles: OQ2, driven by Terrevaste; OQ3 in which Flaco was leading a trio of the Caserne Auvare's burliest male uniforms; and OQ4, the command vehicle, driven by Frankie Lejeune.

Working on the theory that Esquebel would initially head to the Peerless Taxis office to pick up his hidden key, OQs 3 and 4 were already parked downtown.

Frankie watched the cursor on her screen move unerringly on to Avenue Joseph Raybaud.

'It's brilliant.' She squeezed Erica's knee. 'And that's not from page one of the *Positive Reinforcement Handbook*. It really is amazing.'

Erica took the compliment with a modest shake of the head. For all of two seconds.

'I know! And the cursor will continue to flash however much we zoom the map. That will be invaluable later.'

'Absolutely.'

Erica looked up for a moment. A little to their left, an interesting vehicle was slowing for a red traffic light.

'Frankie – look.'

Every patrol officer and CCTV watcher in the city was on the lookout for a white Mercedes long-wheelbase panel van.

'OQ Three.' It was Flaco from the other Caserne car. 'A white Merc LWB just pulling up at the lights. Can't read the plate from here. Come in, Four, over.'

Frankie picked up her handset.

'OQ Four. Yes, we see it. If it has an A-31 plate, Operation Manou's going on temporary hold. Come on, roll forward... Got it. No – no go. The plate is the new type.'

She read out the number. 'And it's local. They could

have changed it, of course, so call it in. They'll probably tell you they've stopped the van several times already this evening but never mind. Over.'

'OQ Three. Copy. Over.'

The lights turned to green. The van pulled away.

'Landing right in our laps?' Erica gave a little shake of the head. 'That's not going to happen, is it?'

Frankie exhaled deeply and returned to the map showing Manou Esquebel's progress along the avenue.

'OQ One. Suspect turned into Maccario. His mobile's in his trouser pocket, by the way. Front right. In case you were wondering. Come in Two. Over.'

'Two. I'll let him turn at the cross junction and then I'm go. Over.'

The women could follow the move perfectly. But then quite suddenly, the cursor veered slowly off the road.

Frankie gave Erica a look. The cursor continued to drift.

'He's turned off, Frankie. Somehow.'

'Are you sure? There's no road shown on the map.'

'I'm certain. It's spare ground or something. It has to be.'

'OQ Two. Where the hell has he got to? Over.'

'OQ One. Can't you see him? Over.'

'Two. No, I can't. Over.'

'One. Fuck – he must have shot off round the back of that building site. Over.'

'Two. Well, get in there after him. He's trying to lose us. Over.'

Erica grabbed Frankie's wrist. Her words came out in a single burst.

'Manou's *not* trying to lose them – he's slowed right down, look. He thinks he may be being followed. It's a test. I'm certain of it.'

Decision time. No gizmo was glitch-proof but in her short career, Erica had never yet let the Brigade down. Frankie picked up the handset.

'OQ Four. Don't chase him. Stop the tail. Now.'

For a moment, radio protocol broke down.

'No, no, no,' Terrevaste said. 'Esquebel might be going off anywhere.'

'Sorry, Captain, but TeeVee's right, we can't just—'

'OQ Four. Listen – I know what's happening. I'm following it on our screen here. Maintain your speed and direction or you'll give the game away. You're stood down, both of you. Over.'

'That's not the right—'

'Four. Do you want me to add "that's an order" to what I'm saying? Because if you do, you're both on a charge. Over and out.'

Frankie rammed the handset back into its cradle. Both women gazed at the cursor.

'He's still crawling,' Erica said.

A few more seconds elapsed. And then, slowly but surely, the cursor began to head back to Avenue Maurice Maccario. It stopped at the junction for what seemed an inordinate amount of time and then continued towards the city.

Frankie hit the talk button.

'OQ Four. Erica one – Foch nil. Over.'

'OQ Three. Awesome, ladies. Uh… over.'

Frankie and Erica couldn't resist a smile.

On the screen, turn after turn brought Esquebel inexorably towards them. Finally, he turned into Rue de Bruges, parked outside Peerless Taxis and went in. 'OQ Four. Okay, we can all see where he is. Let's just sit tight for the moment. Over.'

'OQ Three. Check. Over.'

A couple of minutes later, he came out, drove his cab around to the back of the building and returned on foot. Looking all around him, he stepped off the kerb and walked quickly away down the street.

'OQ Four. He hasn't ditched the mobile so we can still track him. Once he's disappeared around the corner, we'll rendezvous and continue on foot. Craxe? You stay in the vehicle and sweep behind us.'

'Three. Understood. Over.'

Erica kept her eye on the screen as they got of the car.

'I'm on him,' she said, following the cursor. 'Rue d'Alsace, left-hand pavement.' 'Better give Darac an update.' Frankie took over the laptop. 'Want to do it, Erica? I can follow the bouncing ball.'

Back in the squad room, a tired and frustrated team was in need of a lift. Perhaps the call just in from Rue Vaulesne would provide it.

'Alright – thanks for that.' Martinet hung up. 'Still no sign of Corinne Delage.'

Max Perand was loping his way around the desks, doling out coffees.

'She was an accident waiting to happen, wasn't she?' He set down a couple of noisettes. 'Now she's happened. Beard's got rid of her to stop her screwing up anything else.'

When Granot's eyes were tired, they had the look of raisins dropped in crème pâtissière. Tonight, a splash of red wine seemed to have found its way into the mix.

'It's possible.' His words floated away on the ebb tide of a long, exhaled breath. 'Likely, even.'

'Was yours the flat white?'

'Do I look like a drag queen?'

Granot grabbed an espresso.

'Sweet Jesus.' Bonbon tossed his pen on to the pile of papers in front of him. 'Just taken me ten minutes to realise I've been over this case once tonight already.'

Darac's mobile rang.

'It's Erica.'

Heads turned as he put the phone on speaker.

'Looks as if Manou's picked up the key. He's just left the office on foot so he can't be going far.'

'Fantastic. So your device is working well?'

'Of course. And the beauty of it is even if Manou looks behind him, he won't see us. We're not there. We're strolling along quite happily around the corner.'

'*Chapeau*,' Granot said, sharing a smile with Darac. A tired smile but a smile, nevertheless.

'No need for Terrevaste and his mate, then?'

'Frankie stood them down ages ago. In disgrace, practically.'

'Good. Very good. But listen, Erica – things could get rough later. If the guys go in after Manou, you make sure you're well back. Promise?'

'Frankie's already laid down the law on that.' Darac heard a distinct catch in her voice as she went on. 'When we get to wherever Manou's headed, he might be the only one there, you realise.'

'Understood. But if he isn't and things get ugly, you might get hurt. Or protecting you might be the reason one of the guys gets hurt. Stay well back.'

'I will.' She still sounded a little unsteady. Perhaps it was the combination of care and authority in Darac's voice that was getting through to her. 'I... cross-checked Delage's phone records against the others, by the way. There were no matches.'

'Ah. Thanks for trying.'

'The raid – if raid's the word – Frankie's going to call you the minute it's over.'

'Good. Stay safe.'

Darac flipped his mobile.

'Who's in the second car with Flaco – Arnaud, Craxe and who else?'

'Serge Paulin.' Granot gave a nod. 'Rugby player. Big future for him in the game, they think, if he decides to go that way.' He gave Darac a knowing look. 'Of course, he might just be mad enough to try and combine two careers.'

'Whether he's a *sportif policier* or not, it sounds as if they'll get the job done, alright.' Darac raised his espresso cup to Perand. 'Double?'

'More like a quadruple.'

'Good man.' Darac downed it in one and returned to his notes. But after just a few lines, he thought better of it. 'I think we all need a break. Let's take a minute.'

There were no dissenters and for the moment, the only sound in the room was the rattle and hum of the air conditioning. Darac got to his feet, his mind already defaulting to the situation with Angeline. He hadn't yet read the remainder of her goodbye text. But was now an appropriate moment? Would there ever be an appropriate moment? He decided to risk it. Three texts had come in since he had last checked: two from the quintet leader, Didier Musso; one from Marco, the drummer. Safety first. Didier's opener was a list of the numbers he'd selected for Monday evening's band rehearsal. They completed a cycle of jazz suites the quintet had been working on for several months – Thursday's gig promised to be quite something. The other two messages were timed at 9.25 and 9.38 respectively. The gist of them was that Darac was missing another sensational night at the Blue Devil. The guys knew he loved the percussionist Lucas Van Merwijk and his band was tearing the place up. *Okay – crime and shit is important*, Marco asserted. *No question. But we're talking Lucas, man! Rim shots that'll take your head off! One-handed rolls! Clave like you wouldn't believe! The guy's a genius!*

And then Darac turned to Angeline's message. He managed to read one more sentence.

Nothing but rattle and hum in the room. And every so often, an arrhythmic thump.

Bonbon and Granot were standing around like victims of a stun bomb.

'Cancellara won the time trial.'

Granot nodded.

The rattle, hum and thump went unchallenged for a while.

'Sprinter's day today.'

Rattle. Hum. Thump.

'Probably.' Bonbon gave the matter prolonged consideration. 'Hushovd maybe.'

Hum. Thump. Rattle.

'Or that English kid.'

'Cavendish.'

'Uh-huh.'

Thump. Thump. Rattle. Hum.

'I'm going to throw some cold water on my face.'

'Good idea.'

They shuffled out of the room together.

Once they had safely gone, Perand gave Darac a sly grin. 'There they go – the ox and the fox. Like in the kids' books. Or maybe the hog and the...' A look from Darac persuaded him to go no further. 'Chief – don't get me wrong.' A little colour showed through the boy's stubble-blackened cheeks. 'They just look funny together, that's all I meant.'

'Perand, I need to spell something out to you. Because I don't give a shit about matters of form or hierarchy or – fill in the blank, basically – I let a lot of things go. Right? But that doesn't mean I suffer fools gladly, sadly, or in any other way when the chips are really down. At this stage, I don't expect your written work to be anything like as perfect as Granot's or Bonbon's. But I do expect you to record information as clearly and concisely as your ability allows. A murder case report is not the place for jokes, irrelevant comments or ironic little asides about one-horse towns, et cetera. At best, it's an irritation; at worst it could slow things down or even become a source of confusion. I don't want to see any more of it. Understood?'

Perand shrugged.

'Okay.'

Darac held the stare a moment but said no more.

By the time Granot and Bonbon returned, Darac and Perand were back at work. Darac was rereading a copy of a letter Corinne Delage had received from her mother in 1987, just a month before she died. One sentence struck him as particularly resonant, though its meaning wasn't clear:

Corinne, I will never forget the day you became part of our lives, wandering in like a little lost lamb.

Darac sat back, his mind alive with 'what if?' scenarios. He couldn't shake the feeling that in one of them lay the kernel of the whole story.

* * *

Rue Monteverdi was an impressive street in name only. A glorified alley running behind Rue Durante, it was, however, no more than a short stroll from two significant sites: the Peerless Taxis office, and Rue Verbier, home to the prayer room. Manou Esquebel had advanced about halfway along it when he turned into a space shown on Erica's screen as the yard of a small industrial unit.

'This looks promising.' She showed it to the others. 'He can only get out the way he went in.' She switched to a city-view image of the spot. The street boundary to the yard was formed by a head-high wall topped with spikes. Into it was set a gate wide enough to admit a car or a small van. 'Through that gate, in other words.'

Flaco peered at the screen.

'Maybe it's that padlock Florian's key fits – not the door to the unit. Whatever it is.'

Frankie had already dismissed the possibility.

'Wrong kind of key.'

'The wall is handy.' Erica was still buoyant as a beach ball. 'Something for us to hide behind.'

Kevin Arnaud was a big man with a big ego and a small mind.

'We don't hide, Mademoiselle. We take cover.'

'You take cover, sweetie. I'll hide.'

'Toggle back to the tracker map, Erica.' Frankie studied it for a second. 'Can we all see it?' They were about fifty metres away from the target. 'Any questions?'

Serge Paulin put up his hand. He was a powerfully built young man with a confident but sweet persona; the sort of lad every mother hoped her daughter might bring home one day. And with any luck, hand on.

'Might it be easier if I take the laptop?'

'Thanks.' Erica gave the case a pat. 'But I'd better hang on to it.'

'Incoming.' Frankie smiled suddenly, prompting the others to cool it for a moment. As the passers-by came alongside, Arnaud made to kiss Erica – a much-used move because it concealed two faces at once. Feinting deftly to her right, she sought Serge's arms instead. It seemed to have the desired effect. The passers-by passed by.

'Quite a sidestep you've got there.'

'Really?' She re-anchored her hair. 'You'd know, of course.'

'Sure you don't want me to carry the laptop?'

'I'll manage it, thanks.'

Frankie looked up and down the street and then checked her watch.

'Okay, as quickly and as quietly as possible – let's move. Rendezvous at the wall.'

Scooting effortlessly on his toes, Serge Paulin beat the others to it by some margin. There was no sign of a padlock on the gate. Taking up position, he peered around it into the yard. Illuminated by a solitary lamp, it was a paved area bounded by blind walls on all three sides. There was no sign of Manou Esquebel. The industrial unit itself was a small, single-storey L-shaped building with an unfrequented, even disused air. No lights were visible inside. If Esquebel had got in, it couldn't have been via the roller door set into the short side of the L. Paulin would have heard it.

Without warning, a heavy male body landed on him from behind.

'Hi, what are you doing?' The man reeked of spirits. 'Playing *cache-cache*? *I* wanna play.'

'Shhh!'

The drunk immediately put his finger across his lips.

'Do you want the seekers to catch us? Run down to the street at the bottom.'

'To Ruesorrini?'

'To Rue Rossini, yes. Go on. And when you get there…' Paulin gave the man a shove in the back. '…count to five thousand before you move again.'

Like an antique vehicle misfiring into motion, the man's legs gradually picked up the drive as he set off down the street.

Arnaud led the chasers home. Hampered by the laptop, Erica was still some way behind.

'Did you see Manou…' Frankie took a recovering breath. '…go into the building, Paulin?'

'He must have got in around the corner – the far end of the long side.'

'What is this place? Or was, rather?'

'A small workshop, maybe?'

Flaco shot glances over the wall at the building and then behind her.

'I don't get it.' She took a second look. 'The layout and the angle means you could back a car into that far corner and no one would see you go into the building. Not even from directly opposite.'

Frankie checked the angles for herself.

'Yes, you could. So why didn't he drive here?'

Erica finally made landfall.

'He's inside… Over in the far corner.' She took a deep breath in. 'Note to self – get fitter…' She tapped a slender fingertip on the screen. 'He's where the cursor is.'

'Okay.' Frankie signalled the backup car. 'Time to suit up.'

Arnaud gave Erica a look.

'How accurate is that trace?'

'It's a five-metre spread. Of course…' Another breath. 'I don't know how the space is laid out inside the building. But what it means is…' She performed the calculation on the screen. '…he's somewhere between six and eleven metres the other side of the outer door.'

'At the moment.'

'Yes.'

'So let's hope he doesn't move. Or take his trousers off for any reason.'

'Alright, Arnaud.' Frankie fixed him with a look. 'It's thanks to Erica we've got this far.'

'Yes, Captain.'

Craxe joined them from the backup car and handed out the body armour.

As Frankie suited up, her eyes locked on to Erica's.

'Got your radio?'

'Yes.'

'Put your earpiece in and go back with Craxe to the car. Listen in but don't talk to us unless it's absolutely necessary or you might blow our cover. If we lose Esquebel, you'll hear all about it. If we ask you, but only if we do, tell us where he's going. Okay?'

'Yes, Mama.' Erica made a moue. But she did as she was told.

The raid party all set to go, Frankie turned to Flaco.

'Ready, Yvonne?'

'Ready.'

The men shared a grin. Yvonne was 'Flak' to them.

'You all know what to do.'

With weapons drawn, they advanced silently towards the far corner of the yard. Arnaud held the lead position as they approached the door. Each member of the team had a copy of Emil Florian's key. But was this the right door? Anxious looks were shared as Arnaud put the key into the lock and turned it. The door opened.

The space beyond was unlit. Arnaud's torch went on as he stepped quietly inside. The others followed. The air in the room felt like a medium for swimming in rather than breathing. It was a small, shabby space; its only furniture was a quartet of battered old waiting-room-style benches thrown together in one corner. The topmost one was missing its seat, Frankie noticed. A door was set into the far wall. Beneath it, light spilled in a shallow pool. With Paulin and Flaco in close order behind him, Arnaud moved smartly towards it. Muffled voices were heard. One was Manou Esquebel's nasal whine. The other was more sonorous. Frankie's ears pricked up. It sounded familiar. Holding up a staying hand, she slipped past Arnaud and listened at the door.

'Of course it's good to see you,' the voice said. 'But why haven't you brought the cab round to the door? That's always been our arrangement in the past.'

Frankie had heard enough. She nodded to Arnaud and took a couple of paces back. With one kick, the door flew open. The team burst in.

'Police!'

A mirrored wall. Esquebel standing. Half-naked male standing. Half-naked young female lying. Toilet.

'Face down on the floor! Now! Both of you! Down!'

Shaking, the half-naked man sank only as far as his knees. The sole of Flaco's boot did the rest. As she grabbed his hands and cuffed them behind him, urine began to trickle between his legs.

'Keep still!'

Looking exhausted and defeated, Manou remained standing, hanging his head. But then, as if detonated by an unseen hand, his whole body seemed to explode. Fending off his kicks and punches, Arnaud took a couple of blows that might have broken his ribs but for the body armour. It was Paulin who finally quelled the storm, lifting Manou off his feet and charging him hard into the mirrored wall. In a splatter of blood, the miniature muscle man shattered into a hundred pieces and dropped unconscious to the floor. Cuffing him, Arnaud ran an eye over the source of all the bleeding – a gash at the back of the head.

'Deep but not life-threatening.'

He called an ambulance.

The girl was lying on the missing bench seat. Frankie knelt down next to her.

'We need two ambulances, for God's sake.' The girl looked about seventeen and was barely conscious. 'Then phone Forensics.'

'Check.'

The girl began to stir.

'No… I don't… want…'

'It's alright, it's alright. You're safe now.' Frankie hoped her voice would act as some sort of salve because cradling the girl in her arms was not an option yet. 'By the book now, everyone. We owe it to the victim. I'm going to take swabs from her. Swabs that I'm sure will positively incriminate Monsieur André Volpini.'

The girl became more obviously agitated. Frankie came in a little closer.

'There, there, you're safe…'

Flaco's sense of outrage went up several notches.

'This is Volpini? The lycée principal?'

'That's right. Will you help me, Yvonne? Yvonne!'

'Yes… Yes of course.'

'Arnaud – who is she? Come on – the rest of her clothes and things are on the floor next to the toilet.'

He went over to them and picked up the girl's purse.

'Paulin? Arrest Monsieur Volpini. Pay particular attention to your wording. When I've finished with…?' She shot Arnaud an enquiring look.

'Anne-Marie Sosa, eighteen.'

'When I've finished with Anne-Marie, I'll take an initial statement.'

And then she would call Darac.

With Granot and the others listening in, Frankie's report concluded with an account of Volpini's confession to the rape of Anne-Marie Sosa and an unspecified number of other girls.

'He had no choice, we had every conceivable piece of evidence against him and he knew confessing would reduce his sentence slightly.'

'And naming the other five key holders to the room won't harm him, either. Legally.'

'Indeed.'

'Any of them work at the lycée?'

'None. Judging by the addresses, they are all reasonably well-to-do middle-class types, though. The yard and the building belong to one of them – a Thierry Ranson. Armani's organising the trawl, a five-point simultaneous strike.' She glanced at her watch. 'In exactly four minutes, Volpini's friends are going to get an early morning call they will never forget.'

Raul Ormans caught Frankie's eye. Indicating the fingerprint sample he was holding, he mouthed 'Florian's' and pointed to the top of the toilet tank. She blew him a kiss as Darac continued.

'So Manou was the driver.'

'He was on hand both to take the drugged victims to

the room – usually as the result of a call for a cab home – and to drive them away afterwards. He never took part in the rapes themselves, according to Volpini. It seems Esquebel wasn't lying about that, remarkably.'

'Good for him. How long had it been going on?'

'Eighteen long months and we didn't know a thing about it until Emil Florian got himself murdered. R.O.'s just found a print of his here, by the way.'

'Excellent. What did Volpini say about Florian's murder?'

'At the time it happened, Volpini was waiting for him here. They were going to "go hunting" – that was the term he used.'

'Using the water bottle ploy?'

'Volpini had little faith in it. He was going to introduce Florian to the joys of roofies. When he didn't show, he assumed he'd got cold feet. He says he had no idea that Florian had been murdered, and I believe him. Volpini has come completely apart and you know what that does – the bastard hadn't the energy to lie.'

'Bonbon's saying something, Frankie – hang on.'

Frankie caught Ormans' eye.

'Any other prints, R.O.?'

'Some. Remains to be seen how many of them match the other key holders but it's looking promising.'

Darac came back on.

'We're wondering why Volpini went anywhere near the Rue Monteverdi room once he knew we were investigating the murder of one of the key holders. Should have been a sign to stay well away, surely?'

'Except for one thing. After my visit to Volpini, he and the others got their heads together. They realised we may have acquired Florian's key but what good was that to us without an address to tie it to? Nevertheless, they thought it...' her tone supplied the quotation marks, '..."prudent" to discontinue their activities here. But they couldn't just abandon the place – there was video equipment, a computer, DVDs, sex devices, sofa beds and other highly incriminating stuff lying around. So they decided to clear it. Ranson volunteered to do the fetching and carrying and to clean up. Volpini helped him. When they had had enough for the day, all that was left were a few battered old benches. They were going to dump those later. Ranson drove off, dropping Volpini at Bar Brindisi around the corner. Several bars later, he clapped his ravening eyes on poor young Anne-Marie Sosa. He knew he shouldn't but he couldn't help himself. His pockets were stuffed with roofies and he still had the key to the place. Yes, the lovely, soft and springy sofa beds had all gone...' Frankie was starting to really feel it. 'But no matter, Volpini thought, he'd use one of those filthy old bench seats. Well, he didn't want to scrape his knees on the floor, did he? Now all he had to do was wait for the right moment to spike Anne-Marie's drink.' Frankie's stomach turned over as she remembered Volpini had offered her a drink in his apartment.

'You still there, Frankie?'

'Uh, yes, yes... He did it just before she made to leave and then followed her outside. Of course, he was soon escorting her. Feeling out of it suddenly, Anne-Marie was grateful for the use of his arm. How kind a gentleman he was. Then he brought her here.'

'But after he and Ranson had spent all that time clearing...'

'I know it doesn't make sense but you have to realise we're dealing with compulsion here. When the impulse kicks in, rationality disappears. It's a disease.'

'A disease, okay. The Manou angle. How did that work this evening?'

'He phoned Volpini from the taxi office – keeping the conversation bland so as not to alert the dispatcher.'

'Jesus Christ...'

Frankie could picture Darac at that moment – his face a clenched fist as he ran a hand through his hair.

'...That's my fault. I should have had Peerless's phone tapped as well as Manou's own.'

'It wasn't a mistake, it was just a bad break. And you haven't exactly had nothing else to do this last couple of days.'

'Manou.'

'Yes. Volpini was furious with him, he said. He'd tried to call the boy numerous times. Where had he been? Manou said he'd be right along. But he didn't take the car, as usual.'

'Why?'

'Because unknown to Volpini and his associates, he'd spent the last twenty-four hours at the Caserne and he'd had enough. He went to tell Volpini that they could get themselves another driver. He'd only done it in the first place to be able to buy a multi-gym machine, he said. Muscles – can you believe it? He did it for bigger muscles.' She exhaled deeply. 'Well… that's about it from here.'

'Ah. I was hoping you were saving the best until last.'

Frankie gave a sad little shrug.

'That Volpini somehow knew what connects Florian and Agnès? No. Sorry.'

'Too much to hope for. But this is brilliant work, Frankie. Now go home and get some sleep. We'll need you fresh later on.'

'It's only… a quarter to three. I can keep going for at least another half-hour.'

Frankie lived in La Turbie, a thirty-minute drive from the city.

'Sensible girl. See you later.'

She rang off, wrapped things up with the forensic team and then walked out through the yard into Rue Monteverdi.

'My car?' she said to the uniform on cordon tape duty.

'It's been left for you down the street, Captain.' He indicated a line of vehicles to their right. 'That way.' He lifted the tape for her.

'Thanks. Goodnight.'

It was 2.50 am and the air was as hot and thick as soup. Were the pavement not blatted with dog shit, she would have slipped off her shoes and walked the rest of the way barefoot. But even given cool, clean stone, it would have been no walk in the park. A montage of images was running in her head. She got into the car, started the engine and lowered her window. But she felt she couldn't drive away.

She needed to take stock for a moment. She recalled the conversation she'd had with Agnès in the cell block. Might it prove their last? It seemed inconceivable. But...

A man's unseen hand reached in through the window. Frankie jumped as she felt a finger jabbing her shoulder.

'You're it!' The drunk's breath was a 70% proof fire hazard. 'Now *you've* gotta count to five thousand.'

Frankie put the car in gear.

'I'm going home. That's what I'm going to do.'

5.15 AM

It was thunder that finally woke Agnès. A cracking, rolling roar that threatened to bring the heavens themselves crashing down. Crashing her out of one nightmare into another.

At least she was not alone. She felt someone's foot nudging her calf; a hand, its fingers splayed, digging into her side. As her eyes grew accustomed to the dim light, she could make out the forms of several others. All of them were naked, as she was. All of them were shaven-headed, as she was. Nevertheless, there was safety in numbers, wasn't there?

She couldn't tell what kind of structure they were confined in but she seemed to be the only one sitting on its floor. The bodies of her companions were snagged together as if they had been bulldozed into the space.

They were all dead.

As the thunder continued to roll overhead, she tried to scream. But then she heard a sound, a wonderful voice calling to her from beyond the dead.

'They're just dummies, darling. Mannequins from a window display.'

'Papa? Oh, Papa! Thank God. Thank…'

She slipped into darkness once more.

7.28 AM

Flat matte black and with a round-edged shiny black surround, the screen wasn't in itself interesting. In fact, it wasn't even as interesting as the digital thermometer. But oh boy, when it was turned on. He thought of the phrase: 'Her face lights up when she smiles.' She, whoever she was, had nothing on the TV. The whole world came to life in its face.

Cancellara yesterday. The time-trial king. The course wasn't ideal for him but it didn't matter. You'd bet your TV that he'd win it. So later on today, it would be Cancellara that would don the yellow jersey and roll out with the others as race leader.

A rustling of cloth.

It's the fat one! My beloved fat one! I thought she was gone for ever.

'Hello.' That smile. 'You got your TV after all. That's wonderful.'

He blinked once.

'You're enjoying it?'

He blinked once.

'Of course. Perfect for you. And being able to watch your son and everything.'

He blinked once.

'I'm on another ward now but I thought I'd just pop over

to see how you are. May I look at your mouth?'

He blinked once.

The familiar smell of her fingers. The loosening of the plate. He felt air cool his lips. What was happening? He felt air on his lips.

Felt it.

'That's looking much better. Just a little more cream and we're there.'

The smell of the cream. He expected that. Come on, let's feel its greasy softness now.

'And now the gauze.'

He hadn't felt the cream. Another false summit.

'Here we go.'

Warmer. And a covering sensation. Almost imperceptible. But it was there.

'And now the plate.'

Pressure. Tightening. Strong words for what were the most delicate of sensations. But sensations they were.

'Upphhh…'

The fat one's eyes widened. Her mouth fell open.

'What?'

'Upphhh…'

'No. Don't try to speak.' Her face a study in concentration, she looked at the bank of readouts on his monitors. And smiled, excitedly. 'In a moment, I'm going to prick the back of your hand. Is that alright?'

He blinked once.

'I want you to blink once if you can feel it; twice if you can't. I'm going to do it on three. One, two… three.'

He blinked once.

'Yes!' she said, her eyes almost disappearing behind the rising crescents of her cheeks. 'Let's try it again.'

7.30 AM

Yves Dauresse jinked neatly between two whip-cracking towels. A Garde Républicaine shower area was no place for the slow of wit and limb.

'Missed, you sad bastards!'

Roger Lascaux and David Jarret were almost changed into their inspection overalls as he joined them at their lockers.

'I don't know why my bare backside seems to fascinate everybody.'

'Fair play to it.' Lascaux slipped his watch over his wrist. 'It is a decent arse.'

'Thank you, Roger.'

They shook hands.

Jarret was drying his hair.

'Except you've got to remember who the towel-flickers, the ones who hang around in the shower at the end, are. They are benders. That is why they go for it.'

'Any arse in a storm, eh? I thought I was special there for a minute.'

Lascaux gave him a look. He knew just how special the man was. And then he realised something was missing.

'I hate to think where you're hiding my watch.' He held out his hand. 'Give.'

'What? No, you must have dropped it.' Looking for a likely spot, Dauresse finally settled on his riding boots. He reached into one of them. 'Well look at that. Imagine finding it there.'

With exaggerated gratitude, Lascaux took it and walked away.

'Shouldn't wear it on your right wrist!' Dauresse turned to Jarret. 'Lefties. Eccentric people.'

It was Jarret's turn to look Dauresse up and down. Gags, cryptic remarks, unsuspected knowledge, sleight of hand: there seemed to be no end to the man's capacity to surprise.

'They're not the only ones, mate.'

The banter and general horseplay continued through all the routines and rituals that marked the start of the GR's day.

And what a day it promised to be for the three of them.

7.45 AM

The mannequins had been removed by the time Agnès woke for a second time. Or perhaps it was a third. Or tenth.

She was wearing a nightshirt now. It was short, thin and filthy but it covered her nakedness. And there were better messages from her body: it hurt like hell. She was sitting with her back drawn up against the side wall of some vehicle. Releasing an avalanche of pain down her spine, she tried to get up. She couldn't. Her wrists were manacled to a chain that ran through an eyebolt fixed behind her. In the dim light of what she now realised was a panel van, her eyes began to focus more securely. The sharpening image she saw almost broke her heart.

'Thank God you've come back to me.' Vincent's words were shot through with tears. 'Thank God!'

She tried to hold out both arms to him but the chain was too short to allow it. One arm would have to do.

'It's alright, Papa.' Agnès's throat was dry and the effort of raising her voice made it crack. 'It's alright.' She was scared to death but she was even more scared of showing it. 'I'm feeling much better now.'

'Thank God, thank God…'

Their reaching hands were well out of touching range

but the look that passed between them felt strong enough to walk on – a suspension bridge across the nightmare. In her head, Agnès was herself enough now to realise that whatever was happening, it was the product of someone else's madness, not hers.

Thunder rolled overhead.

'We'll get out of here, Papa. We're not going to die trussed up like this. They're out there now looking for us – Darac and the others. The Brigade, *our* brigade is looking. And they'll come through for us, Papa. They'll save us. But we mustn't give up in the meantime. Do you hear me? We must keep going. We mustn't give up. You taught me the value of that. Like so many other things.'

Vincent's head dropped.

'*Come on*, Papa. We're in this together. As always. Let's think about it. Let's think about what we can do to help ourselves.'

For the moment, the thunder rolling overhead subsided.

'There's no...'

'Yes there is! *Look* at me.'

His head remained bowed. When he spoke, his voice was a desiccated replica of itself.

'I meant there's no... toilet or toilet paper. I... had to go just to the side here.'

A proud and fastidious man, her beloved papa, reduced to this. Somehow, Agnès managed to stop herself from weeping. Calling on every resource she had, she spoke out in a strong, clear voice.

'Pee-pee and ca-ca aren't going to kill us, you know.'

He didn't respond.

'Hey – remember when I was a toddler? I don't remember it but you and Mama used to say that when I'd finished on my potty, my favourite game was pouring everything I'd done over my head. Do you remember that?'

He looked up, the slightest smile of recognition lightening his face.

'Yes. For a time, you were the most disgusting child.'

'Bodily emissions aren't going to kill us. And our hair will grow back. Well, mine will. And things could be worse, Papa. Thanks to these gorgeous *bon chic*, *bon genre* nighties, at least we won't have to look at each other's wrinkly old bodies now, will we?'

Vincent gave a little laugh.

'*That's* it. We're not beaten. We haven't even begun to fight.' Rasping the chain through the eyebolt, she looked carefully at the way it attached to her wrist restraint. Whatever the fight was going to consist of, she realised, it wouldn't involve freeing themselves from their manacles. It would be a waste of valuable energy to try. 'We'll get out of this, Papa. I'm absolutely certain of it.'

More thunder from above, rolling in the opposite direction this time.

'The van is parked under a rail viaduct, isn't it? That's why they haven't bothered gagging us.'

Vincent's face seemed more animated suddenly. Anger was a great galvaniser.

'They were wrong, weren't they? The so-called *experts*.

They said the Sons and Daughters of the Just Cause were "a joke". Or a smokescreen.' He essayed the neutral Parisian accent. "They're not terrorists." Well look at *us*! I go to the door. A man in a ski-mask pushes me over, then injects something into my arm. Next thing I know, I wake up in this hell hole. Who do they think has done that? Children?'

Agnès smiled.

'That's better, Papa. Much better. My experience was the same. The injection part anyway.'

'Exactly!'

'But the people who've taken us are *not* terrorists, Papa. What sort of targets are we? And there are numerous other factors. Whoever is doing this is doing it to punish us personally. So who? Come on. Let's get our brains in gear. Who hates us? Who have we wronged? No, let me rephrase that. Who might think they have been wronged by us?'

'No, no, no, it's… terrorists, isn't it? Fanatics. Lunatics. No?'

Agnès calmly returned his look, saying nothing. After a long moment, he shook his head.

'You're right. It's not terrorists.'

'No, it isn't. And that's good news because it's not our field. Whoever has done this is a bank robber, an enforcer, a rapist – a murderer. We're in our comfort zone here!'

A bitter smile played on Vincent's lips.

'That's been our lives, alright.' He shook his head. 'I should never have let you join the Brigade.' The chain rasped through the eyebolt behind him as he raised a hand. 'Look where it brought you.'

'Hey. You didn't *let* me join. I joined. And it was the best move I ever made. Now let's move on. Forwards, Papa, remember? We go forwards. So let's think about those who might have done this. It might help us later.'

'How?'

'What did you always say? "Knowledge is...?"'

She let him complete the phrase.

'"Knowledge is power." It's true, yes.'

'We may find ourselves in a position where we can use that power.'

He looked sheepish.

'I need to go to the... Just to pee this time.'

'Do it. I'll look the other way.'

Agnès's back was an inquisition of pain and turning her head to the side brought a new torment. But she was determined not to show it; not to show any weakness or negativity. *Thank God I'm my father's girl*, she said to herself. The Dantiers had never given in. They had always pushed that little bit harder. Always been winners.

'Are you alright, Papa? All I can hear is grunts. I want to hear a nice steady pssssssssssss.'

Vincent was finding it hard to manoeuvre himself into position. But by moving his left hand as close to the eyebolt as he could, there was sufficient play in the chain to allow his right hand to do the needful.

'I'm alright.'

'Good. And if it turns out to be more of a trickle than a torrent, don't worry about it.'

'It's not coming out at all. Come on, damn you.'

'Listen, Papa. I'm going to go as well, alright? Maybe that will help.'

His whimpering started up again but this time, it wasn't through the effort of moving.

'Sweetheart… sweetheart… You're so…'

'Hey, stop that. Come on.'

'Yes… Yes, you're right. Positive. Positive is the way forward.'

It was all Agnès could do not to cry out in pain as she turned on to her side.

'When we get out of here, I'm going straight to the osteopath,' she said, relieving herself. 'Back's a little sore.'

'You poor darling.'

'There you are. Listen to that flow. No problem.'

Her strategy worked.

'Better, Papa?'

'Better.'

Accompanied by more rasping of chains and grunts from Vincent, they set about righting themselves. For a moment, Agnès thought she might vomit with pain but she held on.

'Now – to work. I can think of at least… five people I sent down who swore they would come for me when they got out.'

More thunder, rolling in the opposite direction.

Vincent suddenly looked stronger.

'Who were they? Bastards.'

'Benoit Greuze is the first one that comes to mind.'

'Greuze, Greuze... Strangled a man he swore blind was burgling his house.'

'He did. *Strangled* the burglar, note. It was obvious he'd lured the man to the house for the express purpose of murdering him – he was convinced he was having an affair with his wife. Greuze always maintained I tricked him into confessing. He's out now. Been out almost a year.'

'He could never organise a thing like this. Without help, anyway.'

'Agreed.'

'Who else?'

As the unrecorded minutes ticked by, the pair began to compile an impressive list of candidates. Eventually, they cast their vote.

'So who do you go for, Papa?'

'Cyrille Monceau,' he said.

7.58 AM

Bodies lay sprawled over desks in the squad room like victims of a mass poisoning. Only Darac, revived by a shower in the Caserne, was awake.

He flipped his mobile.

'Who am I speaking to?'

'Cabriet, Captain.'

The boy sounded about seventeen years old.

'And you've relieved Captain Tardelli's man, yes?'

'That's right, sir.'

'You have the Delage house in clear sight?'

'Yes.'

'Any activity to report?'

'No, I'm under orders to ring you if Madame Delage or anyone else turns up. No one has.'

'I'm coming over. Do you know what I look like? I don't want you ringing me to tell me I'm standing on the doorstep.'

'I do, sir. I've seen you play at the Blue Devil a few times. And I've got some of the quintet's CDs as well.'

Darac was stunned. In almost fifteen years on the force, he had come across only three other officers who were jazz fans.

'Practically unique, Cabriet. That's what you are. We'll get together over a beer and a couple of albums sometime. Or the other way around.'

'I'd love that, sir.'

'I'll see you shortly.'

Darac had read Corinne Delage's letters over and over again; every name in her somewhat scanty address book had been rung or visited; her financial accounts had been scrutinised; and her most recent employer, much to the woman's annoyance, had been disturbed at eleven the previous evening for an interview. One or two call-backs aside, there didn't seem much that could be added to the picture of Delage – not in time to help find Agnès and Vincent. And yet Darac was persisting. She was the key to it, he was certain. He put on gloves, went in through the back door of Delage's house, and called Cabriet.

'Yes, I saw you go round, Captain.'

'Let me know straight away if anyone turns up.'

'Yes, sir.'

The photos. The personal effects. Even Angeline's god-damned soap – Darac intended to look at everything again. Maybe they had missed something.

Twenty minutes went by. Thirty. And beyond. It wasn't until he was on the point of leaving that he noticed the foot stool that lived under a nest of tables in the living room. Sitting on stubby wooden legs, it was a leather drum-shaped object – Delage in furniture form, Darac reflected. More for the sake of completeness than in the hope of finding anything useful, he decided to give it a closer look. Reaching under the tables, he felt its top lift slightly as he pulled it out. The top wasn't just a top. It was a lid. For a moment, he was back with Medusa's plinth. He lifted it off.

'How did we miss this?'

The stool doubled as a work basket. An upper tray contained all the typical accoutrements of sewing. A collection of more diverse objects lived in the compartment below, most of them in need of some sort of repair. Kneeling on the floor, he removed them item by item.

One piece immediately intrigued him. With screw holes cut into lugs protruding from either end, it was a small, flat metal case. A vaguely arabesque design was incised into its japanned upper surface. He wondered what the thing was and why it was in the basket – it didn't appear damaged. A bag containing a couple of matching screws was taped to its rear side.

Holding the base, he slid off its lid. Inside was a rolled-up piece of parchment-like material bearing a handwritten text. The script was exotic. He looked at it for a moment, uncomprehending. But then, although he couldn't remember what such things were called, he suddenly realised what it might be. He took out his mobile and photographed the object from all sides. His mind alive with ideas, connections and possibilities, he forsook the floor and went to sit at the bureau. Turning on an Anglepoise lamp, he directed the beam at the screw holes in the lugs attached to the case.

Getting to his feet, he moved quickly to the kitchen door and carefully examined the frame. Nothing. The door to the staircase was next. Nothing. And finally, the door into the front lobby. No better news there. Now what? He went over to the bookcase. He'd been through it once already, shaking out each title to see if anything had been hidden between pages. This time, his attention was directed to the titles themselves. He scanned them one by one.

'Shit.'

So far, nothing had reinforced the theory that was taking shape in his head.

He flipped his mobile.

'Cabriet – alright to step out of the front door?'

'Have you finished then, Captain?'

'No. I just want to stand on the front doorstep for a minute.'

'Alright. Yes, everything's clear.'

Darac went to the front door and opened it. It took two seconds to find what he was looking for. At about shoulder height on the right-hand side of the doorframe, there were two small holes, one above the other. He offered up the parchment case. The holes in the doorframe appeared in the dead centre of the screw holes on the case's lugs. Another matching pair of holes appeared lower down. He went to the back door and repeated the experiment. Three pairs of matching holes there. He was already calling Frankie as he went back inside.

'Paul?'

'Yes, I'm over at the Delage house. Are you at home, Frankie?'

'No – been back in my office for about an hour or so now.'

'Good. Check your inbox – I've emailed you a couple of photos.'

'Of what?'

'This might seem a strange place to start but you're Jewish by birth, aren't you?'

'By birthright and mess of pottage... Sorry, that's not helpful. Yes I am. Non-practising, of course. And non-believing, come to that. Most of the time.'

'But you know Jewish lore?'

'Try me.'

'What do you call those text-containing cases that Orthodox Jews attach to their doorframes? To attract good luck.'

'To attract good luck and good Nazis, my grandfather used to say. Mezuzoth – mezuzah in the singular.'

'Mezuzah – that's it.'

'Why?'

'Because I think Corinne Delage has one. And it's been attached, taken down and reattached to her front and rear doorframes several times. It's not in favour at the moment.'

'I never thought I'd have anything in common with Corinne Delage.'

'I just want to be sure it's what I think it is before I go any further.'

'You're sounding pretty upbeat... Ah, here we go.

I'm opening the photos now… Okay. The first one *could* be a case. Little untypical, though. No Star of David or anything in the pattern. Now the second… is the text: *Shema Yisrael*. It's a mezuzah, alright.'

'This is it. This is *the* lead, Frankie. Granot and Bonbon are still researching old files. Tell them they can stop. I don't know the details yet but I think I know what's behind this whole thing.'

'What?'

'We pass a plaque commemorating it every day.'

'The… round-up? In '42?'

'The round-up. I've got some people to see and other calls to make but I'll be back as soon as I can.'

He began by calling Adèle Rousade in Archive.

10.35 AM

Darac strode into a squad room that bore no relation to the sleepy, report-strewn mess he'd left a couple of hours before. The news that he was on to something had got around. More than thirty officers and assistants were crowded in. But before he got the meeting rolling, he needed to check a couple of things.

At the back of the room, the projector he'd called up was hidden under the blond blackout curtain of Erica's hair.

'Alright back there?'

'Having to replace the bulb holder. Be a couple of minutes.'

'Did Adèle come up with all the files I asked for?'

'All of them.'

'Good, thanks.'

He found Granot next.

'I'm going to need your help during this. Got a ruler and a pad to hand?'

'Yes?'

'All will become clear in a minute.'

Darac returned to the front of the room. Behind him, the screen had already been set up.

'Okay, everyone.' The buzz subsided. 'While we wait, I'll explain why I've come to the conclusions I have.' His eyes swept the room, engaging with every face. 'Put the following factors together and see what they suggest to you. Corinne Delage was on hand when poison was jabbed into the arm of Emil Florian; and later, playing a more active role, she was there when he finally succumbed to it. Then we learn the frugal, seventy-year-old Delage recently bought a van for €9,500. The money was given to her by a third party – obviously to mask the purchaser's true identity. That van is then identified as almost certainly the one used in the kidnapping of the boss and her father. Now this morning, I learned something we didn't know about Corinne Delage. Frankie's best placed to help us with this.'

Feeling strangely moved, Frankie enlightened the team on the concept of the mezuzah.

Darac took it on from there.

'Thank you. Now clearly, a non-Jewish person could own such a thing, though it's less likely they would display it in the prescribed manner. But there's an interesting aspect to this. A pair of matching screws was taped to it. All four turning surfaces in the slots were chewed-up. I then found several pairs of matching holes in the front and rear doorframes. In other words, Delage had attached, removed and reattached the mezuzah on a number of occasions. I think I know what this on-off approach implies about her Jewishness but let's move on. We know she was a war baby. We're not sure of the true details because her original birth certificate was lost but she was registered as born into a family of tenant farmers, the Groismonts from Grandeville in the Île de France.'

The monologue drying his throat, he went across to the water cooler.

'Last night, Bonbon and I came to the conclusion that the Groismonts were not Delage's natural parents. Reinforcing that theory is a remark Madame Groismont, who was not Jewish, makes to her in a letter. She refers to the day young Corinne came into their lives, and I quote, "wandering in like a little lost lamb." Not "climbing out of the car" or anything like that. "Lost" and "wandering". It suggests she was unaccompanied, doesn't it?' Grandeville is a small, rural community...'

Perand examined his nails for a moment.

'...but it's also a rail head. Land Registry confirms that in the forties, the Groismont farm lay right alongside the principal train line from Paris to the south-east – the line used to transport Jews from Nice to the holding camp at Drancy. The records we're about to view should help us with this but I believe that the girl who became Corinne Groismont was on board one of those trains. I'm contending she somehow escaped from it as it slowed to a crawl or made an unscheduled stop alongside the farm. The authorities sealed carriages and freight vans. But I've just been told that there are numerous accounts of captive passengers cutting holes with concealed tools, even forcing apart planking under the noses of the guards. The picture I have in my mind is of someone, probably the parents, seizing the opportunity when the train was stationary to thrust Corinne through such a crack. She was only a toddler, remember, and tiny. Eventually, she found her way across the fields to the Groismonts' cottage. And there, they welcomed in the lost lamb with open arms. And it seems they kept them open.'

He paused to take another sip of water.

'The letter I quoted suggests that at some point, perhaps towards the end of their lives, the Groismonts told Corinne of her true heritage. They knew full well where she had emerged from – those fucking trains were going past their land on a regular basis. It must have been horrendously difficult for Corinne to hear that truth. And confusing. Suddenly, she's not the grown-up darling of a Catholic farming family, she's a... Jewish orphan of the storm. She doesn't feel it but she knows she is. The repeated displaying and taking down of the mezuzah suggests uncertainty as to her religious identity, doesn't it? There's no copy of the Torah or any Jewish literature in her bookcase, incidentally. And Rabbi Pawel has no knowledge of her ever attending synagogue – I've just asked him.'

At the back of the room, Erica was staring into space.

'Ready yet, Erica?'

'A parent pushing a little thing like her out of the train – can you imagine? Almost like giving birth to her a second time.' A shake of the head. 'Sorry. A few more seconds, that's all.'

'Any more questions before we start looking at things?'

No takers.

'Alright, we've got facts and so far we've got little more than informed speculations linking them. But now we come to something about which there is no speculation and it tightens up the whole chain. Adèle has unearthed case files relating to the round-up, detainment, screening and deportation of Jews from the Caserne in 1942. The first thing we're going to see is a list of the officers who played major roles in the operation.'

'Ready now.'

Erica flicked a switch and the projector threw the image at the screen. It landed on Darac first, trammelling him in a net made of names. He stepped quickly aside.

'Just close that blind behind you,' he said, parking his backside on Perand's desk. 'Make it easier to read.'

The list of names formed up in stark black against white:

> Chief Inspector Crutte, Albert
> Inspector Medenville, Jean-Francois
> Sergeant Letcheberia, Pierre
> Officer Dantier, Vincent
> Officer Djourescu, Adam
> Officer Lourthe, Simon
> Officer Bertrainde, Carl

'Dantier.' Armani almost spat out the name. 'Vincent the Good and Wise Dantier.'

Darac took out his notebook.

'He, Djourescu, and Lourthe, I think it was… yes, Lourthe, all young officers, received commendations for their efforts. Djourescu was a real star, apparently. Top marks in everything. Rounding up Jews was just another opportunity to shine. They arrested over a thousand men, women and children in just two days.'

'Makes you feel proud, doesn't it?' Bonbon took a sweet out of his pocket, then put it back. 'And it happened in these very buildings.'

'Less of the piety, *please*.' Granot's dissent had an unfamiliar sharpness. 'Imagine the pressures on them. Don't suppose they enjoyed doing it. Despite the commendations.'

The colour had drained from Frankie's cheeks.

'You're right, of course. But "I was only following orders" has a certain ring to it, don't you think?'

Granot wasn't the most sensitive of individuals but he hadn't the heart to press the point.

'And,' she went on, 'not every officer in France toed the line. Some deliberately lost paperwork; others carried out more active acts of resistance.'

Granot couldn't let that go.

'And what happened to them? And to their families?'

Darac shook his head.

'There's no time to debate moral questions now. Let's concentrate only on the case. Any questions before we move on?'

Flaco raised a hand.

'How did Delage get to know Vincent Dantier had

been involved in the round-up? Just because of his age? Or something more concrete?'

'Good question.' Darac ran a hand through his hair. 'I don't know. And I don't yet know where Emil Florian fits into this.'

'Here's a possibility.' Perand stuck out his long chin and scratched it. 'He doesn't fit into it. He was just the wrong man in the wrong place – a random victim to try out the poison on.'

'A walking crash-test dummy?' Darac stared off for a moment. 'I like the freedom of your thinking but it's far too risky, isn't it? Let's press on.' But he took a deep breath instead. As chills raced each other down his spine, he told himself to essay calm efficiency and get on with it. 'We're going to look at two other lists and compare them. Erica – bring up page one of the first, please.'

As a page of names and ages formed on the screen, Frankie's grandfather's words came back to Darac: *Mezuzoth attracted good luck and good Nazis*. 'These are the names of all those who were eventually deported from the Caserne to Auschwitz.'

'Jesus Christ.' Bonbon exhaled deeply. 'Look at the ages of some of them.'

'The detainees were given the option of handing over their children.' Frankie put a hand unconsciously to her bosom. 'There were organisations who took them and looked after them. But I've heard that a lot of parents thought it was a trick and kept their children. Tragically, as it proved.'

Darac kept a concerned eye on Frankie as he continued.

'It's easy to make mistakes with lists, right? We need something foolproof and I can't think of an easier way of doing it, so, Granot – you've got a pad and a ruler there?'

'I have, yes.'

'As Erica brings up each page, note down the name of any child with a DOB between 1936 and '42 – the span is just to give us a bit of leeway. Tear off each entry as we go so each name has its own strip of paper. Then when we get to the end, we'll distribute the strips evenly around the room to make it easier to match the names to the second list we're going to see. That way, none of the names...' He almost said, 'can fall through the cracks'. 'None of the names can be overlooked.' He stared at the screen. 'Okay, on page one here, there are... none at all. Good. Page two, Erica.'

By page twelve of the first list, Armani could no longer look at the screen. Giving Frankie's shoulder a squeeze en route, he went to the window and stared out.

A roll call of names gradually coalesced.

'That's the last page,' Erica said, her voice almost inaudible.

Armani went back to his place as the distribution of the names began. At the end of it, virtually everyone in the room had become the proxy guardian of a child. Darac suspected that the name of his charge, Paul Stefan Gartos, was one that would remain with him. For his part, Armani had cast only a cursory glance at his own strip of paper. Alexander Jacob Markowski was a name he didn't want to remember.

His heart rising in his chest, Darac took another sip of water. And then another.

'Now it gets harder. We're going to see that initial list of names again. This time, in date order, the details of what became of the children is recorded.'

As each page came up, anxious eyes scanned the list. Every so often, there would be a sigh, an "oh no" or a shake of the head, and a strip of paper would be laid gently down. It was on page eleven that Darac let go of Paul Stefan Gartos.

Armani made it through to the final page of the inventory. But then there it was. Alexander Jacob Markowski had not been spared.

'No!' Crushing the strip into a ball, he turned to Darac. 'You think that was easier? Do you? Jesus!'

'I meant easier logistically, Armani – that's all.'

No one said anything for a moment.

His expression a curious mixture of concern and surprise, Granot looked across at Darac.

'All the names are… well yes, accounted for. The girl who became Corinne Groismont was not on board any of the trains.'

'She must have been.' But Darac wondered if he had made a serious error. An error that was wasting valuable time. 'I would have staked anything on it.'

'She wasn't there, chief.'

Frankie raised a hand.

'The plaque outside commemorates 1942. But we should probably look at 1943, as well. The '42 round-up targeted Jews from around Europe who had fled here looking for sanctuary. The poor souls underestimated the reach of Vichy. But by '43 when the Nazis themselves were in charge, the situation changed. I know from my grandfather that *local* Jews were the targets, then. There were deportation quotas; bounties paid to anyone who would identify them; local hotel rooms turned into torture chambers. It was worse than before. Appalling.'

And it would have been appalling to have reacted to the revelation with anything but disgust. But Darac felt a sense of release, nevertheless.

'Thank you, Frankie,' he said. 'Those are the lists we need.'

He punched buttons on Perand's desk phone. As he waited, he watched Armani straightening his screwed-up strip of paper with an ironing motion of his fist.

'Archive? Get me Adèle.'

11.13 AM

Every so often, the light had flashed. And now it became more regular.

I'm breathing, *he said to himself.* Breathing under my own steam.

The blonde one. Talking over him, as usual.

'What's the backup rate set to?'

'Twelve,' *the black one said.* 'And the total rate is reading sixteen.'

The blonde one's face. Big and beaming. Coffee breath that could de-grease a chain.

'Clever boy, breathing by yourself. But we're going to keep a watch on you, alright? Because the machine is still doing most of the work. And we want to see you take over completely.'

I'll move my fingers. That will impress her.

'Look at him go! There'll be no holding you back soon, will there? You'll be able to breathe, move… And you'll be able to talk – not just blink yes and no. You'll be able to say anything you like. Are you looking forward to that?'

Oh yes. He was looking forward to that very much indeed.

He blinked once.

11.33 AM

Erica flicked the switch.

'The blind again, please.'

Another page. Another river of tears flooding in from the past.

As Granot noted down the first of the names, Bonbon lowered his head into his hands.

'Bills of lading.' He massaged his forehead. 'Human freight.'

Frankie sat forward as if prodded from behind.

'Look at the bottom of the page.'

For a moment, the group was too stunned to say anything. Erica refocussed the image. No, they weren't seeing things. The entry referred to a family of three who had been arrested and dispatched to hell within one working day: 10 October 1943.

> Djourescu, Adam: DOB 9/7/20
> Djourescu, Elena: DOB 16/4/21
> Djourescu, Olivie: DOB 30/08/40

'But he was one of the arresting officers the summer before.' The words were Flaco's but she was speaking for everyone. 'The commended one, the high flyer.'

Perand shook his head.

'He certainly paid for arresting his own kind. And the rest of his family paid with him.'

Bonbon turned to Granot.

'Who arrested *them*, I wonder?'

'Fucking hell!' Armani threw a hand at the screen. 'Jacques Sevran selling photos of me and some of the others to the boys is shit, isn't it? But sending a brother officer and his family to their deaths? That can never be forgiven.'

'What was that?' Granot stopped writing. '*Did* Seve do that? We thought he'd just accepted a bribe. To fund his wife's care.'

'That may have been the reason he was arrested – so what? He's done a few things, I hear. The rat.'

'The Seve issue can wait,' Darac said. 'Carry on, Granot.'

The procedure proved even more gut-wrenching the second time. As the inventory accounted for child after child, the sense of loss in the room was palpable. But as the torture finally ended, a solitary hand rose into the air. A hand clutching a strip of paper.

'I've still got little Olivie Djourescu.' Frankie's cheeks were damp with tears. 'She never made it to the holding camp at Drancy.'

A collective sigh. Smiles. Even a smattering of applause.

As ever, Granot sought to point out the dangers of jumping to conclusions.

'You know, someone like Frènes would argue that all this tells us for certain is that Olivie went missing somewhere between Nice and Drancy.'

Armani brought his hands together and shook them emphatically.

'Don't forget the lost lamb scenario at the Grandeville farmhouse.'

'It's suggestive – absolutely. But as yet, we just don't have enough to be sure little Olivie is that lost lamb: the one who became Corinne Delage.'

'Yes we do.' Darac pointed to the screen. 'Look at the dates. You were right, Erica: Olivie/Corinne's arrival at the Groismont farm was like a second birth. 10 October 1943 was the date of the Djourescus' deportation to Drancy, right? On the re-registered birth certificate, the Groismonts cited 10 October 1940 as Corinne's DOB. They kept the day her young life began again as her birthday.' He turned to Granot. 'Good enough?'

'Good enough for me.' He gave Darac an approving nod. 'I taught you well.'

Knowing what the exercise had cost her, Darac gave Frankie a look.

'Thank you. And thank you, everyone.'

As a buzz went around the room, Darac was already on the phone to Archive.

'Adèle – we need everything you've got on Officer Adam Djourescu. Prioritise anything that links him with Vincent Dantier. They worked together until October 1943. Soon as you can, please.' He put down the phone. 'Let's take a break. We're in for another wait, I'm afraid.'

As the minutes ticked by, every new sound out in the

corridor drew eyes to the door. And then, a full half-hour after Darac's call, a uniform wheeled in a trolley laden with files. The team got to work on them like maggots on a rabbit carcass. It was Erica who came up with the first find.

'Here are Adam Djourescu and Vincent Dantier's ID photos from '43.'

She projected them side by side on the screen. Idealistic, talented, confident – the young officers looked out into the squad room as mute witnesses to the search for the truth that connected them.

'You can see Corinne Delage in Djourescu's face,' Frankie said. 'Quite clearly.'

Perand looked up from his work for a moment.

'You can. Difficult to feel much sympathy for him, though. The biter got himself bitten, that's all.' Interpreting a lack of dissenting voices as encouragement, he felt emboldened to continue. 'And we're punching the air because little Corinne fell through the cracks in the system and was saved. But look at how she turned out. The woman's a witch.' He looked meaningfully at Frankie. 'And that's despite being brought up in an obviously – what's the term? – "supportive family environment".'

'But look at what had happened to her before then.'

'Probably doesn't remember a thing about it.'

Frankie skewered Perand with a look.

'So would you be happier if she had died?'

'No.' He avoided her eyes. 'But maybe we wouldn't be looking for the boss now if… that had happened.'

'We'll have to debate nature–nurture some other time.'

Darac didn't look up from his file. 'Connections, leads –
that's what we're looking for.'

'I don't believe…' Flaco threw down her pen. 'This…'
She stared at the file in front of her as if it was evil. 'On
the morning of the day of their arrests, Elena Djourescu,
who was seven months pregnant, gave birth in their
apartment. Unsurprisingly, the baby was stillborn. Just a
few hours later, after *that* experience and in *that* weakened
condition, she was arrested. And with her other child and
her husband, she was shipped off…' Her eyes seething
with the injustice of it, she shook her head. 'Yes, I can see
the parents hacking holes in the train carriage to try and
save the one child they still had. Hacking holes with their
bare hands, if necessary.'

Frankie was over her tears.

'I would have,' she said, setting her jaw as she stared
at the screen.

Punctuated by phone calls, cross-checks and updates,
five further minutes of digging went by. Ten minutes.
Fifteen. And then several things happened at once.

Granot's watch was showing 12.17 as he gathered
the stack of papers he'd been working on and set it aside.
Spotting that Darac was on what seemed like a significant
call, he decided to favour the others with his conclusion.

'Not good news.' Granot's take on *sotto voce* was
something all his own. 'Vincent is the only officer or
member of the admin staff working at the Caserne in '43
who is still alive. There's no one we can talk to about the
rising star who was Adam Djourescu.'

Perand shrugged.

'From all those years ago? It was always going to be a waste of time.'

Granot shared a look with Armani. The boy was seriously getting on their nerves.

'Excellent. Ring me back when she gets in, will you, monsieur? Thank you.' Darac hung up and gave the air a decent right uppercut. 'There may be no one left who was *here* but there is somebody still around who knew Djourescu. A Madame Albertine Laseige lived in the same apartment block at the time of the family's arrest. Lives over by Musée Chéret, now. That was the building's concierge I was talking to.'

Perand had further wisdom to impart.

'I wouldn't get your hopes up just because the old dear's out somewhere, chief. My grandmother's almost never in and she thinks De Gaulle's still president.'

'Thanks, Perand,' Darac said, making his way over to Frankie's desk. 'I would never have thought of asking the concierge about her fitness to talk to us.'

'Hey, kid?' Armani's smile was as sweet as gelato. 'Go fuck yourself.'

Darac parked his backside on Frankie's desk.

'When I get the call, it would be a great help if you came too.'

'I'd like to but...' She indicated the pile of material still in front of her. 'Who'll do this?'

'Me, if you like.' Perand shrugged, nonchalantly. 'I've nearly finished my lot.'

'Uh… Okay. Thank you.'

'Guys? This report's quite something.'

All eyes turned to Bonbon. His scrawny frame was arrayed with such spectacular awkwardness in his chair, it was as if he had crash-landed on it from above. But that was the way he sat when he was wrapped up in something. Righting himself, he speed-read the last couple of sentences, gave the pages a flick with the back of his hand and tossed them on to the desk.

'So – thanks to what we've learned about Corinne Delage, we've all been suspecting that it was Vincent Dantier who arrested Adam Djourescu on that October day. Right? It turns out *not* to be the case. A Gestapo unit arrested him and his family.'

'See there.' Granot essayed a sage nod. '*Not* Vincent. Christ, we're so quick to—'

'Just a minute, just a minute… Yes it was the Gestapo but they were acting on a tip-off. The informant was identified neither by name nor initials – as they often seem to have been – or a Nazi hunter may well have found him or her years ago. Instead, there's an oblique reference to the number 287.' Bonbon's tawny colouring turned a couple of shades redder. 'Two Eight Seven. Ring any bells?'

'How about his warrant-card number?' Repeating 287 like a mantra, Frankie scanned the data on the screen. In vain. 'Nix that.'

Darac had several suggestions.

'Car registration? House number at the time? Marriage certificate…'

'None of the above.' Bonbon got to his feet. 'Just nipping to Agnès's office. Back in a second.'

No one spoke. After some moments, Perand turned to Granot.

'So what do you think now? Bonbon must be on to something.'

'What do I think? What I think, son, is that if you turn out to be one tenth as good an officer as Vincent Dantier…'

Bonbon returned brandishing a framed photograph.

'This is not a documented image, just a personal snap and therefore untraceable.' He held it up. 'I must have seen it a thousand times.'

'We all have,' Darac said, studying it. A companion to the photograph he'd found in Agnès's dining room, it showed a young, shirt-sleeved Vincent shaking hands with a superior who was handing him his newly won sergeant's uniform. 'I'm still none the wiser.'

But then he saw it. Behind Vincent, the number on his open locker door was just legible.

'Two eight seven…' Granot shook his head in disbelief. 'Oh no.'

Armani voiced what most of the group was thinking.

'The bastard *did* sell his mate down the river. The whole fucking family, in fact. How could the father of Agnès D. have done that?'

Darac's phone rang.

'Madame has returned?' He stood, giving Frankie the nod. 'We'll be there in fifteen minutes.' He hung up. 'Ready?'

Frankie picked up her bag.

'We'll update you the minute we know anything.'

As they signed out at the desk, Officer Charvet's eyes told them all they needed to know about the way he was feeling.

'There's some progress.'

'You'll get there.' The look he gave them both was sincere. But it conveyed more hope than certainty. 'I know you will.'

Darac nodded. Hope was catching, it seemed.

'We need copies of the flyers of Corinne Delage and the bearded man.'

'I've got some under here.'

'Just one of each. And could you cut off the bottoms? We don't want the text.'

Frankie glanced at the doctored Delage flyer as they made for the door.

'She's bitter and twisted, all right. But there's no wonder, is there? What does Perand expect?' She turned to Astrid's drawing of the bearded man. 'I haven't actually seen this yet… Wow. What a talented girl. Assuming it's a good likeness, of course.'

Bzzzzzzzut!

Despite the heat, Darac put his arm around Frankie's shoulder as they took the steps down.

'I'm sorry you had to go through all that, Frankie.'

'It was tough for us all. And you? How are you coping?'

'Same as everyone else, I guess. Tired. Pumped up. Desperate.'

'I didn't mean that.'

She gave him a look of such tender concern, it gave him an odd sensation in his stomach.

'Ah. Ask me about Angeline after.'

'After what?'

'After we've saved Agnès.'

12.44 PM

Twenty-five kilometres away in Monaco, all was set for day two of the Tour. The hard-nosed hilarity of the promo caravan was already on the road. Back at the start, the team buses had inched their way through the crowds. Bikes, rigid and precise as surgical instruments, had been washed, geared up and fine-tuned. The riders, bellows-chested, skinny-armed, had donned their suits of lurid Lycra and warmed up. Team bosses, the *directeurs sportifs*, had issued their final instructions for the day. The riders had then signed in, formed up, heard but not listened to the dignitaries' speeches, and were all ready to roll out on the first long stage of the race.

Behind them was a motorised armada of team cars, press, TV, neutral service, doctors and many others – hundreds of vehicles in total. On the start line itself was the car of the race director. Ahead of that, the forty-five-strong squadron of the Garde Républicaine was preparing to head off along the route.

The whole world was watching.

Astride their machines in the centre of the front row were Yves Dauresse, David Jarret and the blue-eyed boy, Roger Lascaux – the three musketeers of the unit. That was how they saw themselves: a band of brothers in shirt-sleeved uniforms and shades. Or rather, that was how two of them saw themselves. The third had a very different perspective on things.

Dauresse gave his throttle a tweak.

'So today's the day we were supposed to get blown up, yes?'

Jarret seemed more tense than usual.

'You did that one yesterday. Twice.'

'Did I? Must be getting old. What do you reckon, Lascaux?'

The voice of the squadron commander broke in their earpieces.

'First positions, gentlemen. Over.'

As clutches were let out, 45,000 ccs of power purred gently forward.

'What was that, Dauresse?'

'I said, do you think I'm getting old?'

'You?' Lascaux adjusted his shades. 'You're never going to get old.'

12.45 PM

Madame Albertine Laseige opened the door to the limit of its chain.

'Bonjour, madame. Captains Darac and Lejeune of the Police Judiciaire.' Wearing reassuring smiles, they held up their IDs. 'May we come in?'

Like a tortoise sticking its head out of its shell, Madame Laseige slowly craned her neck into the crack. With damp but alert eyes, she peered at their photos and then at them.

'I've been expecting you.' The old woman's voice was surprisingly strong. 'The concierge mentioned you had called.' She opened the door and, leaving Darac to close it, walked in a rocking motion back into the apartment. The slightly burnt smell of stove-top coffee wafted in from the kitchen as they followed her into a greenhouse-hot sitting room.

Frankie slipped off her jacket.

'Don't be alarmed, madame. We're not the bearers of bad news.'

'Bad news for someone, I imagine. Or why would you be here? But there will be time for that later. Please – sit.' The old lady indicated a deep-cushioned sofa covered in a floral chintz print. 'You can drape your jackets over the end, if you wish. The temperature in here is fit only for reptiles and old ladies.' She brought her hands together decorously. 'But you'll take coffee and gâteau?'

The offer came across more as a command but Darac remained standing.

'Under normal circumstances, we would be delighted…'

'And these are not normal circumstances?'

'I'm afraid they're not,' Frankie said, sitting. 'But we'd love to take coffee and gâteau with you, madame. Thank you.'

Darac gave her a look before turning to Madame Laseige.

'Then may I help you in the kitchen?'

'No, no. I may be ninety years old, Captain Paul Darac of the Brigade Criminelle – you see, I did read yours and Francine's identity cards – but I am quite capable of providing refreshment in my own apartment. Thank you.'

Having laid down her marker, Madame Laseige tottered into the kitchen.

Frankie smiled.

'She might have clammed up completely if we'd tried to rush her.'

'Coffee.' Darac sighed. 'And cake.'

'You run on coffee. And be grateful for the cake, it will probably be our lunch.'

In the kitchen, the mocha pot began to spit and bubble, allowing the pair to speak freely. As they waited, they took in the photographs on Madame Laseige's sideboard, snapshots of another life: the lithe, cheeky-faced child; the shiny young bride full of hope and promise; the proud mother hen with her chicks.

Frankie indicated a collage of school photos.

'She was a schoolmistress, look.'

'She still is.'

'If I live to be ninety, I hope my mind is as sharp as hers. Behave.'

All went quiet in the kitchen. Darac was on the point of investigating further when Madame waddled in carrying a tray containing two small espressos and two large slices of *gâteau mocha*.

'You were a teacher, madame?' Darac said, behaving.

'Yes, I put in over thirty-five years at the chalk face. Happy days. Most of them.'

'Beautiful wedding photograph, too.' Frankie rose to help her. 'Some time in the forties?'

'Easier if I do it myself. No, it's 1938. I was nineteen, Albert twenty-one.' As if she were out of practice, she essayed a smile. 'Yes, Albert and Albertine, I'm afraid. Peas in a pod.' She set down the tray and retired to a straight-backed chair facing them. 'You'll find cake forks and serviettes in the cupboard beneath.'

'1938?' Frankie found them. 'Actually, it's an event that occurred just a few years later that has occasioned our visit today. Are you not joining us, madame?'

'No, no – gâteau is for guests only and I've referred to the coffee pot once this morning already – before my constitutional. The early forties? What possible interest could there be in that for the police now?'

Darac downed his coffee in one and fished the flyers out of his jacket pocket.

'So no one has written or phoned or been to see you recently to talk about that time?'

'No.'

'Not this young man, for example?' He rose and handed her Astrid's drawing. 'He's in his late twenties, we think.'

She looked at the drawing most carefully. And then shook her head.

'Or this lady? Corinne Delage is her name.'

She repeated the performance.

'No. As I said, no one at all has contacted me about... that period. Until now.'

Darac and Frankie shared a look. The news was a crushing disappointment.

'Have you seen either of them in any other context?'

She obliged them by looking once more.

'Not the young man.' She handed it back. 'Nor... Madame Delage, I think you said her name was. As far as I know, that is.'

Darac kept his eyes on hers.

'Would you be surprised to hear that as an infant, the person in the photo you're holding was known as Olivie Djourescu?'

Madame Laseige's skin turned to parchment.

'Water, madame?'

Without waiting for a reply, Frankie hurried into the kitchen.

'No. No. It can't be Olivie.' The old lady's hands closed around the arms of her chair like bird's feet on a perch. 'It can't.'

'Take your time, madame.'

She took a deep breath.

'It's not possible. It's not!'

'Not possible because they took her – the Nazis? Along with her parents?'

It was as if movie clips had begun to play in Madame Laseige's head, scenes from a hellish past.

Frankie returned with a cup of water.

'Take a sip, madame.'

Holding the cup to her lips with one hand, she felt the old lady's pulse with the other. A look told Darac to be careful. He nodded. But they had only so much time.

'I can see this is terribly difficult for you, madame, and I wouldn't press you if time weren't so short. The lives of two people might be saved *today* if we can leave here with a better picture of what happened back in 1943. So please, answer our questions if you can.'

Madame Laseige took another sip of water. Gaining some strength, she let go of Frankie's hand and picked up the flyer.

'This is Olivie, you say?' Her forehead was crazed in doubt. 'No. How?'

'I assure you that it is. She escaped from the train that took her and her parents to Drancy.'

'Escaped?'

Her damp eyes wide, she turned to Frankie.

'It's true, madame. Olivie was saved.'

'She... *survived*?' Overwhelmed with the joy of it, she looked more closely at the image. 'I can see it *could* be her, I suppose, but...' She blew her nose. And then smiling more freely than before, she shook her head. 'Oh, I wish Albert were here. This would have made him so happy. After all this time, to learn that both children got away. It's wonderful. May I keep the photograph?'

'Of course.' Frankie jetted Darac a look. '*Both* children?'

'Yes – what other child was there, madame?'

The question seemed to restore something in her.

'Ah. You don't know.'

'No, we don't.' Darac's hopes began to reform. 'Tell us.'

Frankie rejoined him on the sofa as Madame took a long, slow sip of water. When she began to speak, her words had the quality of a rehearsed monologue, one she hadn't delivered in a long time.

'There were two women in our block who were pregnant that summer – Elena, who already had Olivie, and Louise, who at that point was childless. Elena was spirited, earthy. Lovers by the string, I shouldn't wonder. Not that I ever saw any of them. I rather liked her. Louise was altogether plainer. Quieter. Very determined though, in her own way. And rather clever. The two of them had been on no more than cordial terms before the pregnancies but being due to deliver within a short while of each other, they inevitably became a little closer. Not confidantes, I don't think, but sharing that time can draw the strangest people together.' In some distant echo of the phenomenon, she turned to Frankie and smiled. 'Do you have children, my dear?'

'No.' She kept her gaze level. 'I'm afraid not.'

'I'm sorry.'

'No, no. Please go on.'

There had been a further dimension to the trauma Frankie had gone through at the meeting? Darac had always assumed that she had simply not wanted children. Now it was absolutely clear to him that it was a source of pain to her that she didn't, or perhaps couldn't have them. His heart went out to her; but his head had to go back to Madame Laseige.

'Our apartments were all on the top floor. I wasn't particularly close to either of them but as a young mother myself, I was there as a sort of midwife's help when Louise gave birth. It hadn't been a difficult pregnancy but something went wrong towards the end and the baby came early. He was stillborn. Just a matter of hours later, Elena gave birth to a healthy little boy. I wasn't present at that.'

Darac and Frankie shared a look. In the report Flaco had read, it was Elena Djourescu whose baby had been born prematurely and had died.

'And... then.' Madame Laseige stiffened. 'Vehicles braking hard in the street outside. Doors slamming. Hammering. Shouting. I will never forget the look on Adam Djourescu's face as he ran past me on the landing, heading for Louise and Marcel's apartment. He was carrying his newborn son in his arms, a little squirming bundle of life. The soldiers got into the building. They went to the stairs immediately. They knew where they were going. The sound of boots getting ever closer. Before they swarmed on to the top landing, Adam ran past me heading back to his own apartment. He was still carrying a bundle.' Tears welled and spilled. 'But this one wasn't squirming…'

Frankie drew her hand to her mouth.

'…And then they took them – the soldiers. To the trains. We never saw the Djourescus again.'

It was only as her monologue ended that Madame Laseige realised she had been clutching the picture of the grown-up Olivie to her chest. She held on for a moment longer, then with a flicker of a smile, set the flyer down next to her.

Darac stirred uncomfortably in his seat.

'I'm afraid I need to make sure we've got this right, madame. The Djourescus exchanged their live baby son for Louise's stillborn one?'

'They did, the poor, poor things. And it worked, as it were. As far as the records showed, Elena had given birth to a stillborn son; Louise, a healthy baby boy.'

Darac nodded as if he were gathering routine information.

'And that baby grew up to be called?'

'Jean. Jean Florian.'

'Jean Florian. I see.'

He gave Frankie a look. She picked up the baton.

'Louise Florian went on to bear a son who did live, did she not?'

'Indeed she did. But there was a lot of heartache in

between. It must have been seven… eight years later that Emil came along.'

'You gave Emil's name a slight emphasis, there. Do I infer…?'

'Emil was indulged. Spoiled rotten, in fact.' She gave a sad shake of the head. 'When I think of how they came by little Jean. And what a lovely boy he became – cheerful, full of life. But sweet also. Always helpful, always happy to run errands.' She smiled. 'I can see him now tearing off on his bike. But after Emil came along, he may as well have never existed as far as the Florians were concerned. He was their own, of course. A biological child.'

'He was neither loving nor sweet – Emil?'

'Oh, he seemed it. He could act it. But he was the sort of boy who enjoyed pulling the wings off butterflies when he thought no one was looking. Clever but cowardly. It was his parents' fault – they ruined him.'

'What become of Jean?'

'I'm sure he realised even as a youngster that he wasn't wanted. And of course, it changed him. In retrospect, one sees it as a classic progression. There was naughtiness at first. And then more extreme forms of attention-seeking. Finally, the situation having eroded still further, he sought escape.' She lowered her brow suddenly. 'Neither of you have touched your *gâteau mocha*.'

'I'm sorry,' Darac scooped a forkful. 'What form did the escape take?' He put the loaded fork back on to his plate.

'Cycle rides. Oh, I don't mean buzzing to the shops as

he'd done as a little boy. I mean going off for days at a time.' She leaned forward slightly, raising her eyebrows. 'Jean left home as soon as he was able – when he was sixteen. That same summer, he cycled the entire route of the Tour de France. Sixteen years old! That is what neglect can do to a child.'

'When was the last time you encountered any of the Florians?'

'In about… 1961 or '62, it would be, I bumped into Louise in Cours Saleya. She told me that Jean had never once written after he'd left home. To any of them. Do you know what I said to her?'

'That you…' Darac held back, realising he was playing over Madame's solo. 'What did you say?'

'I said that I didn't blame him for a second. Our conversation ended there and that was the last time I ever saw any of them.'

'Madame, what you've shared with us is utterly invaluable. But I have to take you back to that horrendous day in 1943 just once more, I'm afraid.'

'Very well.'

'The Gestapo. Did anyone at the time, or later on, come to that, have any theories about who had tipped them off about the Djourescus?'

'Theories? New ones by the day. But I doubt any had substance. My Albert himself was even suspected for a time – if *suspected* is the word. Whatever may be said now, not everyone shed tears over the destruction of the Jews. Many welcomed it. Shamefully.'

'Indeed.' Darac gave Frankie a glance. 'Did you ever meet any of Adam Djourescu's brother officers?'

'No, no.'

'Or just see any of them around the apartments, perhaps?'

'Very occasionally. You have to remember that one seldom entertained one's work colleagues in that way, back then.'

Darac flipped his mobile and selected the photo album.

'I'm thinking of one in particular.' He showed her Vincent's warrant card photo from 1942. 'I know it's a lifetime ago but do you remember this man? Vincent Dantier is his name.'

'No, I'm afraid not.' She performed a double take. 'Vincent, though, you say?'

'You recognise the name – perhaps in connection with the tip-off?'

'Not in connection with that. And as I said, anyone and everyone was named as the informant at one time or another.'

'Then?'

'I remember it in a slightly different context. I was always puzzled by something Adam shouted as he ran back from the Florians' apartment carrying the… in that awful situation. I haven't thought about it in years, but now I do, I realise I may at last have the answer.'

'Go on.'

'He shouted: "Thank you, Vincent." Shouted it most vehemently. But Louise's husband was Marcel, not Vincent. But now I know that this Vincent was Adam's friend, do you think that he was there at the time? Do you think it might even have been his idea to exchange the living for the dead?'

Darac answered as neutrally as he could.

'I think that was exactly his idea, madame.'

'Ah.' She smiled. 'All these years and I've finally got it.' She looked exhausted, suddenly. 'All these years.'

They had got what they had come for. And more.

'Paul? I think we should leave Madame in peace, now.'

'Yes indeed.' He gathered up the crockery. 'I'll take the tray back to the kitchen.'

Her mind elsewhere, Madame Laseige tacitly granted the indulgence. She turned to Frankie.

'Why are you asking these questions? And whose lives may be saved as a result of what I've told you?'

Kneeling next to her, Frankie took her hand.

'Would you allow us to return when the case is over, madame? We will be in a position then to explain everything.'

'Alright. Thank you.'

Darac returned from the kitchen.

'You've broken the case for us, madame – a case that goes all the way back to 1943.'

He bent and kissed her on both cheeks. 'Thank you. We'll see ourselves out.'

'Goodbye.'

They left her staring into space, as if the whole of her life since that day in 1943 were playing on a screen in the corner of the room. As Frankie closed the door behind them, Darac flipped his mobile.

'Granot? Get on to Paris again. We need to find and question Jean Florian. Immediately.'

1.15 PM

The smell of their waste would have made them throw up had there been anything left in their stomachs. The Dantiers had had no food or water since their incarceration began.

'Where are they?' Vincent's voice was barely audible over the trains thundering above. 'Your precious Darac and his people?'

'That's not helping us, Papa, is it?' Agnès was feeling weak now and even the slightest movement sent sharp, penetrating pains through her body. But she wasn't finished yet.

'"Is it?" I said.'

Vincent didn't answer. Agnès closed her eyes.

'Let's go through it again.'

Vincent looked across at her.

'What's the use? We've been over and over it. And what good will it do us if we do come up with the culprit? Supposing it is Cyrille Monceau? Or one of the Brosses? Or that stupid idiotic bitch? What are we going to do – radio the info into the Caserne? Look at me! When they come in here to kill us, it won't matter who it is, will it?'

Agnès opened her eyes and turned her head slowly towards him.

'I'm sorry!' He wept. 'Forgive me. It's the uncertainty. It's not knowing when these bastards are going to come.'

Another thought had occurred to Agnès. Perhaps the bastards would *never* come. Perhaps they were going to leave them to drift into unconsciousness and death. It was the outcome she feared most. A confrontation, however summary, offered at least some hope of bargaining with their captors. One reason for compiling a list of suspects with her father had been to ensure their minds kept active and focussed on something positive. Selecting the most likely candidates from that list had had another purpose. If a showdown did come, Agnès wanted to be ready with arguments, entreaties and promises geared specifically to those people. There might be seconds to say something that would hit home. And even if it delayed the inevitable by just a few moments, it might be within those few moments that Darac and the team arrived to save them.

She realised she needed to work on her father once more. It seemed that he was at last beginning to come apart, and that she couldn't bear.

'If our captors do come before Darac gets here, I'm going to try to stall them, Papa.'

'With what?'

'Words. They're the only weapons we have. That's why I want to be ready with something tailor-made for the task. I know what might work on the Brosses. I know what might work on Monceau. And I'm almost certain I could talk Jacqueline Dutillieux out of... harming us. So let's pool our resources for one last time, Papa – can you think of anyone else who might hate us enough to want to degrade and punish us like this? If we could identify them in advance, it might save our lives.'

He gazed across at her and then lowering his head, looked the other way. The face of his old friend Adam Djourescu came back to him. Adam, the golden boy of the unit. Adam who was destined for great things. Adam who bested him in everything – except keeping his wife Elena happy in bed. Adam who felt so guilty about the round-up of '42. Adam who had shared his guilty secret with his friend. Adam the Jew.

'No,' he said. 'I can think of no one.'

1.28 PM

The Colline du Château was a wooded hump of rock that rose between the port and the old city of Nice, the Babazouk. In postcard-perfect sunshine, the Garde Républicaine officers Yves Dauresse, Roger Lascaux and David Jarret swung their vehicles on to the quayside that wound around its foot and prepared to go to work.

Designated Station 37 on their route plan, a traffic island opposite the marble war memorial, the Monument aux Morts, was their first assigned obstacle. As his two companions waved and rode on, Roger Lascaux throttled back and slowed to a pirouetting stop just in front of it. His arrival created a buzz among the crowd corralled behind crash barriers on either side of the quai – it was a signal that the riders themselves were on their way. Eyes invisible beneath his tinted visor and shades, Lascaux swung a leg over the bike and pulled it manfully back on to its stand. Someone in the crowd waved to him. He waved back.

A couple of bends further along, the Quai des États-Unis split into four lanes. Marking the start of the central reservation dividing the two carriageways, Station 38 had been assigned to Yves Dauresse. He watched David Jarret disappear into the distance as he pulled up at its broad leading edge. Dauresse's job was to wave the riders across to the 'wrong' left-hand side of the carriageway. He parked without ceremony and, ignoring the crowd, immediately checked out the terrain. He saw no problem with the promenade side. But he was exercised by the Ponchette, a wide, flat-roofed terrace of converted fishermen's houses that stood opposite. His eyes went to that flat roof. Rewarding his instinct, a familiar silhouette appeared briefly above an archway that led through to the daily street market on Cours Saleya. It looked like the stumpy muzzle of an MP5 submachine gun. It made sense to him: a couple of hundred metres long and with a parapet to hide behind, the roof made an ideal viewing platform for a SWAT team – the sort of outfit commanded by the GIPN lunatic he'd encountered at the Monaco briefing, Frédéric Anselme. Dauresse gave a false laugh. He had a nut job and an arsenal of MP5s hovering over him. Wonderful. On his open frequency, he heard an instruction go out to TV. There were to be no aerial shots of the Ponchette. That made sense. Why alert the enemy? Or alarm the viewing public? And if something were to go wrong, three-hundred and seventy million people made a lot of witnesses.

A kilometre or so further along, David Jarret was enjoying himself royally. This was the day he'd been looking forward to since the race route had been announced. To his left was the glittering perfection of the Baie des Anges. To his right was the stuccoed elegance of the Boulevard des Anglais's finest hotels. The crowds were two and three deep as he slowed to a stop at Station

39 – a staggered-kerb turn just beyond the Negresco.

His radio crackled into life.

'This is 35. Four-man breakaway cleared. Peloton thirty seconds behind. Over.'

Station 35 was a steep left-hander on the Corniche André de Joly, four minutes away. The message added useful detail to what Jarret could see with his own eyes. As if tethered to the leading group of riders, a helicopter marked its growing proximity. Chomping the disturbed air of its slipstream, a second helicopter was keeping pace with the peloton immediately behind. And there were others, he noticed, circling serenely above them.

Jarret felt the crowd lift as he dismounted. Here and there, foam rubber hands were donned; inflatable thunder sticks were brandished. He looked back along the road, his eye drawn between the crash barriers to a reassuringly distant vanishing point – reassuring because it meant that the riders would be in his sights for a number of seconds before he needed to act. As always, he had the best seat in the house for their arrival. A head-on shot.

He looked all around him. The crowd was thicker on the city side of the barriers. Not much room to move. Peering through the filigreed canopy of the palms, he checked out the hotels above. As far as he could see, their balconies were scantily occupied: most of those wanting to watch the race had ventured down to the street. He turned his attention to the broad, promenade side of the boulevard. A group dispersing towards the barriers caught his eye. It looked as if some sort of meeting had just broken up. And then he saw it. For a moment, he didn't understand what he was looking at. The sight made him shiver. Snakes. Writhing all around the girl's head.

'This is 36. Breakaway cleared. Peloton twenty-five seconds behind. Over.'

The riders were two minutes away. Jarret jetted a glance down the road and then back towards Medusa. He couldn't see her. She must have taken off the headdress. He scanned the crowd for a matte-white face.

At Station 37, Lascaux had a good sight of the breakaway as they flew towards him.

A full sixty metres away, he could make out the team colours of the four leaders: the orange and white of Rabobank; the turquoise and white of Ag2r La Mondiale; Cofidis's deep red; the blue flower petals of Française des Jeux. Lascaux had eyes like a hawk. His brain was not so acute. He knew what businesses Rabobank and the lottery-sponsored Française teams were involved in. But Cofidis? Ag2r? He had no idea. It didn't matter to him. His contact in the crowd gave him a smile. He smiled back as he turned to face the breakaway. As always, he'd left the holster of his SIG semi-automatic unbuttoned. The safety catch was off. He'd always wondered what it would feel like. One squeeze and it was carnage. One squeeze and he would make history. One squeeze…

At Station 38, Yves Dauresse was sweating so profusely, his flag slipped from his grasp. All those eyes watching around the world. Plus the live spectators. His radio spat out Lascaux's voice.

'37. Breakaway cleared. Peloton at thirty. Over.'

Dauresse's eyes were locked on the Ponchette roof as the lead riders swept around the quai towards him. He could almost hear the safety catches of the SWAT team's weapons flicking off. A madman with a machine-gun battery at his disposal. One false move and there would be shredded flesh everywhere. The breakaway was almost on him as he put the whistle to his mouth and tried to blow.

Further along the boulevard, David Jarret's eyes were still on the crowd. He'd lost Medusa. Where the hell was she? Concluding she might just have moved on, he relaxed a little. But then he saw white-painted hands reaching above the heads of the barrier hangers. The fingers interlocked and slowly lowered out of sight. After an age, they reached up again.

'38. Breakaway cleared,' Dauresse reported. 'Peloton at twenty-five. Over.'

His mind racing, Jarret reached into his pannier and unrolled his flag, a triangle of yellow material bonded to a handle. He peered down the road. Four shapes began to emerge, indistinct at first, as if they were floating above the griddle-hot tarmac.

Thunder sticks began to bang. Foam fingers began to point. Jarret put the whistle to his mouth. Holding the flag in both hands above his head, he began to wave it to and fro.

The breakaway whooshed safely past him. The lead helicopter scudded overhead.

'39. Breakaway cleared. Peloton following. Over,' he said into his radio.

The top of Medusa's head was visible now. She must have put on shoes? She began to glide towards the barriers. Skates. She was wearing skates. She was going to watch the peloton arrive. Jarret turned away.

A dab of grey smudged the vanishing point at the end of the road. And grew wider. It became a flash flood of colour. The crowd began to applaud, bang, wave. Jarret faced the flood as it broke inexorably towards him. A look to the side. Medusa had found a space at the barrier. The second helicopter roared overhead. Jarret began to whistle and wave. The peloton was almost on him. A glance to the side. Medusa was staring at *him*. The peloton was flying past. Their eyes met. Medusa's jaw dropped. The whistle fell from his lips; the flag to the tarmac. He looked to the barriers. There was a space where Medusa had been standing. He needed to think. He flicked on his radio.

'39. Commandant Mohr – do you copy? Over.'

He scanned the promenade as more spaces began to appear.

'Mohr. Affirmative. Over.'

'39. Migraine attack, sir. Visual disturbances…' He continued searching. 'Request stand down. Over.'

'Mohr. Do you require assistance? Over.'

He saw her. Less than thirty metres away. Talking to a man with red pigtails. She seemed anxious to move on.

'39. Negative. Can ride with care. Intend returning to

barracks. Will transfer to tonight's billet when recovered in few hours. Over.'

'Mohr. Stand down. And this will go on your record, Jarret. Over.'

'39. Thank you, sir. I'll see it doesn't happen again. Over.'

He switched his radio on to an open frequency and turned over the engine. As Mohr radioed out the reassigned points to the squadron, Lascaux and Dauresse washed up in the wake of back-up vehicles.

'Migraine?' Dauresse said, pulling alongside Jarret. 'Good skive.'

'Haven't had it in years.' Jarret's eyes were locked on Medusa and her outsized companion. 'Off back to the barracks. I'll be alright.'

Lascaux looked up and down the race route.

'Where are you going to get out of the rat run?'

Jarret indicated an opposed pair of slant-boarded barriers. A uniform stood in front of each.

'One of those gentlemen will do the business.' Medusa still hadn't moved. Jarret told himself to keep acting naturally. 'Well, no explosions or machine-gun bursts to report.'

'I gave the peloton a good strafing.' Lascaux grinned. 'Just to keep them on their toes.'

'Maybe the Sons and Daughters will strike further along.' Dauresse was his easy, swaggering self once more. 'Custard pies or stink bombs is my guess.'

'Could be.'

Medusa appeared to be drawing things to a close.

'Listen, my head's really thumping now, guys. See you down at Brignoles, later.'

Dauresse and Lascaux took their leave, filtering into the convoy before accelerating away towards the peloton. On the promenade, Medusa high-fived her companion, picked up her backpack and began to skate away. She hadn't yet raised her mobile to her ear. That made Jarret's decision for him.

1.36 PM

Darac ran his head under a cold tap before making for the squad room. He found Granot on the phone.

'You're not serious?' He mouthed 'Paris' to Darac. 'You *are* serious. When then?' Granot listened for a second. 'Thank you.' He slammed down the phone.

'That was the Clinique Rendflore near Porte de Montreuil. It's where Jean Florian has been residing for the past three months. In Intensive Care.'

'So he's out of the picture on the ground. Could have planned it, though. Or at least known all about it. Can he talk on the phone?'

'He can blink yes or no.'

Exhaling deeply, Darac ran a hand through his hair.

'Jesus Christ... We could send in a local, I guess. Feed them questions and get them to relay his answer. Frankie – you up for that?'

She interrupted her Evian mid-sip.

'Certainly.'

'I think we'd better do it,' Granot said. 'It'll be at least a couple of hours before he'll be able to speak without impediment, they reckon.'

'Agreed. We can't wait that long.'

Darac's mobile rang.

'Captain Darac? It's Astrid – the mime—'

'Yes, Astrid, if you'll forgive me, we're really—'

'I've seen him. The bearded man…'

Darac smothered the mouthpiece. 'Hey, hey,' he shouted, holding up his free hand. As the squad room fell silent, he put the phone on speaker.

'You've seen the bearded man?'

The room held its breath.

'Yes I have.'

'Can you talk any louder? I can hardly hear you for the… traffic noise?'

'I'm on Boulevard des Anglais – the Tour riders have just gone by and now it's all the team cars and shit. Yes I've seen him but he doesn't have a beard any more.'

'You sure it was him?'

'Absolutely certain.'

'Fantastic – where did you see him?'

'Here. Seconds ago – at the traffic island near the Negresco…'

'Astrid? Astrid, come in.' The phone went dead. 'Shit!' He called her back immediately. No reply. He needed help fast. He checked his address book and dialled another number. 'Santoor? Darac. You know all those DCRI resources you offered to hurl at us?'

'Uh… within reason, Captain, yes.'

'Have you got a chopper over Boulevard des Anglais right now?' Santoor made no reply. 'Don't fuck around. Have you?'

'I'm flying in it as we speak.'
'Good. This is what you do.'

The needle had pierced the soft flesh of Astrid's arm in full view of a hundred people. The drug was the paralytic lancuronium. This time, it contained no delaying agent. Playing his part as theatrically as he could, Jarret took off Astrid's skates, set up her plinth and stood her upon it. A non-living statue. The punters clucked their appreciation at the novel twist in the routine. Jarret unpacked her headdress and put it in place. Astrid stared blindly ahead. He made a show of whispering something in her ear.

'I am truly sorry to have made you a victim, also. But I have something to accomplish that must not be stopped. You died for a just cause, Mademoiselle. The most just cause in history.'

He pulled the bike off its stand and began threading his way between the crowds streaming along the promenade. After a few moments, intermittent snorts from the throttle gave way to a more sustained burst.

Sure that he had gone, Medusa staggered from the plinth. Her slender arms felt as heavy as stone as she raised them to her headdress and pulled it off. Snakes hit the pavement in an explosion of electronic innards.

'Is there a doctor here?' she said, barely able to speak. 'I need help. I've been poisoned.'

Laughter. The spectators were enjoying the whole

fake injection shtick. There was even a fake bead of blood on her arm.

Astrid opened the plinth and with a colossal effort, took out her mobile. The keypad looked kilometres away. Somehow, she managed to enter the number.

Darac's mobile rang.

'Good, I thought we'd lost you. Go ahead, Astrid.'

'He… injected me. Just now.'

'What?'

'He injected… In the arm, I…'

'I've got you. Listen, you're going to be alright, okay? Help will be there any second. A helicopter.'

'I pretended to be… paralysed. But…'

'Don't speak any more. They'll fly you to Hôpital St Roch.'

Quizzical looks were shared around the room. The hospital had no helipad of its own and the standard protocol – landing the helicopter at the old port and then completing the journey by ambulance – would surely take too long.

Darac smothered the mouthpiece.

'Granot – Foch is practically next door. Get them to clear a space on Rue des Postes so they can land on the street. Four good uniforms is all it should take.'

'Yes.' Granot picked up his phone. 'Two, even.'

'It will be there any second, Astrid. So hang on, hear me?'

The sound of blades. Amplified words ricocheted through the roar.

'*Landing. Clear a space but do not disperse. Clear a space. Do not disperse.*'

'There it is now. You'll be in hospital in two minutes.'

'Don't go. Please…'

'I have to make some quick calls. You'll be okay, Astrid. Believe that.'

Back on the promenade, the helicopter landed, scattering the crowd like blown leaves. Two crew members ran towards the fallen statue. Santoor made straight for the spectators.

Darac called Deanna first. His team gathered around like an audience at a gig, he was trading fours with her before the helicopter had even touched down on the promenade. He ended the call by patching her through to the flight crew. Next was A and E at the hospital.

A huge break. It was his neighbour Suzanne who picked up. No need for ID questions or other time-wasting rigmarole. She remained silent as he reeled off everything she needed to know.

'Deanna said to administer the neostigmine immediately. She'll be with you as soon as she can.'

'We're on it, Paul. Out.'

The calls ended, Darac sank down on to the edge of his desk.

'Now we wait. Again.'

Every face was tense. It was Frankie who spoke first.

'What did Deanna say about Astrid's chances?'

'Too many unknown factors. But if she's still conscious on arrival, there's a chance.'

'The poor girl.'

'She helps us – helps us brilliantly – and this is her reward.' Darac stared off, shaking his head. But then something hit him. 'Astrid said she saw the guy "*at* the traffic island near the Negresco", didn't she? Not "just opposite the Negresco", "just past the Negresco" or whatever. But the boulevard is completely closed for the Tour, isn't it?'

Bonbon nodded.

'It was probably just a manner of speaking.'

'Perhaps but this girl's very precise. And she said it before the bastard injected her, remember.'

'But the only guy *at* the traffic island just now would have been a Garde Républicaine officer.'

'What would he have been doing there?'

'Warning the approaching peloton of the obstacle. That's what they do all day when the Tour is on.'

Granot went over to the espresso machine.

'Unless their orders were changed, I can even tell you which officer it was. A lad called David Jarret got that station. We talked about it in Monaco. He was really pleased about it. Prime spot.'

'Jarret.' Darac rolled the name around his mouth. 'Jarret could be Djourescu given a Francophone makeover, couldn't it?'

'It *could*. So could Dauresse, his section leader, come to

that. But this isn't a fruitful avenue. These boys are clean cut. *La crème de la crème.*'

'So was Vincent fucking Dantier.'

Exhaling deeply, Granot shovelled coffee into the holder.

'Anyone join me?'

For once, there were no takers.

'Let's say the perpetrator is this Jarret.' As if propelled by the gathering momentum of his thoughts, Darac shifted his weight forward. 'As a police officer, he could have had access to the files we have. And he could have put the story together – as we have.' He clicked his fingers as an obvious thought struck him. 'He would have had to sign to see them. Archive will have the record.'

'Having to sign for everything.' Bonbon gave a little snort. 'At last it might pay off.'

Darac picked up his desk phone but then put it straight back on to the cradle.

'A problem. If it is this Jarret…'

'It won't be.' Granot shook his head. 'Alright, Vincent turns out to have been a human rat but he's from a totally different world from the GR guys.'

'*If* it's Jarret – how did he tie Vincent Dantier's name to the number 287 on the report? We only got to it via a personal photo.'

Granot held up his hands palms upwards.

'Exactly. And as no visitor to Archive is going to be admitted to Agnès's office…'

Darac was excited again.

'No, it still holds. There's a companion photo in Agnès's apartment. And it's stupidly easy to get into. It took us all of five seconds.'

Frankie nodded, warming to the direction things were taking.

'And we know the kidnapper cased the building at some point, don't we? That's how he knew where the security cameras were in the corridors and so on.'

Darac picked up the phone.

'Just wait.' Granot held up a ham of a hand. 'How did he know to go looking there in the first place? You're putting the cart before the horse.'

Darac smothered the mouthpiece.

'We don't know exactly what he knew to start with, do we? Maybe he knew quite a lot.' He uncovered the mouthpiece. 'Yes, Adèle? I need something else.' He told her what he wanted. 'I'll hold the line.'

Looking tensely at his watch, Darac tapped the desk with a loose fist as he waited. What was happening at St Roch? Did they get Astrid there in time? And if they did, was she hanging on in there now? At least there was a chance. Had he done the right thing? Could he have got her there any quicker? How would Agnès have handled it? Agnès... When this thing was all over, Darac was going to insist she augmented proper security arrangements at her apartment. A ten-year-old child could break into the place.

He glanced at his watch once more. It felt like ten minutes had gone by but it was only two. He scanned the room. Having gone as far as they could for the moment, everyone seemed to be on downtime. Everyone except for Granot, to whom a terrible thought had just occurred. Moving with untypical anxiety, he began scrabbling through the papers on his desk.

'I'm back.'

As Adèle began reeling off a list of names, Darac kept his eyes on Granot. The big man found what he was looking for almost immediately – Astrid's flyer. Setting it down, he arranged his hands around it to mask the beard. Granot's face emptied as if a tap had been turned. Scrunching up the sheet, he tossed it on to the desk like a card player throwing in a losing hand. At that same moment, Adèle read out the name of one David Henri Jarret.

'Thanks, Adèle.' Darac got to his feet. 'Granot?'

'Jarret met both the boss and Vincent at the briefing,' he said, his eyes boring a hole through space. 'Even shook their hands...' He came to, suddenly. 'That drawing's been sitting on this desk for hours. Hours! It just never occurred to me...'

'Why would it?'

The race was on again.

'I need to call Santoor but let's get moving while the trail's still hot. Bonbon and Granot – you organise the ground search for Jarret but no APBs – Jarret may be listening in. Cars, slog squads, our own helicopters, the works.'

'We're on it.'

'Perand – go through Gendarmerie HQ for a photo

of Jarret. Get them to email it to all our guys, fly copies all over the city and on TV.'

The boy got on with it without comment.

'Lartou and Flaco – CCTV and webcams, I guess.'

'Check.'

'Frankie – get back on to Clinique Rendflore in Paris. Conduct that relayed questioning of Jean Florian we were discussing.'

'Right.'

Darac was finally ready to make his call but his mobile rang before he could key in the number.

'Darac? Santoor here. I've questioned the crowd who were watching Medusa. You're looking for a—'

'Garde Républicaine officer, yes, we know. David Jarret is his name. We've got the ball rolling here but what do you have?'

'How did you…?'

'There's no time. What do you have?'

'I'm still on the ground here at the promenade. The helicopter's gone off with the victim. She looked bad, I'm afraid. Jarret injected her in front of several people. Made it look like part of the act.'

Darac ran a hand into his hair and kept it there.

'Jarret tried to stop Astrid alerting us to who he is, right? But he wasn't *as* concerned that several bystanders might be able to identify him later.'

'That's true.'

'So it seems his fear is not so much the threat of capture itself, it's *when* that capture might happen. Wherever he's gone to now, it could be to carry out his mission. We must get to him as soon as we can.'

'This might help you. Jarret's riding a blue Gendarmerie-tagged BMW with a letter P for Paris on the windshield. I've just alerted all... Oh, no, no, no.'

'What is it?'

'I may have just alerted Jarret to the fact that we're on to him.'

'You sent out an APB on an open frequency?'

'I am so sorry.'

Darac felt like hitting something. And all around him, the squad room was alive with abuse and expletives. Some just groaned. Bonbon wasn't alone in reflecting that the man who was carpeting Darac for displaying a photo on his desk had just potentially torpedoed a huge police operation.

'It can't be helped now.' Darac shared a despairing look with Frankie. 'Which way did he go? Did anyone see that?'

'Along the promenade towards the west, initially. After that, no one's sure. But let me get back to you. No more than two minutes.'

Santoor rang off.

'Two minutes is a long time just now.' Darac sought a productive way to fill it. 'Anyone here have Annie Provin's number?'

'I've got her number, alright, but I don't have it.'

Darac's look could have flayed a rhino.

'Cut out the comedy, you fucking clown.'

'Yes, sir.' Perand's swarthy skin coloured. 'Sorry.'

'Frènes has the number, I should think.' Granot was waiting for an answer on his call. 'He's been on her TV show numerous times. They're pretty friendly in a sparring-partner sort of way.' He uncovered the mouthpiece. 'Yes, that's affirmative – every car you have. I *know* the Tour is on…'

Keeping his mobile free for Santoor's return call, Darac picked up a landline phone.

'Monsieur Frènes – Darac. Listen carefully…'

'Captain Dar—'

'Listen! We know who kidnapped the Dantiers. We need someone to review all the TV footage of the Tour's procession along the Negresco stretch of the Anglais. Especially the aerial footage. Stuff from cameras not providing the live feed, even. Annie Provin and her people can do that. Promise her an exclusive on the case if she can get back to us with a lead in the next few minutes.'

He told Frènes what they were looking for and ended the call as his mobile rang.

'Santoor?'

'Not much but something. As we came in to land, the pilot saw Jarret heading up Boulevard Gambetta. He noticed because he thought it odd that a Garde Rép was riding away from the race route while the stage was still going on.'

'Up Gambetta – we'll redirect our ground people accordingly.' He looked across at Bonbon. He nodded back. 'Is the chopper airborne again?'

'Yes. They'll be picking me up shortly.'

'Nix that. Tell them to track above Gambetta *now* – keeping their eyes peeled and you informed all the way. Alright?'

'Check. I'll keep you posted.'

'I'm going over there myself now.'

Darac ended the call.

'Chief?' Perand raised a hand. 'I've got Commandant Mohr holding. He's the GR officer commanding the Tour squadron. I've outlined the situation.'

Perand's printer made an odd burping sound. In halting steps, a photo began to appear.

'Quick work.' He held out his hand. 'Let me have him.'

'The Captain for you now, Commandant.'

His eyes on the emerging photo, Darac took the phone.

'Captain Darac, is it? What is all this kidnapping and murder nonsense? Jarret? It's impossible.'

A maxim of Agnès's came back to Darac: *If you can't pull rank, pull somebody else's.*

'Everyone from Commandant Lanvalle of the DCRI on down is behind us on this, Commandant. Jarret has killed and he's about to kill again unless we can stop him. Quickly, what do you know that might help us?'

Slice by horizontal slice, the top of Jarret's head became visible. The hair was dark brown, and might have been wavy were it not cut so short.

'Are you all sure? It's not—'

'We're sure. Quickly!'

Jarret's forehead. It was quite narrow. Otherwise unremarkable.

'Uh… well he reported sick after the peloton cleared the staggered island at the Gambetta/Boulevard des Anglais turn. Said he was returning to Monaco but he would ride through to Brignoles to rendezvous with the squadron after the stage.'

Jarret's eyebrows. Dark and angled like ticks.

'I see.'

Jarret's eyes. Upside down, they appeared more as an abstract entity than as the 'windows of the soul' concept familiar from pop psychology. Orange-flecked hazel, they reminded Darac of Agnès's. He was seeing her in everything at the moment, it seemed. In everything but the flesh.

'Commandant, I take it your bikes don't carry tracking devices?'

'They do not. We trust our… They do not.'

'Pity.'

Darac concluded the call with a suggestion Mohr call back should he think of anything that might help find David Jarret.

The printer spat out the photo.

'Listen, guys.' Darac held up the shot. Everyone put their call on hold. 'I'm heading out to Gambetta now. I'm going to cruise around.' He brandished the photo. 'Obviously, this man could have gone more or less anywhere from there but at least I'll be out on the streets when the breakthrough comes. Those of you with a finite task: complete it, update everyone and then join me out there. Those with ongoing tasks: assess whether you need to remain here or whether you could carry them out just as well on the move. If you can – you join me, too.' He gave it a beat. Was there anything else? 'Flaco?'

'Captain?'

'The white van paperwork. Do you have that list of rented lock-ups?'

'Yes, I do.' She reached for a loose wad of heavily highlighted pages. 'It's this lot.'

'I know all of them had an initial visit. Were there any inconclusives, any call backs?'

'Several but I think they've all…' She flicked through the pages, looking for any white spaces. '…been done now. No, hang on, there are a couple… Three altogether. Adèle has put them down for a revisit this afternoon but that won't happen with this big push.'

'Let me have the addresses.'

1.52 PM

The rail-thin one. Holding a phone handset. And in the background, a policeman holding a second phone. The blond one was lurking around also. What was going on?

'Hello there, Jean. How are we doing today? Alright? Move your fingers for me.'

He moved them.

'And the other hand... That's it. Lovely! Just need your own breathing to come up that little bit more and then we can take out that nasty tube, can't we?'

He blinked once.

The thin one's sad face.

'Now this isn't easy for me but we all have things to face from time to time. Things that are really difficult and the Lord knows you've had your share these last three months. Well, for most of your life off and on, really.'

Ye gods.

'But two days ago, life sent something else to you, my darling.'

Get out of my face, woman. Can't you see they're coming up to a sprint? Points for the Green Jersey up for grabs. What with David forgetting to give me a wave on TV, the day's turning out a bit shit.

'Yes. Something really bad happened to your brother, Emil.'

Don't tell me the pathetic little bastard has gone under one of those nice new trams? Or choked to death on a piece of socca? That would turn my day around in an instant. Turn my life around. Well, partly.

But then far darker possibilities began to occur to him.

'I asked them if it could wait just a couple of hours but they said it was urgent. I'm sorry, darling. We're here to hold your hand. Listen to the lady on the other end of this phone. She sounds lovely, doesn't she, officer?'

'Uh... I suppose she does, yes.'

'But what she has to say to you isn't so nice, Jean. She's a police officer too. She's going to talk to you to explain things first and then she's going to ask you a series of questions. They are questions about your son. It seems he's responsible for Emil's death and... for other serious crimes since. We can hear the questions too. When you hear them, answer them as you normally do and the officer here will tell the lady what you said. What you meant to say, I mean. Let me just move this TV out of the way. You don't want it at the moment.'

No. For once, he didn't. He didn't want anything except to wind back the clock. He should never have told David what Emil had revealed in that barbed, sneering letter he'd written just twelve short months ago. Announcing that their father had now followed their mother into the grave, Emil had told Jean not to expect so much as a sou in the will.

He could remember whole sections of the letter verbatim. 'Why is there nothing for you? Because you are not a true Florian. I know all about your real mother and father. Especially your mother!' That exclamation mark. Hateful. But then the nub: 'My mother told me the whole thing. You see, you were a Jew baby, given away at birth.' Jean would never forget how he'd felt as Emil went on to recount the story of Officer Adam Djourescu and his wife Elena; the couple whose betrayal at the hands of a brother officer consigned them to the gas chambers of Auschwitz. The only thing Emil's mother seemed not to have known was the full identity of the informant. Jean would just have to make do with the forename – Vincent.

Yet Jean had to pass the revelation on to David. The boy needed to know the fate of his true grandparents. And it explained so much else. It explained why the Florians had treated Jean like a piece of shit once Emil came along. It explained why he had gone on to treat his own wife and son like pieces of shit.

Jean had never blamed his wife for leaving him and taking David with her. He hadn't blamed her for reverting to her maiden name of Jarret. He hadn't even blamed the pair of them for hating him. It had been too late to explain things to his wife; she had died years before. But with David, the neglected son who had disowned him, there had been a chance of redemption. Jean had never had any thought of avenging the original crime, he had sought only to win back his son. David had evidently had different ideas.

What a price Jean had paid. By sharing Emil's revelations, he did get David back; but by sharing them, he might have lost him for ever.

Cold plastic smothered Jean's ear. The thin one was right – the woman's voice on the line was soft and beautiful. But it gouged a hole the size of the Verdon Gorge in his heart.

1.56 PM

Neither had spoken for hours. Having to raise their voices wasted too much energy. When the moment came, Agnès wanted to be ready. Or that was how the period of silence had begun. Now, the first seeds of doubt were taking root. Perhaps it would be better, she'd begun to think, if they just gave in. Let the flies take over completely. And how wrong had she been about the harmlessness of their waste? Leave the stuff another day or two and see what it might achieve.

She kicked one foot against the other, sending a searing pain into her spine. She was furious with herself. That sort of thinking was a one-way street. She would not give in.

The silence wasn't helping. She needed to end it. Trying to manufacture some mucous with her rasp-dry tongue, she moved her head in an agonising arc towards her father. A false errand. He was asleep. It *was* just sleep, wasn't it? A chill washed over her like ice water. She peered hard at his chest. The nightshirt was moving. Never mind about breaking the silence. It was best to conserve energy. Just concentrate on getting through the next minute. And then the one after that.

The fattest of the flies finally came in to land on her leg.

She retched. A positive sign. The thing was too high up her shin to kick away. Bringing more pain, she drew back her foot, lifting the knee. The fly rode the rollercoaster. She would have to use a finger to flick it away. Pulling the chain through the eyebolt behind her, she extended a hand. Nearly. Nearly. Her eyes watering with the pain, she finally managed it. Success! She had shooed away a fly. It looped the loop a couple of times and returned.

Leave it. It doesn't matter.

Forty seconds to go… Thirty…

The thunder overhead subsided momentarily. A gap in the trains. She understood that there was a world of interest in the subject if she could just muster the energy to think about it. She heard a lighter rumble. More of a whooshing sound, in fact. Lorries? It made sense – the Cannes–Menton line ran in tandem with a switchback of highways through a long swathe of the city. The heavy rumbling started up once more, slow at first and then speeding up. It meant the train had pulled out of a station. Probably. Think about which station. Rumbling speeding up; rumbling slowing down. The rumble almost never maintained the same momentum throughout. So it was a station where nearly every train stopped. Nice's Gare Thiers was the principal candidate. No sooner had the theory formed than a continuous rumble challenged it. But it wasn't moving fast. A freight train wouldn't stop at the station, she realised. She considered the thunderous volume of that sound. And the accompanying shockwave. It was as almost as if the rail tracks had been laid on the roof of the van. The whoosh of the road traffic, though, was far less distinct. Yes, they were holed up near Gare Thiers, all right. The viaducts carrying the rail bed were very low on either side of the station – several metres beneath the highway. There was an explanation for everything.

Into the next minute…

With a graunching metallic sound, the back door of the van jagged open. Light flooded in, burning her eyes. Now! Assess. Speak. Bargain. But all she could see was a silhouette behind the bruising beam. Vincent cried out. The silhouette swung the torch at the sound, silencing it.

'What a stink,' the silhouette said. A female voice. 'But it won't be long now.'

With a reverberant clang, the door slammed shut.

Tears lubricated Agnès's voice.

'Papa, are you alright?'

The reply was no more than a mumble.

'Papa!'

'I'm alright.'

Braving the inquisition of her spine, Agnès turned her body towards him.

'Papa, the woman's voice? I recognised it.'

'Yes?'

'It was Corinne Delage.'

Silence.

'Corinne Delage, Papa. Do you know that name? Do you?'

'Sorry, my darling. I've never heard of her.'

At last, Vincent was telling the whole truth.

2.13 PM

Two lock-ups down; one to go.

Set to the Brigade's encoded frequency, Darac's car radio was alive with traffic. The messages followed a pattern. Possible sighting of Jarret reported; sighting investigated; sighting proved negative.

He slowed on Avenue des Fleurs, checking out a broad echelon of motorcycles parked at the kerbside. With one ear on the output from the radio, he called Granot on his mobile.

'Yes, chief.'

'Anything further on Astrid?'

'She's still fighting but... I'm not sure she's winning.'

'Come on, Astrid, come on. Anything from the TV people?'

'They're running stuff but nothing's come of it yet. Annie Provin herself led the footage review – on camera, of course. And they did find a clip of Jarret but it doesn't add anything to what we already knew – he's heading north on Gambetta, going out of frame at Rue de la Buffa. They're broadcasting the clip in split-screen on their news channel, alternating it with the shot we have of Jarret. It's great coverage but she's claiming it merits the exclusive

Frènes promised her. He's already told her it doesn't unless a viewer gives us a lead from it.'

Darac cleared the echelon of bikes. None was a blue GR BMW.

'We've got the whole fucking world looking for Jarret. Surely somebody will have seen where he went.'

'Hundreds will, chief, and we'll talk to them. It's whether we can act on what we find out in time. We've got almost none left.'

Darac turned into Boulevard François Grosso and headed north towards the rail/road viaduct.

'Later, Granot.'

He rang off, restoring the radio chatter to centre stage. Parked against the viaduct wall was another posse of bikes. One caught his eye. He raised his shades. It was big and blue. Slowing, he glanced at the shot of a GR machine Granot had printed off for him. Attracting a fusillade of horns, he stopped the car under the viaduct and went to investigate. It was a BMW of a similar spec. But it was a civilian's bike. He got back into the car as a message from the DCRI helicopter crackled noisily in.

'Magnan sweep completed. Target not sighted. Commencing St Augustin sector. Over.'

His mobile rang. The incoming number was Deanna Bianchi's.

'Deanna?' He held his breath.

'I know it's all systems go but I have something you need to hear.'

His grip on the steering wheel tightened.

'Go on.'

'Astrid's going to live. And although there are complications, as you can appreciate, I'm fairly confident she'll make a full recovery.'

Darac punched the wheel. And then let out a long breath.

'She's already spoken a few words and that's why I'm ringing now. The perpetrator was riding a blue motorbike with a letter P for pancreas on the windshield. That is what you're looking for.'

'Thanks – we got that info and more elsewhere. David Jarret is the guy's name. But she's some girl to have picked it up while being attacked, right?'

'Her ability to stand stock still helped save her life. It slowed the take up of the lancuronium while convincing the poisoner it had taken instant effect. Fortunately, he didn't realise that if it had, she would have toppled over straight away.'

'So how close a thing was it in the end?'

'Had the helicopter taken three minutes to get Astrid to St Roch rather than two, I might be examining her in very different circumstances now.'

'Another sixty seconds and she would have died?'

'Another thirty, even. It was that close.'

'Thirty seconds? Jesus Christ...' He went to a different thought. 'How do you think Jarret got hold of these drugs?'

'Most likely stole them from a hospital, clinic, or possibly even from an ambulance. Neither lancuronium nor neostigmine is a controlled drug, you know. So if some went missing, nobody would have notified the police. All they would have concluded is that some fool nurse had smashed a few vials on the floor and hadn't reported it.'

'Jarret's father's been in an ICU for the past three months.'

'There you have it. But listen – any breaks in the hunt for Agnès?'

'Not yet, Deanna.'

Darac swung the Peugeot into Boulevard du Tzarewitch. Against the cerulean sky, the domes of the Russian Orthodox cathedral glinted like Fabergé eggs. The road turned back towards a cluster of road and rail bridges. Somewhere beneath them was the final address on Darac's list.

2.15 PM

Adrenalin had loosened Agnès's tongue. But her words still emerged as a parched croak.

'Delage. Corinne Delage... Think, Papa. Think because I'm at a loss. She has no grudge against either of us that I can see. She's a racist, that much is clear. I warned her to co-operate with one of our juniors who is black but all this just for that? No. Obviously not. We let her go. And the Caserne didn't even deal with her earlier...'

The back door of the van flew open. Two blinding lights. Two silhouettes. One was Delage. The other was far taller, slimmer.

'Yes!' Vincent said, his chain rattling through the eyebolt as he extended one hand to the newcomer. 'Thank God!' He wept. 'We're saved... Water – give us water, for God's sake!'

'There's no water for you.' Delage's voice was a slap in the face. 'Not to drink.'

As the taller shape shone his torch at Vincent, Agnès's scrunched eyes picked out odd details of a uniform. She didn't trust it. Delage had locked the door on them and then returned with help? No. It didn't make sense. She tried to make out the face gradually filling in behind the silhouette.

'As the laws of this country stand… you are guilty of a very serious offence but if you let us go without further harm, I can assure you—'

'Shut up. Shut up, you filth!'

The shout reverberated in the rank air. A male voice. What men were in Delage's life? Agnès couldn't think of any.

'Yes, you and Corinne shouldn't have kept us in this condition but I repeat…'

Crouching, the silhouette advanced behind the beam. Spittle splattered across Agnès's face. A hand swatted her head to the side. Pain hotwired her neck to her coccyx.

'No!' Vincent cried out. 'Do what you like to me but don't touch my daughter!'

'Let me put the electrics on, David. I want to see better.'

Ignoring the pain, Agnès turned her head towards her attacker. Bulbs in the ceiling came on. The torches were extinguished. In a thin bluish light, she saw him clearly.

'You?'

David Jarret smiled.

'Yes, me. A trusted police officer. Incredible, isn't it?'

Agnès tried to put her mind in gear but it stalled. She had no handle on this. There was nothing to go on. Nothing to connect.

'And I fooled you, didn't I?' Delage sneered as she threaded her arm through Jarret's. 'Fooled all of you. I knew who Emil Florian was, alright. And I knew what had happened to him. I knew everything.' The sneer disappeared. 'Tell David I fooled you. *Tell* him!'

'You fooled us,' Agnès parroted, thinking hard.

'Hear that, David? I did do some things right.'

Jarret's eyes were boring into the motherlode that was Vincent Dantier.

'Me and David planned it together. We were going to get Emil at home but he went out sooner than usual. I knew his route. I knew he'd go to Rue Verbier.'

Jarret's eyes hadn't moved.

'Be quiet. How I managed to shake your hand at the briefing…' He got in closer. 'So how does it feel, Vincent? To be lying here in your thin little nightie?'

Delage gave a delighted little chuckle.

'Lying with your stinking shit just centimetres away? And just out of reach – your beloved daughter lying in *her* stinking shit, vulnerable, abused, uncomprehending? Degrading, isn't it? Painful. Desperate. Hopeless – that you have come to this.'

Delage clapped her pudgy hands together.

Vincent's eyes clotted with grief.

'Water. We need water.'

'Water's coming. I repeat – how does it feel?'

'It feels… execrable; so if you could…'

'Yes? Go on. Finish what you were going to say. If I could do what?'

'David?' Agnès winced as she shuffled her bottom back against the van side. 'You killed Emil Florian.' She swallowed, trying to make spittle. 'But Florian was a rapist, did you know that?'

Jarret and Delage shared a look. And then the old

woman let out a disbelieving snort.

'No he wasn't. He was a rotten bastard alright but—'

'Be quiet. Go on, Filth.'

'Florian *was* a rapist.' Agnès was beginning to feel a little encouraged. 'A rapist of children, indeed. Killing him might even be interpreted as a citizen's moral duty. So there's every chance that your punishment for that crime would be relatively slight. However, harming my father and me will not be interpreted so leniently. I cannot imagine what you, a respected officer, expect to gain by this.'

He gave Agnès a humouring look.

'Can't you?'

More delight for Delage. Agnès persisted with her point.

'David, if we're going to resolve this, you have to release us…'

'We're going to resolve it, alright. Vincent – tell your daughter what this is all about.'

The old man's head was on his chest.

'Look at me, Papa. Don't let go.'

'I don't know… what this is all about.'

'You don't know?' Jarret's eyes were burning. 'Let me help you.'

'Look at me, Papa.'

Vincent slowly raised his head. But he kept his eyes forward.

'The story starts with a family named the Djourescus. Adam was a contemporary of your father's here. A contemporary at the Caserne, I mean. He was bright, wasn't he? Accomplished. Beat you to the André Fonsec Medal in

'41. Beat you to everything, in fact. And you couldn't stand that. But you got your own back on Adam, didn't you?'

'Don't… listen to him, darling.' Vincent's voice sounded false, almost other-worldly. 'It's nonsense.'

'It's not, you arsehole!'

Delage kicked Vincent hard on the knee. He let out a keening sob and sagged forward.

In a rattling of chain, Agnès extended a hand towards him.

'Papa! Don't! Be careful.'

Jarret turned to her.

'He's lucky he got a kick in the knee. Because for what he did next, a kick in the balls would have been more fitting.'

'No – don't tell… He's lying, darling.'

'I know, Papa.'

'It's time we got rid of this stink. Go organise the showers.'

'Alright, David.' Delage climbed happily out of the van. 'Hope you brought towels.'

Her mind still struggling to put a coherent story together, Agnès peered through the open door. They were in some sort of workshop. A roller door was less than ten metres away. She prayed for a hiatus in the thunder overhead. With the van door open, a loud scream might just summon someone.

'Adam had a wife. Elena. Pretty little thing, wasn't she, Vincent? His pride and joy. Your papa tried to get her into bed. She laughed at him.'

In the midst of her terror, Agnès began to gain strength. Her father, behaving like that? It was ludicrous.

'I don't see where Emil Florian fits in with this but you're what – Adam Djourescu's grandson? And you've staged this hideous charade because you've believed some lie from nearly seventy years ago?'

'It's not a lie.' Jarret got in close to Vincent once more. 'Elena, my grandmother, and Emil Florian's mother Louise used to talk about you, Vincent. They thought you were pathetic. They laughed about you and your little, very little, wiles and ploys.'

Vincent returned the look, saying nothing.

Overhead, the thunder began to subside. Agnès swallowed hard, trying to make spittle.

'But I'm jumping the gun.' Jarret jumped out of the van. 'Enjoy!'

The thunder was almost gone. Now was the time. Agnès filled her lungs. But before any sound came, a jet of water hit her in the chest, a crushing, lung-bursting shock. She tried to turn, to hunker down, to make herself as small as possible. Pulling against the chain, she drew a deflecting arm in front of her, a skinny strut against a flaying plume of pain. Momentary release. And then the jet hit her in the face. She tasted salt as her head wrenched back. She couldn't lower it. There was no escape. She couldn't breathe. She was drowning. On and on the torment continued. Another salvo in the face. And then it stopped.

She lay on her side, broken, heaving, spluttering. Vincent stared at her, his mouth opening and closing uselessly.

'Better?' Jarret handed the nozzle to Delage as their

victims' waste drifted on the tide out of the van. 'Watch your footing there, Auntie.'

'You make them all nice and clean.' Delage shook her head as she carried the hose away. 'And this is all the thanks you get.'

Jarret climbed into the van.

'And you want to be pristine for the journey, don't you? It's going to be fun. The van's going to the pleasure park. I think that's what they called it, didn't they, Vincent? In the camps?'

Agnès felt Jarret's hands grab her shoulders. She almost blacked out at the pain as he yanked her upright.

'What's this I hear you say? Camps? Oh yes. You see, filth, in October 1943, your father sent my grandparents and my aunt there to the best of the lot. Auschwitz. It proved a letdown, though. Not so much fun. Forced labour. Gassing. Bodies shovelled into heaps. Not mannequins – real people. Burning. Smoke. Ashes.'

Still recovering from the water jet, Agnès could only manage a single word.

'No.'

'Yes.' He went back to Vincent. 'Tell her.'

Vincent looked into Jarret's eyes.

'I was following orders just as your grandfather did the first time. He consigned countless Jews to their deaths in '42.'

Jarret got in closer.

'*He* followed orders. *You* acted on your own initiative. You informed on him. Informed! And you did it just to gain an advantage at work. To no longer be second best.'

Vincent's head lowered. Jarret's eyes slid to Agnès.

'That's right, my grandparents died in choking agony because your lovely father, a man you so worship, saw a chance to get rid of a rival and advance himself in one fell swoop. All the pain and suffering just for that.'

Making a monumental effort, Agnès took in a long breath.

'It isn't true, David.'

'It's true, alright. They suffered every conceivable torture because of him.' A wilder look shone in his eyes. 'Shall I rape her, Auntie? Just for good measure?'

Delage thought about it.

'Why not?'

'No!' Vincent screamed.

Closing her eyes, Agnès painfully drew in her legs. The van shuddered as Jarret's boots banged down closer. She felt leather scud against her knees.

'Go on, David. What are you waiting for?'

'Leave her alone! Please God!'

'Give it to her.'

'Maybe I... No. She disgusts me.'

It was Jarret's boot kicking Agnès's legs from under her that finally made Agnès cry out in pain. She lost consciousness for a second or two. When she opened her eyes, Jarret was crouching in front of Vincent.

'How did that feel? Eh? I could have avenged the family by just killing you. But for you to really suffer, you had to see your own flesh and blood suffer.'

'Please.' Vincent swallowed. 'No more.'

'Of course, to begin with, I had only your forename to go on. But I got there in the end. Should have joined the Brigade, shouldn't I? Oh – there's one final thing. Your plan didn't work quite as well as it should, monsieur. As you can see, my aunt was given another chance. And so was my father, the not-stillborn baby who took on another life as Jean Florian. You didn't know that, did you? It was a life that was ruined and in turn ruined other lives. But it was through him I embarked on this long journey.' Jarret stared hard into Vincent's shattered eyes. 'What do you think of that, Vincent?'

'A son?'

In her corner, Agnès recoiled as if punched. There was a strange longing in her father's eyes, and a catch in his voice.

'All these years, I've had a…'

'What?' Jarret slapped Vincent's face. 'What are you saying?'

Agnès was sitting open-mouthed, her head shaking.

'You're lying,' Delage said. 'You never had my mother.'

'Whose child do you think she was carrying? It wasn't me your mother used to laugh at, David. It was your—'

'Shut up!

He grabbed the collar of Vincent's sodden nightshirt, pulling his head forward. He slapped him again, harder this time.

'Papa – no, it's not true. Say it isn't. For God's sake!'

Vincent turned to Agnès.

'I… I was thinking of others. I couldn't tell… your mother… Look, David – you couldn't kill your own grandfather, could you? And Aunt Agnès? We could get you off the charge. Get you off the whole thing.'

Agnès began to weep.

Jarret threw Vincent's head back and jumped out of the van.

'Very clever. You almost had me convinced there for a moment. But you are very definitely not my grandfather. And my only aunt is Corinne, here…'

Delage smiled, as if David's confirmation guaranteed the truth of the assertion.

'She and my father are going to get together when this is all over, by the way. He doesn't know it yet. I've kept the fact that his big sister survived a secret from him. Too ill. But when he's stronger, what a reunion that will be.'

'I knew *where* I'd come from, you see,' Delage said, as if chatting with friends over a coffee, 'but until David came to see me, I had no idea of *who* I'd come from.'

'We… we should be at the reunion too.' Vincent essayed a smile. 'Yes – the family all together.'

'Oh yes, we'll do that.' Jarret gave one last smile. 'But first, it's the pleasure park for you two. Have fun!'

The door slammed shut.

Overhead, rail tracks and roadways led off one another in Escher-like complexity. Between the ground-shaking rumble of the trains and the Doppler-shifted whoosh of the traffic, Darac was having difficulty hearing his radio. He upped the volume as he headed towards a row of lock-ups built into adjoining arches at the far end.

A pick-up was parked outside the first of them. Inside, a bald-headed man in overalls was stripping a pine chest of drawers. He cast Darac a suspicious look through his goggles as he got out of the car.

Agnès's weight was hanging on the chain. Using resources she didn't know she possessed, she levered herself upright and stared across at her father. They were going to die, she knew that. But first, she needed to know that her whole life hadn't been based on a lie.

'The story you told. It wasn't... true?'

He looked back at her.

'I... I was just trying to get us out of this. Do you really think I could have...'

A sound from above made them look up. They hadn't noticed the small circular panel that was set into the roof. It disappeared suddenly. A flexible hose protruded tightly through the resulting hole. The van's engine started.

'Oh no...' Vincent whimpered. 'No!'

A choking fug of exhaust fumes began to spew into the space. Vincent turned to his daughter for what he knew would be the last time.

'God... has forgiven me for everything I did. Can you, Agnès. Can *you*? Agnès!'

Agnès tilted her head back and opened her mouth.

* * *

The smell of solvents coming off the blistering wood was overpowering.

'Afternoon, monsieur.'

Darac showed his badge and then retreated a couple of paces.

'Georges Dupont.' The man took off his goggles and rubber gloves. 'Don't get any ideas, this isn't a business – this chest of drawers is mine.' As he spoke, a lit cigarette stuck resolutely to his bottom lip. 'Just thought it needed a spruce-up.'

Several similar items of furniture were stacked at the far end of the workshop.

'Put that out, will you? We're likely to go up in smoke.'

'Never happened yet.' But he complied, saving the stub for later. 'What do you want?'

'Do you know the other owners of these lock-ups?'

'Well, I have this one and the one next door. The one after that's empty. Then there's Monsieur Flaubert and the one on the end is Madame Masoude's. I haven't seen her in a long time. Husband used to be a gardener. There's mowers, tools – all sorts in there.'

Darac showed Jarret's photo to Dupont. He shook his head.

'No. Never seen him.'

Darac showed him Astrid's flyer.

'Monsieur Flaubert,' he nodded. 'Nice young man.'

A thrill shot down Darac's spine. He jetted a glance at the lock-up's roller door. Water was seeping out from under it. The streets around were crawling with backup and regulations demanded he call for it and wait. He remembered Astrid's thirty seconds.

He jumped into his car. Power sliding around a wide arc, he put space between himself and the lock-up and then floored the pedal. Feeling a huge surge of energy, he held his arm in front of his eyes as he aimed at the dead centre of the roller door. In an explosion of noise and flying debris, he smashed through it. A section came away in one piece, somersaulting into the air as the Peugeot slewed to a juddering halt beneath it. He saw a hose snaking from the van's tailpipe. There was no time for preparation. Only to act.

Disconnect the hose. Locate Jarret.

The door section still teetering on its long side, Darac used it as a shield as he dived out of the car and rolled towards the tailpipe. He yanked off the hose. Exhaust fumes poured into his face. The driver's door flew open. A fan of flame from the cab. The thud and whine of bullets. Darac returned fire. The fizz and crack of fracturing glass. He threw open the back doors of the van, releasing a choking fug. No time to check on the occupants.

Protect victims from crossfire. Get away from tailpipe.

A tool cabinet stood against the side wall. Bullets chased him like a lit fuse as he ran and threw himself behind it. A second volley ploughed a furrow of blood along his left forearm as he raised both arms to fire. He felt no pain as he squeezed off another barrage. More flame. More thud. For the first time, Darac got a sight of the shooter. It was Jarret, alright. Jarret shifted his position in the cab. Where was he? More whines. More thuds. Another squeeze. A red haze. The windscreen turned to spray-painted ice.

Secure the weapon. Attend the victims.

From his new position, Darac couldn't see the van's passenger door. It opened as he ran to the cab. Reaching over the bloodied figure of Jarret, he turned off the engine. No pulse. No need to secure the weapon. Darac holstered his own gun and hurried to the rear of the vehicle. Through the dispersing fumes, the muzzle of Jarret's weapon suddenly appeared. Behind it were the small, shaking hands of Corinne Delage. He jetted a glance into the van. Hanging half-out of the back door, Vincent was unconscious, not apparently breathing. In the far corner, an Agnès-like shape was coughing. Darac's heart lifted.

'Reattach the pipe.' Delage's eyes were seething, her blanched face spattered with blood. 'Now!'

'There's no point reattaching it. They're already dead.'

Still aiming the gun at him, Delage's eyes slid sideways. Now was the moment, the only chance he might get. He dived headlong towards her, knocking the gun from her grasp as a bullet ripped past his ear. She fell back, her head slamming hard against the concrete floor.

The weapon finally secured, the rescue could begin in earnest. Holding the hem of his shirt over his mouth, Darac jumped into the van and went straight to Agnès's sodden, rag-covered body. Her shaved head was radish red and she was barely breathing. Her wrists bound, he took the pulse in her neck. Weak and erratic. She had stopped coughing. Good sign or bad? He flipped his mobile and mobilised the medical teams. Now he needed to free her and get her outside into the air.

He realised that he could give her basic mouth-to-mouth if she stopped breathing but if her heart stopped CPR didn't look possible – her shackles meant she couldn't be laid on her back.

A voice called across the death and the destruction.

'And you were worried about my cigarette?'

'Get in here, Dupont. I need you.'

'I don't know about that. What the fuck's been going on?'

'The man you know as Flaubert is a murderer and a kidnapper. He's in the cab. Dead. In his pockets, I hope is a padlock key. Bring it.'

'You do it – I'd rather watch her.'

'I'm not leaving her side. Get the key.'

Dupont advanced tentatively into the space.

'Shit, there's one on the floor here,' he said, tripping over Delage.

Beyond the body, a camp bed was set up. The old woman's overnight things were laid out on it.

'Hurry. There are lives at stake.'

'Alright – I'm doing it, I'm doing it.'

Agnès coughed once more and then choked, a convulsing heaving of the chest. The pulse in her neck began to race. Kneeling down, Darac pulled her torso against him. He began applying rhythmic pressure to her back. As he did so, a milky discharge dribbled from her mouth against his chest and then gushed out in a torrent. Slowly, the coughing subsided. Her skin began to lose its livid colour.

A key landed at Darac's feet.

'Pay you a lot in your job, do they?' Dupont shook his head. 'Jesus.'

Darac put the key in the padlock. It opened.

'Bit too late for the man. He's a goner.'

Darac unfastened Agnès's shackles. Cradling her in his arms, he rocked back on his heels and rose. By the time he'd carried her outside, the first of the ambulances was already pulling into view.

11.15 PM

Charlie Mingus's 'Goodbye Porkpie Hat' drifting dreamily in his slipstream, Darac stepped out on to a roof terrace thrumming with all the sounds and scents of the Babazouk night.

The breeze blowing off the Baie des Anges felt a little fresher this evening. After three long days of pressure-cooker heat, it seemed things were at last beginning to cool off. He set down a cold beer on his tile-top table and subsided into a chair. Only half voluntarily, his head fell back. The sky was crystal clear and he spent several moments just staring at the stars. The universe's reputation for inspiring profound meditation was overrated, he concluded. The holocaust? What help was the universe with that?

His thoughts returned to Agnès. The immediate prognosis was good – doctors were confident she would make a complete physical recovery. But Darac recognised she was going to need all her fortitude to deal with the rest of her trauma.

A Steri-Strip covering his bullet-furrowed left forearm, he reached for his beer and took a long, contemplative draught. It proved only marginally superior to the universe.

Darac turned to thoughts of his own father. Theirs

was something of a charged relationship but he could not imagine what it would feel like to discover a monstrous truth about a man who seemed to have nothing in his heart but tenderness.

The reflection gave him an idea, one he usually ignored – it was just so much easier to do nothing, to let things slide. He felt exhausted, anyway. He had cold beer, he had the pan-tiled canopy of the Babazouk, and he had 'Goodbye Pork Pie Hat' – that would have to do for the time being. But then the tenor solo hit, cutting through the number's hazy lilt like a searchlight.

'Yes, John Handy,' Darac said, aloud. 'You're right.'

He set down his beer glass and picked up his phone.

'Papa? Hi, it's Paul.'

'Paul – this is unexpected, how wonderful to hear from you.'

'Why – has it been so long?'

It had been, he knew.

'No, no. It's just the hour, I suppose.'

'I only got in a few moments ago. So how are you?'

'Uh… fine. Got a bit fed up of the heat wave but it's better over here this evening.'

'And work?'

'Good. Well, maybe not *good*. But you know the perfume industry. When you're as small as we are, it gets more difficult all the time. You?'

'Oh, not too bad. Listen, I was just wondering if you and…'

'Virginie.'

'Virginie, yes, would be free for dinner soon. Next weekend, maybe. Here. Somewhere fancy. My treat.'

'Wonderful. She's dying to meet you and Angeline.'

Gingerly resting his arm on the table, Darac's index finger began absently exploring the gaps between the tiles.

'Actually, Papa, that's one of the reasons I'm calling.'

THURSDAY 9 JULY

11.00 AM

Darac hadn't picked up a guitar in five whole days. He hadn't made love in almost three months and he couldn't remember the last time he'd actually landed a punch on someone.

'If only by default, I'm improving.'

'I've come to the conclusion that despite all her brilliance, Angeline…' Agnès winced as a nurse adjusted her pillow. '…is an idiot.'

A sad smile played on Darac's lips.

'She's no idiot. I think she's right about most things, actually.'

The nurse took her leave.

'You won't change my opinion. But then I'm biased, aren't I?'

'I think you might be, yes. Anyway, the quintet is playing tonight so I'll soon be indulging in one of my wicked ways. Possibly two if Didier trashes Louis Armstrong again. He's got a terrible blind spot for early stuff.'

Agnès's eyes slid to the dressing which ran the length of Darac's left forearm.

'*Will* you be able to play later?'

'It's only a flesh wound.' He wiggled his fingers freely.

'Pity I didn't lose a couple – it might have helped my Django Reinhardt stuff. Two usable fingers on his left hand – that's all he had to work with.' He shook his head. 'Angeline doesn't believe in heroes. As a concept, I mean.' He smiled, a little more of the familiar lift in his expression. 'Plucky try on Django's part, though, wasn't it?'

Agnès searched for a word of comfort. All that came into her head were platitudes and claptrap. But there was a truth among them.

'Just because it's a cliché doesn't mean that time *isn't* a great healer, you know.'

'Are you referring to my situation or yours?'

'To both, I suppose.'

'There's no comparison.'

'Have you spoken to her?'

'We met for a drink last night. It was a mistake. But at least I know it definitely is over now.'

'I'm sorry.'

'Well… Angeline was precious to me and losing her is painful. But what *you* went through…' He slowly shook his head. 'I can't believe your resilience, Agnès. You are an amazing person.'

She looked far away, suddenly. She was back there. Back in the nightmare.

'Apart from everything else he did, my father… sought to have a woman pregnant with his own child taken away and exterminated. And the only reason he didn't succeed in getting rid of them both – he mistakenly thought – was that the baby had been stillborn that same morning.' It hurt Agnès terribly that her father had seemed to feel a sense of loss at never knowing the son who had, after all, survived; the son he had sought to have killed. 'Mengele? Eichmann? My father was as evil as any of them.'

'Agnès…' Darac left it there. He just didn't know what else to say.

'But should I start feeling bereft at his loss, I can always contact my half-brother, Jean, can't I? Why not? Have a party. Invite good old Corinne as well. If she recovers.' Tears came. Darac leaned forward and held Agnès's shaven head to his chest.

'A clearing shower,' she said, drying her eyes. 'That's what Mama used to call it.'

Darac imagined there would be many more of them in the months to come. He sat back, without thinking, dragging a hand through his hair. He regretted it immediately.

'I've been told it's an irritating habit. Must seem especially so at the moment.'

'No, not at all.' She stroked her skull. 'I rather like the feel, actually. I may even keep it like this.'

'It… suits you.'

'It does not.'

'No, it doesn't.'

She managed a smile. Nothing was said for a moment.

'Could you handle one final point about the case, Agnès?'

'I think so.'

'The non-credible threat. I still don't understand why Jarret put it together that way.'

'Ye-es… Well, we know he wanted to exact revenge on… my father. That was his first objective. I think a second one was to discredit the Police Judiciaire as a whole – as a punishment for what its forebears did – and didn't do – back in the war.'

'To get the Press and everyone saying: "The stupid idiots took no notice of the threat and look what happened – two of their own commissaires wound up being…"'

'Murdered,' she finished, matter-of-factly. 'But I suppose he didn't dare risk making the threat so credible that Paris would have thrown everything at him – it might have scuppered his first objective.'

'Stop and search, extra surveillance – both would have made it more difficult for Jarret to carry out the abductions. And there would have been other difficulties. Yes, I suppose it makes sense in a twisted sort of way.'

'The threat part of his plan was quite well conceived, I think. Had my father and I both been murdered, it would have looked really bad for us.' She smiled. 'Looked bad for the Brigade, I mean.'

'And I suppose a third objective was to point the finger of blame for the outrage at the Muslim community – or why use the "Just Cause" tag? A terrorist organisation of *any* persuasion would have served to deflect us away from the personal motivation for the abductions.'

She looked far away once more. 'Race… Blood… Why can't people ever seem to get beyond that? In some ways, it's the saddest thing of all.'

In the corridor outside, the sound of approaching

voices was the signal for Agnès to reach for Darac's hand.

'Before the others come in, I want to say something.'

'There's no need.'

'Yes, there is. You came through, Paul. When everything else was crumbling around me, you came through. I will never forget that.'

He'd always been taught to accept thanks gracefully.

'I… think you're after another foot massage.' He gave Agnès's hand a squeeze before withdrawing it. 'Seems like years ago, that, doesn't it?'

She managed to raise a smile as the rest of the squad filed into the room.

For the next half-hour, fat was chewed, gossip was passed on. Updates were issued on everything from Jacques 'Seve' Sevran's likely fate to Corinne Delage's improving medical condition. As it came time for everyone to leave, Agnès had another speech to make.

'I know how tirelessly you all worked on this. The fact that it mattered so much to you matters hugely to me. Thank you.'

'I wasn't doing anything that weekend anyway.' Armani's was the loudest voice in a chorus of disclaimers and gags. 'You're getting out in about a week, right? If you want to make it up to us, you can take us to the Chantecler. The à la carte menu.'

'Then it will be *socca* all round. See you all soon.'

Darac and Frankie were the last to leave.

'Are you going to be alright, Agnès?' Frankie asked, exchanging goodbye kisses.

'Oh yes. I'll be fine.' Her eyes were far away. 'I'm a Dantier.'

Later that afternoon, Darac went looking for his team in the squad room. He found them sitting around the TV, engrossed in the day's Tour stage. Only Perand, seeking refuge at the coffee machine, was *hors de combat*.

'Espresso, chief?'

'You read my mind.'

Before Darac could say anything further, his mobile rang. He sat, and leaning back in the chair, put his feet up on a desk.

'This is Frènes.'

'Monsieur.'

'Captain, I'm calling to inform you that your disciplinary hearing regarding the incident in the Marguerite car park is set for two weeks today. 11 am. That's the 23rd.'

'Eleven on the 23rd. Right.'

'And just because Mademoiselle Lamarthe has arrived at, or been steered toward, the opinion that any combat-trained officer disturbed without warning would react as you did, I must nevertheless caution you that…'

As Frènes continued, Darac's eyes strayed to the TV screen. A knot of riders was rounding a turn at full speed. At a traffic island ahead of them, a Garde Républicaine officer waved a yellow flag. The peloton flew past.

As Perand handed Darac the espresso, Flaco gave him a wave from her desk.

'Can I have a word when you've finished?' she mouthed.

He gave her a beckoning nod.

'I have another date with the authorities for your diary, Captain.'

'Uh-huh.'

'Although the DCRI officer Lieutenant Efe Santoor has opted to drop some of the allegations against you, there is still a whole catalogue of practice deviations, rule infractions, and outright misconduct charges to answer. The hearing is set for Tuesday the 28th at 10 am.'

'Ten on the 28th. Right.'

'And something to be borne in mind here…'

Flaco scowled sweetly as she handed him a clipboard. Darac ran an eye over the clamped pages. Sponsorship forms. The girl was climbing Kilimanjaro. Frankie had pledged thirty euros.

'Jesus.'

Frènes concluded his briefing on the DCRI hearing and then turned to another topic.

'And just to inform you of another matter, Captain. Your investiture of the Police Medal of Honour is set for 4pm on the 31st.'

'Four on the 31st. Right.'

Darac ended the call, put himself down for thirty euros and got to his feet.

'Thanks, Captain.'

'You're welcome.'

He turned to the TV watchers.

'If I could have your attention for just one moment,

guys? And everyone else? Thanks. Ever since the sweep was drawn, my possession of a certain piece of paper has created what could only be described as a frenzy of interest. Increasingly hard sums of cash have been offered for the passport to ultimate success that is ticket number twenty-one, Signor Alfredo...'

'Alberto...' a number of voices chorused.

'Alberto Contador. Here is *my* final offer. As some of you know, Thursday nights are quintet night at the Blue Devil.'

'We *all* know.'

'Thank you, Bonbon. Tonight, we are going to do something really special. During the first set, we are playing the whole of Duke Ellington's Far East Suite. Ellington. Tunes, right? Sing-along time. It's worth coming just to hear "Bluebird of Delhi", trust me.'

From Erica to Granot, every face was looking at him as if he were an escaped lunatic.

'The second set is devoted entirely to suites by Sonny Rollins and Ornette Coleman. That is one unique evening of jazz. Now, I am prepared to swap my sweep ticket with anyone here who will come along to the gig. *Swap* – no cash required. All it will cost you is fifteen euros to get into the club.'

'Couldn't we just pay and go away again?' Armani said.

Bonbon shuffled awkwardly.

'Swap your ticket – not *give* it? I did draw Lance, you know.'

Granot had the look of a discomfited warthog.

'How long would the thing go on for?'

Swatting the reluctant trio aside, Darac turned to Flaco.

'You'll swap your ticket to come to a jazz gig, won't you? Ellington? Rollins? Coleman? Geniuses, the lot of them, and if I say so myself, the quintet's pretty damn good. We're going to be a ten-piece for the night.'

'Tonight? Can't. Sorry, Captain. Training.'

'Erica?'

'I'd love to… I'm lying. Look – the problem is, I really can't stand jazz.' She scrunched her face. 'Sor-ree.'

'Can't stand it. Uh-huh.' Making an effort, he regrouped, smiled and turned to Perand. The young man shook his head before Darac got a word out.

'Just not my thing, Captain. Too…'

'Keep it to yourself.' Running a hand through his hair, Darac turned to the whole group. 'You know there's a kid over in uniform who's already going to this gig – Patrick Cabriet. No inducements. Just knows a good thing when he sees it. I've got a good mind…'

In the manner of someone offering the ultimate sacrifice, Armani stepped forward.

'No, no. I tell you what – I'll do it. Yes – I'll swap. Why not? And come to the whole gig. There. How bad can it be?'

Armani drew admiring glances from the room.

'You won't regret it.' Darac smiled as he handed him the slip of paper bearing the magic number twenty-one.

'There you go.'

Bowing graciously, Armani put his hand in his pocket and gave Darac his own slip in return. Darac opened it.

'Who's your new boy, chief?'

In Granot's handwriting, the slip read: *Alexander Jacob Markowski*.

Suddenly, the air con was the only sound in the room.

'No, that's… mine,' Armani said, at length. He held out his hand.

Darac folded the paper neatly and gave it back to him.

ACKNOWLEDGEMENTS

Producing this series of novels would have been an infinitely more difficult task without the sage counsel, encouragement and support of my wife Liz, and my immediate family, Rob, Clare, Katey and Bryan. For giving unstintingly of their time and for their invaluable insights, my thanks go to Susan Woodall and Alex Carter. For their many kindnesses, I'm indebted to Lisa Hitch, Sarah Burton and Boris Blouin. Special thanks go to Katherine Roddwell for her translation work both from texts and during in-situ interviews with officers of the Police Judiciaire in Nice.

Finally, for their expert guidance, warm thanks to my agent, Ian Drury at Sheil Land; and my editor at Titan Books, Miranda Jewess.

ABOUT THE AUTHOR

Peter Morfoot has written a number of plays and sketch shows for BBC radio and TV and is the author of the acclaimed satirical novel, *Burksey*. He has lectured in film, holds a PhD in Art History, and has spent thirty years exploring the life, art and restaurant tables of the French Riviera, the setting for his series of crime novels featuring Captain Paul Darac of Nice's Brigade Criminelle. He lives in Cambridge.

BABAZOUK BLUES

A CAPTAIN DARAC NOVEL

PETER MORFOOT

Captain Paul Darac of the Brigade Criminelle is forced to abandon his jazz quintet mid-show by the call to a possible murder. He and his officers arrive on the scene to find the mutilated corpse of a woman, although her cause of death may not have been a sinister one. Initially routine, the case deepens and darkens into a complex inquiry that threatens to close in on Darac himself. But allegiances past and present must be set aside to unravel a tale of greed, deception and treachery that spans the social spectrum. It is among the winding streets of his own neighbourhood in Nice's old town, the Babazouk, that Darac faces his severest test yet.

AVAILABLE APRIL 2017

BOX OF BONES

A CAPTAIN DARAC NOVEL

PETER MORFOOT

It is Carnival time in Nice, and for three weeks the boulevards are alive with dancers, jugglers and musicians. Amidst the colour and pageantry, Captain Paul Darac of the Brigade Criminelle is investigating a series of suspicious deaths. He and his team reopen a closed case that may provide new insights, but their own lives are in danger as they uncover a story of terrifying ambition and betrayal.

AVAILABLE APRIL 2018

THE BLOOD STRAND

A FAROES NOVEL

CHRIS OULD

Having left the Faroes as a child, Jan Reyna is now a British police detective, and the islands are foreign to him. But he is drawn back when his estranged father is found unconscious with a shotgun by his side and someone else's blood at the scene. Then a man's body is washed up on an isolated beach. Is Reyna's father responsible? Looking for answers, Reyna falls in with Detective Hjalti Hentze, but as the stakes get higher and Reyna learns more about his family and the truth behind his mother's flight from the Faroes, he must decide whether to stay, or to forsake the strange, windswept islands for good.

PRAISE FOR THE AUTHOR

"Unmissable and thrilling fiction… a tough-talking, brutally honest lesson in the harsh realities of youth crime."
Lancashire Evening Post

THE BURSAR'S WIFE

A GEORGE KOCHARYAN MYSTERY

E. G. RODFORD

Meet George Kocharyan, Cambridge Confidential Services'
one and only private investigator. Amidst the usual jobs
following unfaithful spouses, he is approached by the
glamorous Sylvia Booker. The wife of the bursar of Morley
College, Booker is worried that her daughter Lucy has fallen
in with the wrong crowd.

Aided by his assistant Sandra and her teenage son, George
soon realises that Lucy is sneaking off to the apartment of an
older man, but perhaps not for the reasons one might suspect.
Then an unfaithful wife he had been following is found dead.
As his investigation continues – enlivened by a mild stabbing
and the unwanted intervention and attention of Detective
Inspector Vicky Stubbing – George begins to wonder if all the
threads are connected...

For more fantastic fiction, author events, competitions,
limited editions and more

Visit our website
titanbooks.com

Like us on Facebook
facebook.com/titanbooks

Follow us on Twitter
@TitanBooks

Email us
readerfeedback@titanemail.com